More Than a Dream

Books by

Lauraine Snelling

* 5 books in each volume

LAURAINE SNELLING

More Than a Dream

BETHANYHOUSE

MINNEAPOLIS, MINNESOTA

More Than a Dream
Copyright © 2003
Lauraine Snelling

Cover design by Dan Thornberg, Design Source Creative Services

Scripture quotations are from the King James Version of the Bible.

Published by Bethany House Publishers
11400 Hampshire Avenue South
Bloomington, Minnesota 55438

Bethany House Publishers is a division of
Baker Publishing Group, Grand Rapids, Michigan.

Printed in the United States of America

ISBN 978-0-7642-0863-8

The Library of Congress has cataloged the original edition as follows:

Snelling, Lauraine.
    More than a dream / by Lauraine Snelling.
        p.   cm. — (Return to Red River ; 3)
    ISBN 0-7642-2319-4
      1. Journalists—Fiction. 2. North Dakota—Fiction. 3. Minnesota—Fiction. 4. Epidemics—Fiction. 5. Floods—Fiction. I. Title. II. Series: Snelling, Lauraine. Return to Red River ; 3.
    PS3569.N39 M67   2003
    813'.54—dc21   2002152648

DEDICATION

To all those readers whom I meet

at the HostFest in Minot, North Dakota, every fall.

Thanks for your pleasure in my books

and the laughter, stories, and hugs

you share with me there.

Mange takk.

See you next year—

God willing.

LAURAINE SNELLING is an award-winning author of over 60 books, fiction and nonfiction for adults and young adults. Her books have sold over two million copies. Besides writing books and articles, she teaches at writers' conferences across the country. She and her husband, Wayne, have two grown sons, a bassett named Chewy, and a cockatiel watch bird named Bidley. They make their home in California.

Bjorklund Family Tree

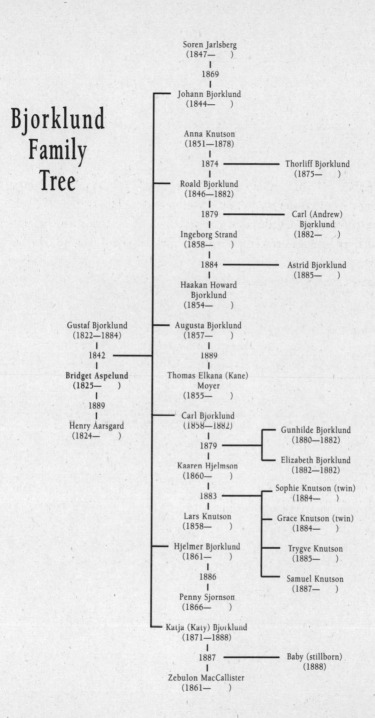

Soren Jarlsberg
(1847—   )

1869

Johann Bjorklund
(1844—   )

Anna Knutson
(1851—1878)

1874 ——————— Thorliff Bjorklund
(1875—   )

Roald Bjorklund
(1846—1882)

1879 ——————— Carl (Andrew)
Bjorklund
Ingeborg Strand (1882—   )
(1858—   )

1884 ——————— Astrid Bjorklund
(1885—   )

Haakan Howard
Bjorklund
(1854—   )

Gustaf Bjorklund   Augusta Bjorklund
(1822—1884)   (1857—   )

1842 ———————   1889

Bridget Aspelund   Thomas Elkana (Kane)
(1825—   )   Moyer
(1855—   )
1889

Henry Aarsgard   Carl Bjorklund
(1824—   )   (1858—1882)
Gunhilde Bjorklund
(1880—1882)
1879 ———————
Elizabeth Bjorklund
Kaaren Hjelmson   (1882—1882)
(1860—   )
Sophie Knutson (twin)
1883 ——————— (1884—   )

Lars Knutson   Grace Knutson (twin)
(1858—   )   (1884—   )

Hjelmer Bjorklund   Trygve Knutson
(1861—   )   (1885—   )

1886   Samuel Knutson
(1887—   )

Penny Sjornson
(1866—   )

Katja (Katy) Bjorklund
(1871—1888)

1887 ——————— Baby (stillborn)
(1888)

Zebulon MacCallister
(1861—   )

CHAPTER ONE

Northfield, Minnesota
June 1895

Elizabeth Rogers stared at the drifting white priscilla curtains without seeing them.

"Elizabeth, did you not hear me?"

She turned at the sound of irritation in her mother's voice. "Sorry, Mother, I was studying." *Liar, you were worrying, and you claim not to be a worrier.* The little voice that seemed to reside on her left shoulder made her feel more irritated than her mother sounded. She stood and crossed to the dark oak door that was open only a crack. Perhaps if she'd left it open all the way, she could have heard better. She stuck her head out to see her mother's careful coiffure rising as she came up the walnut stairs.

"Dr. Gaskin is waiting for you in the study." Annabelle shook her head slightly, a frown wrinkling her forehead under the dark corkscrew hair wisps she'd curled about her face. "Did you know he was coming?"

Elizabeth took her turn at shaking her head, her brown hair twisted into a bun at the very top of her head. "He knows I am preparing for final exams, so it can't be for a house call unless we have a woman in real distress." Since Dr. Gaskin now had a well-trained nurse, he hadn't requested Elizabeth's services to help with birthings as often as he had in the past, something she missed at times like this. With her final college exams only days away, she'd planned on using every moment for reviewing her lecture notes. Medical schools wouldn't be able to use her grades as an excuse to turn her away. She made her way down the staircase at her mother's side. "Did you have Cook bring him coffee?"

"And gingersnaps, his favorite cookie. He looks mighty serious."

Elizabeth picked up the pace, although if he'd been in a hurry, he'd have suffered no compunction about letting the messenger know. She entered the study in a swirl of dimity skirts, the unseasonably warm weather begging for light clothing.

"Good day, Dr. Gaskin. How nice of you to come by."

"Good day to you, m'dear. You look more lovely every time I see you." Dr. Gaskin wiped cookie crumbs from his recently grown mustache. His hair had grayed to nearly white in the two years since his wife died, and the lines cut deeper from his nose to his chin, the mustache giving him the look of an aging walrus.

"Flattery will get you nowhere—or everywhere, depending on what it is you want." Elizabeth dropped a kiss on his everbroadening forehead. She and her mother had wondered if the reason he had grown a mustache was because of the breadth of shiny space on the top of his head. Elizabeth and the doctor had long since passed the point of mentor and student and had become more like a niece with a favorite uncle. She picked up the silver coffeepot on the silver tray. "More?"

"Only if you are having some."

"Then I shall." As she picked up the coffee server, her hand shook so badly she was forced to set it back down immediately. The server rattled the tray.

"Are you all right, my dear?" Dr. Gaskin leaned forward, his brow wrinkling in concern.

"I-I don't know." Elizabeth grasped the offending hand with the other. She rubbed it, then shook it out. *What's happening? I've never had something like this before.* She flexed her hand, made a fist.

"I'll pour. You sit down. Does it hurt? Prickle like it went to sleep?"

She shook her head while taking a seat on the other end of the horsehair sofa and accepted her filled cup with the other hand. "No, none of those things." Now when she lifted the cup from the saucer, it was like nothing had happened. Her hand worked fine. She smiled his way. "See, I'm fine." All the while she spoke and sipped and smiled, she tried to figure out what had happened. Her hand must have just gone to sleep. But it didn't feel that way. "Now, what is it I can do for you?"

"I think it is more what I can do for you."

At his response, her eyebrow arched. "Really?"

He watched her over the rim of his cup. "Have you been accepted at any of the medical schools yet?"

She nodded. "The Woman's Medical College of Pennsylvania, but that's not really where I want to go." She reached for one of the cookies.

"I know. You want to study in Minneapolis."

She nodded. "Same as always. You know me. Once I get my mind set on something . . ."

"Like a bulldog you are."

"Well, I'd think you could come up with something more flattering than that." She held out the cookie plate.

"Could, but . . ." He leaned forward to take another cookie and dunked it in his coffee before the tidbit disappeared into his smiling mouth. "Your cook sure makes the best cookies in town."

"Ah, you can say good things about her cooking, but I get called a bulldog."

"Tenacious is what you are and what you need to be for what you want, but . . ." He slanted his bottom lip slightly to the left and sucked on the skin, a sure sign he was struggling with something.

Come out with it. I know something is bothering you. She kept her thoughts to herself, knowing that he would get around to the subject in his own good time. If only she could learn to do that with everyone,

11

especially Thorliff Bjorklund. There was something about that young man that removed the bars of propriety, so she just spouted out whatever she was thinking. Her lack of restraint had caused some heated verbal disputes. Her mother called them battles, but a battle usually had a winner and a loser. She and Thorliff did not argue to win or to lose, but for the pure pleasure of sparring, even though at times his bullheadedness nearly drove her to distraction. Was that because of her own bulldog tendencies, as the doctor so gently put it? She leaned back against the cushion, wishing as she often did that she had longer legs so she could sit back and still keep her feet on the floor. Or not look like she was reclining rather than sitting properly, as her mother would comment.

Had Dr. Gaskin's mind wandered? That seemed to be happening with more frequency since the death of his extremely capable wife and best friend, Helen. She'd had that wonderful gift of making everyone around her feel better for the visit. Elizabeth knew that as much as she missed Helen, Dr. Gaskin had nearly gone down with grief, even to overuse of the bottle. So what brought him by today?

"I talked with Dr. Johanson."

"Oh." Dr. Johanson was the new doctor, *new* meaning he'd only been in town four years instead of growing up in Northfield. From what she'd heard he was building a practice that was beginning to support him, his wife, and their two children. Not that there wasn't plenty of work in town for two doctors, but people were stubborn and didn't take quickly to someone new. *Come on. Tell me what's on your mind. I'm wasting precious time.* Sometimes being polite took more strength than fighting for a woman's life in the wee hours of the morning.

"And he agrees with me."

"I see." *No, I don't. Talked to him about what?*

"We agree that between us we could train you to be a doctor as well as any medical school could. He says he's learned most of his medical knowledge since he went into practice anyway. You could assist in surgeries, and we'd make sure you got every possible opportunity. You know that. Why, you've already operated, set fractures, birthed babies, diagnosed all kinds of ailments. You go to school and you're going to be taking steps backward." His tone intensified and he leaned forward. "Besides, there's all the guff you'll have to take. Too many of those teachers don't want women in medicine. They don't think women are capable."

Elizabeth listened beyond the words. She knew he wanted her to take over his practice one of these days, and she also knew that he wanted what he thought was the best for her. Dr. Morganstein had offered her the same opportunity at her women's hospital in Chicago, where she had spent six weeks working herself to a stick the summer before. *But my, oh my, I learned a lot.*

"Will you think about it?" He tried to keep the pleading out of his voice, but his eyes gave him away.

Elizabeth sighed. To say she'd think about it just to make him feel better seemed more like a lie than a comfort. She looked up from studying the cup she held in both hands, her thumb hooked through the handle. Right now the forget-me-nots her mother had painted so carefully didn't help. "I have thought about studying with you—I've thought about it a lot. I could do that and take more training with Dr. Morganstein too. So why am I so convinced that medical school is the best way for me to go? Is it a dream? Is it because I like a challenge? I know that I love school—the classroom, the competition, the discussions." She set her cup in the saucer balanced on her knees. "I know one major thing. If I worked here with you, I would probably never have a chance to dissect a cadaver so that I really learn nerves and muscles and the internal organs. I want to know what the brain looks like, and the lungs." She paused and rubbed her chin. "But do I need all that, or is it my insatiable curiosity that drives me? As you've so often said, medicine is changing all the time, and there are more changes to come. It seems to me that the more I know, the better a doctor I can be. Am I way off the path?"

"No, lass, I don't think you are off the path at all. And you are right, I we—cannot give you all that. Your Dr. Morganstein cannot either. But know that if you can't get into the school you want, you have an alternative." He set his saucer and cup down on the tray. "And now that I've given you even more to think about, I'll let you get back to your studies. Sure do wish one of these colleges here in town had a medical program. You'll let me know when you find out anything more?"

"Of course. Other than Mother and Father, you'll be the first one I'll tell." She showed him to the door and took his hand before he stepped outside. "Thank you, Dr. Gaskin. I appreciate all you've already taught me. Without you I'd be a neophyte, most likely without the courage to even dream."

"If I hadn't encouraged you, most likely you'd be playing piano on the concert stage and making your mother extremely happy. Tell Cook thank-you for the cookies. She had no idea I was coming, yet she baked my favorites."

"I will thank her for you." Elizabeth watched him stride down the walk to the street, where his horse dozed in the shade of a huge maple. How much easier it would be to just give in and stay at home. She pushed her newly cut fringe up off her forehead. One of her slight rebellions and a mistake in this heat. Back to her books. She trailed one hand along the banister as she climbed the stairs, counting each one just as she had done as a child. Birds sang outside, calling to her through the open windows. The grand piano in the music room begged for attention, since she hadn't played for over a week. Sitting at her desk, she studied three pages, realized she had no idea what she'd read, and read them again. She got up and made a trip to the necessary, returned to the books, got up and stood by the window, and watched the shadow leaves dancing on the lawn.

"Elizabeth Marie Rogers, get back to work! This is downright silly. You have no time to waste, and you're acting like a three-year-old." She made a face at herself in the mirror and sat back down at her desk. She puffed upward to fluff her fringe. It would be cooler down in the study. She gathered her books and papers and trudged down the stairs, taking the seat behind her father's desk. Three more pages, actually the same three pages.

"Oh, you've come down here. Can I get you something?" Her mother paused in the doorway.

"No, thanks." Now Elizabeth remembered why she had stayed up in her bedroom.

"It's nice out in the backyard. I think we'll have dinner out there. Cook has made chicken salad, one of your favorites."

"That's nice." Elizabeth kept her finger in the text and gave her mother the kind of smile that said, *Thank you for your concern, but please go away so I can study.*

Annabelle took the hint, and again Elizabeth had no one to blame but herself for her preoccupation as her thoughts meandered once again from her textbooks. What was happening with medical school? Dr. Gaskin had opened the basket of snakes she'd been trying to keep contained. She abhorred worrying, but at times like this it snuck out, snagged her by the stockings, and wouldn't let go. *I don't want a medical school that teaches only theory. I've already had plenty of lectures and I can read books on my own just as well. I want to learn all that I can firsthand.* That would include dissecting a human body, more than one if possible, and studying with a group of students, learning from and with one another. Such training would be superb. She'd read somewhere that the human body was the best teaching tool for anyone who wanted to be a first-rate physician. That same article had mentioned that artists sometimes learned anatomy the same way for their paintings.

She'd also read about the scandals of grave robbers digging up the newly buried and selling the bodies to medical schools or to others who wanted to buy one. Some states had passed laws to prevent grave robbing, but like anything else, the thieves had to be caught first. The only other source of cadavers was criminals or indigents who died without someone claiming their bodies.

The cooler room didn't help her to concentrate.

Why hadn't she allowed her mother to bring her something to drink? Leaving her books on the desk, she wandered toward the kitchen, stopping by the grand piano to trail her fingers over the keys. Playing the piano had always comforted her when sad, calmed her when excited, and soothed her when restless. Like now. She sat down and let her fingers find their own song. Rippling waters, singing birds—the notes flowed and danced in a breeze of their own making. After about ten minutes, she held the final note and laid her hands in her lap.

But instead of rising, Elizabeth opened a piece of music she'd been working on. It was a sonata by Chopin that she had struggled with. She couldn't seem to master the intricate fingering. Taking the first six measures, she played it through slowly, setting the metronome to count the beats. And played it again, changing the emphasis. Liking that better, she played it through four more times before going on to the next several measures. She concentrated solely on the music, listening for the meaning, for what she wanted it to say. Note by note, rest by rest, the effort erased everything else from her mind. Her hair loosened from the bun she'd pinned into place, perspiration trickled down her spine, and yet the music beckoned her on. After playing the entire piece through again, she took a deep breath and nodded with satisfaction as the final chord faded.

"Dinner is ready." Cook stood in the doorway. "I didn't want to disturb you. It's out on the verandah."

"Thank you." Elizabeth smiled, feeling cleansed from the inside out. "I'm famished."

"Good. Thorliff Bjorklund came by a bit ago, and now he is out visiting with your mother." Cook started to leave, but spoke over her shoulder. "You might want to fix your hair first."

Elizabeth raised a hand to find curls dangling over her ears. "Thank you. I'll be out shortly." She trotted up the stairs wishing she had time for a real washup, just now aware of her dress sticking to her. Jehoshaphat, her gold-and-white cat, lay curled in the middle of her bed and yawned, showing teeth and tongue when she blew into her room. He uncurled in the way of all felines, arching his spine and stretching limb by limb. Elizabeth stroked his back and cupped her hands around his face, dropping a kiss on his pink nose.

"Here, I've been working away, and you've spent the morning snoozing. What shall I do with you? Were there no mice to chase?" The comment made her smile. Jehoshaphat had no more idea what to do with a mouse than she did with a crochet hook. She washed, changed into a green-and-white gingham dress, brushed and tied her hair with a green ribbon and, humming, made her way back down the stairs. Amazing what learning a new and complicated piece of music did for her mind. Right now she wished she could go back to studying. But soon, after

16

all, Thorliff needed to go back to work too. And he had final exams same as she did. Just that his weren't the last ones before graduation.

"And how are you today, Thorliff?" Elizabeth said, stepping out onto the verandah. "Ready for tomorrow?"

Unfolding his more than six-foot length, he stood and shook his head. Thorliff Bjorklund had come to Northfield, Minnesota, to attend St. Olaf College two years earlier and had started working at her father's newspaper, the *Northfield News,* in exchange for room and board. Now he wrote for the paper as well and was a trusted employee and confidant of Phillip Rogers. Through shared meals, walks up the hill to college, and working together at the paper, he and Elizabeth had become good friends. "I brought you a copy of an article I read on women in medicine," Thorliff said with a smile.

"Oh?" Elizabeth glanced over her shoulder as he held the cast-iron chair for her. "And what is their opinion?"

"You should stay home and raise children."

"Thorliff Bjorklund, then why did you bring it for me?" She glared at him, ignoring her mother's *tsk* of remonstrance.

His arched eyebrow pushed her instant ire up another notch. "I've already read more than enough editorials with that bias, thank you." She shook out her napkin with more force than necessary and spread it in her lap. "I thought you were planning to keep your nose to the books today."

"I was, but your father asked me to bring some things over for your mother, so here I am." He took the offered bowl of chicken salad from Annabelle and helped himself. "Sounded to me like you were trying to beat the piano into submission. Having a hard time studying?"

"You have such a way with words." Honey dripped from her words— rancid honey.

His chuckle made her chew on her lower lip to keep from smiling. She didn't dare to look at her mother, knowing the frown that rode her brow. *Just what I needed. Piano time and a sparring match with Thorliff.*

She took the bowl and dished up her own salad before passing it to her mother, who had started the basket of rolls around. When she glanced up, she caught Thorliff staring at her, his eyes blue as the skies above and the dappled shade of the oak tree catching glints of gold in his hair. "What is it?"

"Nothing. You remind me of my little sister in that dress."

Elizabeth could feel a blush start on her neck. Leave it to Thorliff. She sucked in a breath and huffed it out. "Have you decided what you'll do when school is out?"

He nodded. "Your father has convinced me to stay here so we can put *The Switchmen* out in time for fall."

"And your family?"

"They won't be happy, but they'll understand. I warned them of the possibility at Christmas."

"Astrid will really miss you." Elizabeth thought of the little girl she'd learned to see through Thorliff's tales of life in the Red River Valley.

"I know."

Elizabeth glanced at her mother, who was shaking her head.

"It's hard when our children leave home. After having Elizabeth gone so long last summer, I know how your mother feels." Annabelle buttered a roll. "I so wish . . ." She stopped and sighed. "At least your mother still has others at home."

Ah, guilt. How you sting. Elizabeth and Thorliff exchanged glances. *Why did one person's happiness so often seem to come at the expense of another's?*

CHAPTER TWO

Blessing, North Dakota

"But, Mor, I want Thorliff to come home so bad."

"I know. Me too." Ingeborg Bjorklund put her arm around her ten-year-old daughter as Astrid turned to lean into her mother's chest, both arms around her waist.

"I don't like Mr. Rogers."

"You don't know Mr. Rogers. How can you like him or not?" Ingeborg smoothed wisps of nearly white hair back off her daughter's forehead and leaned her cheek on top of her daughter's head, an act that would not be possible much longer unless she stood on a box. *Ah, child, you are growing so tall and capable. Where has my little Astrid gone?*

"Well, he made Thorliff stay in Northfield. We need him here with us."

"That's the way of jobs. You might have to be far away from home to do your work. Look at Onkel Hjelmer. He has to travel around some. And during threshing season, Far is gone and Onkel Lars too."

"But that's different. They come home again when the threshing is done." Astrid tipped her head back so she could look into her mother's face. "I'm afraid Thorliff will never live here again. Like Tante Solveig, we'll only get letters and never see him again. And Northfield is lots farther than where Tante Solveig lives."

Ingeborg cupped her daughter's strong jaw in her hands and smiled into her eyes, eyes the Bjorklund blue that proclaimed her heritage. "If Thorliff doesn't come home, one of these days we will go to Northfield and visit him."

"You mean that?" Astrid's face lit up like the sun peeping over the horizon. "Really?"

"It is something to think about." Ingeborg ran her tongue along her front teeth and let her thoughts chase after. "I could call on businesses in Minneapolis that sell our cheese." Her stomach clenched at even the thought of such audacity. But if they were to turn more of their acreage over to hay, pasture, and grain to feed more milk cows to produce more cheese, they would need to add new customers. Would Haakan want to go along on a trip like that? Could both of them leave the farm for that long? Of course they could. Lars and the others would take over all the milking and run the cheese house. It would have to be before or after harvest, and then Astrid would be in school again. Would Pastor Solberg allow her to be gone for a few days? And Andrew? "Uff da. So many things to think about."

"What do you mean?" Astrid looked over her shoulder to the door, where the cat meowed to be let in. "I'm coming, Goldie, just be patient."

"Oh, about a trip like that. So much more than just going to see Thorliff."

"Someday maybe we could go see Tante Augusta too. South Dakota isn't that far away."

Ingeborg tweaked her daughter's nose. "You think you want to travel all over like that?"

Astrid nodded. "I want to go to Chicago and New York and Norway and—"

"Really?"

"Ja. Mr. Moen talked at school about Norway and the mountains and the fjords and all. I asked Bestemor about Norway too, and she told me about her home there. We could visit Onkel Johann and Tante Soren."

Ingeborg closed her eyes as a pang of homesickness, so acute that she had to catch her breath, stabbed her in the heart. Her parents were getting up in years, like Bridget, and while she had always told herself she would see them next in heaven, suddenly the urge to see them in this life seemed as necessary as breathing. Letters back and forth had grown further apart through the years, and she'd never been able to convince any of her family to emigrate. Not like the adventurous Bjorklunds. Only Johann, the eldest Bjorklund son, had remained behind, and he held the home farm, deeded to him as the primogeniture laws ordered. While Roald, her first husband, who had died in a North Dakota blizzard, had grumbled about such laws, once he'd claimed the land they now farmed, he'd never looked back. In truth, neither had she. Until now.

What would it be like to go home to Norway for a visit? She thought on the words. Was Norway home any longer? She gave a mental shrug. Not really. This rich land they farmed was home of both her mind and heart. She watched as Astrid opened the door and picked up the orange-and-white striped cat, his fur impeccably groomed, his feet so white he appeared to have floated over dust or mud without touching down. Goldie's purr could be heard clear across the room as Astrid held him under her chin and rubbed his ears and cheeks.

Like her older brother Andrew, Astrid had a way with animals. They gentled at her touch and voice, even the cows and pigs. The horses came when she called them, and the chickens flocked around her feet, knowing she always carried a scattering of oats in her apron pockets. Only Astrid could pick up the barn cats, who were friendly just at milking time and never tolerated more than a quick pat or two.

Ingeborg often wondered at the many gifts these two children of hers had been given and what would happen to both children and their gifts as they grew older. Watching Astrid with the cat, smiling at the picture they made, she scolded herself. *You know better than trying to think ahead like that. Jesus said we should let the day's own trouble be*

21

sufficient for the day. You'd think I'd have learned that clear down to my toes by now.

But thoughts of the possible trip didn't leave her. They took up residence in the back of her mind, popping out at strange times to cause her to stop again and think. *When I get it thought out, the next step will be to talk it over with Haakan. Father God, is this something you want me to do, or is it that prowling jackal sending me dreams that I ought not to own?* She glanced around her kitchen. Fresh yellow-and-white gingham at the windows, braided rag rugs on the dark blue painted floor, the chest that she and Roald had brought from Norway painted in rosemaling patterns. A big black stove. Such riches for which she was grateful. She sighed. Was one ever grateful enough?

"Astrid, would you please bring in some buttermilk and sweet milk both? I think a chocolate cake would be just the thing for dinner. Oh, and some cream. We can whip that for the frosting."

"Anything else?" Astrid paused at the door and looked over her shoulder. The sun glinted off the fine white hairs that haloed the top of her head, and her skirt swished well above her ankles. Another indication of how much she had grown.

"No, I have the ham baking, and we'll make scalloped potatoes from those poor shriveled things that made it through the winter." Ingeborg shook her head. "Ah, the thought of new potatoes . . ."

"And peas. Some are blooming already. How come the weeds grow so much faster than the vegetables and the wheat?"

"You ask that every year."

"Ja, and you always say God made it so, and so it is. That means you don't want me asking anymore."

Ingeborg made a shooing motion, her hands fluttering in front of her. "I need the buttermilk." Astrid's laughter floated back over her shoulder and mingled with her mother's chuckle as the girl leaped from the top step to the ground.

"Uff da. Such a child."

Even though in the past she had pleaded for more children to fill their house, God had seen fit to send her and Haakan only one. But she knew her second husband loved their two strong sons as if they were from his own loins. He'd told her so with such firmness in his voice and touch that she'd never questioned him again. Thinking of Haakan made her reach up and tuck trailing strands of hair back up in the two braids that circled the crown of her head.

Astrid returned, laden with the milk jug and the crock of buttermilk, set them on the table, and watched her mother creaming the butter and sugar. "You want I should help in here or go on back to the weeding? The sweet corn needs hoeing too."

Or you could bake the cake and I could go outside. Oh, to be outside with the sun beating down on her back and chasing away the winter cold that still seemed stuck in her bones. But she glanced at Astrid, who shifted from one bare foot to the other. "You go on outside. I'll get this in the oven and join you."

"Mange takk, Mor. You are so good." Astrid dashed out of the kitchen just in case her mother might change her mind, her long braids flopping against her back. As soon as she had returned home from the last day of school two weeks earlier, her shoes came off for the summer, only to be worn to church on Sundays.

Ingeborg finished mixing the cake, poured the batter into the greased and floured pan, and checked the temperature gauge on the oven door before adding more wood to the firebox. She slid the cake into the oven and placed the bowl and wooden spoon in the dishpan full of water keeping warm on the back of the reservoir. She had a good hour before she'd need to put the potatoes in.

The garden beckoned, and Ingeborg followed its siren song.

She stood a moment on the top porch step of the white two-story house and, shading her eyes with her hand, stared across the fields to where the men, including her younger son, Andrew, were cultivating the acres they had planted to corn this year in order to have more cattle feed. With wheat prices down and shipping prices up, cattle, both beef and dairy, looked like a better crop all around. They'd kept all the piglets too, since more whey could feed more pigs, and more pigs going to market would add to the income.

Diversifying from wheat to other crops took courage and unending discussions.

She reached back into the porch and snagged her wide-brimmed hat from the nail where it hung most of the time, even when it should have been on her head. Sunbonnets, straw hats, heavy skirts—sometimes she remembered back to the ease of wearing britches in the days when she and Kaaren fought to save the land after their husbands died. Britches would make kneeling to weed the garden far more simple.

But she'd promised Haakan she'd wear skirts instead of the men's pants she had been forced to wear in the early days while trying to save the farm, and so she would. She took the other hoe that leaned against the post and attacked the weeds in the potato patch, hilling up the rich black soil around the growing plants so the new spuds would not get sunburned. While the hat shaded her eyes and neck, it kept the breeze from blowing through her hair. There was always a trade-off.

"We need rain." Ingeborg glanced west in the hope there were thunderheads amassing.

"I know. Far said we might have to haul water again." Astrid looked up from weeding the carrots, a job that had to be done by hand.

"Are you thinning those as you go?"

"Mor."

"Sorry. I keep forgetting you know all about gardening by now." After one row Ingeborg's shoulders already felt the bite of muscles unused to the push and pull of hoeing. The fine dirt crumbled beneath her feet, bare like her daughter's. Give Red River dirt a steady drink of water, and it would turn to black gumbo that could be slick as ice and bring horses and humans both to a stop when it clung to hooves, boots, and wheels. Give it just enough moisture and it could grow anything. She chopped the weeds out, leaning over to pull pigweed too close to the four-inch-high plants. Quack grass, the bane of her existence, also needed to be pulled out; the slightest bit of root left in the soil would take over the patch seemingly overnight.

Sweat trickled down her back. She squashed a potato bug with the back of the hoe and checked other plants. Wasn't it early for potato bugs? Bugs and weeds, drought and hail, all the forces that fought to keep them from getting a good harvest. And grasshoppers. Another drought year could possibly bring that scourge again.

A meadowlark trilled off in the hayfield and robins hopped and foraged behind Astrid, keeping a safe distance but making sure no worm dug back down beyond beak level. Barn swallows dipped and stole the mud from around the watering trough to build their nests along the overhang of the barn and shed roofs.

Ingeborg inhaled the heady scents of spring sliding into summer. Fecund earth, mint from the patch she'd planted in an old tub so it wouldn't take over the garden, green grass, daisies, and cottonwood leaves, the breeze as it blew over the water trough and surrounding mud bringing the smell of cows and manure, all a rich potpourri of farm and growing life. She dug into her midback with her fists and rolled her shoulders back and then forward.

A hawk's *scree* floated from above, and she and Astrid immediately looked toward the chicken yard. Ingeborg shaded her eyes to find the bird spiraling against a blue so intense that the few clouds cottoning the heavens glistened white. Astrid sprinted for the chicken yard to chase the hens out of harm's way. While a full-grown hen was pretty big for a hawk to kill and carry, the chicks and half-grown stock were fair game.

"I've got to get the potatoes on," Ingeborg called to Astrid, who waved back at her. The inside of the house felt dark after the brilliance of the sun, but the smell of chocolate made her hustle to the oven. She pulled the cake pan out and frowned at the edges pulled away from the pan and slightly crispy. "Uff da, good thing we have plenty of cream. How could I go off and forget the cake like that?"

The cat blinked golden eyes at her from the chair cushion where he liked to curl up and sleep. He yawned, tongue pink and teeth shards of white, then closed his eyes and tucked his chin back into the fur of his front legs.

"Sorry to bother you, Goldie. Don't you think you could look for the mice on the porch instead of laze your days away like this?"

His ears twitched along with the tip of his tail.

Ingeborg peeled the shriveled potatoes and sliced them into the cast-iron kettle. She dusted each layer with flour, salt, and pepper, wishing she had onions for flavor. The ones in the garden weren't large enough to eat yet. With the potatoes stacking to an inch from the top of the kettle, she poured in milk to almost cover the potatoes and added a layer of thinly sliced cheese to top it off. She took out the roasting pan that held the ham and slid the kettle in. She opened two quarts of canned string beans into another kettle and set that on the back of the stove to simmer until the potatoes were done. They had at least an hour until dinner.

Buttermilk, butter, and flour turned into biscuits as she stirred, added, kneaded, and patted the dough out to an inch thick to be cut with a round cookie cutter. Sliding those onto a flat cookie sheet, she cleaned up her powdery mess, dropping the leftover flour into a crock she kept on the warming shelf for gravy. She frowned at the overly browned cake. What would her mother say about such sloppiness? Well, at least it wouldn't go to waste. That would be far worse than being slightly burnt.

Glancing out the window she saw Astrid still on her knees in the garden. Should she go back out or set the table and let Astrid keep weeding? She opted for setting the table, knowing her daughter would rather be outside. "Like mother, like daughter."

Goldie meowed and rose in an arch to stretch every muscle and ligament. He leaped to the floor and padded over to the door, where his chirp suggested she should open it for him. When she didn't come immediately, he raised his voice in a commanding meow.

"I'm coming."

Suddenly a call rang out. "Tante Ingeborg! Come quick!" The urgency in Sophie's cry made Ingeborg throw open the door to answer her niece.

"Dear God above, what's happened now?"

CHAPTER THREE

Northfield, Minnesota

"I don't know what I'd do without you." Phillip Rogers, owner of the *Northfield News,* a weekly paper, looked over the top of his glasses.

"Thank you, sir." Thorliff glanced over to see his employer leaning against the doorjamb. The windowless printing room was located directly behind the office, where a high counter separated the patrons from Phillip's desk. A large plate-glass window fronted on the sidewalk, allowing the customers to frequently ignore the Closed sign if they saw lights on and someone working inside.

"You've spoiled me, that's all. I thought last summer was about the longest I'd spent in my business, even after Mrs. Rogers came in to help. With you and Elizabeth both gone . . ." He paused and shook his head. "While the new press was supposed to make life easier, with all the new business, it's just . . . well . . . busier."

"I know." Thorliff Bjorklund wiped the sweat from his brow with the back of his hand. He'd spent half the night studying for final exams, had taken one this morning, and was back in the pressroom where the printing press created more heat than the furnace ever did, especially on this hot June day. He watched as the paper feeder again ran smoothly, the printed handbills stacking up like they were supposed to. No matter how new the machine, it had to be watched carefully to catch a problem before paper, ink, or precious time was wasted. The pungent odor of ink permeated his very pores.

"How many more exams do you have to go?" Mr. Rogers picked up one of the handbills for the political rally, checking to make sure the proper amount of ink was laid down.

"Three. Two tomorrow, one the next day."

"And then you can be here every day?"

"Until school starts again in the fall."

"Good. Good for me, but I'm sure your folks aren't real happy."

"No." Thorliff thought of home, milking the cows, working the fields, of Astrid, who he knew was heartbroken because her older brother wasn't going back to Blessing for the summer. While he'd not yet received a letter from his family, he figured one would be arriving shortly. One he would not want to read. Choosing to stay in Northfield had not been a hard decision but one that made him sad when he thought of home. And he knew his being gone was a hardship for those he loved.

"What are we doing after this run?" He took the stack of handbills and set them on the bench kept to the side for that purpose.

"I thought we'd start on your book next."

Thorliff stopped and stared at his employer-cum-mentor. "Really?"

Phillip nodded, his glasses catching a glint from the lamplight. Or was it a twinkle in his eyes? "We can do the pages first since we haven't designed a cover yet. I've been waiting until I could afford a binder, and that will be coming next week. Never thought I'd go from newspaper printing into the book publishing business too. And all because of you. We'll be able to do booklets for the county, and the Fire Department has asked me to print them some. One of the professors from Carleton came in the other day and wanted me to print up his family story. I'm sure there is a market out there for some book printing, and once we get real good at it, I'll begin to advertise." He slapped the printing press with one hand. "And to think I went all those years without this, all because I didn't want to use my wife's money. Moral of the story—don't let pride get in your way, son. Bible's right when it says, 'Vanity of vanities; all is vanity.' "

Thorliff checked the paper roll to make sure they had enough. "The Bible also says that pride goes before a fall." He grinned at his employer.

"Thank you, Mr. Bjorklund."

The bell tinkled over the door, announcing a customer. While Thorliff stayed with the press, Mr. Rogers headed for the front desk. When the print run finished, Thorliff stacked the handbills and tied them in bundles of twenty-five. The mayor would be handing them out at the Fourth of July celebration. Politicians always had something to say, it seemed. Even when it wasn't an election year.

My book. All those chapters of The Switchmen *will be bound together into one volume.* The year before Thorliff had proposed a story to be run in the paper a chapter a week, and Mr. Rogers had taken him up on it. The final chapters ran the summer before and had even been picked up by a paper in St. Paul. Over the winter he'd edited it and rewritten portions he wasn't happy with, knowing that eventually Mr. Rogers planned to bring it out again in book form. They'd had many requests and sold even more newspapers than during the Christmas season when they ran a contest for the best holiday stories. The second year they did that had outdone the first.

The first volume they had printed after the advent of the new press was a compilation of the winning Christmas stories. By adding those that had received honorable mention, they'd produced a slim volume for each year. Overnight the books became collector's items, especially when the readers began shipping their copies as far away as Norway and Germany.

Thanks to Mr. Moen, a Norwegian writer visiting in Blessing, several of Thorliff's stories had appeared in newspapers in Norway. Now he'd had a request for more. Perhaps this summer he would find time to do more writing. The printing business didn't run from dawn to dark like farming. Thorliff thought about Ivar Moen, the man who'd come to America to talk to Norwegian immigrants about their experiences in the new land and fallen in love with Anji Baard. Anji, who'd at one time been promised to him.

He jerked his wandering mind back from that track. While he'd forgiven her for what he thought of as her perfidy, even though he knew the sorrows she'd been through with her mother and father dying most likely contributed to her change of heart, sometimes the pain made his heart clench. Life sure didn't match the dream he'd had at his graduation from high school.

"Thorliff, when you're done with that, would you please go on out to the Creamery and pick up their advertising copy?" Phillip stopped in the doorway. "Stop by the house on your way back. Cook has packed us a basket, so we don't have to stop the press. I'm going to start the typesetting while you're gone." They'd been working on the design and layout for Thorliff's novel in their off hours.

"Sure."

"Oh, and take the bicycle. I parked it out back." Since purchasing one of the latest bicycle designs, the horse and buggy came out only on Sundays if the family wanted to go out in the country for a drive. The bicycle became the favored mode of travel, including riding around to get stories like the barn fire at the Olsens' the week before and the baseball games between Carleton, St. Olaf, and other teams in the area. Thorliff had played first base on the team this spring and, thanks to his hitting, helped win a couple of the games. When someone asked him where he got his skill, he'd said in the cow pasture at home.

Enjoying the cooling breeze as he pedaled his way along, his thoughts returned to the challenge Reverend Mohn had given to all the students the final day of classes. He'd read the Beatitudes from Matthew, his rich voice making the word *blessed* one of great desire and approbation. Thorliff knew them well, since Pastor Solberg in all his school years had insisted on his students memorizing large portions of the Scriptures. But memorizing and what he'd heard that day were two different things entirely, although knowing the words helped understand the challenge.

"My challenge to each of you is that you choose one of these Beatitudes and live it out. Let it permeate deep down into your heart and soul so that you check your thoughts and actions against the words of Christ Jesus our Lord and Savior. What does He mean? Not only what do the words mean, but what is Christ saying to you? How can living the Beatitudes make a difference in your life?" He paused to let his words sink in and then began to pray. "Father God, I ask thee to reveal thy words to our hearts and souls that we might live lives that honor thee. As Christ taught those crowds upon the hillside of Galilee, so teach us now. In thy name we pray, amen."

He opened his eyes and looked around the room, meeting each of their eyes. "Now, each one make your choice, and I'll look forward to our discussions on this topic with those of you returning in the fall. God bless you today and always and especially as you finish preparing for your exams."

"You don't suppose he really means for us to choose one," Benjamin, Thorliff's best friend at the school, turned to ask Thorliff as they filed out of the room.

"I think he does. You know he always says to study the particular so you can understand the general. Which are you going to choose?"

"I'm thinking of 'Blessed are the poor.' You can't get much poorer than me. I have not a dime left in my account or on my person."

Thorliff thought of the account he'd opened with the hundred dollars given to him at his graduation by Mr. Gould. More than half of it was still there because Mr. Rogers paid him beyond room and board for his work at the paper. Should he offer to help Benjamin come fall?

"What about you?"

"I'm not sure. For some reason my first thought was to choose 'Blessed are the pure in heart.' Perhaps I'll undertake that one."

"I'm not even sure I know what pure in heart means. You know, this is going to cause consternation all summer. What if I learn nothing over the summer on my Beatitude, and when Mohn asks me in the fall, I just look stupid?"

"Knowing Reverend Mohn, he's going to be praying that we all learn our lessons from this, or he wouldn't have made the challenge." Thorliff shifted his books to his other arm. "I'm going up to study. You coming?"

31

"No, I've got a meeting with Professor Ytterboe. He asked to see me." Benjamin rolled his eyes. "I'm sure it's not good."

Thorliff's thoughts came back to the present as he pedaled the bike onto the road leading to the Creamery, the largest commercial establishment in Northfield. Milk was hauled in from the surrounding dairy farms, bottled, and delivered by horse-drawn wagon to the houses of Northfield. The cheese they made didn't begin to equal that which was produced on the Bjorklund farm in Blessing.

"I'm here for the advertising copy." He nodded to the woman behind the desk.

"One minute." She turned back at the doorway. "That was some hit you made the other night. I thought that ball was going to fly clear to St. Paul."

"Thank you. I caught it solid is all." He could feel his ears heating up.

"You catch it solid more than most. I'll be right back."

Thorliff looked around the office, wrinkling his nose at the sour smell that came from the processing plant. Two weeks earlier he'd written a piece on the Creamery and the new equipment they'd recently installed.

"Here you go. And thanks for coming by. Mr. Warren liked your piece, by the way."

"Tell him thank you for me." Thorliff touched the brim of his hat. "Have a good day." Out the door and back onto the bike, he headed for the Rogerses' house, the envelope with the advertising copy in the basket attached to the handlebars and weighted by a stone. The rain the night before had washed all the dust off the leaves, so the maple, oak, and elm trees that dappled the street with shade wore a patina of green so sparkly he needed the shade of his straw boater to protect his eyes. Eyes that matched the blue of the skies, Bjorklund blue as they called them at home. He waved to two small children playing in a front yard and ignored a small dog trying to sound like a big one while being protected by a newly painted white picket fence. A boy in knickers and a flat hat raced him, keeping a hoop rolling in front of him with the regular application of the stick in his hand.

"You have to go faster than that." Thorliff pulled ahead, turned the corner, and rode into the Rogerses' drive. The two-story brick home was set back from the street with the front yard shaded by oak and maple trees taller than the house. Roses and honeysuckle perfumed the air, a yellow-and-black butterfly flitting from blossom to blossom. Thorliff leaned the bike against the back porch railing and leaped the three steps to knock on the screen door.

"Come in," Cook called.

Thorliff did as told and sighed in relief. "Ah, so nice and cool in here."

"Not if you come near this stove." Cook, who never had regained her robustness since before the measles attack the winter of '94, smiled in spite of her brusqueness, which Thorliff knew by now to be a put-on to cover a tender heart.

"I'll stay away from it then. Smells like you've been baking up a storm." He inhaled the scents of ginger, lemon, and pork roast, all overlaid with the aroma of freshly baked bread.

"It is our turn to bring cookies for the after-church social. And you know how they like my lemon bars, but Pastor put in a special request for gingersnaps, so I made those too. Here's some of each for the office." She handed him a wrapped packet and a covered basket. "And here's your dinner. What this world is coming to when a man is too busy to come home to eat is beyond me."

"We're starting on my book this afternoon."

Cook stopped and shot a firecracker smile over her shoulder. "Now, don't that beat all. Congratulations, young man. That is an honor certainly earned. I want a copy of my own, you hear?"

"I hear. I'll save you the first one off the binder."

"No, the second. You keep the first one for yourself. That is a milestone known by only a few."

"You're right. Thank you for the reminder. Miss Elizabeth studying?"

"From dawn to dark and thereafter." Cook handed him several gingersnaps. "I say if she hasn't got it by now, she's not going to get it."

"She wants top grades, hoping that will make a difference at some of the medical schools she's applied to."

"It would make a difference if she were a man instead of a woman. Those men in charge don't know up from down. She's already a good doctor, thanks to Dr. Gaskin. What does she need them for anyway?"

Thorliff took the safe path and kept his opinions to himself. Not that he didn't think Elizabeth would make a good doctor—he knew she could do anything she set her mind to—but still, real doctoring seemed to be a man's profession. After all, what man would want a woman doctor operating on him?

Not that he'd want anyone cutting on him, but if an operation were necessary . . . He thought back to Agnes Baard, who'd had something growing in her belly for the last years. That something had eaten her alive before their very eyes. Could a doctor have taken it out so that she could have lived longer? His mother had suggested it to her, as had others, but Agnes had been adamant. What God had sent her way was for her to endure, and endure she did. Breaking her children's hearts in the process.

Would his life have been different if Agnes had lived?

One of those questions without answers. *No looking back,* he ordered himself. *You vowed, no looking back. But your mother acts as the doctor in Blessing.* The thought sounded an awful lot like his father Haakan's voice. But Mother wasn't a young woman, and besides—He cut off the thought, knowing this was not a topic to bring up with Elizabeth.

"Okay, here's the lemonade. I will see you back here for supper?"

"Mange takk." He looked at the parcels, wondering how he was to carry them all on the bicycle. "But no, I will be studying from the time we close up until I get done. I'll just eat the leftovers."

"Well, don't blame me if you never fill out. I try to feed you enough."

"I won't. Thanks again." He juggled everything to open the screen door and, once outside, set the jug and the cookies in the basket and hooked the handles of the picnic basket over the handlebars. Whistling the catchy tune of "A Bicycle Built for Two," he pedaled back out the drive and down the street toward town.

"Hey, Mr. Bjorklund, that was a right fine article on the abuses of the railroad last week. But why aren't you running another story like you did last year?" Old Mr. Henry Stromme, who lived one block away from the Rogerses, called from his rocking chair on the front porch.

"Thank you." Thorliff coasted to a stop and braced with his feet. "I had no time to write the story this year, but we're thinking of one to start in the fall."

"Good, good. I'll be looking forward to it." He pointed a shaky finger in Thorliff's direction. "You going to run the contest again at Christmastime?"

"We're contemplating a Thanksgiving contest this year. What do you think?"

The old man nodded, his head keeping time with his rocking chair. "You think folks run outta Christmas tales?"

"No, just something different." Thorliff set one foot up on the pedal. "Glad you're happy with the paper."

"Near's I can figure, Thanksgiving ain't nowhere near important as Christmas."

"True."

"You ask me, and I'd say stick with Christmas."

Thorliff thought a moment and couldn't stop the grin. "You don't by any chance have a story you're planning to send in?"

The old man cackled like a hen just off her nest, announcing to the world that she laid the best egg ever. He slapped his knees and shook his head. "You be one smart young feller to figure that out. I might be. I just might."

"I'll tell Mr. Rogers your opinion." Thorliff waved and pedaled off. "Best to you."

"And you." Another cackle followed him down the street.

Thorliff parked the bike behind the newspaper office and entered through the back door, hanging his hat on a peg in the wall by the door to his room. He glanced longingly at the bed that had hardly been slept in for the last few days and continued on to the office, where Mr. Rogers was waiting on someone at the counter.

"Ah, Mr. Bjorklund, I've been meaning to ask you . . ."

He turned from setting the picnic basket on the desk and smiled in the direction of the woman crowned by a broad-brimmed straw hat that dipped seductively to the right. He couldn't see her face because the window light threw her in shadows, but he'd recognize the voice anywhere.

"Yes, ma'am, Miss Simpson? What can I do for you?"

"I was wondering, are you going to write another story for the paper? We just adored the one last year."

Why a woman her age fluttered her eyelashes at every person in pants was beyond him, but he kept a smile in place no matter. "You'll have to ask the boss here. After all, it is his paper."

"Oh, you silly boy, of course Phillip will run another story if you but write it." She tapped her fan on the top of Phillip's hand lying on the counter.

Thorliff could feel the laughter rising both within himself and the man next to him. "We'll do our best, ma'am."

"That we will." Phillip Rogers pushed a receipt across the counter. "Thank you for your advertisement. I'm sure the town will support your ladies' social. Anything to help our more unfortunate brothers."

"And sisters." She turned to leave, but her hat bobbled and flopped, so she had to grab it with one hand. "Good day, gentlemen." With that, she sailed out the door.

Phillip turned to Thorliff. "You better get crackin' on that story. Miss Simpson has spoken."

"Strange, but that's the second one today. Old Mr. Stromme hailed me—"

"From his front porch?"

Thorliff nodded.

"From whence he rules Northfield?"

Another nod. "I guess. But he insisted we need another Christmas contest this year—along with another serialized story."

"If I had a dollar for each request . . ." Phillip shook his head. "You're king in Northfield, young Bjorklund. You better enjoy it while it lasts."

CHAPTER FOUR

"I'm done!"

"Me too!"

Meeting on the front steps of Old Main, Thorliff and Elizabeth stared at each other, both noting the circles under eyes, the sag of weary shoulders. The broad lawn lay like a smooth skirt around the distinctive mansard-roofed brick building.

"I want to sleep for a week."

"I'd take one good night. I have to start writing the new story tomorrow." Thorliff reached for her bag, and Elizabeth was too tired to even protest. They walked down to the shaded path that led to town, grateful for the breeze that rustled the leaves above them. Rainwater from showers the night before still lay in puddles in the hollows, but soon the heat would drink them dry. Thorliff inhaled the fragrance of rain-washed leaves and grass. Daisies nodded where the sun poked through the covering. Blue and purple violets peeked out from under the bushes, too shy to push their way forward like the sun-loving daisies.

"It surely does smell good, doesn't it?" Elizabeth followed his lead, only stopping to sniff again where a particularly delightful perfume caught her nose. "Ah, honeysuckle." She turned her head, following the scent like a hunting dog on point. "See, over there." She pointed to a shrub polka-dotted with the fragile white blossoms blinking in the dancing shade.

"You want one?"

"Of course." She started forward, but Thorliff stopped her with a cautionary hand.

"Might be poison ivy in there." Keeping an eye out for the attractive leaves, he picked a sprig of honeysuckle and brought it to her.

Her thank-you wore a well-washed gown of grudge. Frequently sniffing the fragrant offering, she strolled down the path, forcing Thorliff to keep his pace sedate or be rude and go on ahead. There was more than one feminine way to get even. "So do you have your new story all figured out?"

"No, but I'm working on it."

"What's the general idea?"

"A continuation of *The Switchmen* with Douglas now head of his own company and seeing things from the other side. A sort of Horatio Alger's story."

"I think you need more female characters to draw in more women readers."

"Hmm." Thorliff rubbed his chin, an unconscious imitation of Haakan in deep thought. "Makes good sense."

"Well, can you believe that? Mr. Bjorklund can take a suggestion from a mere woman." Elizabeth batted her eyes.

"You don't simper well, so forget it."

"Thorliff, you are the most insufferable—"

"Miss Elizabeth." He loaded extra emphasis on the *Miss*. "I am too tired to argue with you or even carry on a decent conversation, for that matter, so sniff your posy, and we'll go at it again tomorrow."

"Or the next day when I finally wake up." Elizabeth stifled a yawn. "I never did simper well."

"Not enough practice." He held the back door open for her and followed her into the kitchen, which seemed huge for its emptiness.

"Where's Cook?" He set Elizabeth's satchel down on one of the red-cushioned chairs by the turned-leg table. A vase of roses nodded in the center of the red-and-white checked tablecloth.

"I have no idea." She saw a note on the counter and crossed the room to read it aloud. "Thorliff's dinner and supper are in a box in the icebox. There is salad for your own dinner. Your mother is at the ladies social at the Lutheran church, and I have gone to the market. There are extra cookies in the cookie jar if Thorliff cannot make it to his room without food. Cook." Elizabeth pointed to the cookie jar. "Help yourself."

Thorliff did and, leaning against the counter, devoured three in close order while Elizabeth fetched his string-tied box. "Thanks." He took it and headed for the door.

"Remember, add more women." Her advice trailed him outside as he picked up the pace to his usual half-trot, and with legs the length of his, he passed the block quickly. He glanced at Mr. Stromme's porch, but the rocking chair sat empty, forlorn, as if not knowing what to do with its spare time. He kept going for half a block, ignoring the voice inside, but finally turned around and took the stairs to the old man's house in one bound. He rapped on the screen door, staring into the long hallway toward the kitchen. There was no response. He rapped again. "Mr. Stromme, are you all right?"

Again only the silence of a waiting house answered.

Thorliff set his school satchel and dinner box in the chair and leaped to the ground to trot around the house to the backyard. It was empty of human habitation, but the wheelbarrow sat out, rake and fork showing there had been a plan for work.

"Mr. Stromme?" Thorliff looked around, checked the tool shed, then mounted the back steps. *Do I go look for him or assume he stepped over to the neighbors?* A voice demanded from inside of him: *Go look.* He opened the screen door, the screech of hinges needing oil the only sound. Calling every few moments, he checked each room downstairs, then mounted the stairs. "Mr. Stromme?"

He found the old man lying beside his bed, fully dressed, his eyes imploring him to help. One side of his face drooped like melted wax, and drool puddled on the floor under his cheek.

"Oh, Mr. Stromme, I am so sorry. Do you have a telephone?"

A slight shake of the grizzled head, so slight that had Thorliff not been watching, he would have missed it.

"Do your neighbors?"

Again that minuscule movement.

"Then I shall run back to the Rogerses' and call the doctor from there."

One clawlike hand scrabbled on the painted floor.

"I'll hurry. I know. I don't want to leave you alone either, but if I see anyone, I'll send them up." Leaving the man was one of the harder things Thorliff had ever done. Old Mr. Stromme's eyes haunted him as he ran the distance, pounded up to the back door and, not bothering to knock, charged into the kitchen.

Cook, eyes wide and mouth agape, turned abruptly, dropping her recently purchased potatoes onto the wooden floor. "Wh-what?"

"I have to call Dr. Gaskin. Old Mr. Stromme is on the floor. I'm sure he's had a stroke." The words trailed back from over his shoulder as Thorliff strode to the telephone in the hall. He picked up the receiver, set it back in the prong, and cranked the handle on the side of the wooden box. Picking up the earpiece again, he said, "Hello?"

"Central."

"We need a doctor at Mr. Stromme's. I just found him on the floor upstairs." He could hear Miss Odegaard ringing the doctor's number before he finished his sentence.

"You go on back to be with him while I get the doctor there," Ina Odegaard said.

"Thank you." Thorliff hung up and headed out the front door to save a few paces.

Cook was halfway down the drive with a basket over her arm. She handed it to Thorliff. "A cold cloth for his head. I'll be right behind you."

Thorliff ran back down the street, bursting through the gate, taking the steps two and three at a time, then pounded into the bedroom.

The relief in Mr. Stromme's eyes burned the back of Thorliff's throat. He knelt beside the old man and, taking the cloth from the basket, laid it across his forehead. "Would you be more comfortable if I put a pillow beneath your head?" Never had he realized eyes could say so much. He took a pillow from the bed, picked up the man's head, and slid the pillow in place, straightening his shoulders and laying the clawed hand across the sunken chest. "Are you cold?"

Again Mr. Stromme responded with a blinking of the eyes. So Thorliff reached up to take down the knit afghan to cover him, all without letting go of the other hand, as if he had any choice.

Cook came panting up the stairs, stopping in the doorway with a hand to her chest to catch her breath. "H-how is he?"

Thorliff gave a slight shake of his head and settled himself on the floor beside the patient, gently returning the faint hand squeeze from Mr. Stromme. *Lord, please help this poor man. Here, he lives all alone and has always been so spry and busy. Who will tend his garden and take care of him if he . . . Where would he . . . Lord, this is a mess.*

"The doctor is here." Cook touched his shoulder and motioned to the doorway.

"Thank you."

Mr. Stromme's eyes fluttered open, and he tried to speak, but when only guttural sounds came out, his eyes shifted to terror again.

Dr. Gaskin nodded to Thorliff and knelt by their patient. "Ah, Henry, what have you done now? I know, I know. You didn't fall or anything." While he talked, he applied the stethoscope from his bag to the man's heaving chest. "Your heart sounds good. You been having headaches lately? No? What about vomiting? Any dizziness?" He stopped and watched Henry's face. "Dizzy today or other days?"

Thorliff felt the man's hand clench, whether a spasm or in response to the questions he didn't know. Poor old man.

"Well, we'll move you over to the surgery where we can keep an eye on you and see if we can get your limbs moving again. I know you're feeling panicky right now, but I've seen lots of folks with a condition like yours improve. It will just take time and work on your part." Dr. Gaskin glanced over to Cook. "Why don't you get some quilts or blankets so we can make a pallet in the wagon. And you, young man, go fetch Old Tom. He's working at my house today. Tell him to bring his wagon."

"Yes, sir." Thorliff gently released the old man's hold on his hand and smiled into the watery eyes. "It's okay now. Dr. Gaskin is with you. Don't you worry. I'll be back." Down the stairs he went and up the street to the Rogerses' again to call the surgery and leave a message with Nurse Browne.

"I'll send Tom right over, and tell Doctor I'll have a bed all ready," said the efficient nurse.

"Thank you." Thorliff hung up the phone and leaned his head against the wall. All this going on and Elizabeth slept through it all. She'd probably be downright cranky with him for not letting her know, but she'd looked ready to melt into a puddle. He thought of the bed waiting for him in the cool back room of the newspaper office. Oh well, he could sleep later. Visions of the old man's pleading eyes propelled him back out the door and wearing a path to Stromme's house door.

"He sure took to you," Doctor said a bit later when the wagon bearing the old man to the surgery pulled out.

"He'd call to me from his rocking chair, telling me when he was happy with my story in the paper and other times when there was something he wasn't too happy about."

"You mean he raked you over the coals?"

Thorliff half shrugged. "Me or Mr. Rogers or the mayor or the president . . ."

"Or anything else he thought you might like to know. As if you were responsible for it all."

"I guess he figured since I work for the newspaper, I might be able to fix something."

"Henry Stromme has been a pillar of the community for more years than I care to count. Back in his younger days he ran the grain elevator down by the river. Since they put him out to pasture, he's kept half the town supplied with tomatoes and cucumbers, all kinds of good things from his garden. But this past year he was too stove up to even do much of that. Arthritis is a mean thing, crippling a person. Henry still managed to keep abreast of all the happenings, including all the gossip. In spite of no phone, he hooked on to the Northfield grapevine."

Thorliff listened, nodding when appropriate and wishing he could have done more. "What'll happen to him now?"

"I'm hoping we can get him moving around some. If not, we'll move his bed downstairs to the parlor and get someone in to help. Knowing him, he'll be one cantankerous patient, but Nurse Browne will charm him into behaving. Hopefully we can get someone in to take care of whatever he needs done."

"No family?"

"All gone before. His wife died four, maybe five years ago." As they talked, the doctor put his bag back together, and Thorliff folded up the afghan and laid it back on the bed. They walked downstairs to meet Cook coming from the kitchen.

"I cleaned up for him, put things away, figured it might be some time before he gets to come home again." She wiped her hands on her apron, making *tsk*ing sounds. "Anything else I can do?"

"Not that I can think of. Thank you." Dr. Gaskin patted her arm.

"You're welcome." She closed the door behind them as they stepped out on the porch.

"Look at that dog carrying that box." Doc pointed to a shepherd-type dog hightailing it out of the yard with a box in his mouth.

Thorliff glanced over to the now empty rocking chair, his book satchel dumped on the floor. "That's my meal box. Hey, drop that." He leaped off the steps and chased after the dog, which after a glance over his shoulder at the shouting chaser, picked up the pace and left Thorliff behind shaking his fist.

"I'll fix you another." Cook could hardly talk from laughing. Between her and the doctor, the food nabber might have been the funniest thing to happen in Northfield in a month.

Thorliff stomped up the walk. "Stupid dog."

"Smart dog, far as I can tell. Everyone in town knows Cook here is one of the best, even the local canine portion of our fair city."

"Fair city, my foot." Thorliff sank down on the top step, panting to catch his breath. "People ought to keep their pets at home." He glared up at the two chortling in glee. "I don't see this is so funny." But he had to fight to keep his grin from showing. The dog had looked like a cartoon character carrying off his dinner. The box was bigger than his head. "Hope he enjoys it." Actually he hoped the dog would get a stomachache. And here he'd spent his time taking care of Mr. Stromme. He shook his head. "There's just no justice." He slanted a look out of the corner of his eye to make sure the two above him were still enjoying themselves at his expense. Neither one of them had occasions to laugh like this often.

"I better get on over there and check on my patient. I'm sure Nurse Browne and Miss Haugen have cleaned him up and gotten him as comfortable as he can be by now. Hopefully after he sleeps awhile, he won't wake up worse. That happens sometimes, you know."

"Poor old dear." Cook patted Thorliff's shoulder as she passed him on the steps. "I'll send Old Tom over with another packet for you; just you be careful this time to not go laying it around for someone or something to snitch it."

"Mange takk."

"Velbekomme." She fluttered a hand at him when she reached the sidewalk.

"Now there goes one fine woman."

Thorliff stood and walked to the buggy, the horse sound asleep between the shafts, the breeze causing the sun and shade to polka all over its dark back. "And to think Elizabeth slept through this whole thing. She'll be some bothered that no one woke her."

"I'm not telling her, that's for certain, and if Cook has a lick of sense, she won't either." Dr. Gaskin chuckled again as he stepped into the buggy. "You want a ride?"

"No thanks. That's out of your way." He swung off toward the newspaper office, this time hoping no one tried to catch his attention. By now, thanks to Ina Odegaard, the town operator, everyone in Northfield knew there had been an emergency at the Stromme house. And those without phones would hear about it over the back fence grapevine nearly as fast.

"So, I hear that you're the hero of the hour." Phillip Rogers looked up from the editorial he was writing.

"How long did it take for you to find out?"

Phillip held up a sheaf of papers several thick. "Long enough to write this about how the people of Northfield are so quick to help others in distress. I included those who helped put out the grass fire south of town, several other incidents, and you, of course, as the man of the hour."

Thorliff groaned.

"What made you go check on him?"

"I tried to ignore that little voice inside, but it yelled so loud I turned and went back. It looked like he'd been out working in his garden and must not have felt well so went up to lie down. He never made it to the bed—almost but not quite."

"Well, thank the good Lord you listened. He might have died there without help."

"If it's as bad as it looks, he might wish I hadn't shown up."

Phillip shook his head. "Well, God must have a reason for keeping him around awhile longer. Listening to that still small voice takes practice."

"Still, small, my foot. It was yelling fit to be heard clear across town."

"I hear you had a bit of a mishap after."

Thorliff blinked and took a step back. "You heard about the dog taking my dinner? Already?"

"Mrs. Norlie was down the street and saw the whole thing. She was laughing fit to bust her corset when she came in here." Phillip leaned back in his oak chair until it sent up a shrieking. "Moral of the story—don't ever try to hide anything in this town. You'll be found out for sure." He sat forward, and his chair squeaked in relief. "You want to go back and get another box or just go home with me for dinner?"

"Old Tom is bringing it by. I want to get the first chapter started today if there is any way." *And if I can keep my eyes open.*

Phillip nodded, his pen racing across the paper. "Good, good."

Thorliff took his satchel back to his room and tucked it under the bed. He wouldn't need it until fall now. What a way to start the summer. He thought of the letter he would write home. They'd laugh for certain sure. What other crazy things would he have to write home about? And what did pure in heart *really* mean?

CHAPTER FIVE

Blessing, North Dakota

"Sophie, what happened?" Ingeborg threw open the door as she spoke.

"It-it's Trygve." Sophie Knutson, Ingeborg's niece, leaned over to suck in another breath, then straightened. "He fell out of a tree." Brushing hair that held small sticks and bits of grass in its wavy strands off her face, she looked toward home. "Mor thinks his arm is broken. I thought sure you heard Sammy screaming."

"I'll get my basket." Ingeborg spun back into the house and snatched up the basket she kept packed with emergency supplies, including several wood splints that Andrew had sanded smooth so they would cause no slivers. This wouldn't be the first broken bone she had set through the years.

"I'm coming too, Mor." Astrid came running from the garden.

Sophie, worry crinkling her amber eyes, took her aunt's hand and pulled. "Come, he's hurting mighty bad."

"So how come Sammy was screaming?" Ingeborg strode swiftly across the small pasture.

"He was in the tree too. Trygve had gone up to help him down."

"I see. They're at the house?"

"Ja."

"All right then, Astrid, you go get Andrew to bring over some ice. That will help a lot. Needn't be a big piece." Andrew would chop off a chunk of ice they'd cut from the river during the winter and stored in the icehouse, well insulated by thick layers of sawdust.

"I will." Astrid set off at a dead run.

Ingeborg and Sophie hurried up the steps to the two-story house that had been added on to so that now it housed all the students of the deaf school along with the Knutson family. With most of the students gone home for the summer, the house seemed huge.

"In here, Ingeborg." Kaaren beckoned from the downstairs bedroom. "I didn't dare try to set it alone."

Trygve lay on the bed, his face white with a green tinge, one arm, already swollen, propped on a pillow. Sammy sat on a stool beside the bed, sniffling every time he looked at his brother. "My fault. It's my fault."

Grace, Sophie's twin who was born deaf, took the cloth off his forehead, dipped it in cool water, wrung it out, and lovingly laid it back in place.

"Well, Trygve, this is sure going to put a bump in your summer." Ingeborg smiled at her nephew as she gently probed his arm. When he yelped, she nodded. "Broken all right."

"What are you going to do?" Trygve's voice quivered.

"I am going to hold your shoulder, and your mother is going to pull until we hear that old bone snap right back in place."

"Do you have to?"

"Ja, if you want to be able to use your arm right ever again."

"Oh. It's going to hurt bad, huh?"

"I'm sure, but you're a big boy. You want a stick to bite down on?" He shook his head.

Ingeborg took a brown bottle out of her basket and pulled the cork out with her teeth. "Sophie, go get a cup of water to mix with this. That will make setting it easier on him." The girl scuttled out of the room

47

while Kaaren and Ingeborg both studied the arm. "Good thing it's not at the elbow. A forearm like this will heal real quick."

"Will I be able to go swimming?"

"No, nor milk cows."

"But don't worry, you can hoe with one arm and still pull weeds." Kaaren took the cup of water from Sophie, mixed several drops of the brown liquid in the water, and held the cup to her son's mouth with one hand while she propped his head with the other.

"Ugh."

"I could have put some honey in that." Ingeborg pushed the cork back in the bottle.

"Anyone who falls out of a tree is strong enough to take his medicine straight."

"But, Mor, I went up to help Sammy down." Trygve started to raise up to state his defense but yelped instead. He eased back down, glaring at his painful arm.

Kaaren turned to her younger son. "And what is your excuse?"

Sammy tried to become part of the stool on which he sat. "I-I saw a bird's nest, and I wanted to see the babies," he muttered into his knees.

"And you were going to go way out on the limb to see them?"

He shook his head. "I thought if I got higher, I could look down. And then I saw how high I was and got scared."

"And how come Trygve fell?"

Sammy shrugged, the suspender on his skinny shoulder sliding down his arm. With an unconscious gesture, he thumbed it back in place. Growing into his brother's outgrown clothing sometimes took a bit of time.

Kaaren turned back to her son in the bed. "How come?"

"I got up to him, and he kicked at me. He wouldn't let me help him, so I was hurrying back down to get Andrew or Pa and a ladder."

Sammy flung himself off the stool and into his mother's aproned skirt. "I-I'm sorry. I didn't mean for Trygve to get hurt. I was so scared."

Kaaren patted his head. "And how did you get down?"

"I-I—he screamed and c-crashed through the b-branches, and he was hurt, so I had to help him. I went down as fast as I could, and his arm and . . ." Hiccupping sobs punctuated his slurry of words. "I-I am s-so sorry." Tears soaked her apron.

"I know you are, but sometimes being sorry after a bad thing happens isn't enough. You need to think ahead and not make foolish choices." Kaaren nudged him back toward the stool. "You sit there now and see what we have to do to help Trygve. Let this be a lesson the next time you do something without thinking. I think you will have to take over the chores he cannot do with only one hand."

"Even feeding the pigs?"

"I expect so."

"I think he's drowsy enough now that we can set it," Ingeborg said.

The screen door banged and Andrew charged into the room, a chunk of ice in a gunnysack over his shoulder. "Where do you want this?"

"In the pan in the dry sink. Chip off enough to pack around his arm. Sophie, you go hold the dish towel for him. We'll lay his arm in that when we get it set."

Ingeborg and Kaaren exchanged glances and each took her place. "Now this is going to hurt, but we'll do it as quickly as we can. You can help us most by lying still." Ingeborg laid her hands on the boy's shoulder and elbow while Kaaren took his wrist in both hands.

"Now." Kaaren leaned back, and in one smooth pull they heard the bone click back together.

Trygve clamped his teeth on a scream and lay back, sweat popping up on his forehead.

They could hear Andrew chipping ice and Sophie saying something that made him laugh. Grace took the cloth and, dipping it again, wiped Trygve's brow and patted his cheek. "You be better." She spoke slowly, carefully forming the sounds she could not hear. While her hands were fluent in speaking, her mouth was still learning.

"Here you go." Andrew brought the towel and ice and handed it to his mother, who folded it into a square and slid half under the boy's arm, laying the rest on top.

Trygve nodded. "Thank you," he said in the slurred way of a drug-induced almost sleep.

"You must not move your arm. We'll bind the splints in place in a little bit. Do you understand?" Ingeborg touched his cheek and received a brief nod.

"I'll stay." Grace glanced from her brother to her mother. Her fingers flew as she continued. "I won't let him move."

"All right." Kaaren stroked the hair back off her son's forehead and turned to Sammy. "You stay and watch too. Tante Ingeborg and I are going to have a cup of coffee, and then we'll come and splint this."

"Where's Astrid?" Ingeborg asked Andrew after sitting down at the table.

"She took over the team for me so I could run fast. I need to get back out there. She was so worried about Trygve." Andrew snagged two cookies off the plate on the counter and with a wave headed back out the door, leaping from the top step of the porch to the ground. "Mange takk."

They heard the words fly back as if carried by the breeze his speed created.

"He has grown so much this year, I can't find my little Andrew anymore." Kaaren poured two cups of coffee and set them on the table. "Sophie, you need to get the table set. They'll be up for dinner soon."

"Where's Ilse?" Ingeborg took a ginger cookie and dunked it in her coffee.

"Gone to help Penny for the day. They had a shipment come in for the store, and Penny needed someone to watch the babies."

"I could have sent Astrid."

"And I could have sent Sophie, but neither of them want to be nearer to George McBride."

Her comment made them both smile. Ilse, orphaned by her parents dying on the ship, had come to them when Bridget Bjorklund, the mother of their first husbands, emigrated from Norway. Now Ilse was Kaaren's right-hand woman, both helper and teacher at the School for the Deaf, which Kaaren had founded several years after the birth of the twins. Kaaren had determined that Grace, never having been able to hear, would somehow learn to communicate with the hearing world in which she lived. David Jonathan Gould, a friend from New York, had sent Kaaren a book on a newly developed sign language, and many of the residents of Blessing learned to use it because Pastor Solberg taught signing at school.

The two women caught up on whatever news each had heard and in a few minutes returned to the sick room, where Trygve snored with little puffs of breath. They eased the ice away, laid the padded splints on either side of the tanned arm, and bound them in place with strips of old sheets.

"I'll put a sling on him when he wakes." Kaaren turned to see Sammy sound asleep on the floor by his brother's bed. She nodded and Ingeborg came around the bed to see him too.

"Some of us seem always to need to learn our lessons the hard way."

"Ja, that is so. But thank you, Lord, this lesson was no harder than it is. When I think what could have happened . . ." Kaaren closed her eyes. "Thank you, Jesus, for watching over my boys."

Several days later Ingeborg called to Astrid, "I am going over to visit Metiz. Please take the cake out when it is finished."

"I will." Astrid looked up from the dress she was hemming. "How long?"

"Check it in fifteen minutes or so. I just put more wood in the fire." Ingeborg untied her apron and hung it on the hook.

"You want me to frost it?"

"No. I think we'll put applesauce on it. Applesauce always goes good with gingerbread."

"If I know Andrew, he'll smell that gingerbread clear across the field and come in for a piece."

"Tell him it is for dessert. Dinner will be ready at twelve-thirty. He can wait that long." Ingeborg picked up the basket that she'd packed with cheese, strawberry jam, and two slices off the ham now in the oven and headed out the door. Something inside her had said she should go

51

check on Metiz. Metiz had been living on the land when they home-steaded it. She was of Lakota Indian and French Canadian ancestry. As a healer, she had shared knowledge with Ingeborg, and they had become fast friends. Ingeborg strode the trail to the river, thinking back to when they'd driven the cattle down to water and hauled water for the house. Ah, what a time-saver the well had been, and still was, for that matter. Water was something never to be taken for granted.

Metiz' house sat under one of the few remaining big oak trees, not far from the bank of the river. She had rabbit hides tacked to the outside walls, drying so she could tan them to make mittens, vests, and even a hat or two, all to sell in Penny's store or to give as gifts. Vests of the softened skins, with the fur side either in or out, were prized among the children of Blessing. Deer antlers hung on pegs on a post so she could turn the horn into knife handles. Either Hjelmer Bjorklund or Sam Lincoln would make the blades for her at the blacksmith shop. Penny ordered special steel for the knife blades, tempered so it would hold a fine edge. The knives were of such caliber that Penny could sell all that Metiz made and had customers waiting for more.

"We need another dog," Ingeborg said to the crow that announced her coming. "Days like this I miss Paws as much as Andrew does." Paws, the dog given to Thorliff when the Bjorklunds first moved to Dakota Territory, had died more than a year ago, leaving a hole in all their lives. The crow flew off, screaming "intruder" as he flapped his wings.

A meadowlark sang, the notes hovering on the breeze as if loath to die away. Ingeborg whistled a close proximity to the lark's song, but the bird failed to respond.

"Guess you didn't like my rendition, eh?" *Thank you, God, for such a glorious morning. Since Metiz is sitting in her rocker working away as usual, perhaps you called me out to hear the meadowlark and enjoy the bluebells.*

"Ho," Metiz called from her chair. "You come."

"Did you need me?"

"Need? No." She shook her head, the dark hair gone nearly white and worn in two braids tied by a bit of thong. "Want, yes." She held up a deerskin vest she was beading with bits of porcupine quills and tiny glass beads she traded for. The black hairs from a deer's tail wove a minute dark design just below one shoulder seam.

"You do such beautiful work." Ingeborg fingered the rust and tan beads and the few blue ones that added more color.

"Need more beads for moccasins. Traded for elk hide. Good for moccasins. Harder to get now. Tell Andrew thank you for rabbit skins."

"I will." Ingeborg sank down on the lip of the low porch. "I brought you some extra supplies."

"No need."

"I know." The two smiled at each other, the peace of two longtime friends settling upon them. "Are you feeling all right?"

Metiz shrugged. "So-so. Hands, feet still work."

Ingeborg knew from the limp Metiz now wore all the time that the arthritis that bent her fingers had most likely settled in her hip too. But it would have to be pretty bad for Metiz to complain. She walked a bit slower, appearing smaller winter by winter, but like the rest of them seemed to blossom again come summer. The weathered boards of her house melded into the shade of the tree so that it looked as if it sprang from the soil like the grandmother oak above.

The house was just one large room with a door on either end, because that was the way she wanted it—"to let the river through," she'd told Haakan when he insisted they build her a better house than the shack she'd built herself for her and her grandson Baptiste. With Baptiste now married to Manda and raising and training horses in Montana with Manda's adopted father, Zebulun MacCallister, Metiz was growing older alone but for her friends, chiefly the Bjorklunds.

"You been fishing lately?"

"No. Andrew brought me fish last week, along with the rabbits. He good boy."

"Yes, he is. If only he would ignore Toby Valders."

"He bad."

"I hate to call him bad. He just had a poor beginning, living on the streets of New York like that. Reminds me to never take all that we have here for granted." Ingeborg leaned against the post holding up the shed-roofed porch.

"Toby Valders . . ." Metiz shook her head slowly. "He mean inside."

"Now, Gerald isn't. He's a good boy, works hard to help his folks. Haakan said he'd take Gerald on the threshing crew this year if he wanted to go." Gerald was the older brother of the two. They'd hitched a ride on the train and got off in Blessing to forage for food. Penny caught them trying to steal food from her mercantile.

Metiz folded the vest she'd been working on and placed it in a basket beside her chair. She grunted as she pushed up to stand, then disappeared into the cabin and returned with a letter. "Please read."

"Of course. When did this come?"

"Yesterday. When I take knives to Penny."

"Why didn't you stop by?"

Metiz' thin shoulders lifted slightly. She sat back in her chair. "Tell Andrew I have present for him."

"Of course I will." Ingeborg drew the paper out of the already slit envelope.

"Dear Grand-mère,

I am glad you have someone to read this to you. We are doing good here. Plenty of foals born this spring. We trapped more wild horses too, so the herd is growing. We built a cabin of our own not far from the main house. We will be bringing horses early this year while Manda can still ride. We will have a baby late in the fall. I wish you could see the mountains. The game here is like it used to be along the Red River.

Your grandson,
Baptiste

PS: Manda sends her love and wishes you could be here to help her birth this baby."

Ingeborg looked up to see Metiz smiling and nodding.

"Good news."

Metiz nodded again, ever chary of her words. "Good they come. Make papoose board."

"We'll get started on diapers and baby things. Oh, Martha Mary will be so excited. May I take this for her to read?"

Metiz nodded. "Bring back."

"Of course. Letters are precious." She carefully folded and put the paper back in the envelope. "And to think Baptiste wrote. Usually men let their wives do the letter writing." Especially those like Baptiste who never were enamored of school. "How I would love to see the mountains. That's one thing I miss about Norway. The mountains. Some had snow all summer long, so high and majestic they were. And some dove right into the fjords. Such blues—sky and water—and snow so white it shadowed azure. In the summer we would take the cows and goats and sheep up to the high pastures to graze, and all the milk would be turned into cheese." Ingeborg's eyes flew open. "Speaking of cheese, I must get home to finish making dinner. Are you sure there is nothing else you need?"

"No. Mange takk."

"Velbekomme." Sticking the letter in her pocket, Ingeborg set out for home. She stopped and looked back. "Have you seen any ripe strawberries yet?"

"No, but soon. Good year for berries."

"Good."

After saying good-bye and promising to return the letter, Ingeborg headed back across the field. The icehouse with its blocks of ice buried in sawdust reminded her that they hadn't had ice cream for some time, and now with the warm weather, ice cream would be a real treat. She paused for a moment, glancing back over her shoulder. Something was bothering her about Metiz. *What, Lord? What is it?* A shiver started at her toes and worked upward. She closed her eyes, seeing Metiz rocking in the chair, another of the chairs built by Uncle Olaf. Was it her face? Nothing came to mind. Her voice? The way she moved? But Metiz had been getting a bit more bowed year by year. What was different? Or was it nothing, her mind trying to worry in spite of all her good intentions?

"Uff da. I'll think about this later." When she entered the house, she inhaled the ham and ginger fragrance.

"Please ring the bell." Astrid set the roasting pan on the cool end of the stove.

"You are that close to ready?"

"We will be by the time they get here."

Ingeborg glanced around her kitchen. The table was set. Potatoes steaming on the stove, the last of the dried bean britches simmering with salt pork, bread sliced and on the table along with the butter.

"You are going to make some man a wonderful wife someday." She set her basket on the counter. "But please don't be in too big a hurry."

"Mor." Astrid shook her head, her grin giving lie to the remonstrance she tried to inject in her voice.

"Well, I wasn't gone that long." Ingeborg took out the knife and gave it a couple of swipes on the stone before beginning to slice the ham. "Oh, I didn't ring the bell."

With another rolled-eye look, Astrid headed out the screen door to clang the bar around the iron triangle. She shaded her eyes to look out in the field, seeing Andrew already turning the team toward home. He stopped to unhitch the cultivator. In the far cornfield, Hamre did the same. Soon haying season would start, and she knew her father was down in the machine shed making sure the mowers were in good repair and the sickle bars sharpened. Between Haakan and Lars, the Bjorklund equipment was always ready for the next job. Astrid had overheard people's comments on the success of the Bjorklund/Knutson farms, and always she felt a surge of pride.

After the men washed up and everyone took his place at the table, Haakan bowed his head for grace. "Heavenly Father, we thank thee for the food before us and for the hands that fixed it. And Lord, if you could see fit to send us some rain, we would be most grateful, as would the fields. In your son's holy name, amen."

As they passed the platter and bowls, each one helping himself, Ingeborg paused. "Andrew, Metiz asked if you would come by. She has something for you."

Andrew looked up from pouring gravy on his potatoes. "What?"

"I have no idea. She didn't tell me."

Andrew glanced at Haakan. "I'll go over right after we eat."

Haakan nodded. "You been running a snare line for her?"

"Not lately. I'll set one up again."

"She heard from Baptiste." Ingeborg picked up the letter she'd set by her plate and read it to them.

"That's all he said?" Haakan cocked his head and grinned at his wife. "A man of few words, our Baptiste. It will be good to see them."

"I thought to take this over to Mary Martha this afternoon. She is always asking if we've heard from them."

"She gets more letters than anyone, thanks to Manda." Andrew reached for another roll. "Hamre, how's your section coming?"

"Good. Once more with the cultivator," responded Hamre Bjorklund, who had immigrated with his great-aunt Bridget and was known never to use two words when one would do.

"We're going to have to chop out those thistles before they take over the entire field. I'll sharpen up the hoes after we eat. Get Grace and Sophie and Trygve to help too." Haakan added, "Oops, not Trygve with that broken arm."

"You want Mr. McBride too?" Andrew asked. "I saw him over at Onkel Lars's."

"I thought he was working with Olaf."

Andrew shrugged and looked toward Hamre.

"He is working two days a week at the furniture store." Hamre went back to eating.

"I'll go ask him." Haakan nodded to Astrid. "Please pass the potatoes."

When the meal was finished, Haakan didn't bother with his pipe but set off for the Knutsons' house across the small pasture, which was the fenced field between the two homes. Andrew headed for Metiz' cabin after suggesting to Hamre that he sharpen the hoes. Years earlier he had learned that Hamre did nothing on his own but was willing to do whatever someone suggested. He'd have gone out to continue cultivating without complaining but without seeing other things that might need doing. He never initiated conversation either, so unless someone spoke to him, he lived in a word-free world.

Andrew kicked a rock-hard clump of black dirt ahead of him. He whistled a tune, his thumbs hooked into the front pockets of his pants.

What a perfect day to go fishing. But then, any day was a perfect day to go fishing. Wouldn't his mother love a string of perch to fry for supper? In spite of a full stomach topped off by gingerbread, he could taste the crispy fried fish. Now if Baptiste still lived around here, he'd have brought them strings of fish, or a mess of squirrels or rabbits, or a deer if he'd have seen a buck. Farming took too much time away from hunting and fishing. He remembered stories his mother told of the early days when the sky had been black with migrating ducks and geese. She said you only had to aim at the sky and surely you'd hit at least one. While Andrew doubted the flocks were that thick, his tante Kaaren had corroborated his mother's stories, and Tante Kaaren never exaggerated when telling stories like his mother often did.

He whistled a three-tone call that Baptiste had always used to announce his presence and waited for Metiz to come out of her house.

"In back."

"Okay." He followed her voice, and when he stepped around a woodpile that needed splitting and stacking, he saw her sitting on a bench on the back porch, a basket at her feet, something black and brown and furry in her lap. "How are you?" He nodded toward the wood. "I'll come split and stack that as soon as I can."

"This for you." Metiz stood and held out a squirming puppy.

"Really?" Andrew crossed to the porch and took the puppy in both hands. "Look at his feet. He's going to be a big dog." Andrew gathered the bundle of wriggling fur and pink tongue into his chest. "Where did you get him?"

"A member of my tribe. He say I need dog. I say you need dog."

"He looks like someone spattered gray and black and brown paint all over him." The puppy chewed on Andrew's thumb, his tail whipping in ecstasy. "And one white foot. Does he have a name?"

"No, you name."

Andrew sat down on the bench beside Metiz. "You sure you want to give him away?"

She nodded. "He need longtime home."

"You planning on going somewhere else?" He glanced at her out of the side of his eye and caught her shrug.

"One never know."

"Well, I must get back to work. Thank you for my new friend here."

"You most welcome. He meant for you."

Andrew, puppy in his arms, headed for home. "How did she know, Mor?" he asked after showing Ingeborg his gift.

"It wouldn't be hard to figure out, knowing how much you loved Paws. But Metiz senses things. She always has."

"Did she say anything to you about going somewhere?"

"No, why?"

"Just . . . I don't know. She said the puppy needed a longtime home, and when I asked her if she was going somewhere, she said, 'One never knows.' Strange, isn't it?"

Please, God, don't let it be what I fear.

CHAPTER SIX

Northfield, Minnesota

Playing the piano was more soothing than a cool bath.

Elizabeth let her fingers trail over the keys, rippling from chord to chord and melody to melody. She closed her eyes and let the music seep into her muscles and bones, trickling into her soul, where it began the needed healing, mending the rents and tears of finals week, of not hearing from the school she wanted, of missing Thornton. Thornton Wickersham the Third, whom she originally thought to be pompous and boring but had instead become a good friend, who insisted she take time to laugh and play.

She hadn't thought that would be the case, but today the croquet set almost brought her to tears. They'd played many a match on the back lawn, and now she regretted trouncing him so soundly. His latest letter lay open on the piano, where she could partially read his writing. He sounded both happy and sad. Rejoicing in the ministry and broken-hearted at the poverty. He was having a hard time with the languages, and the man he'd gone to serve with had been sent to the States on a medical furlough. He wrote:

> I wish I had been able to accompany him, if for no other reason than to see you again, my dear friend. Your letters are like a drink of water in a parched land.

Guilt sliced like the finest surgical steel. She had written so seldom. The activities of her senior year had taken over her life, as had trying to get into a medical school closer to home than Pennsylvania.

> We need medical missionaries here far more than the likes of me. Some days I cannot fathom why God brought me here, yet other times it make sense, like when I hear the children singing "Jesus Loves Me" in their own language, knowing I taught them the tune and the words that Pastor Weirholtz translated. Pastor Weirholtz was born here to missionary parents and grew up speaking like a native. He studied for the ministry in America and returned to this place he calls home to teach these poor people how to read and write. School is so important, and in the learning, we teach about Jesus Christ.

Elizabeth found herself playing the simple tune and singing along with the music. "Jesus loves me! This I know, for the Bible tells me so. Little ones to him belong; they are weak but he is strong. Yes, Jesus loves me!" She didn't bother to dash away the tears that for some unknown reason streamed down her face. "Yes, Jesus loves me! Yes, Jesus loves me! The Bible tells me so."

Her hands stilled. Her head bowed. "Lord, I know that you love me. But the question is, do I love you . . . enough?" Her whisper floated on the breeze that lifted the sheer summer curtains and dried her tears. "Can I ever love you enough? You say to love you with all my heart, soul, strength, and mind. How can I do that?"

Her hands wandered back to the keyboard, this time finding their way to hymns that flowed one after another as if joined by a chain of notes. Darkness crept into the room, dancing with the music, peeking at her from the other side of the piano, spinning and dipping like a little girl lost in the loveliness of song.

When the last note drifted away, her father's voice brought her back to the room, to the moment. "Thank you, my dear. I had no idea how much I needed that."

"Me too." She reached up and, picking up the sheets of paper, rose and handed him the letter. "From Thornton."

"You don't mind if I read it?" Phillip reached for the letter.

She shook her head. "Did I make the right decision not to follow Thornton to Africa?"

"I believe so. You didn't love him."

"I know. And I knew it then. Good night." She bent down and kissed his cheek.

It is so easy to wonder, she thought as she climbed the stairs to her room. *Did I do not only the right thing but the best thing? Best for Thornton as well as for me?* She continued pondering as she got undressed. *I'm just sorry Thornton got hurt in the end. He wasn't supposed to fall in love with me. We were only pretending.*

She and Thornton Wickersham, Pastor Mueller's nephew who had attended Carleton for his final year, had agreed to act as though they were falling in love so that the girls at Carleton would leave him alone and her mother would quit trotting out eligible young men for her. All Annabelle wanted was for her daughter to marry, preferably well, and become a concert pianist—instead of a doctor. Elizabeth desired neither, believing she could not manage both a medical practice and a family complete with husband.

She sighed as her full cotton batiste nightgown slipped over her head. Why was it that people got their feelings hurt so easily?

Looking back, she had to admit she and Thornton had enjoyed many good times together. And now there was no one with whom to share ice cream or croquet or bicycle riding or walks down by the river. Most of her friends had already married. She corrected that. Her two friends. And they had moved away. She'd not taken time during college to make new friends, instead concentrating all her efforts on her studies, working for her father, and assisting Dr. Gaskin whenever he asked.

Before turning out the gaslight, she read one chapter and one psalm in her Bible, a habit she'd formed while in grade school after a missionary came to their Sunday school. He'd told them how important it was to learn God's Word while they were young and challenged them to stay in His Word daily throughout their lives.

The missionary had been from Africa.

So why not teach Thorliff to play croquet? He's a good baseball player. Surely he can learn to hit a wooden ball on the ground.

With that thought in mind, she said her prayers and rolled over, the moonlight tracing intricate shadows on the floor of her room, a mockingbird singing, perhaps mistaking the bright moonlight for sunshine.

I'm thanking you, Lord, for the school you will send me to and for the chance to learn patience—she rolled her eyes at that one—*and for the full knowledge that you know what is ahead. I just wish you would give me a glimpse.*

With her mother now in charge of the accounts at the newspaper and Thorliff working all summer, Elizabeth had no reason to rush in the morning, so she ate her breakfast out under the oak tree in the backyard. When she finished, she cut some deep red roses for the house, arranged them in vases, and set one on the narrow table in the entry hall, another on the piano, and a third on the dining room table.

Not knowing what to do next, she went into the kitchen. "You need anything from the market?" she asked Cook.

"No. I've already been." Cook gave the pie dough on the table another pass with the rolling pin.

"Oh. Do you need some help around here?"

"Not that I can think of." Cook flipped the dough into the pie plate. "All your things ready for graduation?"

Elizabeth ticked them off on her fingers. "Dress is pressed and hanging ready, thanks to you. Also petticoats. Menu planned for the reception afterward. Guests invited." She looked up. "Anything else you can think of?"

Cook added the home-canned peach pie filling. "No, nothing."

In reality her mother had been the one to plan the reception. Had it been left to Elizabeth, she'd have been content with the one at the school.

"Just think, as of tomorrow afternoon, I will be a college graduate." She leaned against the doorjamb.

"And that is a major accomplishment." Finished crimping the edges of the pie, Cook trimmed the crust and slid the pie into the oven, wiping the perspiration from her forehead with the edge of her white apron. She returned to the floury board and began rolling again.

"If there is nothing you need, I think I'll take a book outside. I haven't read for pleasure for so long, I'm not sure I will remember how."

"I'll bring out lemonade."

After fetching *The Red Badge of Courage* by Stephen Crane from the library, Elizabeth made herself comfortable on the chaise lounge in the shade and read the first page. By the third page, her eyelids felt as if they were attached to fishing weights. She forced herself to read another page and had no idea what she'd read before the book flopped on her chest and her eyelids refused to rise again.

"So here's our sleeping beauty." Her father's voice brought her back from a lovely stroll along the river, a handsome man beside her. Who he was, she had no idea because she hadn't been able to see his face.

She stretched both arms above her head, too far to trap the yawn that caught her unawares. "Oh, I was having such a nice dream."

"With a Prince Charming, no doubt." Phillip took the chair at the table and drained the waiting glass of lemonade.

"That was mine."

"Too bad. I was working while you were snoozing away the day. Thorliff is joining us for dinner, so you might want to freshen up a bit." He reached over and lifted a fallen leaf from her hair. "I'm glad to see you resting. You've earned it."

He pulled her up with one hand, and together they strolled into the house.

"What are you doing this afternoon?" Elizabeth asked Thorliff a little while later as they were eating the peach pie still warm from the oven.

"Working at the paper." Thorliff wiped his mouth with his napkin. "Why?"

"Do you know how to play croquet?"

"No."

She turned to her father. "I think he should learn, and I should be the one to teach him . . . today."

Phillip gave her one of his my-daughter-can-have-her-way-today-since-she-is-about-to-graduate-from-college smiles and nodded to Thorliff. "The princess has spoken. Surely you wouldn't mind an afternoon learning to play croquet? You are due a day off anyway."

"But I was going to write on . . ." Thorliff stared from the complacent smile on Elizabeth's face to the helpless shrug of his employer. "All right, if you say so."

"You needn't act like you are being punished. After all, it's a game for fun." Elizabeth folded her napkin and stuck it into the silver napkin ring by her plate.

"Give it all you've got, son. She is a good teacher but a go-for-the-jugular player."

"Now, Phillip . . ." Annabelle shook her head and looked up toward her eyebrows. "Don't listen to a word he says, Thorliff. He so loves to tease."

"Have you ever won a game off her?" Phillip looked over his glasses at his wife, his eyes twinkling behind his spectacles.

"No, but then we all know how abysmal I am at anything athletic. She got all her prowess from you, dear."

"Well, I haven't won more than one or two matches since she was ten. She hits me into the rose garden or the fishpond every time. Did you know lilacs are mean and vicious creatures that delight in flaying shirt sleeves and hide?"

"Father, you are going to scare Thorliff off, and then you will have to take his place."

"Spare me, Lord." Phillip clasped his hands and looked heavenward.

Elizabeth, the twinkle in her eyes matching that of her father's, held out her hand. "Come on, Mr. Bjorklund, surely you have not lost heart."

He stood and pushed his chair back up to the table. "If I don't return, you know where to find me, ensnared by the lilacs or still hunting my ball in the pond."

"Oh, never fear. It's easy to rake them off the bottom. The pond isn't that big." Her merry laugh preceded him out the kitchen door and into the backyard where the wickets were already in place.

"Have you really never played before?"

He shook his head. "Guilty as charged. We don't have many smooth lawns like this on the farm, in fact no lawns at all. I did learn to play badminton up at school."

"Well, I'm afraid skill in one does not contribute to skill in the other. Which color do you want?" She pointed to the mallets and balls in the wheeled wooden cart.

"Ah, blue."

"Good. Red is my favorite. The purpose of the game is to roll your ball through each of those wickets." Her hands waved the pattern to follow. "And through those final three to hit the peg before I do. On the way if you hit my ball with yours, you can knock me out of the playing field, thus my father's comments about the vengeful lilac hedge or the waiting pond. A good player tries to keep the other off the field as much as possible."

"I can see that." Thorliff contemplated the playing area, the tip of his tongue massaging his right cheek. "Could you please show me how to tap the ball? Surely there are tricks in that too?"

"Of course. I'll start from the beginning. You hold your mallet so . . ." She positioned her hands on the stick of the mallet. "Then you make contact with the ball like so." Her ball rolled obediently through the first three hoops. "Now you try."

Thorliff stationed his feet like she had, held the stick the same, and tapped the ball, and it rolled through two hoops and out before the third. "Hey!"

"You have to hit it straight on." She tapped her ball again and it rolled toward the next hoop, stopping close to straight on.

"May I have a few practice shots?"

"Of course." She leaned on her stick, the mallet providing a good brace. "Hit away."

After five or six practice hits Thorliff announced himself ready to play.

"Good. I'll concede one thing since this is your first time. I won't knock you into the pond, the lilacs, or the rose garden, all right?"

"All right." Thorliff tapped his ball through the first three wickets this time and overshot the first single by only a foot or so.

"Very nice."

By the time they'd played half the course, they were fairly close in play. When she bumped his ball, she glanced toward the pond and grimaced. *Oh, how fun that would be. Why did I ever offer him that promise?* She glanced over to see Thorliff watching her, a half smile on his mouth and a twinkle in his eyes.

"Are you sure you've never played this game before?"

"As your father said, you are a good teacher."

"You didn't answer my question." She heard the tendency her voice had to snap.

"No, I have never played croquet before, but I did try golf once. We read about it, took sticks out in the field, and batted at the puffballs. They didn't roll well, so Andrew carved us a ball out of a hunk of wood. That thing could fly, until it broke in half. Then we wrapped it with string, and it really flew. Right into the river. End of game."

Elizabeth studied him, questions racing through her mind like kids just out of school and just as noisy. What a creative family they were, those Bjorklunds. Did they really not have much of anything, as he had so casually mentioned? What was life really like on that North Dakota farm of his?

With a sigh, she tapped his ball a few feet out of the playing area and won the game by one stroke.

"Is it proper to put your foot on the ball like that?"

"House rules?"

"Ah." His eyebrows waggled.

"My father said it was so, and so it was so."

"Very well said, Miss Rogers." Thorliff dropped his mallet back into the proper slot on the cart. "Thank you for a most enlightening afternoon."

"Can you not find time to play another round?"

"Not today. But you can count on another match, perhaps Sunday after church?"

"A good time." She looked toward the house when she heard a door slam. "See, Cook is bringing refreshments. Her timing is impeccable."

"Of course, all she has to do is glance out the window when you crow in triumph."

"I didn't crow."

His eyebrows rose as one.

"Well, perhaps only a little crow."

When they sat at the table with their lemonade, she asked, "You are coming to graduation, aren't you?"

"I promised to cover it for the paper."

"Is that your only reason?"

He studied her as if trying to figure out what she wanted. "Why else?" At the glint in her eye, he added, "And to see you graduate, of course."

"That's better." Her smile brought an answering one from Thorliff. He reached for another cookie and sat back in his chair.

Elizabeth nibbled on her bottom lip. "Have you been thinking any more on the challenge Pastor Mohn gave that day?"

Thorliff nodded. "And you?"

Elizabeth continued to worry her lip before answering. "He has such a gift for striking one right in the heart. I tried to ignore it since I'm not coming back here to school, but it isn't that easy."

"I know." Thorliff sipped from his glass. "I've gone through all of the Beatitudes and considered each one. After I figured out the real definition of each one, that is. They are not easy."

"No, that is for sure. I went back and forth between mercy and pure in heart, finally settling on mercy. I thought that is something I need in the medical field. What about you?"

"I decided on pure in heart."

68

"And?"

"And controlling my thoughts is not easy. Paul said the same, that we should take every thought captive."

"But thoughts and heart, they aren't the same."

"They are if you go back to the Greek. Jesus did not offer an easy thing, and Pastor Mohn understands that." *And since he's a man, perhaps I could talk with him. Here, even just talking with Elizabeth, my mind . . .* He shook his head.

"What?"

"Nothing. I need to get going." He stood and nodded. "Thanks for the lesson."

That night at supper they discussed Thorliff's new story and how the printing was going on *The Switchmen*.

"I told Thorliff I think he needs a strong female character or two so that more women will want to read his story." Elizabeth steepled her fingers under her chin, her elbows propped on the table. A look and a throat-clearing from her mother made her remove her elbows from the table.

"You think women haven't been reading *The Switchmen*? That's who we heard from mostly." Phillip leaned back in his chair and stroked his mustache.

"That's because men don't usually tell you if something is good, only if it is something that doesn't please them." Annabelle raised the silver coffee server, but they all shook their heads.

Phillip studied his wife, then glanced at his daughter. He turned to Thorliff. "So do you have any ideas for such a character?"

"Or two," Elizabeth added.

"I can figure some out. Both young men are of marriageable age, and . . ." His voice faded.

Elizabeth watched him, having learned that the look on his face meant he was off in the world of his latest story. She and her father exchanged a smile, knowing that he did the same thing when writing his editorials.

"Ah, thank you for supper." Thorliff stood and sketched a slight bow. "I will see you at the ceremony tomorrow."

They watched him leave before Annabelle rang for Cook. "We'll have tea out on the verandah, please."

"And I challenge you both to a game of croquet." Elizabeth stood and took her father's arm. "Come along, you need the exercise. Mother?"

"I, ah . . ." Annabelle sighed. "All right, if you insist, but if either of you knocks my ball into the roses, the lilacs, or the pond, I shall quit. Immediately."

The sky darkened with thunderclouds just as people were gathering for the graduation ceremonies. With guests filling the chairs and the faculty lined up to parade in front of the sixteen graduates, Reverend Mohn took his place at the podium.

"Before we begin let me announce that if the rain doesn't hold off, we shall recess inside to the auditorium. But in the name of the Father, the Son, and the Holy Spirit, we shall begin with the processional." He nodded to the band instructor, who raised his arms, and marching to "Holy, Holy, Holy," the procession began.

Elizabeth looked at the young woman marching beside her. Both of them tightened quivering chins and stepped out on the right foot, just as they had practiced.

The last diploma was handed out, and Professor Mohn, usually rather loquacious, had quickly concluded his speech before the clouds warned them with a sprinkle. By the time they'd all made it inside, the last ones looked a bit damp. Thunder growled and lightning slashed, but the exuberance inside the auditorium drowned it all out.

Thorliff observed all the graduates with their families. He watched as Professor Ytterboe drummed up financial support to keep the college going. Would it be that way in two years for him, with his family gathered around, rejoicing? Would he even make it through the next two years, or did God have something else in mind for him?

CHAPTER SEVEN

June 19, 1895
Dear Thorliff,

   I hope you are enjoying your summer in Northfield. We are sure missing you here at home. Our big news is that Metiz gave Andrew a puppy. He is the funniest thing. Andrew was wishing you were here to help find the perfect name. He   the puppy, not Andrew—has one white paw, and the rest is black and gray and brown all mottled together. He is so small we cannot let him outside by himself yet in case a coyote would grab him. Oh, Mor named him after all. His name is Barnabas—Barney—because he follows us all over. He loves to chew on anything he can get his mouth on. Far says he will be better when he gets his permanent teeth. I didn't know that puppies had baby teeth and then got their big teeth just like we do. I know about kittens though, since we have so many. I hope his new teeth aren't as sharp as his baby teeth.

   Mor and I got to take care of little Gus and his baby sister yesterday. Tante Penny says Gus can run faster than a jackrabbit.

He is such a happy little boy. He will be two in October and can say all kinds of things now. He is so smart. He calls me "Astid" because he cannot say his r's yet. And little Linnea looks just like a doll. She's such a happy baby. I wish you could see them both.

Mor says we will come to visit you sometime this summer. I cannot wait. I want to see your school and the newspaper and have ice cream at Mrs. Sitze's like you wrote about. I wish Far and Andrew could come too, but they said there is too much work to do here for everyone to be gone at the same time. I will have a surprise for you when I come.

Please write to us more often. I miss you so much. Are you writing another continuing story for the newspaper? Did Elizabeth graduate? Is she going to medical school? Don't you do anything for fun?

Your sister,
Astrid

Leaning against the column in front of the post office, Thorliff read the letter a second time. Yes, he should write home more. He promised himself he would do that in the evening and headed back to the newspaper office, the mail for the business under his arm. Getting the mail was one of the jobs he had taken over for the summer.

"Hey, Bjorklund, you have time for a soda?"

"Sorry, not now. I'm working." He waved back at one of the students he knew from school. Between his writing for the paper and playing baseball on the St. Olaf team, he'd become quite well known in Northfield.

"Another time, then?"

"Sure. You know where to find me." He waved and picked up his pace again. Living in town was certainly different from on the farm, Mrs. Sitze's Ice Cream Parlor being one of the niceties of town living.

The bell jangled overhead when he entered the newspaper office.

"Thorliff, how long since you've seen Mr. Stromme?" Phillip asked in greeting.

"Three, four days. Why?"

"Doc just called. He says Henry is asking for you, as well as he can ask. You better go on over."

"You've figured out how to finish setting up the binder?"

Phillip waved the booklet he was reading. "I will soon. You'd think they'd send someone out with a machine like that to make sure it is set up right and to give us some instruction."

They'd spent one day cleaning out the storeroom to have a place to set up the new machine, moving the old printer and various other castoffs to the unused side of the carriage house at Phillip's home.

Phillip had patted the archaic printer and smiled at Thorliff. "When the time comes, I will give you a real good deal on this old lady. Of course you'll be so spoiled then with the one we have now that it will feel like going backward, but I know what it's like starting out. There's never enough money for all the things a new business needs. Besides, there's a lot of good wear left in the old girl. If you haven't forgotten how to pick type, that is."

Thorliff nodded. "Starting a newspaper sounds overwhelming, but in a few years Blessing will be big enough for a newspaper."

"Have you mentioned this to your folks yet?"

"No. Perhaps right now it is just a dream, and knowing Astrid, she'll be after me all the time to tell her when."

"You could always stay here, you know. The way we're growing, I need full-time help. Don't know what I'll do when you go back to school."

Thorliff cut off the memories cascading through his mind like a creek in snow melt and retrieved his hat from the rack by the door. "I'll be back as soon as I can."

Clapping his hat back on his head as soon as he stepped out the door, he righted the bicycle.

"You go right on in," Nurse Browne said when Thorliff entered the surgery at Dr. Gaskin's house. "He's been waiting for you and not too patiently, I may add. Once that man gets something in his head, he doesn't let go." She shook her head. "You have to listen real hard to understand him, but he has improved since the last time you were here."

Thorliff nodded. "He's trying real hard."

"He's trying all right, trying my patience and that of Miss Haugen too. But that stubbornness is what is pulling him through, and I need to remind myself to be grateful for that." She *tsk*ed with a slight frown. "Things could be so much worse."

With that Thorliff walked down the walnut-paneled hall to the third door on the right, one of three bedrooms where Dr. Gaskin housed patients when they needed extra care. Thorliff knocked and pushed the door open enough to peek in to see if Mr. Stromme was awake.

A grunt and a garbled phrase told him that not only was the old man awake but his mood was not one of cheer.

Thorliff stepped into the room. "I came as soon as I could." He crossed the room and reached to shake the extended but shaking hand. "You're looking better."

"Huh!" Mr. Stromme's normally cheerful face had not yet regained its balance and welcoming smile. With half a face to smile with and the other half no longer rigid but now slack, he appeared lopsided, as if a child had been sculpting and got bored with the project before finishing it.

Thorliff listened carefully, watching the man for any clues. "You are most welcome. I would have come yesterday, but Mr. Rogers sent me out on an assignment. Nurse Browne says you are improving every day. Would you like to go outside?"

The frown and headshake said more than the words. "That's fine. I just thought sitting in the sun might make you feel better. It always does me."

When Mr. Stromme pointed to a chair next to him, Thorliff sat down and leaned forward, elbows on his knees.

"I . . . wa . . . t . . ."

Thorliff nodded and waited for Henry to continue.

"You . . . to . . . li . . ." The rest of the thought trailed into gibberish.

"You want me to . . ." Thorliff left the sentence hanging, hoping Mr. Stromme could finish it.

A nod. And a grimace. Henry slammed his hands on his quilt-covered knees in frustration.

"Easy. I'm in no hurry. Just take your time, and we'll figure this out." Thorliff leaned back in his chair. Thoughts of his story tickled the back of his mind while he tried to decipher the mixed-up sounds.

Mr. Stromme closed his eyes, took in a breath, and started again. "Lii . . . wii . . ." He tapped his chest with one finger.

"Live?" Thorliff grasped at the first word that came to his mind. At the nod he continued. "Live with me—I mean you?"

Another nod and a deep sigh of relief.

Oh, Lord, what do I do now? "But I already have a home down at the newspaper."

A knock on the door interrupted what the old man tried to say.

"Ah good, Thorliff, you're here. I wanted to talk with you." Dr. Gaskin entered the room with a smile. "How are the two of you doing? Henry, you been telling him your idea?"

"He said he wants me to live at his house."

Dr. Gaskin nodded. "We know you have a job, but Henry here says he doesn't need someone there during the day. His neighbors will help him if he needs it. He's agreed to put a telephone in so he can ask for assistance. But he shouldn't be alone at night, just in case. So that's where you come in. If you will sleep there, help him if needed, that will bridge the gap. At the rate he is progressing, I don't think this needs to be a long-term commitment, more like until school starts again. Right, Henry?"

Mr. Stromme nodded, relief showing in his eyes.

Thorliff rubbed his chin with one finger. "I would need to talk this over with Mr. Rogers, since he hired me especially to be there at night. But there have been no instances of trouble again, and perhaps he'll agree. I don't have to keep the furnace going right now."

"Y-you . . . w-wan . . . to . . . h . . . ?" He clenched his teeth and slapped his knee twice.

"Take it easy, Henry. The harder you fight it, the more difficulties you will have. Relax and let the words come."

Mr. Stromme gave a slight nod and sighed. He tried again. "He . . . p."

75

"Yes, I want to help you if I can." Thorliff reached over and took the old man's good hand. "I'll let you know as soon as I talk with Mr. Rogers."

"Tan . . . k . . . y-you."

"You are most welcome, but I haven't done anything yet." He left the room and slipped out the back door so he wouldn't have to go through the waiting room again. How much help would Mr. Stromme really need? Getting undressed and to bed? Help dressing in the morning? Meals? No, Dr. Gaskin said others would take care of that. *But I have to write in the evenings. Just when I think things are settling down so I can get more done, something like this happens.*

Guilt gnawed at his heart like a dog on a shank bone. Here, he should be grateful for a chance to help someone out, and he was grumbling instead. Not that the decision was his to make.

He climbed on the bike and pedaled back to the newspaper office. Best to get this over with immediately.

But if you don't do it, who will? His inner voice could be such a nagger at times.

When he explained the predicament to Phillip, the newspaperman crossed his arms over the back of his head and leaned back in his chair, making it shriek like a child in pain.

"The only problem I see is getting ahold of you if we have a story you need to cover."

"Dr. Gaskin said a telephone would be put in." Thorliff leaned a hip on the edge of the desk.

"Do you want to do this?"

"Not particularly, but if this could help him get back on his feet, I'm willing to help."

"You could write there, but you'd need to find out what else you would be doing." The chair shrieked again. "How about you try it, and if it doesn't work out, we'll look to another way to solve his problems?"

"Thank you. I'm not even sure when this would start."

The bell tinkled over the door, drawing their attention.

A woman entered and, after closing her ruffled parasol, minced her way over to the high counter that divided the office from the reception area. She flashed a brilliant smile at each of them, her upswept eyelashes beating against high, rounded cheeks. Everything about her appeared rounded but for a waist so tiny Thorliff could hardly keep his eyes on her heart-shaped face.

"I'm looking for Mr. Thorliff Bjorklund." Her voice purred like a kitten being stroked.

"I am Thorliff." Clearing his throat took two swallows.

"Ah, but I expected someone more . . . ah . . ."

"Older?" Phillip's smile dimmed in comparison to the brilliance of hers.

"To be frank, yes. Are you indeed the author of *The Switchmen?*"

Thorliff paused to settle himself. "Yes." *Can't you think of anything more witty or bright than yes? Repartee is needed here.*

She extended her hand, palm down, wrist limp, as if used to being bowed over. Or kissed. The thought of which sent Thorliff's heart into overdrive. *Pure thoughts, pure thoughts,* he mentally screamed at himself.

"I am Mrs. Karlotta Kingsley, of the Kingsleys of Chicago."

Thorliff wanted to look to Phillip for some kind of assistance, but he couldn't take his eyes off the beauty mark on the outside corner of her right eye, thus keeping his gaze from her cupid's bow upper lip and other portions of roundness. He could feel the heat blazing up his neck.

"We have just moved to Northfield, and I am suitably impressed with the culture here, especially the quality of the newspaper for running such a delightful saga."

"Ah, thank you. I'd like you to meet my employer, Mr. Phillip Rogers, publisher and editor." Thorliff stammered only slightly, much to his relief.

Phillip stood and bowed over the hand now extended to him. "Charmed, I'm sure. Now, how can we be of service?"

"We are moving into the Wilson house, and I would like to receive your paper. I also heard that you are publishing *The Switchmen* in book form?"

"Yes, we are in the process now."

"Ah, delightful." She turned her attention back to Thorliff. "I was hoping that I could invite the author to tea so we could discuss how he got started. Perhaps you would give me a few hints, as I dream of becoming a writer myself."

Thorliff's throat felt like the victim of a North Dakota dust storm.

"Of course Mr. Bjorklund would be most delighted to have tea with you. You may leave a message here as to the day and time. We do our best to make new folks feel welcome in our *delightful* town."

Thorliff sent Phillip a pleading glance before smiling back at the woman before him. Why did he feel like a sacrificial lamb or what he assumed a sacrificial lamb might feel like?

"I would indeed be delighted." *Not that I have any advice to offer, but . . .*

She extended her hand again, the softness of it covering slender bones. Thorliff mimicked his employer with a slight bow.

"Thank you, gentlemen, and Mr. Bjorklund"—she tapped his upper arm with the tip of her closed fan—"I look forward to our time together." With another incandescent smile, she turned and minced her way out the door, her dark hair trailing from under the brim of her pert hat.

"Well, her prow sure came through that door before the rest of the ship." Phillip fanned his face with a paper from his desk. "Whew."

Thorliff choked on what he was going to say and hoped the heat he could feel flaming his entire body could be attributed to the coughing jag. Inhaling, he could still sense her perfume hanging in the air, despite the smell of printing ink.

Had a twister just blown through the room or what? *And what about my pledge to purity of heart? Father God, I want to see you.*

CHAPTER EIGHT

Late June

"Telephone," Annabelle said, coming into the study. "It is long distance."

Elizabeth looked up from the letter she was writing. "For me?" *Who would be calling me?* she thought as she laid down her pen. She followed her mother out the door and gave her a questioning look.

Annabelle shook her head and continued on to the kitchen, leaving Elizabeth alone in the hall with her call. She picked up the dangling earpiece and spoke into the trumpet-shaped mouthpiece. "This is Elizabeth."

"Good. I decided to take advantage of this newfangled instrument and save myself the time of writing a letter."

"Dr. Morganstein! Oh, how wonderful it is to hear your voice."

"Ah, you recognize me in spite of all this fuzzy noise on the line. How are you, my dear?"

"Restless. It's already been a week since graduation, and I've received no word yet from the medical school in Minneapolis. I've been accepted at the Woman's Medical College of Pennsylvania, as I wrote to you."

"What's wrong with that school? It has a fine reputation."

"But not as good as Johns Hopkins or Harvard, and they have both turned me down. As you said last summer, at the men's schools I would receive better and more complete training, even at the college in Minneapolis, which is so much nearer to home."

"Time is running out."

"I am well aware of that. Father thinks I should send a letter of acceptance to Pennsylvania, and then I can cancel if I am accepted elsewhere."

"Sound advice. A bird in the hand, as the old saw goes."

"It seems like a settling for, if you ask me." Elizabeth knew she sounded more than a mite cantankerous, so she tried to change the tenor of her voice. "How are things at your hospital?"

"In dire need of more hands, which is why I resorted to the telephone. Can you possibly come work with us again this summer? I know your parents are dreading your leaving and want to spend every possible moment with you, but, Elizabeth, I need you—desperately. And you know you will receive training far beyond what even your first year in medical school will give you."

Elizabeth closed her eyes, remembering the heat and humidity of Chicago in the summer. It had taken her weeks to catch up on her sleep, and yet never had she felt more alive and useful. If she'd had any doubts as to her calling, her time at the Alfred Morganstein Hospital for Women dispelled them like dew under a hot summer sun.

"I . . . I will have to talk with my parents." *I know Mother will be disappointed, but she is at the office enough now that she'll be too busy to realize I am gone.* While Elizabeth knew that was an exaggeration, she reminded herself that she had already mentioned that she wanted to return to the hospital for a while this summer.

And Annabelle had only sighed, not harangued her as in former days.

"Call me back tomorrow if you can. Here is the number."

Elizabeth repeated the number to herself as she said good-bye. She hurried to the study to write it down. Having paper and pencil by the telephone would be a good idea, although here in town, all they had to do was ask Miss Odegaard for whomever they wanted.

Before going to find her mother, she sat down and pulled a sheet of paper from the stack her father kept in the right-hand drawer. Taking her father's advice, she wrote her acceptance letter, signed it, addressed the envelope, and rummaged for a stamp. None. She folded the letter and inserted it in the envelope, each motion feeling like another nail pounded in the wall, the wall enclosing her with only one door out and that labeled Pennsylvania. She'd mail it after talking with her mother and before catching her father at the office. Sometimes it was better to talk to her parents separately so that she didn't feel ganged up on. Not that they were always in agreement, but right now she needed all the support she could find, not a list of the negatives.

"You do what you must," Annabelle said after some discussion. Sitting under the oak tree with the roses and daisies in glorious bloom and a slight breeze with just enough breath to cool them made Elizabeth wish she didn't have to go to Chicago either. *I don't have to,* she reminded herself, *it's just that I can't not go. I'm needed there and here. . . .*

She tuned back in to what her mother was saying, guilt nibbling at her heart because she wasn't content with being the "at home" daughter Annabelle desired.

"If we can work in a shopping trip like last year, we can have you ready to leave for medical school in September. That is when the new year starts for schools of this nature too, isn't it?"

"It will for me, but as far as I understand, people can begin any time they start a new unit." Elizabeth pushed her chair back and got to her feet. "I'll be back after a while. I have some errands to run."

"Tell your father I will be down later." Annabelle smiled at her daughter, the kind of smile that said I'm really going to miss you.

Elizabeth inspected her upper eyelashes and her fringe, a new feature that she still wasn't quite comfortable with, be it that short hair fluffed on the forehead was all the rage or not.

Why was it that now that she and her mother were getting along better than they ever had, she was about to leave home? Another of those things to ponder in the middle of the night when sleep was cavorting off somewhere else instead of bringing its healing blessings to her busy mind.

Her father's agreement with her mother that they would support her whichever school she decided to attend should have helped, but it didn't.

Once at the office, she stopped at her father's desk and waited for him to look up from what he was writing.

"Yes, my dear?" His smile made her wish she wasn't considering leaving sooner—for a heartbeat anyway.

"I had a telephone call from Dr. Morganstein and . . ."

His nod encouraged her to continue. "And she wants me to come now. She needs another pair of hands desperately."

"And?"

"And I'm asking for your permission to go. Mother said she understood, if we could have a shopping trip again."

His slight smile matched her own. "She does love to go shopping in Chicago."

"So you don't mind?"

"Of course I mind. I was looking forward to our croquet matches and evening concerts." He leaned forward. "But, my dear daughter, you must do what you must do. I thank you for asking my permission, but you are a grown woman now and must make your own decisions. Do you want to go?"

"Of course."

"Then you will go with my blessing."

When she came around the desk, he stood quickly enough to open his arms to gather her close. He kissed her forehead and sighed. "Have I told you lately how proud I am of you?"

"Not for a day or two." She could hear his heart thudding, a sound she had laughed about as a little girl sitting in his lap. How often he'd said that she was in his heart, and she'd giggle and say, "No, Daddy, I'm right here. Your heart is in there." And she'd push a fingertip into his shirt.

Now she looked up into eyes that matched her own. "I am the most blessed that you are my father. Thank you for everything."

"You are welcome."

The tinkling doorbell took his attention, and she left his side to meander down the hall to the necessary where she used the hand towel to mop her eyes. She stared into the mirror. "Am I doing the best thing?"

Elizabeth entered the pressroom and watched Thorliff add more ink and start the press running again. If anyone would give an honest and mostly unbiased opinion, it would be he. When he came to stand beside her, still keeping an eye on the press, she laid out her concerns for his evaluation.

"Do you think I should give up on the school closer to home?"

"No, why? You are going to Chicago again to the hospital, right?"

She nodded. "I've just been invited back."

"But she told you last summer that she would love you to come again."

"I know, but things change in a year."

"I doubt the change is ever in the favor of a hospital. There are always more than enough sick people to treat."

"Thorliff, you are so pragmatic. Is this a gift, or is all your family that way?"

Thorliff decorated his chin with black ink as he thought about her question.

"Growing up on a farm, you have to accept things the way they are. The wheat grows or it doesn't; the rain falls or it doesn't. You do the best you can and wait on God for the harvest. But if you don't plant the seed, you can be sure there will be no harvest. Seems to me you've planted the seeds and now you are waiting on God for the harvest."

"Waiting is hard."

"The hardest part. But you've got tilling to do at the hospital."

"That's one way of putting it. But then you won't have anyone to beat you at croquet."

"But by the end of the summer, if I can find someone to play against, I will be a formidable opponent."

"You will get that much better by the end of August?"

"Yes, I will." He picked up one of the printed sheets to check the ink quality.

"That's a signature of your book?" Elizabeth was pleased she had picked up some of the terms for book printing. Each sheet of paper would have eight book pages printed on both sides, so the paper had to be turned over and printed again. It would be folded and cut later.

He nodded. "We're printing a thousand on this first run to see how it goes. After all, most of the people around here have already read it."

"I don't think that's enough. You'll be back to the presses within a couple of weeks, if not before that."

"As the old Jewish saying goes, 'From your mouth to the ears of God.'"

The bell tinkled over the door to the office, and Thorliff stuck his head around the corner to make sure Phillip was still out there to wait on the customer.

"Who is it?" Elizabeth asked, her curiosity aroused by the red she could see climbing Thorliff's neck and face. His Adam's apple bobbed as he plastered himself against the wall.

"M-Mrs. Kingsley."

"Oh, the new woman in town. Father mentioned her at the dinner table. Mother, of course, knows of the Chicago Kingsleys. Why don't you want to see her? Father said she seems very nice."

"Ah, excuse me, I need to check on the . . ." Thorliff fled down the hall.

Elizabeth stared after him, shaking her head. *Whatever is the matter with him?* Still shaking her head, she ambled out to the front office.

"Oh, there you are, my dear." Phillip turned from chatting with the woman on the other side of the counter. "Mrs. Kingsley, I'd like you to meet my daughter, Elizabeth. She has just graduated from St. Olaf College and this fall will be on her way to medical school."

"Oh, how wonderful. I graduated from one of the first classes at Bryn Mawr College in Pennsylvania. My father is unusual, like yours. He felt a woman was entitled to just as good an education as a man."

Elizabeth nodded. "I'm happy to meet you too. What brought you to Northfield?" She kept her eyes slightly downcast, the better to study the woman without being blatant. Lovely dimity dress, obviously sewn just for her in order to fit that rather extraordinary bosom and waspish waist. Her parasol, bag, everything matched, including the ribbon bow on the leghorn hat.

Elizabeth gave a mental rundown on her own appearance. Dress a bit faded and severely out of style, no hat, parasol nonexistent, shoes dusty from a walk by the river. The only new thing she wore was the ribbon tying her curls back off her face. Improper, her mother would say.

She brought her attention back to the woman in front of her.

"Pardon me, I think I went woolgathering. I missed the first part of your question." *How embarrassing.* She could feel the heat flaming her cheeks. *Now I know what Thorliff felt like.*

"I said my husband is starting a new department at Carleton, and I was just asking which medical school you are going to. I didn't think too many of them took women. I know they do in Europe but not so much here."

"It's a problem. I've been accepted at Woman's Medical College of Pennsylvania, but I'm hoping to go to the Northern Medical School in Minneapolis."

"Ah, you want to be closer to your young man here in Northfield?"

At Phillip's not quite discreet snort that turned into a genteel cough, Elizabeth blinked and tilted her head as if she might not have heard right. "My young man?"

"Well, surely by this time one of the eligible men of the area must have put in his bid for courting you." She shot Phillip a smile that invited him to be part of her conspiracy.

He shrugged as if to say "humor her, she's a guest" when Elizabeth glanced his way.

"You and my mother will no doubt become bosom friends. That has been her dream since I was little. My dream, however, is to become a doctor, and I see no way I can have a medical practice and be a wife and mother also." There, that ought to settle her inquisitiveness.

With one hand on her now heaving bosom and the other extended to Elizabeth in an imploring gesture, Mrs. Kingsley rolled her eyes heavenward, as if pleading the interference of the Almighty. "Oh, my dear, dear girl, surely you don't mean that. Why, if our young women don't carry on the banner of profession and marriage both, what will happen? All of the babies will be born to those without either the intelligence or the wherewithal to rear them properly. We will become a nation of the lower classes and unschooled immigrants. It is our duty as educated women to show what we are made of, the sterner stuff of American progress."

Elizabeth dared not look at her father. She could feel his laughter bubbling below the surface. While he managed to keep suffragette news out of the *Northfield News,* he kept abreast of political change on all fronts. And this newcomer made wonderful parody material, the kind of thing he loved to use in his editorials and encouraged Thorliff to do likewise.

"I . . . I'll see what I can do about that." Elizabeth kept a neutral expression on her face, the polite smile her mother had taught her through hours of remonstrating when a young Elizabeth had managed to offend her sensibilities in public.

"Excuse me, but I have several more errands to run before I go home to pack. I'm going to be working in the Alfred Morganstein Hospital for Women this summer like I did last year." She nodded to their guest. "A pleasure to meet you, Mrs. Kingsley. I hope you find your time in Northfield a delight." *Now I even sound like my mother.*

"Thank you." Mrs. Kingsley turned her attention to the man behind the desk. "And now, Mr. Rogers, is that young man here, Mr. Bjorklund? I promised him some articles from a paper in Chicago."

Elizabeth stepped quickly through the door so that she didn't have to hear her father's response. After all, Thorliff had been there and would most likely be in the back. However, she had heard the door to his room close sometime earlier. Something about the woman sent him into a dither, that was for sure.

She pondered that thought on her way to the post office, then to the drugstore, and the grocer, where she picked up some eggs and lemons for Cook, who was determined to serve all her favorite things, like lemon meringue pie, before she left. Knowing that she'd hardly find time to eat once she got to the hospital, she didn't try to talk Cook out of her mission.

Back home she found she'd missed her mother on her way to work at the newspaper.

"I'm going up to pack." Elizabeth laid the parcels on the table. "Is there anything else that you need?"

"No." An answer abrupt even for taciturn Cook.

"The mail hasn't come yet?"

"No."

"Are you all right?"

The nod came with more force than necessary. Cook sliced a lemon in half with one whack.

Elizabeth crossed the room to where Cook worked at the counter. "You knew I would be leaving home one day."

A whack for the next lemon, then a wrench of the wrist on the glass juicer so that the juice spurted rather than just oozing into the basin.

Elizabeth sighed. "I'm going to miss you too." She rested her head against Cook's shoulder, feeling sinews of steel rather than the comfort of younger years. She waited until she felt the shoulder relax and then rubbed her cheek against the wash-softened calico of Cook's dress. "Those lemons smell so good." She sniffed again. "And so do you. You've always smelled good, as far back as I can remember. Cinnamon and flour and vanilla. I think they've permeated your skin and clothing. Your apron always smells of starch and the wonderful fragrance it picks up out at the clothesline. All the smells remind me how you've been here whenever I needed you. What a blessing you are to our family. What would we do without you?"

"You can count on my never giving you a chance to find out. And you can quit sweet-talking me now." Cook's voice had the bite of lemon juice, but the quaver sneaked past her crust and bubbled over like filling from an apple pie in the oven. She turned and gave Elizabeth a quick squeeze.

"I washed and ironed those dresses you took with you last year. Uff da, you have nicer clothes than those. You better not let your mother see what you are packing."

"I am taking another trunk of city clothes for when she comes. There is no sense ruining my frocks with blood and spills that happen in spite of the white aprons we wear. Dr. Morganstein wears only dark skirts and white waists, all covered with the ubiquitous aprons. I thought of wearing just the apron over my chemise but . . ." She stopped at the gasp that she'd hoped to evoke. She patted Cook's shoulder. "I just thought about it, that's all." She left the room, whistling, secure in the knowledge she'd taken Cook's mind off the coming departure.

"Whistling girls and crowing hens . . ." followed her across the music room.

"Always come to some bad ends," she sent back.

"It won't be long until you come for me and we go shopping," Elizabeth said to comfort her mother the next day at the train station. "You know how fast the summer went last year."

"I know." Annabelle wiped her nose with a square of calico. "You will write . . . at least once a week?"

"Or perhaps I shall call on the telephone."

Annabelle shook her head. "What is this younger generation coming to?"

"They're getting ready for the twentieth century, my dear." Phillip patted his wife's hand, tucked securely within the crook of his arm.

"All aboard!"

Elizabeth hugged her mother and father and accepted the conductor's hand to assist her up the stairs. She waved and made her way to the first empty seats that faced each other. She'd just settled down by the window and waved again at her parents when the train lurched forward, wheels squealing and steam billowing past.

If only I'd heard from the medical school in Minneapolis, she thought. *I guess I must just gird up my loins as the Scripture says and resign myself to Pennsylvania. I'm sorry, Father, that I'm not more appreciative of your answer. I guess I want things my way again. Please forgive me and help me do my best at the hospital.* She leaned her head against the seat and watched the farmland fly by the window as the train picked up speed. *Stop whining, you goose. After all, what can go wrong under Dr. Morganstein's tutelage?*

CHAPTER NINE

Blessing, North Dakota
July 1895

Rain veils drifted across the plains.

"Please, Lord, let it rain right here on us." Ingeborg and Astrid stood at the edge of the garden watching the dancing gauze, the darkening sky, and listening for the thunder, yet so faint as to seem only a murmur, a figment of the imaginative ear.

June had received only one visit from the life-giving rain, and now the land, baked under a brassy July sky, panted for the water that tantalized and then blew over.

The breeze that fluttered the sheer curtains hanging from the sky kissed their faces with cool lips and lifted hair pasted in curls on their foreheads and necks. Ingeborg opened her mouth to taste the breeze.

Lightning forked the western sky. Purple shadows leaked sunshine in shimmering spears of gold, then snapped the trapdoor shut as black triumphed over royal purple.

"It's coming closer." Astrid glanced up at her mother. "We could run to meet it."

"Where's your father?"

Astrid shrugged. "Over at Onkel Lars's I think." She listened for the banging of metal on metal. The men were back at their eternal job of keeping the machinery running and were now getting it ready for the harvest.

The wind blew cooler.

Please, Lord, no hail. We look to have a good crop this year. Please let us harvest it. Ingeborg sniffed again. Nothing smelled fresher than rain. Even the trees seemed to be raising their branches in supplication.

They heard it before the drops splattered the dust, drumming on the hard-packed earth, the shingles of the barn, and finally their faces.

Astrid stuck out her tongue, tasting the wetness, then arms in the air, she twirled and dipped, her hair plastered to her head and rivulets coursing down her face. "Come on, Mor, dance with me." She grabbed her mother's hands, and they danced to the music of the rain.

Giggles vied with chuckles; laughter broke free not to be stifled by the thunder that crashed directly overhead. Instead of running for the house, the two faced each other and raised their joined hands to the heavens in praise of the downpour.

A bark behind them brought Astrid running to the porch steps. "Oh, you poor baby, come play in the puddles." She scooped the puppy up in her arms and, spinning around, found puddles for stomping. Barney licked the raindrops from her neck, making her giggle again. She swung him in her arms, cradle style, until he leaped to the ground and landed in a puddle with a *woof*, his pudgy body immediately a ball of dripping mud.

The rain continued to pelt the ground and form puddles in the ruts and hollows as the thunder and lightning drifted eastward, over the river and beyond.

"Mor, let's wash our hair."

"Better hurry, or it might be gone."

Astrid flew into the house for the rose-petal soap she'd received for her birthday and, grabbing towels, left them on the porch to keep dry.

The two of them rubbed the soap into their drenched hair, and after Ingeborg scrubbed and sculpted Astrid's, the girl did the same for her mother. Wearing foam-formed turbans, they dipped water out of the already full rain barrel under the downspout at the house and rinsed each other soap free.

Standing on the porch, their heads wrapped in towels, they watched the rain continue to soak into the thirsty ground.

"I can hear the trees sighing in delight."

"And the garden," Ingeborg answered. She slid an arm around her daughter's shoulders and hugged her close, both of them shivering now in the breeze tugging at their wet clothes.

"We better get dried off."

"I don't want to miss a minute of it." Astrid leaned her head against her mother's upper arm. "You think it will ruin the hay?"

"Not if the wind doesn't knock it down. So far we can rejoice in the gentleness of it. Such a gift, a perfect rain."

Astrid shivered again, so hard that her teeth clicked together.

"You're cold."

"I know, and it feels so good." She turned her head to look up to her mother. "You think Thorliff gets to play in the rain anymore?"

"I don't know." Ingeborg wrapped her other arm around her daughter. "But I'm sure grateful we got to."

"Me too."

"Oh, the windows!" Ingeborg spun around, and they both headed for the west windows to slam them shut. They spent the next half hour mopping up rainwater from the floor and laughing all the while.

The rain continued through the night until the rooster's crow chased it away.

While she stretched her arms over her head and pushed her toes toward the bed's foot, Ingeborg inhaled the rain-washed air blowing in their bedroom window.

Haakan propped himself up on one elbow, the better to see out the window. "Guess we won't be cutting hay today."

"I guess not."

"Ah, well. It wasn't quite ready anyway." He lifted the long braid she wore at night and sniffed. "Your hair smells good."

"Washed in rainwater." Shivers tickled her middle.

He trailed a finger down her nose and rested it on her lower lip, moved it to her chin, and kissed her. "You smell good."

Some time passed before he called to Andrew to come get started with the morning chores. After they went out the door, Ingeborg found herself humming as she rattled the grate to reveal the remaining embers. A good rain made everyone happy.

Galloping hooves pounded up to the house. The sound set the hairs on the back of her neck upright, a frisson that made her head for the door.

"Mrs. Bjorklund, come quick." The call, accompanied by a fist thundering on the screen door, made her hurry.

"What is it? Oh, Mr. Nordstrum, how can I help you?"

"It's my boy. A cow kicked him, and he banged his head on the wall. There's blood coming from his ears."

"Go to the barn and ask Andrew to hitch up the buggy. I'll get my things together." Ingeborg spun around to see Astrid entering the kitchen and reaching for an apron from behind the stove.

"I'll take care of breakfast, Mor. You go."

Ingeborg snatched her medical basket from its place in the closet and swiftly checked to see all was in place. *A head injury. Oh, Lord, whatever can I do? Ice. Would ice help? Do I need Metiz? Lord, please give me wisdom and lay your healing hand upon this child.*

While she waited for Andrew to back the horse between the shafts, she recalled seeing Robbie Nordstrum playing with Trygve after church last Sunday. The two looked enough alike to be brothers and thought of enough mischief to make up for three families.

"You want anything else, Mor?" Andrew snapped the last trace in place.

"I'm thinking ice could help. Do we have any left in the icehouse?"

"Some. Pa was saving it for the Fourth of July celebration."

"Better to save this boy's life. Bring some as soon as you can." Ingeborg climbed up on the buggy and flapped the reins. "Get up, boy."

Water splashed out of the ruts as they trotted out the drive, the wheels throwing up mud behind them. What rain hadn't soaked into the thirsty ground had turned the upper layer of soil to the slippery gumbo that clogged wheels and weighted down horses' hooves. The sky sat upon the earth, creating fog pockets in the hollows and turning the world gray. A thin line of gold in the east promised that the sun had not forgotten to rise but at the moment was bowing to the hovering clouds for dominion.

The rich smell of rain-soaked earth lent life to the breeze, with the dust washed from air and plants. Ingeborg exhaled worry about the injured boy, leaving him in God's gracious hands, and inhaled renewed rejoicing for the life-giving rain.

The horse's flared nostrils and heaving sides told of the weight of hooves and buggy by the time she stopped him in the farmer's yard.

"Here." Mrs. Nordstrum flapped her apron as she called from the back door of the soddy that had yet to be replaced by a frame house. The couple had moved to Blessing the summer before and, like those before them, had built the barn first. They'd bought the farm from a family who had given up and moved back East like others who'd been chased away by the drought.

Ingeborg stepped down from the buggy, taking care to walk on grass so that she would not slip in the mud. Even so, she slid once, catching her balance by a bit of arm waving, her basket cover flapping in the motion.

She scraped the bottoms and sides of her shoes on the steel plate embedded upright between two blocks of wood and entered the soddy.

"How is he?" she asked.

"The same. He just lies there. He don't answer when we call him, not even a flicker of an eye." Betty Nordstrum wrung her hands, her lip quivering, her voice cracked by fear. A little girl, still wearing the shift of babyhood, peeked out from behind her mother, one thumb planted firmly in her mouth. A baby whimpered from the basket set on the table. Ingeborg had helped the baby into the world not much more than a month earlier. She followed the mother to the bed in the lean-to at the back of the lime-washed rooms. Kneeling beside the bed, she laid a hand on the boy's forehead. No fever.

"Could you bring a lamp in here, please?"

"Oh, sorry. I sorta get used to living like a mole. The bleeding from his ears, that stopped. I washed it away. As if that could help him. Oh, God, please . . ." She gnawed on the knuckles of her fisted hand and hurried from the room, swinging the little girl up into her arms.

The boy's skin felt damp, clammy, and at the moment Ingeborg removed her hand, he went rigid, which was followed by an arching of his back that sent him nearly off the bed. Tremors shook his entire body, his limbs flailing, one knee catching Ingeborg in the side.

"Oh, Lord God, help us." She breathed the prayer as she leaned across the boy's body to stop the thrashing. "Lord God, please be merciful to this child of yours, to this family."

"What's happening?" Betty rushed back through the door, the lamp held high in one hand, her other clamping the toddler on her hip.

"He's having a fit." Ingeborg dug in her basket for a piece of smooth-sanded wood. When the boy's jaws relaxed enough for her to check his tongue, she inserted the piece of wood between his teeth.

"What's that for?"

"To keep him from swallowing his tongue or biting it if he convulses again." Knowing full well there would be more, she beckoned the lamp closer and lifted one eyelid and then the other. One pupil looked black, the other nearly invisible in the light. She checked his ears, but his mother had washed them well. His breathing filled the small room, echoing from the corners.

"Where is Mr. Nordstrum?"

"He had to finish the milking. He'll be here soon."

"Someone will be bringing ice as soon as they can. We'll pack it around his head to see if we can reduce the swelling." She thought a moment. "Perhaps we should take him over to the icehouse."

"Is . . . is he going to die?"

"I don't know. I pray not."

The boy arched again, his face a rictus of distress. His mother stifled a scream, and the child on her hip let out a wail that brought an answering one from the babe in the basket.

"What's happened?" Mr. Nordstrum burst through the doorway. "Is he dead? Is our boy gone?"

"No." Betty turned and burrowed into her husband's arms.

He looked over her head. "How is he?"

Ingeborg finished feeling the back of the boy's head. "He might have a cracked skull, and I'm sure there is swelling in his brain from the blow. Andrew is bringing ice, but I think we would be wise to take your son to the icehouse. All I really know to do is to pray for him and try to get the swelling down."

"Is that what is causing him to jerk around like that?"

"Ja, I am afraid so."

The man left his wife and knelt by the bed, stroking the hair back off his son's forehead. "Ah, my son, my son. I am so sorry. I should never have let you milk that cow. You are so little." He bowed his head, silent sobs shaking his shoulders.

Ingeborg laid a hand on his back. "You mustn't blame yourself. Accidents happen in spite of all our good intentions."

"B-but he's such a good boy."

"I know." *Oh, Lord, what do I say? Please heal this boy and comfort this family.* She closed her eyes, remembering how sick she'd felt inside when three-year-old Andrew got lost in the tall grass. Surely she could have done something more. But God had sent Wolf to care for Andrew and bring him home the next morning. The sight of the great gray wolf with Andrew clinging to his side, baby fists buried in the rough gray fur, had never disappeared from her memory. Nor the joy at seeing her mosquito-bitten son come home. Please, Lord, bring this boy back from the land of pain where he wanders.

The baby left off crying, and glancing up, Ingeborg realized Betty had turned her attention to the other two children, her gentle murmur only faintly audible above the heavy breathing of the boy on the bed.

"Mor?" Andrew appeared in the doorway, a dripping gunnysack in his hands.

"Go and crush part of that ice block in a towel and cover the rest with quilts to keep it from melting," Ingeborg instructed Mr. Nordstrum. "We'll pack the ice around Robbie's head."

"Okay." The man did as asked, glancing back over his shoulder as if fearing his son might die in the meantime.

"Can I help in any other way?" Andrew stood at her side.

"Not that I can think of. Oh, go by Pastor Solberg's and let him know what has happened."

"I brought the wagon for the ice, and I have to clean off the wheels first. The mud sure sticks. And it is raining again."

"Why don't you ride one of the horses and then come back for the team?"

"Good idea."

"How much ice is left in the icehouse?"

Andrew shrugged and extended his hand about three feet off the ground. "Not much."

"If the ice helps, we'll take the boy there and keep him cool and quiet." She could hear the thud of the side of the ax on the ice block. Within moments the father returned and handed Ingeborg a towel of crushed ice, already dripping.

She folded the towel over, making an ice pillow, and gently raised the boy's head and shoulders so his father could place the pillow underneath.

Nothing changed, but Ingeborg knew the value of patience. Her stomach rumbled in the meantime.

Several hours and several seizures later, Pastor Solberg arrived and, after greeting the family, took his turn kneeling at the bedside.

"Any change?"

"I think he is slipping into a coma." Ingeborg kept her voice low so the others wouldn't hear.

"Ah, Lord God, hear the prayers of your children." Pastor Solberg laid his hand on the boy's chest and bowed his head. "Hear us, holy Father. You know the pain of this family and the pain this child is feeling. Only you can restore him to health and wholeness, and we plead the saving, cleansing blood of Jesus to bring Robbie back from wherever he is."

The boy twitched but on only one side of his body now, his back not arching off the bed like it had before.

"Is that an improvement?" Pastor Solberg whispered with a look up to Ingeborg seated in the chair beside him.

She shook her head. "I don't know. I think we should move him to the icehouse."

They loaded Robbie in the back of the wagon on a pallet of quilts, with his head cushioned by a down pillow and the last bits of ice. By the time they had him bedded on top of the sawdust-covered ice, his breathing had evened out, the tremors nonexistent.

Ingeborg waited on each breath, willing him to keep breathing. Betty Nordstrum clung to her hand with one and patted her son with the other.

As the hours passed, Ingeborg closed her eyes and ears against the sound of each breath and instead concentrated on the alternate drumming and pattering of the rain on the roof and the splashing of the runoff into the water-filled grooves worn in the sod.

Hours passed. Neighbors came and went, some to pray, some to bring food, all to offer encouragement. Mr. Nordstrum took the children home, accompanied by Ilse to oversee the house while Mrs. Nordstrum remained with her son.

"I am going home for a bit, and then I'll return," Ingeborg said, feeling the boy's forehead again. Still cool, and while shivers twitched his body now and then, they were indeed shivers and not tremors. She could tell the difference.

"Is there anything I can do?"

"You can rub his arms and legs. When I come back, we'll take him off the ice and see what happens."

"He is so cold."

"I know." Ingeborg wrapped her arms around herself. *Me too. But, Lord, with no change, is this not good?* Hope stirred like a kitten replete with milk and yawning before sleep.

"I'll bring you back something to keep warm. And coffee."

"Thank you."

The overcast sky made it seem much later than it was. Lights beckoned from her house across the land. A horse and rider loped across the field.

"How is he?" Pastor Solberg stopped his mount beside her.

"The same."

"And that's good?"

She shrugged. "At least he is not worse. I'll be back in a little while."

"I brought a lantern."

"Mange takk." Breathing in the damp air as she walked, Ingeborg felt renewed, as if she breathed in life itself. "Father in heaven, making this boy well again is such a simple job for you. Say the word, and he will sit up and be himself again. In the meantime, teach me what to do for him."

Listen.

She glanced over her shoulder to see who had spoken, the sensed word was so clear. "I am listening."

Rest.

"Rest? That is what he is doing." Only the sounds of her feet on the earth and her own breathing filled her ears as she approached her house.

"How is he?" Astrid looked up from stirring gravy when Ingeborg entered the kitchen.

"The same. I thought to bring back coats for Mrs. Nordstrum and me. It's cold over there, and we are not lying on the ice." *Please, God, let me do the right thing.*

"You going to eat supper before you go back?"

"No, I'll just gather what we need. Pour some coffee in a jar for me, please."

Astrid wrapped the jar in a dish towel to help keep it hot and put the jar, cups, sliced bread, and cheese in a basket to hand to her mother when she was ready to go out the door again.

"You want the wagon?"

"Yes—the little one. Or the wheelbarrow—that's what I'll take."

Astrid retrieved the wheelbarrow from the garden and folded the coats and quilt into it, setting the basket on top. "If I can do more, tell me."

"I will. What you can all do is pray for Robbie during grace."

"We will."

Ingeborg looked longingly at the lighted windows from the barn but trundled the wheelbarrow back toward the icehouse, her brisk stride warming her from the inside out.

A puddle of yellow light surrounded a lantern set on the higher sawdust-covered blocks of ice. Robbie still lay without moving on the first shelf. The icehouse huddled low to the ground, its snug, thick walls filled with sawdust, which also covered the remaining blocks. With care they would last until August or even September. The people of Blessing could buy ice in the summer, usually for making ice cream, or as in this case, for use in caring for an injury.

Darkness hovered around the puddle of light, shrouding it like a dark cloak that would smother the boy who lay there. Outside, the dark hovered like a friend, but not in the icehouse this evening.

"Any change?" Ingeborg asked as she handed Betty Nordstrum a heavy wool coat.

"No."

A whisper echo sighed in the heavy rafters.

Pastor Solberg clapped his hands against his shoulders. "Let's pray together before I leave. Mrs. Nordstrum, you take Robbie's hand, and Ingeborg, you lay your hands on his head. I'll stand right here with my hands on your shoulders. Remember the promise Jesus gave when He said, 'Where two or three are gathered together in my name, there am I in the midst of them.' " At their murmurs of assent, he continued. "Father God, thank you for sending your son to show us how to pray. He commanded us to meet like this, and we know, Father, that you love this little boy far more than even his mother and father are able. Please bring your healing power to work here. Take away the pain. Let Robbie wake up again and be taken home to his family with rejoicing. Father, we thank thee and praise thee that thou hast heard our plea. And for your mercy, we are thankful. In your son's precious name, amen."

The two women murmured their amens, and Pastor Solberg stepped back. "I'll leave the light here with you. The real light along with this lantern."

"Thank you. That was real pretty."

As the pastor left, Ingeborg returned to the wheelbarrow and brought the basket over to Mrs. Nordstrum. "I brought you some coffee and something to eat."

"Thank you." Betty accepted the cup of coffee and held it between both hands.

Haakan came out to the icehouse in the early hours of the morning and finally convinced Mrs. Nordstrum to go to the house with Ingeborg for a few hours rest.

"Just a pallet on the floor," Betty pleaded, but Ingeborg took her upstairs to share Astrid's bed.

Some time later Haakan woke his wife when he crawled back in bed. "Mr. Nordstrum came to spell me. I'm not sure because the light was so poor, but I think the boy is responding."

"Really?" Ingeborg started to throw the covers back, but he stopped her with a hand on her arm. "His father is there; actually, both fathers."

Ingeborg snuggled back into bed and after only a "Please, Father" fell back to sleep.

When she entered the icehouse a bit later, Metiz sat beside Mrs. Nordstrum.

"My husband went home to do the chores. I couldn't sleep no longer."

"I come." Metiz sat cross-legged in front of the boy.

"I was going to get you in a bit."

"Good. I think time to take him off ice."

"All right."

"You sure?" The mother looked from one woman to the other, apprehension tightening her face.

"We can always move him back on." Ingeborg lifted the boy and nodded to the others to move the quilts. She was just settling him back on the rearranged pallet when she heard a sound, a faint whimper from Robbie. His eyes fluttered; he shivered.

"Oh, please, God, please." Betty took his hands and began massaging them again. "Robbie, can you hear me? It's your mother."

A slight nod.

"Easy." Ingeborg laid a hand on Mrs. Nordstrum's shoulder. *Please, Lord, please,* she echoed the mother's prayer.

Robbie sighed. "I-I'm cold."

"Oh, thank you, God. Lord above, you brought our son back to us." Mrs. Nordstrum stroked Robbie's hair back from his forehead and cupped his pale cheeks with her hands.

Ingeborg swung open the door when she heard the rooster crowing. A gray line in the east said the night had passed, and this morning now there would be a little joy with the daybreak.

"Mor!"

She looked up to see Andrew on horseback galloping across the field. "The Vaswigs. They need you to help with their baby."

Ingeborg waved to him and hugged Mrs. Nordstrum. "God be with you. I'll be back as soon as I can. Keep talking to him, and rub his arms and legs."

"You go help the others. You're a good woman, Mrs. Bjorklund. Thank you for all you done." Mrs. Nordstrum handed her the basket of medical supplies.

Ingeborg turned to Metiz, who was already moving toward the door. "Will you come with me?"

The two mounted the horse when Andrew threw himself off. "Please, God, let this go better than the last."

CHAPTER TEN

Chicago, Illinois

"Arsonist Sets Tenement Fire."

Elizabeth stared at the headline through eyes bleary from lack of sleep and tears. Four people from that fire died on her watch the night before, and there were several others hovering on the border. Fourteen others would live but would be horribly scarred.

"How could anyone do such a thing?" She slammed a fist on the tabletop, knowing there was no answer and right now no one else in the room to venture a guess.

"Miss Elizabeth, they need you." Patrick stopped in the doorway, his skinny shoulders even more stooped than the summer before. Even though Patrick's official title was janitor, he filled in where he could, as the hospital was chronically understaffed.

Elizabeth nodded as she stood, tightening her apron while she followed him out the door. Even the few minutes off her feet had helped.

"Where?"

"The surgery."

"Now what?"

"An accident with the trolley car. Woman said she was pushed."

"Oh, how can people be so cruel to each other?"

"They're not like that where you come from?" Their heels clacked on the hall floor and down the stairs, his with a bit of a shuffle from a hip injury years before, hers the determined stride of one avenging angel. She slammed the swinging door open and crossed to the sink to begin scrubbing. The bite of carbolic acid stung her nose and ate at the rough skin on her hands. No matter how much glycerin she rubbed in, scrubbing with the harsh soaps left her hands red and chapped.

"Need you now!" Mary O'Shaughnessy, head nurse for the surgical unit, stuck her head around the corner.

Elizabeth shook out her dripping hands, stood still for Mary to tie a clean apron in place, and pushed through the door to the surgery.

"I need you to assist. Dr. Morganstein is tied up in the other room." Dr. Fossden looked at her over his glasses. While he looked more like an aging gnome than a highly trained specialist, the speed with which he wielded a scalpel continually amazed her.

"What do we have?" Elizabeth took her place across the operating table from him.

"Compound fracture of the right tibia, various lacerations, and possible internal bleeding. That's what you and I are taking care of now, the leg later. Ready?"

She sucked in a deep breath and nodded. "Ready."

"Good. I'll section, you suction. Make sure the clamps are secure when you use them. When we find the bleeder . . ." He drew a line on the woman's abdomen with the scalpel and followed the red line with a deep cut. As soon as the abdominal cavity was open, blood spurted, dousing them in red spatters.

"Clamp!" Dr. Fossden dove in with both hands, feeling for the pulsating bleeder since he couldn't see. One nurse wiped the doctor's face and glasses and another did the same for Elizabeth. The sweet but pungent smell of blood filled her nostrils while she tried to sponge enough away to clear the operating field.

"Got it. Follow my fingers in."

The blood stopped spurting and a nurse suctioned the field.

Elizabeth did as he ordered, locating the now flaccid blood vessel between his clamped fingers.

"Above and below?"

"Yes."

She clamped first one and then the other, refusing to allow the shaking in her knees to transmit to her hands. Never had she seen so much blood flow like a fountain, the woman's lifeblood pumping out over the hands and sheets and onto the now sticky floor.

"Okay, clean us up so we can really see what we are doing here." The doctor's voice snapped through the bustle.

One nurse removed his glasses and washed them in the sink while another turned Elizabeth's face toward her with a gentle hand to mop her up.

"Just like your mother used to do, eh?" A slight Irish lilt lingered, telling of her origins before Chicago.

"Thank you." Elizabeth peered into the abdominal cavity where one side of the artery to the right leg was missing half an inch of the interior wall.

"Can you stitch that back together, missy?"

She looked up to see a smile that not only stretched his cheeks but lit his eyes. "I, ah . . ."

"You're a fine seamstress. Hop to it."

Elizabeth held out her hand, and a nurse laid a curved surgical needle threaded with the finest catgut on her palm.

"You can do it," she whispered to herself to stop her shaking hands. *Please, Lord, keep me steady here, no mistakes. Just like back home when the Swenson boy nearly sliced off a finger.* She tried to take the first stitch, but the artery slid away from her.

"You have to take a deeper stitch than that, enough to get beyond the damaged tissue."

"All right." Her second attempt made it through, and within minutes, she had the sutures snugged into place.

"Let's loosen the clamps nice and easy now, and at the slightest leakage, tighten them again."

Elizabeth swallowed, eyed the handle of the clamp, sucked in a calming breath, and released the pressure on the upper one as the doctor did the same with the lower one. Blood swelled the artery again, filling and flowing with nary a drop of red.

"That's the way." Dr. Fossden beamed at her, his white caterpillar eyebrows dotted in red. "Close her up so we can get started on all the exterior lacerations. She'll look like a patchwork quilt, but if she can make it through the night—"

"Won't she need a transfusion?"

"I have someone standing by just in case."

Elizabeth glanced down at the floor. How could anyone live with such great loss of blood? She held out her hand for the next needle and began stitching the incision in the abdominal wall.

Some time later, time that felt like hours rather than minutes, the doctor laid aside his needle, waited for Elizabeth to tie off one final stitch, and nodded to her. "You did a fine job, young woman. I'd do surgery with you anytime."

Elizabeth could feel her cheeks redden at the compliment. "Thank you for the privilege."

"You are most welcome, and now, Nurse, remove the ice packs and let's get at that leg." He turned to the nurse monitoring the ether drip into the cone over the patient's face. "How's she doing?"

"Sleeping like a babe, heart steady in spite of all that blood loss. She is one strong lady."

"Good. Miss Rogers, you begin." He indicated the area where the shattered tibia had broken through flesh and skin.

Elizabeth swallowed hard. "M-me?"

"Is there any other Miss Rogers around here?" The twinkle danced behind his glasses.

"N-no." *Steady legs,* she ordered. *You can't collapse now.* She turned to the nurse beside her. "May I have a drink of water, please?"

"Of course, dearie." With a smile the woman left and returned with a full glass, including a chip or two of ice. She held it for Elizabeth to drink, then patted her shoulder, the motherly gesture both comforting and encouraging.

Elizabeth looked across the patient to the doctor. "Ready?"

At his nod the nurse slapped a new scalpel in her hand. She made the initial incision.

"Oh." Elizabeth stared as the scalpel hit the floor. She clenched and flexed her hand. "I'm sorry." Her mind flashed back to home when she'd been so shaky with the teacup.

"Ready?" The nurse held out another scalpel.

Elizabeth shook her hand hard. *Please, God.*

"Are you all right?" Dr. Fossden waited. "Good. The artery is fully functional, which is why there was a lack of bleeding from this wound compared to what it could have been. First we need to remove all the separated bone splinters and pretend this is a jigsaw puzzle. Once the field is cleaned out, we'll retract both ends of the bone and see if we can fit it back together. The swelling will increase, but by keeping the ice around and under, we might be able to alleviate some of that."

While the doctor explained what to do each step of the way, Elizabeth used tweezers to pluck away errant bone fragments. "Can any of these be put back, if we can find the right place, I mean?"

"That would be a good idea, but I'm afraid we'd be asking for more risk of infection than we are right now. Back in my early days during the war, we just sawed off a leg like this and prayed the patient didn't die of gangrene. We've come a long way since then, but still . . ."

"You think she'll be able to walk again?"

"If we do our job right and God takes good care of the rest."

"And she stays off her feet long enough to heal properly." The nurse beside Elizabeth mopped the perspiration off Elizabeth's forehead again. "That's always the problem."

"All right, this looks as clean as it is going to get. Miss Rogers, you take the foot, and I'll do the hip. Nurse, you do what you can to ease those pieces back in place. On three, steady pulling, no jerks, pull straight."

Elizabeth felt someone beside her and turned to see Patrick's smiling face.

"Together," he whispered.

When the doctor reached three, she grasped heel and upper foot, pulling both carefully and firmly, grateful for Patrick's strength along with her own. *Lord, please make my hand work. What's happening to me?*

"Enough, hold it." Two nurses worked over the leg. "Ease off slowly. Good."

"Patrick, make sure the weights are rigged in place so we can move her to her bed before she wakes up."

Elizabeth looked up from the bone that now lay together, albeit with missing pieces. "Weights?"

"We have devised a weight and pulley system that will keep the tension on this break so it can heal cleanly. It also keeps the patient from getting out of bed or even moving around. We will put sandbags along her side also to keep her immobile."

"For how long?"

"Six weeks at least."

"What about her family, if she has one?"

The doctor shrugged. "We do what we can."

And there will be no charge if there is no money. Elizabeth took the offered needle and began closing up the wound.

"Not too tight now, we need to let it drain, like the abdomen."

She nodded. Weariness beyond anything she remembered assailed her as she tied off the final stitch. She propped herself up with rigid arms on the surgical table.

"Are you all right?" Nurse O'Shaughnessy slipped an arm about her waist.

"In a moment."

"Help her into the scrub room. Patrick, bring in a chair. Elizabeth, you need your head between your knees—now."

She felt herself half walking and half being carried to the chair. As she sat down, someone pushed her head down between her knees. Her apron smelled of blood and disinfectant. Her stomach pitched and tossed like a small boat on rough seas.

The bite of smelling salts cleared her head.

"Breathe!" The doctor's voice came firm but gentle in her ear.

She sucked in a deep breath and coughed on the fumes. Raising her head was impossible with someone's hand firmly planted on the back of her neck.

She sniffed again, her eyes and nose both dripping, and dried her eyes with the edge of her apron. "I'm fine now, really I am." She sniffed again.

"Good, then come up easy."

Mortification burned her face and flamed her neck. She forced herself to look up, much preferring to slither out under the door and up to her room.

"Did I look that bad?"

Again that twinkle in his eyes. "Yes. You were whiter than that apron of yours when it is clean."

"I am so embarrassed."

"Ah, child, don't be. You did an excellent job, and it was hot enough in there to boil water. I'm going to suggest we get some fans to blow over chunks of ice to cool that room. I read about that somewhere. And that refrigeration they have now—I read about a new device that is small enough for here. I shall have Althea install one. While she hesitates to spend any money for the good of the staff, it will help with patients too."

Elizabeth turned to thank the nurse who'd been fanning her with a folded newspaper.

"Dr. Rogers, you are needed on the burn ward."

Elizabeth turned with a start. Dr. Rogers! How wonderful that sounded. She gave the messenger a questioning look.

"After what you did in there, you surely can be called Doctor, can you not?"

Elizabeth shrugged, untied her apron, and tossed it in the laundry basket while at the same time reaching for a clean one. How much cooler she would be if she could jettison the skirt and petticoats she wore beneath it. Cooler but definitely not proper. She clenched and straightened her right hand. What if Dr. Fossden had not been there to take over?

By the time she collapsed on her bed that night, she'd delivered a baby, cared for her burn patients, ordered more morphine for the unspeakable pain they were in, set a green-stick fracture on a boy who fell out a window—said his older brother pushed him—and found time to comfort a little girl who had witnessed a beating. Her father was now in jail, and her mother was asleep in the ward after surgery.

For the first time since starting work a week earlier, Elizabeth got a full night's sleep. And this was to be her day off. A note that had been slipped under her door asked her to meet for dinner with Dr. Morganstein and Mrs. Josephson, her benefactress from the hotel where she and her mother had stayed two years before and would again when her six weeks with the Alfred Morganstein Hospital for Women was up.

Elizabeth washed and dressed, wishing for her tub at home where she could soak up to her neck with fragrant bath salts and bubbles to float down her arm, which of course would mean she had time for such luxuries. At least the water felt cool on her skin, and she no longer wore freckles of dried blood.

I must be grateful for the smallest mercies, she reminded herself while fixing her hair in front of the mirror. Today, a mercy is that I do not have to wear that triangular kerchief on my head. She fluffed her fringe and then the rest of her hair, running her fingers through the weight of it and flipping it in the air. The motion tingled her scalp and let a breath of coolness blow in. But before leaving the room, she knotted it into a bun set high on the top of her head, keeping her neck free to absorb any cool air that strayed her way.

On the way down to the dining hall, she swung by the office to see if she had any mail. Two envelopes lay on the desk, one with her name penned in her mother's handwriting. Seeing the Northfield stamp, she felt a slight stab of guilt. She'd not written home other than that brief note to say she'd arrived. She slit open the envelope and removed a sheet with her mother's name printed at the top.

July 2, 1895
Dearest daughter,

I know you are working so hard and long that you have no time to write, but I have wonderful news for you, at least in your estimation. You have been accepted at Northern Medical School in Minneapolis. It makes me happy for you to have a dream come true, and for the rest of us, happy that you will be closer to home than Pennsylvania. I have enclosed their letter so that you may write back your acceptance. I've also included the address for the school on the East Coast so you can send your regrets.

Everything is going along well here. Thorliff has moved into the Stromme place to help out with Henry's care until school starts, and then surely there will be another young man who needs a place to stay and earn his room and board.

Cook says to tell you that she will have your favorite things ready for you when you come home, which to all of us, cannot be any too soon. I am looking forward to our Chicago shopping expedition like we did last year. I covet our times together.

Your father sends his love. Oh, and remember the family whose boy died of the croup? She had another baby. He's healthy and it was an easy birth. Dr. Gaskin was pleased.

Another piece of news—I keep running on here. Your father and I made the final decision to change churches. We are now members of the Congregational Church. Pastor Johnson is such a good friend and a fine example of a humble man of God. So opposite from Pastor Mueller. I know this news will please you.

If you cannot find time to write, you can always call on the telephone, and we will gladly pay the charges. We can get some use out of the thing besides calls from here to the office.

Always remember that I love you.

Your mother

You are not to feel guilty for not marrying. You are not to feel guilty for not marrying. Elizabeth repeated the words as she opened the next letter, which was from Thorliff, of all people. She stared off into space, thinking of her mother's inferences and her own certainty that marriage was impossible.

But why is it impossible? The little voice sounded so reasonable. *Male doctors are married.*

But Dr. Morganstein isn't. The inner discussion picked up the tempo.

Perhaps she never met a man she wanted to marry. You haven't.

She glanced at the envelope in her hand. Her mother's words teased their way past her defenses. Marrying a good friend is a good basis for—Elizabeth cut off further thoughts and ignored the slight feeling of warmth. Surely it was due to the weather and not any thoughts of Mr. Bjorklund, as if not using his Christian name would keep him at arm's length. As if he'd ever been any closer than arm's length, which was absolutely proper. She almost stamped her foot for emphasis.

Whatever is the matter with you today? When there was no answer, she began reading.

July 3, 1895
Dear Elizabeth,

 I hope all is going as you wished at the hospital. I have to admit that the office and your home are strangely silent with you gone. Your father mentioned the other night after supper how he misses your playing the piano. Dr. Gaskin has been asking after you when he calls on Mr. Stromme. I have moved into his house to help for now. He has regained some of his speech and spends most of his day on the front porch, where half the town calls on him. One almost never sees him sitting by himself. I help him down there before I leave for work, and he holds court all day. I have been practicing my croquet. Your father and I play a match most evenings after supper when I eat there instead of with Mr. Stromme. I know we hear a lot of the local news at the paper, but Henry gleans it all. One just has to listen a bit more carefully than before the stroke. Dr. Gaskin is most pleased with his progress.

 I had a letter from home, and Astrid is hoping and praying they can come visit me this summer. I end up feeling so guilty that I do not go home, not like I have had any time to do that. Things are so much busier at the paper with all the new printing contracts. The new press has made such a difference in the amount and quality of printing we can do, as you well know. Your mother has suggested that we put a line of cards and stationery into production. You must admit that poses intriguing possibilities. I read that Mark Twain is lecturing in Chicago. I hope you can find time to go and then tell me all about it.

Oh, and congratulations on your acceptance in Minneapolis. I know you will turn a staid place like that upside down.

Your friend,

Thorliff

Elizabeth tapped the edge of the envelope on the side of her finger as she entered the dining room. A basket of muffins sat by the coffeepot kept warm by a small fat candle burning on the stand under it. A bowl of canned peaches, a pitcher of milk, and a pan of oatmeal above another candle gave her choices to make. The quiet of the room seemed more important than the food. At the first bite she realized how hungry she was and thought back to the night before. Had she eaten supper or not? Not, she decided as she spooned in the oatmeal, alternating with bites of muffin and sips of coffee.

When nearly finished she took out the pad of paper she'd stuffed into her pocket in the office, along with a pencil, and wrote to her parents, to Thorliff, Dr. Gaskin, and to Thornton. She'd respond to the medical schools next but needed ink to write those letters.

She thought of going outside for a walk but chose instead to return to her room for a nap before dinner.

"Ah, you look rested again." Dr. Morganstein met her at the door to her private quarters. "I was growing concerned for you."

"Thank you, but as Shakespeare said, sleep knits up the raveled sleeve of care. Sounds like I was looking pretty raveled."

"But not now. Ah, the resilience of youth. Come, Issy is already here and looking so forward to a good visit with you."

Arm in arm they entered the sitting room that looked more like a garden room with its white wicker furniture, green walls with white trim, blooming geraniums on the windowsills, and spider plants flowing over white stands. Three violets topped a chintz-covered round table, along with framed pictures of family members. A large oval picture of a little girl sitting on a bench seat, hands and ankles crossed and a bow in her hair, caught Elizabeth's attention.

Dr. Morganstein's gaze followed hers. "Ah, that is my sister at age five, most likely the only time she ever sat that still."

"I thought it might be you."

"We did look a lot alike. I am the elder and tried to keep her within bounds."

"At which she failed miserably." Issy Josephson, eyes twinkling over her pince-nez glasses, shared a smile with Althea and joined them in front of the portrait. She reached for Elizabeth's hand and cupped it in both of hers. "You know, ever since I saw you at the hotel, I have felt a new surge of joy for living. You are contagious, my dear, and I thank you for that."

Standing between the two women who'd been friends for far more years than she'd been on the earth, Elizabeth wanted to put her arms around their waists and hug them both. And so she did, surprising them as much as herself.

"Dinner is served," announced the smiling maid. "And Mrs. Cuvier says you should hurry so the soufflé don't fall."

"Well, we surely don't want a fallen soufflé." Dr. Morganstein turned them in the direction of the dining room that, in lieu of the dark walls and heavy drapes of the current fashion, looked as bright and airy as the sitting room with its white walls and green trim.

Arm in arm they made their way to their chairs, Elizabeth taking in the discussion going on around her.

"But how can you add another wing when there is no space left now?"

"I think we must buy the building next to us on the north. I have inquired, and the owner would be willing to sell."

Issy snorted. "For an exorbitant price, I am sure."

"No, it's really quite reasonable, considering."

"Ah, a landlord with a heart? Now that is a novel idea."

"Actually, he came to me. You see, someone he loves was treated

113

here, and he feels we are doing a good job of improving the community. Personally, I think he had an encounter with our living Lord, and it changed something in him. He's been making improvements in another building he owns down the street."

They sat and opened crisp white napkins to lay in their laps.

"Well, I never." Issy shook her head. She turned to smile at Elizabeth. "About like a leopard changing his spots, wouldn't you say?"

From what Elizabeth knew of landlords in neighborhoods like this one, she had to agree. "Would that it would happen to more of them."

"Issy, will you say the grace today?" Dr. Morganstein asked and then bowed her head.

"Holy Father, hear our prayers. Bless this food that it may give us the strength to carry out your will. In Jesus' precious name, amen."

As soon as the maid set the soufflé in front of Dr. Morganstein, Elizabeth leaned forward.

"I have some wonderful news."

"Good, I like to hear wonderful news." Dr. Morganstein laid her hands in her lap the better to listen.

"I have been accepted into the medical school in Minneapolis. I won't have to study at the women's school in Pennsylvania after all." She stared at her two friends, wondering at the look that passed between them. "What? Are you not pleased?"

"Yes, yes, of course. It's just that—"

"Just that we have good news too," Issy interrupted her friend. "Tell her, Althea."

Dr. Morganstein dipped into the soufflé to begin serving the meal. "I will as soon as we have our food in front of us."

Waiting had never been one of Elizabeth's strong suits, but manners won out and she took a deep breath to calm herself.

"Now, then. You know the building we were discussing a few minutes ago?" Dr. Morganstein now wore a more serious look.

Elizabeth could feel the tension run up her neck. "Yes."

"One of my plans for it is to open a medical school of my own. We have room there for classrooms, including one large enough to build a cool room for the cadavers and have dissecting tables for ten specimens. That would accommodate twenty students. I have a benefactor who is willing to set up the entire laboratory, including an apothecary."

Elizabeth laid a hand on her middle to keep it from leaping and dancing.

"You really mean this?"

"Of course, you think I would tease you?" When the young woman shook her head, the doctor continued. "I have five students ready to enter; you would make six. I wanted to wait until I was more sure of the possibilities before telling you. If all goes well, we could open the doors this fall. In the meantime we could start classes here in the basement. Patrick will have to move things around, but we do have room."

Elizabeth sank against the back of her chair. "I believe I better write another thanks but no thanks letter this afternoon. I know my mother will be disappointed since Minneapolis is closer to home, but . . ." She clasped her hands to her chest. "To be able to study here with you, with cadavers too, and the hospital . . ." Her voice trailed off.

"Before the year is out, I predict there will be others clamoring at the door. You will have to expand even before you have completed the initial plans." Issy tasted the soufflé. "Ah, delightful. Now let us eat before the food is ruined and we hurt Mrs. Cuvier's feelings."

While the conversation lasted into the evening, Elizabeth went to her room still bubbling with questions and excitement. To be one of the first graduates of the Alfred Morganstein Medical School would indeed be an honor.

The next morning she entered her first examination room to find Moira Flannery, the young Irish woman she'd seen the summer before.

"Why, hello. It is good to see you again."

"Ah, Doctor, and you have come back to help out again?"

"I have, but I'm not a real doctor yet, just an assistant. How can I help you today?"

The woman patted her swelling abdomen. "Just came to make sure all is right with the bairn."

Elizabeth nodded. "I see. And you have how many children now?"

115

"Two; one was stillborn in between."

And what has happened with that wife-beating husband of yours? Elizabeth kept that question off her lips and from her face, nodding instead and checking for more bruises without appearing to be doing so.

"Me man, he's been back to work, so things, they are better."

"Good." After checking the heartbeat of both mother and fetus, Elizabeth studied her patient. The yellowing bruise she saw on the woman's upper arm could have come from banging into something. "You must take good care of yourself. Drink milk and eat red meat." Was she naturally pale, as were so many with red hair, or was it the heat or . . .

"Thankee, mum. I think I am about seven months along."

"That seems about right. Let us check you again in a few weeks."

"I will."

As the woman left the room, Elizabeth wrote her notes on the chart. *Please, God, help that man keep his temper. Let him indeed be changed like she has said.*

CHAPTER ELEVEN

Northfield, Minnesota

"Ah, there you are, Mr. Björklund."

Thorliff looked up to see Mrs. Karlotta Kingsley bearing down on him. What was there about her that made him so uncomfortable?

"Good day, Mrs. Kingsley." He touched the brim of his straw boater, a recent acquisition at Rudy's For Men. He'd bought it when Phillip sent him to the store to interview the owner for a recent article on local businesses. Rudy had given him a cut rate since he was writing for the paper. That same article had earned him a free soda at Mrs. Sitze's Ice Cream Parlor.

"I just spoke with dear Phillip, and he said you were just the one to attend the social I am sponsoring to earn money for the Missionary Society. The good book says that those of us who have must share with those less fortunate. Don't you agree?"

He nodded but only slightly. "I . . . I need to be going. I . . ."

Before he could make a break past her, she took his arm and turned to accompany him, the swell of her prodigious bosom brushing his upper arm.

Struck by a hot poker, he tried to withdraw his arm and only succeeded in bringing about another contact. Heat flared up his chest to his neck and face, hot enough to lift his hat and let it sail away on the windless air, the wind he needed so desperately right now and which for a change had taken time off. Not a leaf moved in the elm trees shading the sidewalk. The thoughts he was trying to keep pure—weren't.

At any other time there would be mothers with baby carriages, businessmen, children playing hoops, someone to whom he could apply for assistance.

No one in sight.

Every time he tried to put some distance between her and his arm, she moved with him. *Lord above, help me. What am I to do?*

"So you will attend, then?" She tapped his arm with her folded fan.

"I . . . ah, I suppose so." *How can I get out of this? Fake an illness?* "When did you say this soirée will take place?"

"Tomorrow night."

"Are you certain Mr. and Mrs. Rogers will not be attending?"

"Oh my, yes, they will be there, but dear Phillip said that he would rather attend as a guest and not have to worry about writing it up. He said that is what he has you for."

Phillip Rogers, I know you are my boss, but I also thought you were my friend. He swallowed, knowing that his Adam's apple must be beet red. Blood-beet red.

"Dear Mr. Bjorklund, I have a favor to ask of you." She turned, and it happened again. Was it deliberate? The thought sent another burst of heat headward.

"And what is that?" His voice cracked on the last word.

"Would you please read over some of my writing and see if it might be publishable?" She tapped him again with the fan that hung on a braided cord around her wrist.

He glanced down into eyes green as grass. She batted long, up-curved eyelashes of such thickness to seem as fans of their own. He couldn't take his gaze back; he felt as if a corded line held him in place. His heart picked up speed and he felt a stirring in his middle.

"Ah, that might be more in the area for . . . for . . ."

A slow sweep of those lashes and her eyes pleaded with him, shimmering a language of their own.

"Ah, I guess I could do that."

"That would be such a kind thing." Her voice now held the breath of awe, as if he had bestowed a gift of immense magnitude.

His swallow had a hard time passing his Adam's apple.

"Thank you." Sweet intoxication tickled his nose from the perfume she wore, like lilies of the valley and roses and something darker.

"You . . ." He swallowed. "You are welcome."

"Shall we say this evening then, Mr.—No, I feel that we are becoming such friends. May I call you Thorliff?" Her voice purred like a kitten stroked by a loving hand.

"I . . . ah, y-yes."

"And this evening it is?"

"That will be fine."

"Then I must be on my way. Thank you again and bonjour." She fluttered her hand as she turned and walked back the way they had come. He watched her undulating hips bringing a sheen of moisture to his upper lip.

He wiped it away with his handkerchief. "Surely has gotten hot today," he muttered as he continued back to the office.

"Mrs. Kingsley was here looking for you. I said you would cover her soirée."

"I know." Even he could hear the disgruntlement in his voice.

"Ah, she found you?"

Thorliff nodded and wandered back to the printing press he'd been cleaning before being sent on an errand. *She found me all right. How does one keep pure in heart with a woman like her on the loose?*

"Where are the stamps and the mail?" Phillip called from his desk.

Thorliff jerked straight up from checking the ink level and then flinched. "I'll go get them right now." He fled out the front door as though a swarm of bees were chasing him.

119

After closing up the shop because Phillip had gone home earlier, Thorliff trudged up the street to the Stromme house. He'd much rather have stayed in his back room at the newspaper, but he'd promised to help Henry Stromme until they found someone else. He hoped that would be soon, though Henry made it clear he would prefer that Thorliff stay.

Trying to put a pleasant look on his face, Thorliff turned up the walk to his temporary home.

"Hey, young man, good to see you." Pastor Johnson rose from the seat facing Henry and extended his hand. "Sounds to me like you've been doing a good job with this old codger here."

Henry's barking laugh and half smile showed his agreement.

"H-he be good." The speech came slowly, but it came and was getting better week by week.

Thorliff took the old man's extended hand and squeezed gently. "Come on, squeeze back." He nodded at the returned pressure. "Good, good. Did you have someone help you today?"

"Ja, t-two." Henry held up two fingers.

"Well, Henry, I'll come back tomorrow and read to you again. Pretty soon you'll be able to turn your own pages, you wait and see." Pastor Johnson stood. "Mrs. Norlie brought supper over. It is in the kitchen. Henry says he can pretty much feed himself now. That is great progress."

"Once we got him out of that bedroom and back out on the porch, he's gotten better daily," Thorliff said. "His porch sometimes looks like the neighborhood social hall, what with half the women in town bringing him cookies and lemonade."

"Mrs. Gartley brought strawberry-rhubarb pie. We managed to leave you some." Pastor set his hat back on his thinning blond hair and, after patting Henry's shoulder, ambled down the walk.

Henry pushed with his arms and after a struggle made it to his feet. He grabbed the cane by the chair with his good hand and allowed Thorliff to hold open the screen door so he could go in.

"Tha-s."

"You are welcome."

Henry slowly made his way down the central hall from the front parlor, recently converted into his bedroom, to the kitchen at the rear where he sank onto another chair with a sigh.

"You're getting stronger every day." Thorliff lifted the lid on the cast-iron kettle on the still-warm stove. "Um, smells good. Are you hungry?"

Henry half shrugged.

"Too much pie and cookies." A cackle greeted his teasing. "I'll dish up, and you tell me when to stop."

Later, with them both finished eating and the kitchen straightened up again, Henry motioned to the box of dominoes that resided in the middle of the table.

"Sorry, but I have a meeting tonight, so I need to help you get ready for bed now. Not sure how long I'll be."

Henry sighed, and the one shoulder rose and fell in the usual shrug.

"If you're still awake when I get back, we can play a game then."

"Goo-d." The old man struggled to his feet and shuffled back down the hall.

Thorliff offered as little help as necessary because Dr. Gaskin continued to stress that Henry needed to do as much for himself as he was able and if anyone helped too much, they were doing him no favor. Waiting and watching the struggle were painful.

Thorliff's fingers twitched to assist. "We need to give you a shave in the morning. Can't have you looking scruffy for all your girlfriends."

The dry cackle always made Thorliff smile too. In spite of his difficulties, Henry Stromme managed to keep his sense of humor.

"I'll be back later, then. You need anything else?"

Henry shook his head and waved his good hand.

"No, use the other."

Slowly the hand obeyed, rising from the top of the sheet that covered Mr. Stromme and moving from side to side.

"Good for you. Guess Dr. Gaskin isn't going to have to come every day to beat you with a stick after all." Thorliff left with the cackle of glee ringing in his ears.

I'd rather stay here, he grumbled to himself as he made his way to the Kingsley home. *How'd I let myself get talked into this?* But the thought of bewitching green eyes and a memorable perfume made him pick up his feet a little faster in spite of himself. He slicked his hair back and adjusted his collar before ringing the doorbell at the brick house that could closely be called a mansion. If he remembered right, the Kingsleys had bought or perhaps leased the house from one of the founding families of the town. The children had moved on, and the old folks passed away, leaving a house that needed a family.

"Yes?" A white-capped maid answered the door.

"I'm Thorliff Bjorklund, here to see Mrs. Kingsley."

The young woman eyed him up and down, a slight smile tugging at the corner of a cupid-bow mouth. "Won't you come in?" She stepped back and indicated the same with one hand. "They are out on the verandah. Follow me." She closed the door and led him down a hall, through a large open room with dark, grand furniture, through open French doors, and announced, "Mr. Bjorklund is here, ma'am."

"Ah, Mr. Bjorklund, so good of you to come." She beckoned him to join them and turned to the man beside her. "Dear, this is the young man I told you about who works at the newspaper office. He wrote a book too. Mr. Bjorklund, this is my husband, Edmond Kingsley."

Edmond Kingsley looked up from the book he was reading, marked the place with one finger, and stood to shake hands.

"I heard you go to St. Olaf. Shame. We could use you at Carleton."

"Thank you, sir, but I think I shan't switch. I hope you like it here in Northfield."

"The town seems pleasant enough so far, but for the finer things of life." At Thorliff's questioning glance, Mr. Kingsley added, "Like the theater, the opera, and the symphony. I do appreciate a good museum also." His accent spoke of the East Coast, but Thorliff wasn't sure from where.

"Minneapolis and St. Paul aren't all so far by train." Thorliff realized he'd made a gaffe by the raised eyebrows and a look he could only interpret as condescending. *Ah well, I'm sure he will be real popular with the students at Carleton!* But Thorliff kept his thoughts from his mouth and he hoped from his face. He started to defend the choir and band at St. Olaf but decided to let it ride. "It is good of you to support the Missionary Society."

Kingsley waved a dismissive hand. "That is my wife's interest, not mine. I hope you can help her with her writing." He glanced down at his book, obviously wanting to get back to it.

"We'll leave you then, dear." Mrs. Kingsley took one step toward the house. "Can I send anything out for you?"

"Something to eradicate these pesky mosquitoes. One can hardly enjoy the solitude with them whining about." He sat back down and reopened his book.

"Come, we'll work inside where the light is better." She strolled beside him, her perfume teasing his nostrils again.

"Would you care for something to drink? We have wine, whiskey, or if you'd rather, iced tea or lemonade."

"Nothing now, thank you. I need to get back as soon as I can to make sure Mr. Stromme is all right."

"Mr. Stromme?" Karlotta paused in reaching for a stack of papers on the library table.

Thorliff explained his position as she sat on the horsehair sofa and patted the seat beside her.

"The light is better here."

His fingers accidentally brushed hers in the transfer, sending a shock up his arm, making him choose a chair on the other side of the whatnot table that held the lamp. Trying to swallow again took effort.

In spite of her compliments on his suggestions for her writing and her repeated offer of refreshments, he fled Karlotta Kingsley's presence as soon as he could manage.

Back home, Thorliff lost two games of dominoes to Henry, and after rolling around in his bed in that restless land of neither waking nor sleeping for what seemed like hours, he finally drifted off. Only to wake with his heart pounding at the dream he'd had of Mrs. Kingsley.

He drained a glass of water from the pitcher he kept near and sat on the edge of the bed, head propped in his hands.

*Whatever in the world is the matter with me? Lord, forgive me. She's a married woman, and I—*He chugged another glass of water, feeling instead he should pour it over his head. If there had been a cow tank nearby he could have thrown himself into it to cool off. He picked up his Bible and turned to Matthew, chapter five, and read: "Blessed are the pure in heart: for they shall see God." Thorliff repeated it out loud with his eyes closed. *However will I get my thoughts under control?*

"What's the matter with you?" Phillip asked the next day. "You're lower than a centipede."

"Nothing. I'm fine." Thorliff thought a moment. "I would really rather not attend the soirée tonight. I mean, I have not the proper attire, and . . . ah . . . I need to stay with Mr. Stromme, since I have agreed to help him and . . ." He could think of nothing else to say.

Phillip steepled his fingertips and studied Thorliff over the top of them.

Thorliff could feel the heat rising from neck to face; his ears blazed.

"Your suit will be fine; just give it a bit of a brushing. Henry can manage for a few hours on his own. What is it that is really bothering you? This will be a good opportunity for you to mingle with the upper echelon of this town. There are people attending tonight who already know you because of what you've written here at the paper and through your book, but meeting them personally could be beneficial down the road. Who knows how."

"I just . . . I . . ." *Please, Lord, get me out of this.*

"I think you better plan on going."

Thorliff felt his shoulders sag. How could he say no? "All right."

"Eight o'clock."

"I know."

"And, Thorliff, just be your normal, respectful self. Women like Mrs. Kingsley lose interest as quickly as it starts."

"Thank you, sir." *He does understand.* Thorliff nodded slightly. *I wish Elizabeth were here.* The thought surprised him, but then he realized this had not been the first time he'd thought that since she headed for Chicago. After this was over, he promised himself he'd write her another letter, never mind that he'd yet to receive an answer to his first. He glanced at the calendar on the wall. Nearly four weeks before she'd be home.

The way things were looking, this could be a long summer.

"You must go through the greeting line," the young maid whispered that night as she escorted him into the foyer where a carved walnut stair curved gracefully, drawing the eye to the two-story windows behind it. Mr. and Mrs. Kingsley stood side by side, he in black tie and cutaway coat with tails, she in an emerald green gown with a heart-shaped low-cut neckline.

Thorliff felt like he'd swallowed a baseball. He tried to look everywhere but at the bare skin above the lace-trimmed edge of the bodice.

"Good evening, Mr. Bjorklund. It is good of you to join us." Karlotta fanned herself idly, her eyes sparkling behind the pleated lace and silk confection. Her eyelashes swept down and up again.

"Ah, thank you." He'd read of sweaty hands but never before had the sensation been so overpowering. He half bowed, but that only brought him closer to her.

"Ah, there you are, Thorliff." Phillip to the rescue. "I see you've met both the Kingsleys." He nodded and smiled, at the same time easing Thorliff closer to a group of men, some of whom were also wearing less formal attire.

"Are you all right?" Phillip asked as they finally turned and sauntered toward the group.

"I . . . ah, of course. Why?" Thorliff wanted to loosen his necktie, but he refrained under the strictest self-discipline.

"Annabelle sent me to retrieve you, saying she thought you needed help."

Thank you, Lord. Whatever you tell me to do for Mrs. Rogers to return this favor, I shall do with my utmost ability. "I will thank her myself. And you, sir, for listening."

"Are you sure you are all right?"

"I am now. Who was it you wanted me to meet?"

Thorliff spent the rest of the evening visiting with those people his employer thought necessary and with others who stopped to tell him how much they enjoyed *The Switchmen* and the articles he had written for the newspaper.

"When you chose my daughter to win in the under-twelve-year-old category, you changed her life," said one of the women. "Now she is absolutely certain she wants to become a writer, and her grades have gone up accordingly. I no longer have to remind her to do her homework."

"Thank you, ma'am. She wrote a very good story. I'm glad it has been a help for her." While he smiled and nodded when he should, his mind went leaping off on another tangent. *What if . . . ?*

CHAPTER TWELVE

Blessing, North Dakota

"There must have been a lot of celebrating last year after harvest."

"What do you mean?" Ingeborg rolled on her side to look into her husband's moonlit face.

"Well, the rash of babies you've been birthing of late." Haakan ran a calloused finger down the bridge of her nose.

"There is nothing more satisfying on this earth than helping a baby into this world." Ingeborg smiled at the memory of the night before when she'd ushered a baby boy into his waiting family. Firstborn and a son. The father and mother were both pleased beyond measure.

"The *most* satisfying?"

Ingeborg elbowed Haakan in the ribs. "You know what I mean."

His chuckle banished any shadows in the corners.

Some time later when she was finally on the verge of sleep, Ingeborg thought back to the boy, Robbie, who'd had the head injury and was still alive. She sighed. Tomorrow she would take a loaf of bread over to Mrs. Nordstrum and find out how they were doing.

Ingeborg rolled on her side, laying aside even the sheet. Sometimes she thought of sleeping in the cellar or the cheese house where it was cooler, but Haakan's gentle snores usually lulled her to sleep.

The next morning Astrid came running out to the garden. "Mor, can—" She caught the lift of her mother's eyebrows and started over. "May I go play with Sophie and Grace? Please? We need to go wading in the river."

"Need to?" Again the eyebrows lifted, this time accompanied by a smile.

Astrid nodded. "I heard a bullfrog croaking, and we haven't been to the river in forever."

"What are the boys doing?" Ingeborg pulled a carrot from the rich soil and, wiping it off on her apron, took the first sweet bite. She held it out and Astrid ate the rest. "I meant only to share it, not for you to take it all."

Astrid bent over and did the same, offering her mother the larger end. They both tucked the carrot tops back in under the fluffy row to return to the soil as they decomposed.

"Well?" Astrid said.

"If it is okay with Tante Kaaren, it is with me. Why don't you ask Ilse to go with you? She never has time to play anymore."

"All Ilse thinks about is the deaf school and Mr. McBride." Astrid tilted her head. "Are they getting married soon?"

"Why?"

"Because I saw them kissing out behind the barn."

"Oh. You weren't spying, were you?"

"Mor!" Astrid snapped off one of the last of the pea pods and squeezed it so the peas lay against the heavier seam, lined up like a treasure boat. "Besides, the boys went fishing."

"I think you better play closer to the house," Ingeborg said, knowing the boys' penchant for skinny-dipping after they fished. She rocked back on her heels, her knees on an old gunnysack she kept on a post by the garden for just that purpose. Weeding with the sun on her back and knees to bare toes in the earth always made her feel close to God, closer than church even. No doubt that was why God met his first two human creations in the garden. "Why don't you three go to Tante Penny's and offer to play with Gus and Linnea for a while. I'll give you each a penny for candy. You may take them out of the tin on your way."

"Really?" Forgetting the "need" to go to the river, Astrid leaped over the rows of carrots, beans, and potatoes. The corn was a little too high to leap so she ran through and around it. Her laughter floated back, sweet as a house wren's song.

After weeding the two rows of carrots, Ingeborg rose and dug her fists into her back right at her waist. Ever since the rain the garden had grown inches overnight, as had the weeds. While Andrew had hoed between the rows, one still had to pull the weeds up close to the plants or lose some in the process. She stooped to check the beans, but while covered with blossoms, they weren't ready yet for picking.

She dusted off her hands, picked the dirt out from under her closely cut fingernails, and entered the springhouse to cut a hunk off the wheel of cheese she kept there. That plus the bread sitting on the counter would go in the basket for Mrs. Nordstrum. She had put off the visit until after dinner, but now with everyone off busy on their own, she would hitch up the buggy and go on.

A few minutes later she trotted the horse out the lane, waving at Haakan, who was cutting hay now that the grass had finally dried out enough. The rain had lasted for three days.

She stopped when closer to call to him. "I'm going to visit Mrs. Nordstrum. I won't be long."

He waved to show he'd heard and slapped the reins on the team's rumps again.

"What a good man you are, letting the boys go fishing before haying really starts," she said aloud even knowing Haakan couldn't hear her compliment. But the horse flicked his ears as he trotted along, listening to her and keeping track of everything going on around him. "You know, I'd much rather be riding you than driving you." She thought of how long it had been since she'd gone riding for pleasure or enjoyed the thrill of hunting for their food. Years, would it be?

"Lord, how life has changed these last years. Everywhere we look, there are men working the fields. There are houses, barns, and fences.

And it's only been fifteen years since we left Norway. Counting our blessings takes plenty of time, that's for sure." She thought to her Bible reading that morning, how God's thoughts for his people are more numerous than the sands on a seashore. Not that she'd seen many sandy beaches along the sea. The Norway coast she'd seen was mostly rocks, but she'd seen sand along the river, and she was fairly certain God would count that too. "I will sing praises, O Lord, most high. I will glorify your name." She turned north on the road the men had scraped and widened beyond track width and passed the Solberg place, wishing she were going there instead. She hadn't had a good visit with Mary Martha in a long time. Good thing there was church on Sunday, not only for worship but for a chance to see her friends.

Ingeborg wheeled the buggy into the Nordstrums' yard, stopped the horse by the hitching post, and stepped down, but there was still no sign of life. Perhaps the Nordstrums had gone somewhere. She snapped a rope to the horse's bridle and tied him to the post, took her basket from the buggy, and walked up to the porch. "Anyone home?" She shaded her eyes with her hand to see if Mr. Nordstrum was out in the fields and finally saw him off to the north. Or at least the figure riding the mower behind the horse seemed near enough it might be him. She took the steps to the front door and knocked. Then knocked again. Thinking to leave her gifts on the table, she opened the door and went in.

Dishes still sat on the table, and a boiler of diapers simmered on the back of the stove.

"Mrs. Nordstrum? Betty?" Ingeborg checked the lean-to, which she found was divided into two bedrooms by a flimsy wall with a passage between the two next to the house wall. There was no one in either room, but the dirt smell of a soddy reminded Ingeborg of their early years when the two Bjorklund families lived in one main room.

She returned to the big room and continued back out the door. No one was in the garden, weed choked now since the rain. "Mrs. Nordstrum!" Ingeborg cupped her hands around her mouth to help the sound travel further.

"Here."

She followed the sound to the granary, where Betty Nordstrum sat on a pile of gunnysacks, her baby asleep in her arms, her daughter sound asleep on other gunnysacks, and Robbie curled in the corner, eyes closed and thumb in his mouth as if he too were three instead of eight.

"Are you all right?" Ingeborg kept her voice low to let the children sleep.

"It's Robbie. Sometimes he gets such terrible fits, and this is the only place that seems to comfort him." Betty Nordstrum raised eyes that looked like she'd not slept since they left the icehouse. "I can't leave him alone or he screams. Only sleeps a little at a time. So sometimes we come out here where he used to like playing in the oats. You saw the house?" At Ingeborg's nod, she shook her head. "Can't get nothing done." Her sigh bled despair. "He's like a baby again, needing diapers and all. But he won't let me put them on him. Such a mess."

Ingeborg nodded again. "Well, I come to help, so I will do just that. I'll start with getting those diapers on the line, and what do you want washed next?"

"I can't have you doing that."

"You have no choice. That's what we do here in Blessing, help each other out. Now you stay right here, and perhaps you can take a rest along with your children."

Before long Ingeborg had diapers and sheets on the line, children's clothes soaking, and the kitchen cleaned back up. How she wished she had brought Astrid along. She was needed more here than at Tante Penny's.

I should have come sooner, Ingeborg scolded herself. *I had no idea things were this bad. What can we do to help that boy? What did she mean by fits?*

Thoughts continued to plague her as she found salt pork in the well house and sliced it to fry for supper. She stirred up biscuits to go along with the meat and set potato water and flour to rising for bread the next day.

She heard them coming long before they got to the house, Robbie's plaintive cry tugging at her heart. *Lord, what do I do?*

131

Mrs. Nordstrum laid the baby in a wooden frame with a quilt on the floor. "Mister built that so when he's older he can't crawl out the door." The three-year-old clung to her skirt, and Robbie, holding his head with both hands, sat rocking against the wall.

"Do you have any laudanum?" When Mrs. Nordstrum shook her head, Ingeborg nodded. "I do. Let's give him a bit, enough to make him relax, and if it is pain in his head that is causing all this, that will help." Dropping a couple of glugs in a cup, she added water and handed it to Betty. "Do you have any honey or sugar? Good. Add some of that so it is more palatable."

While Betty followed the instructions, Ingeborg swung the little girl up in her arms and stood rocking her, shifting her weight from one foot to another, all the while crooning the comforting singsong that girls learn at their mother's side as they care for younger children. By the time they are mothers, the rocking and the songs come naturally.

While Robbie made a face, he drank the cup dry and resumed his rocking.

By the time Ingeborg and Betty took another basket of clothes to the line, the diapers were dry and ready for folding. While they pinned the pants and shirts on the rope, Ingeborg asked Betty to describe Robbie's fits.

"Well, he screams and then falls down, twitching and jerking, sometimes flailing his arms and legs, then he wets himself and falls into a stupor. I'm afraid he's going to burn himself on the hot stove or fall and bang his head again." She bowed her head, then raised tear-filled eyes. "You think this is from that clout on the head?"

"Ja, I am sure of it. We'll have to pray that God takes this away too. He kept Robbie alive for a reason. That we know."

"Sometimes I ain't so sure. It's like the stories in the Bible about demons and such. Ingeborg, I am so scared. What if Robbie is like this for the rest of his life?"

Ingeborg put the last carved wooden clothespin in place and picked up the empty basket. "The Lord says to take one day at a time, and that's what we will have to do."

They entered the soddy to find Robbie curled up on his bed fast asleep, the other two playing in the pen, the baby slobbering on his bare toes and May poking at him to make him smile.

"Ah, Ingeborg, how can I thank you. The house hasn't been this peaceful since, well, since the accident."

"I have an idea. Why don't I take May home with me for a couple of days and you give Robbie just a couple of drops from the brown bottle, again mixed with water and honey. Not enough to put him to sleep, but perhaps that will calm him down. And we'll ask everyone to pray for all of you."

"Thank you." Betty looked around her home. "Thank-you seems so little for what all you did."

"Someday you'll do something good for someone else. That's just the way things are. Now, do you mind if I take May with me?"

"If'n you want. I hate to be a burden, though."

"Astrid will love having her. I'll see if I can find someone to come weed for you."

"The mister will be much obliged too. He's been feeling bad because he has no time to help me. You really think the medicine will help our boy?"

"I certainly hope so. I'd best be going." Ingeborg picked up her basket. "I'll check back in a day or two."

Funny, she thought on the way home while dandling the child on her knee and holding the reins with one hand, when things get hard, some pull into their shells like turtles and hide, while others work themselves to exhaustion. Either way, we cut ourselves off from the comfort and healing the almighty God wishes to bestow on us through others. She hugged the squirming and whimpering child closer to her chest.

"Mama . . ."

"I know, baby, I know."

"Ma, where you been all this time?" Astrid came running to meet her when she whoa'd the horse in their own yard.

"I told you I was going to the Nordstrums'." Ingeborg handed the child to Astrid. "May is going to be staying with us for a few days. Her mama's got her hands full with the others."

"Can she walk?"

"Of course, but hold her for a while. She needs a bit of comforting, being separated from her family and all."

"Andrew brought home a string of fish. He's out scaling them now. I started new potatoes for supper and thought we'd cream them along with the last of the peas. Sure would be good if we had ham to go with that."

"Astrid, you are truly a gift from God. You play with her while I go put the horse away. Don't want to stop the fish scaler."

Ingeborg had just started up the stairs to the house when she heard pounding hooves and a "halloo." Only an emergency would bring someone on a hard gallop like that.

CHAPTER THIRTEEN

"It's Mira. She's bleeding bad." Abe Mendohlson fought to slow his runaway fear, but his stuttering speech gave him away.

"Where is she?"

"Home. Here, you take my horse, and I'll hitch up the buggy and bring it to you." He swung to the ground, ready to give her a hand up.

"I need my medicines." Ingeborg looked to the house to see Astrid, child on her hip, bringing out the basket with her medical supplies. "Is there any laudanum in there?"

Astrid checked, ran back into the house with May clinging to her neck only to rush out again. "There is now."

"Thank you."

"Please hurry." Abe threw Ingeborg aboard the horse and ran to meet Astrid, meeting her at the bottom of the steps and grabbing the supplies.

"Is anyone with her?" Ingeborg bent down with her arm outstretched and kicked the horse forward.

"Anji was on her way." Abe thrust the basket at her.

Without bothering to arrange her bunched-up skirts, Ingeborg clapped her legs against the horse's sides and tore back down the lane. If only there weren't so many fences, she could have gotten there more quickly across the fields.

"God, please slow the bleeding, put your hand on her, take away the fear."

I didn't even ask what started the bleeding. Is she in labor? Ingeborg knew the consequences of horrendous bleeding and labor this soon. Mira wasn't due until sometime in August. And here it was only mid-July. What had happened to bring this on? The horse was heaving and throwing foam by the time Ingeborg stopped at the Mendohlsons' soddy.

Anji met her at the door. "I tried to pack her to stop the bleeding, but it's no use."

"Is she having contractions?" Ingeborg spoke over her shoulder, losing no time in getting to the bed.

"Yes. Almost continuous."

Ingeborg sucked in a breath at the bloody bed, the gown, Mira's face so white she could see the blue lines of veins.

"Ingeborg, I . . . I knew you would c-come." Her voice was as faint as her hands were clammy. Pain tied her in a knot again and rolled through, leaving her limp as a used scrub rag.

Ingeborg laid her hands on the belly that should have been distended but only showed a mound. "Lord God, please, we have no way to turn but to you. Help us, Father, help us." She looked over her shoulder to Anji. "Help brace her with your back to the wall. She can hang on to your hands. If we can get this baby born, perhaps we can stanch the bleeding."

"Too soon. Too soon." Mira shrieked with another spasm, the sound trailing off in a whimper. "Too soon."

"What happened? Do you know?" Ingeborg asked Anji.

"No, and Abe was going so fast I couldn't hear what he said. Just came as quick as I could." Anji settled herself at the head of the bed and stroked back Mira's hair with gentle hands. "Do you think . . . ?" Tears flooded her eyes before she could continue. She sniffed and wiped her face with the back of her hand. Laying her cheek on top of Mira's head, she murmured gently. When the Mendohlsons had come to the Baards' to help out when her pa was so sick, Anji and Mira had become good friends.

Keeping one ear for the sound of the buggy, Ingeborg encouraged the struggling woman through another contraction, this one weaker than the last. *God, where are you? Are you listening? What can I do?* She thought of the laudanum in her basket, but while that might deaden the pain, they had to get this baby born before its mother bled to death.

At least bring her husband back quickly. She needs him. That might give her the strength to go on. While the thoughts raced through her mind, Ingeborg continued her gentle ministrations. She dampened a cloth and wiped the sweat from the pale forehead, all the while murmuring encouragement.

Mrs. Mendohlson breathed her last just as her husband burst through the door. He dropped to his knees beside the bed and grasped his wife's hands. "Try, Mira, try. Please . . ." He looked over his shoulder to Ingeborg. "She . . . she isn't . . . ?"

Ingeborg nodded. "She's gone home."

"Oh . . . oh . . ." He put his big hands on both sides of his wife's face. "Mira, please, hear me, Mira."

Ingeborg laid a hand on his shoulder and motioned to Anji, who was now sobbing also, to move away from the bed. The two of them went outside, leaving the poor man to his sorrow.

"He didn't even get to say good . . . good-bye." Anji turned into Ingeborg's arms, and the two of them cried together.

"She was so young, not even as old as me."

"I know." Ingeborg patted her back. "These two have not had it easy, that's for sure. And now he has to raise his children alone." Ingeborg glanced around, for the first time realizing the two were not there.

"Becky took them home to our house. Ossie would hardly leave, crying and wanting his ma, and Julia clung to her ma with both fists."

"Poor little ones." Ingeborg took in a deep breath and, with her arms around Anji, stared out across the fields. Such a high price this land extracted, bleeding some of the farmers dry until they either succumbed to sickness or left for what they hoped would be a better place.

"Come, let us wash up, then after a bit we'll go clean up in there." They walked arm in arm to the well and let the wooden bucket down into the depths. After cranking a full one up, Ingeborg filled the dipper that hung on one of the wooden supports and handed it to Anji to drink first.

If things had gone differently, Anji would have been her new daughter by now, or they would have been planning the wedding and making things for her new home. Hers and Thorliff's. In spite of the hurts caused by the two of them going different ways, Ingeborg knew she still loved this young woman, that Anji would always have a special place in her heart, if for no other reason than Anji was the daughter of her best friend. At the thought of Agnes, gone home what seemed like such a long time ago or just yesterday, Ingeborg's eyes filled again. *Lord, sometimes life is just too hard to bear.*

I will never leave you nor forsake you. The answer came quickly.

I know that, and on days like today you are the only one I can cling to. She stared off to the west, where gray clouds that threatened more rain blocked the stars arching above them. *No rain, please, Lord. So many of the grass fields are cut and drying for hay. Before we prayed for rain and rejoiced when it came. Now we pray for you to withhold it.* She dipped the edge of her apron into the water and wiped her face. So cool, so welcome, and poor Mrs. Mendohlson would never feel it again. Closing her eyes, Ingeborg repeated some of her verses. *"I can do all things through Christ which strengtheneth me." "Surely goodness and mercy shall follow me all the days of my life: and I will dwell in the house of the Lord for ever." Lord, being with you has to be so much better than being here.*

"He's come out now." Anji touched her arm.

Ingeborg sniffed back another freshet of tears and blew her nose. "If you want to go on home, I can manage here."

"No, I'll stay to help. That's what Ma would want me to do."

"I . . . I have to do the chores," Abe said, joining them outdoors.

He braced himself against the soddy wall as if his legs could no longer hold him up.

"Ja, that will be good."

"I'll let Pastor Solberg know." Ingeborg put a hand on his shoulder.

"Thank you." He took a handkerchief from his back pocket and wiped his face. "It's all my fault."

"What is all your fault?" Dreading the answer, the women waited.

"I asked her to help me with the beam for the new granary. I had it all braced, all she . . . she had to do was hold it in place, you know? So simple. Then something happened, and it slipped and fell and knocked her over. She screamed, and I . . . I helped her into the house. She was all doubled over in pain." Tears streamed down his face. "It was all my fault." He closed his eyes and shook his head, as if holding it up would never again be possible. "So you see, if I had gone for Swen or Knute to help me, Mira would still be here. She'd be making supper and laughing with Ossie and Julia, and I would come in with a full bucket of milk, and she would say, 'Supper is ready.'" He stopped and stared out across the land, shaking his head slowly, as if even that were too heavy.

"I will go get one of my brothers to help." Anji looked from the man to Ingeborg, who was also shaking her head.

"Taking care of his animals is a good thing right now." She patted Abe's hand again. "You go and bring in the cows." She spoke as if he were a small boy needing instructions. He nodded and plodded across the yard, stumbling and nearly falling to his knees before righting himself and finally leaning against the barn wall.

"I know how he feels." Anji's eyes swam with tears that glittered in the sun now slanting through the clouds. "It's too heavy. The burden is just too heavy."

"I know. I know." Ingeborg turned and paused in the doorway, forcing herself to go in and begin the final gift she could give this family.

When Anji and Ingeborg had bathed the body and dressed her again in her best dress, they set the sheets and things to soak in cold water and laid out bread and sliced meat for a simple supper. Then closing the door, they set Ingeborg's basket in the buggy, and Anji climbed in while Ingeborg bridled the horse.

"The funeral will be tomorrow?"

"Most likely."

"I could have Gus go tell Pastor Solberg. That way you could go on home."

"Mange takk, that would help so much. I spent all afternoon helping the Nordstrums. She is not doing well, so one of her little ones is at our house."

"Is something wrong with Robbie?"

"Ja." Ingeborg explained what had happened.

"Losing Ma was the worst thing that has happened to me, but when one of your babies nearly dies, and then this . . ." Anji wiped her eyes again.

"Ja, that is worse." *I have done both, and I know. I have comforted others, closed dying eyes, and sometimes the pit yawns before me, but . . .* She sighed and looked to Anji. "This life is hard, but the next one will make up for it."

"Are you sure?"

"Ja, of that I am sure, and I know to the very bottom of my heart that our Father will not let us go. He is always right here." She laid a hand on her chest. "That is the one thing, perhaps the only thing, that I know for absolutely certain sure never changes."

"Thank you. I hope I can be as sure of that one day."

"You can. Your ma was. She told me how she was looking forward to heaven those last months. She had her eyes set on that one prize, and to know that, one must read and believe God's Word. All her life, Agnes did just that, and no better saint do I know of. You do as your mother did, child, and you will grow that same faith."

"I will. I will."

Ingeborg stopped the buggy in front of the Baard house. "How are things here?"

"Swen and Dorothy are near done with their house, so when they move, this one will seem mighty big. She's starting to wear looser dresses.

It will be good to have a baby in the family again. Knute says that after our wedding, Mr. Moen and I can live here too, but I'm not sure what we will do after we return from Norway. Ma always wanted to go to Norway and see her relatives, and now I will be doing that."

"That will be good." Ingeborg ignored the barb that dug in her heart. A silence stretched.

"Do . . . do you think they will like me?"

Ingeborg returned from her own thoughts. "Who?"

"Mr. Moen's little girls. They are living with their grandparents now."

"Oh, Anji, my dear, of course they will like you. Once they get to know you and see how happy you are making their father, they will love you."

"I pray that is so."

Ingeborg could hear the deep breath and slow exhale. "I too will pray that is so."

"Mange takk." Anji stepped from the buggy. "I . . . I am so glad you got there before she . . . she died. I'll go send Gus on his way."

Halfway home Ingeborg felt all her spirit drain right out of her, as if someone had pulled a plug. Holding the reins took more than she could do, so she gave them a turn around the whip stock. She rubbed her burning eyes and slumped against the padded seat. The next thing she knew, Haakan was lifting her from the buggy.

"I can walk."

"You sure?"

"Ja, put me down, but don't let go of me." When her feet touched the ground, she leaned against his strong body. She turned and slid her hands around his waist.

"You've had a hard day."

"Ja." Anything more took too much effort.

"I see we have a guest."

"Ja, thank God for Astrid." Together they mounted the steps to the enclosed porch.

"She is having fun playing Ma."

"Good." A yawn nearly popped her jaw.

"So you can just eat something and crawl into bed."

"I think I must not be as young as I used to be." Ingeborg yawned again.

"Mrs. Mendohlson died?"

"Ja. With the baby never born."

When she closed her eyes, all she could see was blood everywhere.

The next afternoon they added another grave to the cemetery. Just as those burials in the spring when they were finally able to bury those who had died during the winter, this one reminded those living how life could change so swiftly. Mr. Mendohlson stood beside the pine box that Swen Baard had made the night before, his children clinging to his sides. Neither said a word as Pastor Solberg read the service. When he picked up a handful of dirt and drizzled the sign of the cross on the box, a choking sound broke the silence.

"Ashes to ashes, dust to dust. Blessed be the name of the Lord." As Pastor Solberg lifted his voice in prayer and then asked all of them to say the Lord's prayer with him, a little boy's cry, "Ma-a-a, I want Ma," brought tears to those gathered around. Mr. Mendohlson picked up his son, shook hands with those who greeted him and, after thanking the pastor, strode out across the prairie with Julia hanging on by a fistful of his trousers.

"There is coffee and desserts waiting us at the church." Pastor Solberg glanced out at the retreating figure and shook his head. "God be with you."

"Amen," responded those gathered.

Ingeborg had an idea he'd been speaking to the grieving husband more than the others.

"Hear you got a new bull," Haakan said to Swen as he smiled his thanks to Ingeborg for bringing him a cup of coffee.

"Ja, he's a bit of a headstrong one. I've got to put a ring in his nose

and beef up the corral where we keep him. The fool who owned him
didn't dehorn him when he was younger. Now it's going to be a real
mess," Swen had the same tall, lanky build of his father and wore his
manhood like an oft-washed shirt.

"You want some help with that, let me know."

"I will."

Ingeborg finished with her tray. "I hear your house is about
finished."

"Ja, we poured sawdust in the outside walls like you did. Takes more
time but certainly worth it. Onkel Olaf helped me with the insides."
He held his hands out flat. "Never knew I could fit a joint so good.
He's a good teacher."

A house raising was held for them late last fall, so they'd spent the
winter finishing the interior.

As they left, Haakan called to Swen, "You let me know when you
want to cut off that bull's horns."

"I will. I was hoping to wait until fall when the flies ain't so bad."

"Be careful around him, then."

"I will."

"Haakan, those boys are grown men now, you know." Ingeborg
nudged him with her elbow.

"I know, but with their father gone, guess I just figure I better take
his place." He half turned to grin at her. "Giving advice, you know?"

CHAPTER FOURTEEN

Chicago, Illinois

"You're not going to be very happy." The voice slowly made its way through the fog of sleep.

Elizabeth stared at the old man through eyes that refused to focus.

"Patrick?" As if it could be anyone else. Elizabeth knuckled her eyes and looked again to where Patrick's face peeked around the half open door to her room.

"I knocked, missy, but you didn't hear me so I had to call you."

"That's fine. Where do they need me?"

"Surgery. It's that Irish lass you've treated before."

"Oh, please don't tell me . . ." She waved him on. "I'll be right there." She drew a shirtwaist over her head and stepped into a skirt, grateful she'd taken to sleeping in her shift the nights she was on call. With her headscarf between her teeth, she slid her feet into her shoes and snagged an apron off the hook as she exited the room. By the time she reached the surgery, she was fully dressed and ready to scrub.

"We're going to have to take the baby," Dr. Morganstein said as she joined Elizabeth at the sink. "That way maybe we can save one of them, if not both. Scrub quickly."

"What happened?"

"He knocked her down the stairs."

"In her condition? God above, what is the matter with that man?"

"Drink is no giver of wisdom."

"Did he bring her in?"

"No, a neighbor did, but I have a feeling that ruckus I heard is him arriving in all his righteous indignation. You can be sure I've called the police."

Elizabeth swallowed the rage that made her teeth clench. If she let it loose, she would be in no condition to assist.

"They better lock him up, or I swear if she dies, I shall kill him with my bare hands."

"A heavy skillet to the head when he's drunk would do it." Together they entered the surgery.

"Or a shot of rattlesnake venom."

"Feel better?"

"Yes."

"Then let's see if we can help this young woman." They took their places at opposite sides of the table.

"Tell me." Dr. Morganstein nodded to the nurse in charge.

"She is comatose, not responding to pain, but her heart is strong. We can hear the baby's heart also, but it grows more faint. I believe she has broken ribs, one leg fractured, and then of course the blow to the head that is causing the coma."

"Respiration?"

"Slowing. If we don't take the baby now, I'm afraid it will be too late."

"All right. Scalpel."

The surgery began with a swift cut from breastbone to pubic bone, followed by a deeper incision, with Elizabeth and one of the nurses sponging the blood away. When they reached the extended uterus, Dr. Morganstein looked across at Elizabeth. "Have you seen this before?"

Elizabeth shook her head, at the same time clamping the tissue to keep the field open.

"Then watch carefully. This is an operation that will no doubt become a standard procedure when the mother or the baby is in difficulty. I found one with the cord wrapped around its neck, and we were able to save the child. Normal delivery would have strangled it." While she spoke, Dr. Morganstein nicked the sac, and amniotic fluid drenched the table, splashing down onto the floor. She opened the incision further and nodded to Elizabeth. "Take him out, being careful of the cord."

Elizabeth slipped her fingers underneath the infant and did as she was told. Holding him carefully, she waited for him to cry, but instead he lay flaccid and unresponsive.

"Blow in his face." Dr. Morganstein clamped off the cord. "Tip him upside down and right side up again. Move him around."

Again Elizabeth followed instructions, all the time screaming to God. *Save him, Lord, give him life. He doesn't deserve this. Please, breathe into him. Breathe life into him.*

"Swish him in that pan of water. We've got to get him breathing."

While Elizabeth and one of the nurses worked frantically with the baby, Dr. Morganstein and the other nurse stitched the long incision back together.

"Heartbeat is dropping."

"Come on, Moira, you can get through this. Please stay with us."

But in spite of all their efforts, the mother breathed her last, and her baby boy never took his first.

"God, send the father to hell where he belongs." Dr. Morganstein propped her arms up on the edge of the table and, with tears running down her cheeks, stared at the perfectly formed baby boy. "I'm so sorry, little one. We did the best we could, but it just wasn't enough."

Elizabeth wandered out into the scrub room and sank down on a chair.

"If they had gotten her to us immediately, we might have been able to save at least the baby," Dr. Morganstein said, joining her.

Elizabeth looked up, her heart hammering. "How long . . . ?"

"We don't know, but a neighbor found her crumpled at the foot of the stairway, and all the superficial wounds had already stopped bleeding. They thought she was in a faint, but when she didn't respond, they brought her here, four women carrying her on a door."

"I tried to tell her to leave him."

"I know. So did I before you, and we both heard the same thing. 'He's a good man . . .'"

"'. . . when he's not drinking.' Are the Irish really the worst when it comes to liquor?"

"I don't know. I heard someone once say, 'You can always tell an Irishman, but you can't tell him much.' I add, especially when he's in his cups. But then, Patrick is Irish, and so is Mrs. O'Shaughnessy, head of the operating room. And finer people I don't know. So you cannot class all by one or two."

Having washed off all the signs of the operating room, they donned fresh aprons and made their way down to the dining room, where the coffee was hot and the cook fixed whatever they wanted in double-quick time. They were sitting at the table enjoying their coffee when Patrick came looking for them.

"He's back."

"Fine, tell him to take a chair in the waiting room, and I'll be right with him."

"You want me to go with you?" Elizabeth asked.

"No, you take a moment to enjoy your breakfast. We have an hour or so before we begin rounds. I want you to spend some time with the children today. They enjoy it so much when you come."

Just then the door blew open, and Ian Flannery burst in with Patrick tucked underneath his arm. He flung the older man to the floor and advanced on Dr. Morganstein, who stood to receive him.

"I was on my way to see you." Althea nodded to Elizabeth to see to Patrick, who was picking himself up, looking none too steady on his pins.

"Don't move!" The man pointed a finger at Elizabeth.

Dr. Morganstein stepped in front of Elizabeth. "It is I you want to talk with, not she."

"Where's my wife?"

"Where did you leave her?"

He paused. "None of your business. That's what happens with you doctors. You think you know everyone's business." He paused again, his eyes roaming as if looking for something but not sure what. "I ask you for the last time. Where is me woman?"

"And I need not ask you where you left her, because I already know. You threw her down the stairs in a drunken rage and left her there!"

"No, no! I did no such thing." But he stopped again, eyes searching to the right and then the left. "No, I couldn'ta done such a thing. I love me girl."

"Well, I wish you had shown her that love, but because you beat her instead, she died not long after the women brought her here. She never regained consciousness."

"And the bairn?"

"We tried to save him, but we were too late."

"Him? How do ye know that?"

"He was stillborn."

Elizabeth listened as Dr. Morganstein sidestepped telling him about the emergency surgery. What would he do when he found out? What could he do? She glanced at the huge hands clenching and unclenching at his sides. He could do a lot of damage, that was for sure. He had, in fact, sent more than one man to their hospital. Ian had a fierce reputation, especially when he'd been drinking.

"She really is gone?" He covered his eyes with his hands and rocked back and forth on wide-spread feet.

Patrick eased back and slipped out the door to see if the police had arrived.

"I want to take her home."

"We will notify you when we've—"

"You will notify me when I can take my dead wife home so we can be having a funeral?"

"Yes. If you go talk with Father O'Henry, we can fix up a coffin for her."

Elizabeth knew this was not hospital policy, but then she realized it was to save face. This man had no money for even the pine box that Patrick would nail together, and perhaps if they prepared the body and put it in the box, they could keep him from discovering what had gone on.

"If you bring me the clothes you want her buried in, we will take care of the rest."

He studied her through slit eyes. "Why?"

"Why what?"

"Why are ye doin' this? No one ever does something good for the Irish without wanting a pound of flesh in return." His voice had softened.

Had Dr. Morganstein's gentleness conquered his fury? Was she seeing 'a soft answer turneth away wrath' in action? If she had approached Reverend Mueller with the same calm, would she have been able to make a point too, instead of creating an enemy?

"I want to see her." All the agony he'd been yelling around spilled out of his face.

Dr. Morganstein drew in a quiet breath. "Give me a few minutes, and we will have her in a private room. If you will be seated, I will have coffee brought out for you." When he started to sit she beckoned to Elizabeth with one hand. "Come with me."

Seeing the despair on his face, Elizabeth felt a pang in her heart. True, what he had done was despicable, but sorrow was sorrow, and he was grieving.

Grateful that the nurses had already cleaned up the body, they wrapped her in a sheet and moved the stretcher into an empty room.

"I'll comb her hair," one of the younger nurses said. "She was a beautiful woman."

One of the other nurses brought in the baby, also wrapped in sheeting, and laid him in his mother's arm. She stepped back. "Such a waste."

"We did our best, and for us right now that is the most important part. Show Mr. Flannery up and have Patrick wait outside the door to show him out. I don't want him wandering the halls."

He'll most likely head right back to the saloon to drown his sorrows,

149

Elizabeth thought, then flinched at the hardness of her reactions. But not much. "Who will raise those two sweet children of hers?"

"He'll most likely remarry very quickly and then beat up that wife." The older nurse took Elizabeth by the arm. "And I don't apologize for my words either. I've seen this too often. He was most likely born a bully, and he'll die one. God protect those around him in the meantime."

After Ian left, Elizabeth watched as Patrick and two of the nurses readied the pine box and laid Moira and the babe in it. Since Mr. Flannery hadn't returned with a dress for his dead wife, they made the gown they had look as nice as they could. The old man tacked the lid in place and oversaw the delivery to St. Mary's Catholic Church a few blocks from the hospital.

"I'm certainly glad that is over," Elizabeth said to one of the nurses as they turned back to work that had been pushed aside. "Doctor wants me to spend some time in the clinic, so if someone needs me, that's where I will be." She climbed the stairs to the second floor where the noise of the waiting room slapped her on both sides of her head. She passed by the open doorway and continued down the hall to a door that said No Admittance. Pulling it open, she made her way down the corridor with small examining rooms on either side. Babies crying, children whining, mothers at their wits' end either pleading or threatening permanent impairment if their children didn't cease and desist. The heat of the rooms pressed against her, sucking out her sweat like rapacious bloodsuckers. She could feel herself wilting. The basement had been so cool. If only they could move everyone and everything down there.

"Ah, there you are. Doctor said you would be joining us." Nurse Korsheski stuck a pencil in the bun she wore at the top of her head. It joined another, giving her the appearance of a strange kind of fairy with wooden antennae.

"What would you like me to do first?"

"Take that room. There are two very sick babies in there—twins. I'm thinking typhoid, but I'm hesitant to even mention it. How would we quarantine an entire tenement? She brought them here as a last resort. Shame they don't do that as a first resort."

"Will we admit them?"

"That is up to you and if Doctor will concur. Running at both ends they are."

Trying to remember what she had read about dysentery-type diseases, Elizabeth opened the door.

The stench made her gag and hesitate. A young woman sat leaning against the wall, one emaciated child on her lap, the other on a pallet at her feet.

"Ma'am?" Elizabeth spoke once, then louder. "Ma'am."

"Yes, sorry." The woman raised her despair-laden eyes. "Can you please help us? Me neighbor said if anyone could, you would here."

"How long have they been ill?"

"Three, four days. I used the last silver I had to pay a doctor to come, but all 'e did was give me a bottle of some kind of medicine and collect his money. Sign in the window said 'e could cure anything."

Elizabeth, breathing through her mouth, bent over to examine the boy sitting on the woman's lap. She lifted an eyelid to peer into his eye. Yellowed, jaundiced. "Can he keep anything down? Water, milk?"

The woman shook her head. "And if it does stay down, it runs right out the other end. I drag water up from the pump down the street, but I can't keep up with the changing and washing."

Shivers shook the child on the floor in spite of the furnace-like heat emanating from his body.

Elizabeth tried to think of where she could put these poor babies and who would care for them.

"I will stay and care for them if'n you tell me what to do. No one to home who needs me."

"Did you bring the medicine along that the doctor gave you?"

She pulled a brown bottle out of her reticule.

Elizabeth pulled out the cork and sniffed it. Moonshine for sure, and if there were any curatives in it, she'd be surprised.

"I already lost a baby."

"Follow me." Elizabeth picked up both sides of the pallet, cradling

151

the child in the fold, and led the way to a room at the back of the floor. It was barely larger than the single bed that waited for them.

"We will wash the babies first in the water closet and then lay a sheet across that bed. If we put diapers on them, that will help too." She showed the young mother into a bathroom that, simple as it was, made her eyes grow round. "If you will start washing them up, I'll prepare the room."

Elizabeth ignored the thought that she should clear this with Dr. Morganstein as she set a pitcher of water on the stand. Hot as it was, the boys needed nothing more than diapers.

"Oh, Doctor, I canna begin to thank ye. . . ."

"You are most welcome. Your job is to sponge them off to help keep them cool and dribble water into their mouths every half hour or so. I'm going down to see if we have some broth ready." *And to ask if anyone knows of something else to do.*

She saw two more patients, one with boils she was able to poultice and lance, the other with the wheezing she feared to be consumption.

Lord, how many of these people would not be sick were it not for their terrible living conditions? But she didn't bother to voice her plea. Everyone else already knew that was what was wrong.

She'd just returned from checking her hidden family and for an instant had laid her head down on a tabletop when she felt a gentle hand on her head.

"Is there something I can do?" Dr. Morganstein handed her a glass of lemonade. "This is a treat for all of us, so enjoy."

"At home we drink ours out on the verandah under the shade of an oak tree that might be a hundred years old." Elizabeth took a sip. "Ah, good."

"Now we must talk. I learned that you admitted two very ill little boys."

"I gave them one of the back rooms. Their mother plans to stay with them. She washed them up, and they are sleeping right now. I gave her orders to dribble water in their mouths, alternating with the beef broth I took up there. I was coming to ask if there was anything else we can do."

"If it is typhoid fever, they are highly contagious."

"That is why I put them way back there."

"Are they beyond saving?"

Elizabeth stared at the woman across the table from her. "I hope not." Elizabeth shrugged. "Children have amazing powers of recuperation." She waited for an answer, but when Dr. Morganstein continued to stare at her clasped hands, Elizabeth set her glass aside and leaned forward. "Did you want me to send them on their way? Some man with the unlikely title of doctor visited them and took her money for a bottle of nothing. Here we are dedicated to saving lives, and you want me to just shove them out in the street? At least here they are in a clean bed, with clean water. If they have a chance anywhere, it is here."

"Elizabeth, you are right, but if others die because of trying to save those two boys, what have we accomplished?"

Elizabeth tried to force her mind to come up with an answer, but instead she heard someone yelling. The male voice came closer, louder with a drunken slur. " 'Tis all her fault. She told me Moira I was no good!" He pounded on the wall, the echo of the thud chilling her blood. "Ye butchered me wife!"

Elizabeth felt as if someone had grabbed her by the neck and shaken her. Ian Flannery was back in the building.

CHAPTER FIFTEEN

Northfield, Minnesota
End of July

July 23, 1895
Dear Thorliff,

Thank you for your letter. I am too busy to be homesick until I get a letter from home, and then I read with tears in my eyes for wanting to see dear faces. I haven't played a piano for so long that I am afraid my fingers will no longer remember the right keys. But I cannot begin to tell you of all the things I am learning. I assist in surgery almost on a daily basis, depending on what our schedule is. With the heat and humidity of summer, many of our surgeries are to repair the aftermath of fights. What with the drinking of spirits here, which is prevalent, and the hot tempers due to overcrowding and deplorable living conditions, I sometimes wonder if God has turned his eye away from this part of the world and said, "Do your worst and pay the penalty."

So many babies and little children die that it is no wonder the wives are in a family way most of the time. But oh, the heartbreak.

I tried to save two little boys sick with typhoid fever, and Dr. Morganstein reprimanded me rather severely because they were so contagious we could have lost many of our other patients, but they both died within hours of each other. I think the mother wanted to stay with us for the privilege of clean water, a little quiet, and a clean bed. But her husband insisted she return home, no doubt to breed another. I had to scrub and disinfect the room, as well as the bed, afterward. But I would do it again if I could, or rather if I were in charge. But Dr. Morganstein is right, and I must get tougher.

My time here is slipping by so quickly. Two more weeks and Mother will arrive.

Oh, did Father tell you that Dr. Morganstein is planning to start a medical school in the building next to the hospital? She purchased the three-story building not long ago and says she will start having classes in October. She plans to start with ten students and has a room that will be used for the laboratory where cadavers will be available for dissection. I know that sounds macabre, but as you well know from my ranting on about the need to learn the human body from more than drawings in textbooks, I am excited. I have already written to both of the other schools to decline admission there. So I will spend the next two years in Chicago instead of Minneapolis, with no breaks for summer or holidays. Hospitals run both day and night, as I have well learned. Dr. Morganstein says that I am far ahead of most beginning medical students, and she has already given me every opportunity to learn all that I can.

Are your mother and Astrid coming to Northfield in August as they hoped? I am so looking forward to meeting them. When I return I am planning to sleep for three days straight or perhaps a week.

Another little thing: a man here is accusing Dr. Morganstein and me of killing his wife because we did a Cesarian on her to try and save the baby. Oh, a Cesarian is when the baby is removed via an abdominal incision. The police have been here, and we are exonerated, but Ian Flannery will not leave it or us alone. On one hand I feel sorry for him, but not much, because she died after he pushed her down the stairs in a drunken rage. My heart breaks for his two little children.

I am praying he will stop his attacks on us—so far they are only

155

verbal. I really don't trust him. I shall be glad to leave that situation behind. Please don't mention this to Mother or Father, as I don't want to worry them, but I needed to tell someone.

Your friend,

Elizabeth

PS: How is your croquet game coming?

Thorliff reread the part about the angry drunken man. The urge to go there and make sure she was safe almost lifted him from his chair on the front porch of Mr. Stromme's house.

"Bad news?" Henry still spoke slowly and sometimes forgot what he was going to say, but he communicated far better than Dr. Gaskin had ever thought he would. The good doctor had told Thorliff that one evening, claiming it was due to Thorliff's good nursing. Of course, that same evening he'd been giving Thorliff a bad time about Mrs. Kingsley, who managed to show up wherever Thorliff was. At church, at the newspaper office, at the front porch right where he'd been sitting talking with Henry and the doctor. She always had some excuse to be walking by, like needing his expertise with her writing or wanting to introduce him to someone she felt he should meet. He wished she would leave him alone. After all, she was a married woman.

Even at night she haunted him. He'd prayed so often for God to help him keep pure thoughts, he was sure he'd passed the seventy times mark.

"Ja, no. Well, not so much bad news as not really good news. You know what I mean?"

The old man chuckled, ending on a snort. "Not really."

Thorliff changed the subject. "How's your checker tournament going?"

"Takes me longer to play, and sometimes I miss a good move. Never did used to make mistakes like that. Orville is ahead by two games. Pete is one behind me, and John accuses us all of cheating." His pauses between words were becoming shorter.

"Did you walk down to the corner today?"

"I walked to the corner and back twice." Henry held up two fingers.

"Takes me a month of Sundays, but I make it. I been—" he wrinkled his entire face in thought—"c-craving a strawberry soda in the worst way."

"Mrs. Sitze's is pretty far away for walking. How about I borrow a buggy and take you down there?"

"I used to walk that in ten minutes, or less if I was in a hurry." Henry sighed. "But Pastor . . . he reminded me today to be grateful for walking slow when I coulda been stuck in a chair or bed for . . . for the rest of my life." He shook his head as he spoke. "Don't know if I coulda stood that."

Visions of Joseph Baard in such terrible pain for so long made Thorliff clear his throat. "I had a friend once who was bedridden like that after he fell out of the haymow. I wouldn't wish it on anyone. I think you are doing real well."

"But not so well you can move out yet, you know."

Thorliff folded Elizabeth's letter and stuck it back in his pocket. "Can I get you anything?"

"The checkerboard."

"You sure you wouldn't rather have dominoes?"

"One of each?" His sly cackle followed Thorliff into the house.

"Hey, you want some of this lemon meringue pie? Not that there is a whole lot left."

"Sure." He made a cutting motion. "For us both. Mavis will bake another one tomorrow if I ask her to."

Thorliff returned, carrying the domino case under his arm and a plate of pie in each hand. "She the one who cleaned up the kitchen too?"

"Nope. I did that."

"Really?" *I could move back to the newspaper if I had to,* Thorliff thought, *but that will seem mighty lonely again.* Of course it wouldn't matter when school started. He'd have no time to think about being lonely then anyway.

Later that night Thorliff's thoughts went back to Elizabeth's letter. *So do I tell her parents or not?* The thought threatened to turn into a worry. Thorliff lay on his bed, arms locked behind his head. But Elizabeth had confided in him as a friend.

He'd barely fallen asleep, it seemed, when the bells clanged for the fire department. Thorliff bailed out of bed and back into his clothes with the speed of any fireman. He slid down the banister and out the door.

"Go get 'em," yelled Mr. Stromme.

Thorliff jumped on the bicycle he kept propped against the front porch and pedaled toward the fire station. If he got there in time, he could ride on the wagon. He sniffed the wind, which was coming from the west. He could tell by the smell from the Creamery out west of town along the river. The smell of smoke overlaid that of sour milk. Grass fire? Hayfields? *Please, Lord, let it not be a house or a barn.*

The pumper wagon came flying toward him, pulled by six heavy horses. He angled off the road to keep from getting run over and turned to follow them. While there was no way to keep up, the sound of the clanging bell that warned everyone out of the way beckoned him on. He could see the firelight and billowing smoke long before he got to the fire.

Flames were already licking the walls of the barn by the time they arrived. The firemen had the hose down in the well and were pumping the seesaw-looking handles to get enough pressure to get water spouting out the nozzle and onto the flames. Neighbors had formed bucket lines to both fight the fire and soak down the roofs of the house and the other buildings. When one of the firemen called him over, he took a turn on the pump handle, sweat pouring down his face, his hands slipping on the round metal handle. After what seemed like hours and long enough to make Thorliff sure he was going to drop, the fire chief shouted, the men rotated, and someone shoved him aside to take over the pumping.

Thorliff kept from dropping to his knees through sheer force of a will that felt bent like heated angle iron. He choked back a gag and staggered over to join the bucket brigade. Taking the full bucket from one person and passing it to another seemed a cinch compared to the pumping, until his hands blistered. He could feel them popping on the palms of his hands. Winter hands, his pa would say, soft from lack of heavy labor. While the printing press was no croquet match, compared to this it was a Sunday afternoon stroll.

As the barn collapsed in a shower of flames and sparks, the people doused the roofs again and stood back to keep watch that nothing else ignited.

Thorliff walked around asking questions, learning what he needed to know, then returned to the bicycle he'd leaned against a tree trunk.

Pedaling back to town, he kept coughing from the smoke he'd inhaled while at the same time his mind rehearsed the sentences he would write for his newspaper article. Consensus was that hay put up too wet had heated up and burned down the barn. Thankfully all the animals were outside in the pasture, and though the hay and barn were lost, the house and outbuildings were saved. The volunteer firefighters had done a good job.

"How bad?" Henry asked from his bed.

Thorliff told him and then pulled himself up the stairs. Now he really knew what tired felt like. In those minutes between waking and sleeping he figured out a way he could warn Phillip of the possible danger his daughter was in and not really betray a confidence. He hoped it sounded as good in the morning.

By morning he decided he couldn't tell Phillip. Talk about being caught between a burning fire and a cliff. Which was worse?

CHAPTER SIXTEEN

Blessing, North Dakota
Early August

"Abe Mendohlson came by today and asked if I wanted to buy his land."
A ring of smoke floated just above his head. Haakan was an expert at
making smoke rings.

"He's giving up, Pa?" Andrew looked up from the wooden spoon
he was carving as the Bjorklunds all sat on the back steps to catch
a last breath of breeze before heading for bed. Mosquitoes whined,
and flitting fireflies lit up the grass, bright dots of moving light in the
deepening dusk. Barney thumped on the top step in his tiff with the
fleas that bothered him more than mosquitoes.

Astrid slapped one on her arm, leaving a blood splotch. "I hate
mosquitoes." She moved closer to her father. "That's one good thing
about smoke—it chases them away."

"And here I thought you were my favorite girl."

"Pa, I'm your only girl."

"Not really, there's your ma."

"She ain't—er—isn't a girl. She's a woman." Astrid didn't have to see her mother's look to feel it. And *ain't* was such a good word; she could see nothing wrong with it.

"Becky has been over at the Mendohlsons' taking care of Ossie and Julia. She said Ossie cries all the time for his mother. I can't think how bad it would be if something happened to . . . to our mor." She reached behind her for her mother's hand.

Ingeborg laid down her knitting needles and cupped her daughter's head so she could plant a kiss right where the part in her hair left a line of skin less covered.

"The good Lord willing, I plan to be around for a long time." Ingeborg rested her cheek on her daughter's head.

"But Mrs. Mendohlson didn't plan on leaving either. She was so excited about the new baby. Why does God do things like that?"

"Ah, my Astrid, you ask such hard questions. Let me think how to answer."

The western sky wore only a thin line of light right at the horizon, and the farther up one looked, azure deepened to black, and the stars twinkled like the fireflies in the yard. An owl hooted and a nighthawk answered.

Astrid leaned her head against her mother's knees. "Are you still thinking?"

"Ja, that I am. You know that the Bible says all things come from God."

"Ja. Pastor Solberg read that to us. So then how come if God loves us, He sends bad things?"

"But you know that when Adam and Eve ate the fruit of the tree of good and evil, sin came into the world." Ingeborg felt her daughter nodding. *Oh, Lord, please help me here. How can I answer my daughter when I am questioning the same thing at times?*

"Because of sin in the world, bad things happen to us or around us." Ingeborg closed her eyes, praying and talking at the same time. "But God says over and over again that He will be with us, that He will deliver us out of trouble, so we shouldn't be afraid."

Haakan entered the discussion. "Maybe we have to get into trouble so that we cling closer to our Father, just like when you are afraid of something, you hang on to my hand so tight I get fingernail prints on my hand." He blew another smoke ring that stayed in form until a whisper of breeze melted it away.

"Pa, I don't do that anymore."

"No, but you did, and you are still my child, so I think it is the same way with God. He wants us to hang on that tight, and just like sometimes you wandered away from me or your mor, we do the same with God and He uses the bad things to get our attention and bring us back to him."

"Mange takk. Thank you." Ingeborg nudged her husband with her toe.

"I still don't like God's taking Mrs. Mendohlson away from her family like that."

"I know, none of us do." Ingeborg rubbed her daughter's neck and shoulder until Haakan took one of her hands and laid it on his shoulder. Ingeborg took the hint. "But it is good that she and the new baby are together in heaven and having a wonderful time with Jesus."

"Like with our other babies?"

"Ja, with all His children."

Ingeborg thought back to the two babies she'd carried for only half enough time. If only they had lived, she and Haakan would have five children instead of three. If only. She thought they were two of the saddest words in the world.

"You know that report I had to do on heaven?" Andrew's voice came softly from where he sat cross-legged on the ground. The sounds of his carving had ceased as the twilight deepened. "The Bible tells of streets paved with gold and how God lights up the whole place. There will be no more sorrow nor tears, and everyone will be praising God. I don't care so much about gold streets, but I think I will be glad to meet my first pa, and I want to tell Jesus how glad I am that He died on the cross for me."

"You don't have to wait for heaven to tell Him that." Ingeborg rolled her eyes toward her eyebrows.

"I know, but I want to see Him smile, and maybe He will like some of my jokes too."

"Ah, my son, you make Him smile right now." She squeezed back when Haakan took her hand and stroked it with his thumb.

A coyote yipped up the river, and another answered.

"I like to hear the coyotes sing." Astrid leaned her head to the side so her mother could rub her neck more easily.

"Barney doesn't. He just crawled up in my lap." Andrew stroked the half-grown dog.

"How does he know that coyotes are dangerous?"

Ingeborg stared up at the stars. "Astrid, all I can say is God made it so, and so it is."

"And on that I think your mother has answered enough questions for tonight. Morning will come far too soon. Andrew, since we got the haying done so quickly, I think we'll go over and help Swen do some more of the finish work on his house so they can get moved in before harvest starts. He's planning on going with us this time with the threshing machine."

"I wish I could go."

"I know you do, but someone has to stay home and milk the cows and help take care of things around here. I trust you to do that."

"I know, but I still would like to go along."

"So did you buy Abe's land?" Ingeborg asked as they made ready for bed.

"What else could I do? He needs the money."

Ingeborg laid her head on her husband's shoulder. "I love you, Haakan Bjorklund."

In the morning, after chores and breakfast were finished and as the men prepared to leave, Ingeborg brought in the first picking of beans, and she and Astrid sat in the shade to snap them.

"We'll come with dinner, so you tell Anji not to worry about feeding everyone. Kaaren and hers are coming too. We will have a real party today."

"Good. We're about due for a party. Should have told the others."

Haakan finished putting his tools in the wagon bed. "Come on, Andrew, what are you waiting for?"

"I was looking for that horse that Onkel Olaf made for me. I thought Ossie might like to play with it."

Ingeborg exchanged a glance of pride with her husband. Leave it to tenderhearted Andrew. "I think it is up in the attic. I'll go get it." She returned in a few minutes with the cutout horse head on a stick for riding. Olaf had even made a mane out of unraveled rope and a bridle with reins out of scraps of leather. She'd been keeping it in hopes that one day they would have another little one to ride it. Samuel had been the last one to play horsey with it. But after losing the last baby during the winter, Kaaren had not been given another either.

Those ten days of having little May had been such a joy, but her mother coming for her had been even greater. While she knew Robbie wasn't well yet, he was sleeping better, and the rages were less intense. Mrs. Nordstrum had thanked Ingeborg repeatedly for coming to help her when she did.

Ingeborg waved her men off and returned to snapping beans. They would get the first jars canned before they left. And from now to fall, they would be canning and pickling pretty much continuously. She glanced up at the crab apple tree she had planted two years earlier. Perhaps they would get enough to make crab apple jelly this year or at least a jar or two of pickled ones. The blossoms had been such a beautiful pink, dotting the tree like bits of pink sunset cloud come down to rest.

They packed the clean jars, poured boiling water over the beans, added salt, and laid the rubber rings that had been softened in hot water in place. After setting the glass lids on top and flipping the wire bales into their upper grooves, the jars were lowered into the boiler of boiling water. Ingeborg filled water up to the jar necks and steamed them for an hour. At that point the lower bale was locked in place, and the jars boiled for another hour.

"Well, we might not be there right on the twelve o'clock button but near to it." Ingeborg wiped the sweat from her face.

"How come it takes beans so long?" Astrid asked while adding more wood to the firebox.

"Have to make sure the germs are boiled out. Bad beans can kill you."

Astrid eyed the beans with raised eyebrows.

"Don't worry, I check each jar. If it is cloudy at all, we don't eat it."

"I know the chickens do."

Amazing how quickly the kitchen could become a steam room with the stove hot enough to keep the canner boiling and the steam rising from the kettle. They might as well be doing the wash too but for the beans cooking in the boiler.

"Someday we are going to have a room outside with just a roof and a stove. Heard of one somewhere. They called it a summer kitchen. I think it's something they do down South where it is so much hotter and steamier than here."

"I saw in a book on India that there they have fans in the ceiling, but they have a slave or servant or someone to turn a crank to keep the fans moving." Astrid picked up the last bucket to be snapped. "Let's go outside in the shade again."

When they all arrived at Swen Baard's new house, the children leaped from the wagon almost before it was stopped and headed for the front door so they could see all that had been done.

"Sure wish I had that much energy," Ingeborg said with a sigh, lifting two baskets out of the back of the wagon.

"Me too." Kaaren waved at Dorothy, who was washing the windows. Swen's wife, whom he had met in Grafton at one of the dances he and Knute sometimes attended, fit right in with the rest of the community just as if she had grown up there. The eldest daughter of a farmer south of town, she was good for Swen and he for her. Her laughter lightened his seriousness, and his steadiness kept her feet on the ground. Though they'd framed the house the fall before, Swen and Dorothy weren't married until spring.

"Welcome, Mrs. Bjorklund, Mrs. Knutson," Dorothy called. "I have the coffee on. Swen installed the stove last night, so this is our first time to use it."

"Where do you want us to put the food?"

"I set up sawhorses in back in the shade of the house, not that there's much shade anywhere this time of day. But at least there is a breeze outside." She drew her head back in the window and gave the sparkling pane another swipe.

"These young people today sure start out with a lot more than we had." Kaaren nodded toward the windmill that pumped water one way to the water trough for the cows and the other way to the springhouse, where food could be kept cool.

"Ja, and that house is a palace compared to a soddy."

"Won't be all so long until we're doing this for Andrew and Ellie."

"I thought Thorliff and Anji would be the first. So who knows? I'm not counting on anything anymore." Together they carried the baskets and table things around the house to set up for dinner.

"Hurry up, Anji," Becky called out a few minutes later. "Dinner is all ready."

Ingeborg saw Anji walking across the prairie with Mr. Moen. He was carrying her basket and, as usual, was dressed in his dark suit. Did the man never figure out that here on the prairie loose shirts were more practical? As they drew closer, she searched Anji's face for the rosy glow that used to reside there whenever Anji and Thorliff were together, for that look of delight she wore when teasing him, and for her laughter that used to wing its way across the air like the trill of a meadowlark.

All that was missing.

Ah, Anji, if you truly love this man, that is fine, but if you are set-tling for something less than you had before, that is sad. Ingeborg hid her thoughts in the bustle of setting out the last of the food, but she promised herself she would be watchful and do what she could. That's the least she could do to help the daughter of her best friend, who was no longer here to do it herself.

Swen said the grace, and they began passing the bowls and platters of baked chicken, baked beans, fresh green beans, lettuce sprinkled with vinegar and sugar, fresh bread, both soft and hard cheese from the Bjorklund cheese house, and gingerbread with cream for dessert.

"He did well, didn't he?" Ingeborg leaned close to her husband and nodded toward Swen.

"Ja, Joseph can be right proud of his two boys." He shook his head just a little. "Guess I should begin calling them men. They do the work of men and have for years."

"Ja, I guess. And Thorliff too. Wouldn't he enjoy this? I must remember everything and write it to him." When they were cleaning up again, she turned to Anji. "So how are the wedding plans coming along?"

"Good. My dress is finished, and I've sewn enough other things for the trip, I think. Ivar says we can buy some things in New York, but I don't think he has any idea how expensive that would be."

"Now you sound just like your mother. Agnes could stretch a dime into a dollar as good as anyone."

"Do I?" Anji smiled at Ingeborg while her eyes misted with tears. "When I used to dream of getting married, I never thought it would be without my mother and father here. Life just changes, you know?"

"How well I know." Ingeborg thought of the deaths so recently. "And much of it we have no control over. We think we do, but when it comes to living and dying—well, I learned one thing."

"What's that?"

"We need to love everyone around us as hard as we can and not let anger and resentments cause rifts. We just never know what tomorrow or the next day will bring."

"You are so right, but that isn't always easy."

"The best things never are." She patted Anji on the shoulder. "You tell your Mr. Moen that I have something special for him the next time he comes to visit. I always enjoy talking with him."

"He's a good man."

"And he's fortunate to have you."

"Sometimes I wonder."

Ingeborg studied the young woman, who looked off across the prairie as if wishing she could say something else.

"What is it, Anji?" The children laughing and calling in the distance made the silence even more intense. *Might as well ask away; all she can do is think me a meddling nosy neighbor.* "Do you love him—Mr. Moen?"

"I-I care for him." Anji turned to face Ingeborg, tears pooling, sparkling like the dewdrops fired by the sun.

"But do you love him?"

"Is there a difference between love and in love? I-I'm not in love like I was with Thorliff." Her hands crept together and strangled each other. "It is like a whole lifetime has passed since so . . . so much has happened." She used her apron to dry her eyes. A sigh that wept of heartbreak and sorrow hollowed her chest and curved her shoulders, drawing her inward where the soul mourned alone.

Ingeborg wrapped her arms around the young woman whom she loved and held her, wishing for Agnes and her heavenly wisdom. *Lord God, our Father, help us here right now. Please, what do I say?*

"I gave up loving Thorliff. He was not mine to love."

"But—"

"No. I knew if I let him come home, he would never go back, and he is where he needs to be. And I was where I needed to be. And now God brought Mr. Moen into my life, and he needs me. I care for him a great deal, and I know he loves me." She looked into Ingeborg's eyes. "And that is enough, isn't it? We both loved someone else, and now we will be married and build a home together."

"Anji, you have such a heart of love that he is a man most blessed."

"Thank you."

"And will you come back to Blessing?"

"God willing, that is our plan. Ivar says he likes the spirit here. It's not old like it is in Norway. But what do I know? I—"

"You know how to make a home and teach your children and live on the prairie. You know how to love and to laugh, and there is no one else other than Astrid who could take my place helping babies being born and bandaging wounds. Metiz taught me so much, and all that knowledge needs to be passed on to someone younger."

"You are still young." Anji stepped back and looked at Ingeborg as if she'd sprouted a horn in the middle of her forehead.

"Not so young anymore, and that's God's truth."

Anji shook her head. "I remember when you and Mor used to have coffee and what she called a good sit-down, and I wonder if I shall ever have a friend like you. Perhaps I should just stay and—"

"Anji Baard, you look at me." Ingeborg used a gentle finger to turn the lovely young face back to her. "Don't go looking back. The Bible says to look forward to the prize He has set before us. Now, I tell you, look ahead with joy to this marriage, knowing that you are leaving your family here in very capable hands. Between Swen and Dorothy, they will make a home for Becky and Gus, a good home, and you are not to worry."

Anji smiled and slipped her arms around Ingeborg's waist. "Thank you. I didn't know you were a mind reader too, but I am not surprised. I will look forward and not back. I will."

The next day the Bjorklunds had just sat down for dinner when pounding hooves set Ingeborg's heart to racing. *What has happened now?*

"Ingeborg!" Knute Baard screamed her name before his horse came to a halt. "Oh, Ingeborg! Swen was gored by the bull. Come! Please hurry."

CHAPTER SEVENTEEN

Chicago, Illinois

Elizabeth shivered.

"What's the matter? You can't be cold in this heat." Nurse Korsheski shook her head and patted Elizabeth's shoulder. "Now tell me, dear, what is it?"

"I don't know, makes me wonder if I am losing my mind, but I feel like someone is watching me."

"Here in the hospital?"

"Sometimes, and when I go outside. Not that I've gone outside much." *As if I had time or could stand the heat.* Elizabeth sometimes wondered if she would ever be free of the soaking-dishrag feeling again. While her mind knew that winter would come again, right now it seemed as if sticky summer would last for eternity.

But at the same time the days fled past like children on the run from the local bully. The dichotomy of the two made no sense, if she ever had the time to dwell on it anyway. And here with only a week before her mother was to come. Keeping one foot in front of the other eroded her dwindling amounts of energy that never had the time to replenish. And she had dropped a tray of medication the night before. Thankfully it had held the dosages for only three patients. Worry about the strange way her hand had been acting, along with the feeling of being spied upon, gnawed like rabid rats at the edges of her mind.

She held her head still, moving only her eyes, certain that if she looked far enough sideways, she would catch her watcher in the act.

Don't be so silly, she told herself. *There is no one watching you.* But if that was the case, why did the hair stand up on the back of her neck at strange intervals? She was trying to figure out if there was a pattern when Patrick discovered her leaning against the wall, only because the plaster felt cooler than the air surrounding her.

"They need you, miss."

"Surgery?"

He nodded and motioned with one hand for her to precede him.

Shall I ask him? He'll think I am losing my mind. But he'd be the one to know. If he knew, he'd say something. The thoughts reeled back and forth as if caught in a perpetual tug of war.

Elizabeth Marie Rogers, she scolded herself. *You have let your imagination run away with you. Now just stop that and concentrate on whatever lies ahead.*

She stepped to the sink to scrub, listening to the staccato commands from the room next door. Tension emanated from the room at Dr. Fossden's sharp cry.

"We're losing him. Sponges stat!"

Elizabeth ducked into the clean apron the nurse dropped over her raised hands and strode to the operating table, where the head nurse stepped back to make room for Elizabeth. The smell of fresh blood permeated the air and reddened the drapes over the body.

"Gunshot to the abdomen. Thought we got it, and the ligatures slipped." Dr. Fossden nodded to the field. "See if you can grab the other end. It retracted."

Elizabeth could do nothing but go searching for the vein in a sea of blood, like swimming in the dark.

"He's gone." The announcement brought an immediate cessation of action.

Dr. Fossden swore and turned from the table. "I thought we'd pull this one off." He glanced at Elizabeth. "What took you so long to get here? I called for you when we admitted him."

"I-I came as soon as I heard."

"Well, had you been here sooner, we might have saved him."

Elizabeth stopped as if she'd been struck. "But I . . ."

He strode past her without another word, his look withering any resistance she could muster.

She stripped off her apron and dropped it in the dirty clothes bin before stepping up to wash again. *Why did he attack me like that? What did I do wrong? It wasn't my fault I was late. What am I supposed to do? Read his mind?* As the clock ticked off the minutes, her mind ticked into higher gear, fury fueling the flames.

When she was cleaned up again, new apron tied securely, she marched out of the surgery and down the hall, her heels Morse coding her resentment. Patrick waited for her at the corner of the hall.

"He dinna mean nothing by that, miss. Doctor, 'e was upset. That's all."

"Thank you, Patrick, but I am fine, just fine." She marched down to the floor where she was supposed to be dispensing medications. Lining up the bottles on a tray, she added spoons for measuring and a pitcher of water to refill the glasses she provided as chasers. Some of the medicine tasted so vile that only by offering the children a glass of water could she induce them to take the unpleasant stuff. She glared at her hand. *You just better not fail me now.*

She stopped at the first bed and set her tray down on the small table. "Okay, Johnny, as soon as you swallow this, you can have either sugar or water."

"Or both?" The face he made sent the boy in the next bed into a fit of giggles that sent him into a coughing frenzy that had Elizabeth rubbing his back and crooning comfort into his ears as he lay gasping for breath.

"Sorry."

"You didn't mean it." She laid the child back down on his pillows and stroked locks of carrot-colored hair back from his blue-veined forehead. "Better?"

He nodded. "Don't want no medicine."

"Me neither." Johnny crossed his arms over his chest.

Elizabeth stuck her hand down in the pocket of her apron. "Guess I'll just have to give these peppermint drops to boys who take their medicine like men. What do you think?" She opened her hand to show a red-and-white peppermint drop on her palm, then glanced up to see two pairs of eyes staring at the treat.

"I'll go first. I'm biggest." Johnny opened his mouth like a baby bird begging for a worm.

Elizabeth poured the caramel-colored medicine into a spoon and tipped it down his throat, handing him a candy at the same time.

"Eeuuw." Johnny shuddered, his face twisted in a grimace that didn't smooth out until the candy washed some of the awful taste away. "Thankee, Miss Doctor."

"You are most welcome." Elizabeth continued her way down the ward, bribing those who needed medication and using the peppermint drops to comfort those who needed dressings changed. If only there were more she could do to make their lives a bit easier. She knew that when they were well enough to return home, they would lack sufficient food, decent housing, and in many cases, a bed to sleep in. She'd rubbed kerosene in so many heads to free them of lice, she'd lost count.

Once finished with her rounds on the children's ward, she put the medications away and made her way down to the dining room, where dinner would be long done but the cook always kept a plate warm for her.

"Thank you." Elizabeth smiled up to the woman, who wore her abundant hair in a bun and revealed few expressions on her square-jawed face.

A nod was her answer, but as the cook turned to leave, Elizabeth reached out a hand to stop her. "Have you seen any strangers around here lately?"

The woman stopped, thought a moment, and shook her head. "Nein. No one new."

"Thanks." Elizabeth took a bite of buttered bread and smiled her appreciation. While she spoke German well enough to converse with the cook, the one time she'd made the effort, the woman shook her head and asked for English. Finishing the stew in front of her, Elizabeth picked up her plate to return to the kitchen and refill her coffee cup. She would carry it with her and sip while she studied during her designated hour. Ever since she'd announced her intention to open the medical school, Dr. Morganstein insisted that Elizabeth do lessons just as if the school were already in session.

"As far ahead as you are, I am thinking I will start you as a second-year student if you can pass some tests that I will write for you." Dr. Morganstein had peered over her glasses to assess Elizabeth's reaction.

"You mean that?"

"Yes, but we have to think this through. I will hope and pray that you will continue on here after graduation, at least for your two-year commitment and forever as far as I'm concerned."

Elizabeth felt tears spring to her eyes. "I . . . I cannot thank you enough. I mean, that you . . ." She removed a handkerchief from her apron pocket and dabbed at her eyes and nose.

"Elizabeth, you are the daughter I never had." Dr. Morganstein leaned forward. "And beyond that, you are becoming an excellent doctor. A bit hot-headed at times, but all from the goodness of your heart. I am grateful for the privilege of training you, no matter where you decide to practice."

Elizabeth brought her wandering mind back to the present. She opened her medical book to the page where she'd stopped and leaned against the wall to read. She knew if she sat down, her chin would be on the print instead of her eyes reading it. She had the second of three tests tomorrow. And one week before her mother came for their Chicago shopping trip. How could the summer have gone so fast, while some days seemed to last a whole week?

Days later, when she finished her final exam and handed it to her mentor, Elizabeth heaved a sigh of relief. How often she'd taken her excellent memory for granted, the way she'd memorized music since she was small and up through college. Now it had helped her pass these exams with very little preparation. Not only pass but have excellent scores on the first two. This one, however, might be a different situation, since it was mostly essay.

"Are you worried?" Dr. Morganstein indicated the sheaf of papers covered with Elizabeth's fine script.

"No—yes." She shrugged. "A lot hangs on this. An entire year of my life."

"Ah, my dear, don't you realize you already have more training and knowledge than most beginning doctors? You have a college education, three months of hospital experience, plus all the training your doctor at home gave you. You could go anywhere in the country and open a practice right now."

Elizabeth stared at the woman across the desk. "But . . ."

"But you want to be the best, and I want to help you achieve that goal. So you will return in October and begin with the cadaver. You will do more surgeries and see more patients. You will learn more about mixing medications and the latest medical advances I can find for us to implement. And if I have my way, you will teach some of the basic classes such as anatomy and physiology."

Elizabeth felt her eyes widen. "Me? Teach?" Her voice squeaked on the last word. *Oh dear, has she lost her mind? Surely she cannot mean what I just heard.*

"The one who teaches always learns the most. You know that to be true."

"B-but I've never been a teacher." Elizabeth swallowed hard to get past the lump forming in her chest.

"Not to worry. You won't be called on for that until after Christmas." Dr. Morganstein stood and came around the desk. "What time is your mother arriving?"

"Her train comes in about one o'clock, I think, and she will go to the hotel to freshen up before coming here. That's tomorrow."

"Good. I will send an invitation for her to join us in my apartment for supper. I want to explain our new program personally so she will not worry about you."

Elizabeth stood and let out a breath. "You haven't read my exam yet. How can you be so sure I will pass?"

"You would have had to turn in a blank sheet of paper to fail, and when I see how many pages you covered, I know failing is not a possibility." She took Elizabeth's arm. "Now, have you read that latest American Medical Association publication? And I have a letter from a doctor friend in Europe. Ah, the things they are discovering. I've read there's a man in Germany by the name of Wilhelm Roentgen who is experimenting with some new kind of photography that may some day allow us to see bones right through skin and flesh. Is that not amazing?"

The next evening after a delicious supper of fresh vegetables and baked chicken with an orange mustard sauce, Elizabeth fought to keep her eyes open while Dr. Morganstein explained to Annabelle Rogers more about her new medical school and the part she expected Elizabeth to play.

"So you see, your daughter will be the first to graduate from my school, and I will have the honor of bestowing the title of doctor upon her."

Annabelle nodded, her smile still a bit stiff but gracious in spite of her lifelong wish that her daughter would marry well and become a concert pianist, not necessarily in that order.

"I appreciate all that you are doing for Elizabeth, but one thing I would like to say. We can pay for our daughter to attend your medical school so that she can choose where she will set up her practice. Our Dr. Gaskin is hoping she will take over his practice in Northfield as soon as she is trained. In fact, he would turn it over to her now and train her himself."

"I am aware of his wishes." Dr. Morganstein smiled at Elizabeth. "And I'm grateful for all the training he has already given her." She turned her attention back to Annabelle. "We will talk about fees another time when our girl is not so weary. Thank you so much for coming but even more for trusting your only daughter into my care."

"You are most welcome, but I really had nothing to do with it. What Elizabeth wants to do, she generally finds a way." Annabelle looked from the doctor to Elizabeth. "Now, we must be going."

"I will call for a hack." Dr. Morganstein rose and moved into her office.

"You look weary beyond measure. Are you feeling all right?"

"Yes, Mother. A good night's sleep will do wonders." *Especially if I am not half listening for an emergency call.* Although Elizabeth knew she sometimes slept so hard that Patrick or someone had to shake her to wake up. *And I haven't dropped anything lately, so perhaps that problem with my hand has disappeared.*

After they said their good-byes, Elizabeth stood waiting for a moment while the driver assisted her mother into the fringe-topped conveyance. Again the hair on the back of her neck felt like it stood at attention, and she glanced around to see if someone was indeed watching her. Open windows in the tenement across the street framed faces of children and adults. Three men lounged on the landing of a fire escape, their voices raised in what surely sounded like liquor laughter. Children down the street shouted for Bobby to run hard after he hit the ball with the stick. A baby cried; a mother called her children. But no one seemed to be paying her any attention. She climbed in after her mother and settled into the seat, waving good-bye to the doctor, who waved from the top step at the front door of the Alfred Morganstein Hospital, the red brick darkening in the coming gloom.

Less than two months and she would be back. Unless she wanted to come earlier, as Dr. Morganstein had said with the lifted eyebrow of hope and a wishful smile.

Elizabeth turned and looked over her shoulder through the back window of the carriage. A tall brawny man stood on the edge of the sidewalk, appearing to be studying their conveyance. But the light had dimmed, so she was unsure. Could that have been who she'd thought to be watching her?

She slept until noon the next day, showered, then shopped with her mother until the stores closed. In Elizabeth's mind, working the wards all afternoon was less tiring, but she dutifully tried on shoes and frocks and gloves and a new wool coat in a becoming shade of burgundy. At all times she kept a smile in place and made appreciative comments.

The next day passed much the same, finished off by an evening at the symphony, through which she slept for the last half and woke to find her head on her mother's shoulder.

"You could have begged off, you know." Annabelle tucked her arm in the crook of her daughter's.

"I know, but I wanted to hear the music too. There is not much music at the hospital, that's for sure." *Not unless you call the clanking of the metal instruments against each other music.* When she thought of it, it actually was. To her ears anyway.

"Your father is looking forward to hearing you play again." They waited while the doorman hailed them a cab.

Elizabeth trapped her yawn behind a discreet hand. Would her fingers and tired brain remember the notes and reach the proper keys?

The following morning they reached the train station laden with the empty trunk Annabelle had brought now sufficiently full to be able to start a small shop. The hatboxes, stacked three high in two stacks, kept their finds from being crushed. Elizabeth's valise swelled like a pumpkin in the fall, and the books she'd purchased at a newly found bookstore added another box. If she'd had the time, she would have shipped them right to the hospital for use in the fall.

"My, what a marvelous time this has been. If I thought this could happen more than once a year, I would not have been so extravagant."

"Why can't it? Even though I will not have time to come home for the year, that doesn't mean you cannot come to visit me, does it?"

"So very true. I could come, and then you would be forced to take a break to keep your mother happy." The look she gave Elizabeth made the daughter fairly sure she wasn't teasing quite as much as she would have her believe.

Elizabeth motioned her mother toward the open door of the train, where the conductor waited to assist them aboard. "I will want to see you every bit as much or even more than you do me. Just wait."

"Easy, ma'am." The dark man with the wide smile gave them each a hand upward.

"Thank you." Elizabeth kept a smile on her face as she fought the feeling that someone was indeed watching her.

CHAPTER EIGHTEEN

Blessing, North Dakota
August 1895

"Oh, dear God in heaven, save your son Swen." Ingeborg sent a prayer winging upward as she hurried out the door.

"Take Knute's horse." Haakan leaped for his wife's basket and followed her outside. He gave her a leg up and handed her the basket while she shoved her bare feet into the stirrups. Making sure she had a hold on the reins, he stepped back and slapped the horse on the rump.

"I'll be right behind you."

"I'll get the buggy hitched," Andrew called back on his way to the barn.

Ingeborg leaned low over the horse's neck, drumming his sides with her legs. "Go, boy. Faster." She slowed before the lane turned into the road, then kicked him into a dead gallop again. All the while her mind screamed to heaven, "Please, dear God, help us, please." Tears blurred her vision, tears of fear and horror, tears caused by the wind, tears of pain for this family that had so recently lost so much.

"He's at the house!" Gus hollered from his post at the lane, then ran behind her as she galloped on. Pulling the horse to a sliding stop at the gate, she fell into Gus's arms and let him half carry her up the steps and into the kitchen.

"Where?"

"In Pa's bed."

"Get water boiling."

"I have." Rebecca turned from the stove, tears streaming down her white cheeks.

Ingeborg entered the room where Anji leaned over one side of the bed and Dorothy the other. Swen lay on the pillows, his face whiter than snow, a bruise on his forehead a blotch of purple and red. The strain of his breathing filled the room, punctuated by sniffs from the two laboring over him.

"Don't die, Swen. Please don't die." Dorothy stroked his face when his eyes fluttered open.

"Water." A wince followed his croak, and he reached for her with his shaking hand. She took his hand and held it while Anji lifted his head to take a sip of water.

Ingeborg took all this in with a glance that included the bloodstains on the sheet that covered him.

"I . . . I'm cold."

Ingeborg bit her lip, trying to hold back the tears. So many times she'd fought the specter of death, but now she could tell it had gained a stronghold that only a miracle of God would cure.

Anji looked at her, hope lightening her sorrow. "Thank you for coming so soon."

"Ja." Ingeborg lifted the sheet and fought the gagging at the sight. She let the sheet settle back into place.

Oh, God, Father of us all, you know there is nothing I can do. She met Anji's questioning gaze and gave a minuscule shake of her head. Anji reached for her hand and clutched so hard, she dug her fingernails into Ingeborg's palm.

"I . . . I'm sorry." The whispered words floated on the air, like miasma from a swamp.

"We must pray." Anji fell to her knees, her glance to the others encouraging them to do the same.

"Has anyone gone for Pastor Solberg?"

"Gus was to go as soon as he met you."

The pounding of a horse's hooves and the creaking of a buggy told of the arrival of Haakan and Knute.

Ingeborg knelt by the bed, laying her free hand on Swen's arm so still by his side. *Lord, help us.* She felt Haakan's hands on both of her shoulders, his strength pouring into her through the clench of his fingers.

"Heavenly Father . . ." Anji choked on the words. "All we have is you. You are our strength and our redeemer, our healer, our Lord. Please, if you can see a way, bring healing and life back to my brother. This wound is far beyond what we can care for."

Ingeborg's tears dripped to her chest. She watched as Swen's eyelashes lifted and his gaze cleared. He smiled at his wife, only a slight lifting of the corners of his mouth, and raised his hand to touch her cheek. When his eyes drifted closed, he breathed his last. The silence in the room wore a hush as those in attendance waited, hoping beyond hope that God would indeed intervene.

"G-go with God." Dorothy laid her head on Swen's open hand and soaked it with her tears.

Ingeborg gathered Anji into her arms and leaned back against Haakan. Rebecca dug her way into the fold and together they cried for the life so rudely snuffed out, for themselves and what might have been.

Knute stood with his hands on Swen's wife's shoulders. "I'm going to shoot that bull!"

Haakan raised a hand. "No, I will take him home with me. We will cut off his horns and link a chain from the horn stumps and down through the ring in his nose. You cannot afford to destroy him. He is only a dumb animal."

"And if he kills someone else?"

"Has he been dangerous before?"

"No more so than any other. You never trust a bull."

"And right you are." Haakan motioned toward the door. "Come."

As the men left, Ingeborg dried her eyes and turned to Dorothy. "I will wash him. You go in the kitchen and put cool cloths on your eyes. Drink some water and remember what a fine young man he was. While we are deep in sorrow, he is meeting his Lord, and we can rejoice for that. We too will stand in His glory one day."

Dorothy laid a hand on her belly. "Dear Swen, if this one I carry is a boy, he will carry your name." She mopped her tears again and pushed herself to her feet. She stopped at the door. "And this started out to be such a beautiful day."

"I will help you." Anji paused beside Ingeborg.

"No. This is the last I can do for him. You go comfort the others."

Anji left the room, and Ingeborg took the pan of water sitting by the bed, cooled now from the wait. She washed Swen's face and neck and down his chest where they had removed his shirt. She took the rolled bandages from her basket and wrapped them around his body from chest to hip. Going to the hooks along the wall, she took down a shirt and lovingly dressed him in it, closing each buttonhole with fingers gentle as only a mother's hands can be.

When she was finished with the rest of his clothes, Ingeborg stepped back. "Say hello to your mother for me," she whispered. "And tell her, although I know you needn't, that she can be proud of each of you. Such fine folk you've turned out to be." She wiped her eyes again. "Ah, this poor family. Such sorrow to bear." She could hear hammering out in the barn and knew that Haakan and Knute were already making the box.

"Ingeborg?" Pastor Solberg stepped inside the door and joined her at the foot of the bed. "Lord God, help us all."

"I know. So many deaths lately. And . . ." She raised her hands then dropped them back to her sides. "There was nothing I could do. Like trying to hold water in your hand, the life just ran out of him."

"You got here before he died?"

"Yes, for all the good it did. I could do nothing for him. Sometimes I wish we had a doctor here, but no doctor could have helped him either." She turned from staring at the still face, the slight smile still in place. "That bull, to be so vicious, and now Haakan says we will take it home. It's not like Swen was careless around that creature. We all know not to be."

Solberg laid a hand on her shoulder. "I know. Accidents happen. Is there anything I can do for you?"

She shook her head. "Not unless you can turn the clock back and make this all unhappen."

Pastor Solberg sighed. "The Lord is my God, and I will praise him. In times of trouble I will call upon his name. He walks with me through the valley of the shadow of death." He sighed again. "I know nothing but what He says, and I believe every word. I know that my redeemer lives and I know that Swen and Joseph and Agnes are together this day, basking in the light of our heavenly Father."

"I know that too, but right now I am having a hard time accepting it."

"Ja, me too."

Ingeborg wandered into the kitchen to find Anji kneading bread dough as if to beat it into the table. The screeching table legs told the story of punishment being given. Ingeborg wisely left Anji to her labors and wandered outside to find Dorothy with Gus and Rebecca, the three arm in arm with Dorothy murmuring gently to them.

Hammering still echoed from the barn.

"Can I get you something?" Ingeborg hated the feeling of being at loose ends.

Dorothy raised tear-filled eyes and shook her head.

"Where is Mr. Moen?" Ingeborg asked.

"Gone to Grand Forks for a couple of days to talk with some people there."

"Ah, just when Anji needs him most." Ingeborg wiped her nose again.

"Ja, I suppose." Blinking hard, the young wife kept the tears at bay. She stood patting the two younger ones in the same smooth motion, then left them to join Ingeborg on the porch. "You have to talk with Anji. I know she is going to postpone the wedding because of this, and I cannot let her do that."

"But that is proper."

183

"I know but . . ." Dorothy shook her head. "It may be proper, but it isn't right. The tickets for the steamship are bought and everything. She and Mr. Moen need to go and start a life together."

"But . . ." Ingeborg stopped. "Gus and Rebecca can come stay with us until she gets back."

Another shake of the head. "No. I will care for them in my house. Knute will live here." When Ingeborg started to interrupt, she laid a hand on her arm. "Can't you see? That will help me too. I-I cannot bear to be there alone." Her shoulders shook then straightened. "Not yet."

"I do see. I hadn't thought ahead." *And you, poor child, have thought of others in this terrible time. What a fine woman you are.*

"You will help me persuade them?"

"Ja, I will help you."

Some time later, with the bull plodding docilely behind the buggy, Haakan drove them home.

"I wish you hadn't brought him." Ingeborg nodded over her shoulder.

"We have some cows due to be bred. People will have to bring them here rather than the bull to them, that is all. With beef cattle we could just turn him loose in the pasture."

"You think the corral is strong enough?"

"Andrew and I will make sure of it. I don't think this bull is intentionally savage. I think Swen just got between him and a cow. We'll never know." Haakan pushed back his hat, revealing the white line that divided his forehead. With three fingers he rubbed the ridges that grew in both number and depth as time passed. "What a terrible way to die."

Ingeborg woke in the night to find her pillow soaking wet, and it hadn't been hot enough to sweat that much. A cooling wind had liberated the land from the daily heat and blew fresh in the window. She eased out of bed and went to stand in front of the billowing curtains, the air drying her face and lifting her nightdress.

"Are you all right?" Haakan's voice came gently through the dark.

"Ja, I guess. I think I was having a nightmare, but now that I'm awake, it is still here." She used the palms of her hands to smooth the damp tendrils of hair back from her face. "I thought God had blessed my hands for helping to heal the sickness and wounds of Blessing, but now I am beginning to wonder if I've done something wrong and He has taken that away."

"Ah, my Inge, that is sorrow talking. Come here, back to bed. Morning will come too soon, and it will be a hard day for everyone."

But the dark thoughts didn't stop when she returned to bed. *How can he seem so calm when this is breaking my heart? How can I answer a call to help when lately every time I go, someone dies?* She lay still, hoping for an answer and praying she would not keep Haakan awake. Praying also for the sleep that eluded her and sent her mind in circles like Jack the mule used to cut in the grass when harnessed to draw water from the well.

Ingeborg again stole from under the sheet and tiptoed out to the kitchen, shutting the door to the bedroom on her way. She took a spill from the back of the stove and, carefully lifting the stove lid, dug free a winking coal to use to light the spill and that for the kerosene lamp. She took the lamp into the parlor, set it by her rocking chair, and lifted her Bible onto her lap. Reading the Word seemed a better use of her sleeplessness than tossing and turning. She turned to Psalms and flipped to one she knew so well she hardly needed to see the words to be able to say them herself. *"The Lord raiseth them that are bowed down."* *Oh, Lord, that is me right now. Be the lifter of my head, for it is too heavy for me to carry. And my heart. Be thou my vision, my shepherd, my guide.* She flipped the pages to Psalm 23, knowing Pastor would read that at the burial. Tears burned the backs of her eyes and nose. *Poor Dorothy, so alone and expecting the baby. And Anji, Lord, make her see the sense of what her new sister says. It matters not what some of the others say. Oh, Lord, let there be joy for Anji.* She tipped her head back and thought to Thorliff's graduation from high school, the joy on his and Anji's faces, their blushes when teased, their laughter, their dreams. Slowly her eyelids drifted down and she slept with her hands on the Bible and the first twittering of birds calling up the sun that only grayed the east.

Haakan found her there and roused her with a kiss on the cheek. "Why don't you go back to bed for a bit while we do the milking. I heard George already bringing up the cows."

"I need to bake for the funeral." She patted his cheek. "But thank you." Setting her Bible to the side, she let him pull her to her feet and enfold her in his strong arms. They stood together for a moment, savoring the strength of each other and wishing the day was already past.

That evening after everyone else was in bed, Ingeborg wrote to Thorliff.

August 10, 1895
Dear Thorliff,
    I have such sad news to tell you.

She described what had happened the day before, tears blotting the ink in several places.

    We buried him today next to his father and mother. The sight of those three graves is almost more than I can bear. While I know he is with our Lord—if I didn't have that to comfort me, I don't know how I would go on—I still ache for those of us left behind. It was almost like losing a son of my own, and that is beyond imagining. Tonight I am thankful that Agnes went first so that she doesn't have to bear this too.

She stopped to blow her nose and continued.

    The bull is here in the corral. Your father prevented Knute from shooting the poor creature.
    I haven't heard from you in some time, so I hope and pray that all is going well. Won't be long now till it's harvest time. Swen was planning on going along with the threshing crew, so now I

know Hamre will go. Andrew wants a chance to go, but someone has to stay here to help with the work. Some good news. George McBride and Ilse were married at the end of last month. It took us by surprise when they so quickly decided to marry, but there were signs of a romance blooming. Such a rush, but we finished their wedding quilt in time. Onkel Olaf made them a lovely oak bed and trunk. They received so many nice gifts, including several hens and a rooster. George is becoming very adept at doing things around the farm. They are living in Tante Kaaren's soddy, so Hamre is back with us. He never says anything, but I know he was sweet on Ilse at one time too. I wouldn't be surprised if sometime he heads west to go fishing out in the Pacific Ocean. He hears about the fishing fleets, and I can see his interest, in spite of that face of his that shows so little.

I do not think Astrid and I will come visit this year, no matter how much we want to. I just get a feeling I should not be gone, and now that harvest is about to start, my leaving is impossible. We should have come earlier, but the summer has gone by so fast. I wish you could come home even just long enough for me to see your dear face. I am sorry this is such a sad letter.

Love from your mother.

She signed her name and sighed again. Such a time this was for sighing. If only she could convince Anji to go ahead with the wedding. Everyone needed something to lift the heaviness. Much as she hated to admit it, she did especially.

CHAPTER NINETEEN

Northfield, Minnesota

"You finally look rested again." Thorliff stood poised with his croquet mallet, looking indeed like a formidable opponent.

"Thank you, Mr. Bjorklund, for those kind words." Elizabeth fought back a yawn that would put the lie to his words. "Don't you know it is impolite to comment on a woman's health?" *Or the lack thereof?* She'd slept round the clock for two days and then half of this one. And the only reason the purple half moons didn't show beneath her eyes was because she'd powdered them after lying with cool cucumber slices in place for half an hour. Again she fought a yawn. Gracious, he would think her most impolite after her gentle reminder on his behalf.

She eyed the croquet wickets, wishing she hadn't taken him up on his challenge. "I get the feeling you've been practicing while I was gone."

"I needed to become a worthy opponent." He put his foot on his wooden ball that snuggled against hers and swung his mallet. Her ball headed for the lilac hedge as if it might keep going clear through and on to the river about a quarter mile away.

She could just see the red stripe when it finally stopped. "That really wasn't very nice, you know."

"Ah, but so very satisfying. Your father taught me well."

"He should have warned me. After all, I am his daughter."

"And how often have you done the same to him?"

"Beyond counting."

"You can shoot from five feet this side of the hedge. Your father said that is the normal next play."

"Thank you, kind sir." Passing him on her way to the ball, she glanced up to see his incredibly wonderful blue eyes dancing at her. Had his eyes become more blue over the summer? And why was her neck feeling warm? Wishing she had a fan in spite of the cooling breeze, she dug her ball out of the hedge and hammered it back to the playing field. It flew past the wickets, past the beginning post, and rolled to a stop by the wrought-iron chaise lounge under the oak tree. Six more inches and it would not have been playable—again.

"Would you like to call a truce and enjoy the ginger ale Cook is bringing out?"

I'd like to call the game, she muttered to herself but instead she turned a brilliant smile on her opponent. "If you feel the need for refreshment, of course we shall take a break." She thought with longing of the piano waiting for her in the music room. She kept herself from collapsing on the lounger and instead took one of the cast-iron chairs with a rose-patterned cushion. If she were to lie back, that stubborn yawn would have its way, and she would be comatose within moments. Pushing the tray closer to Thorliff, she took a glass with her other hand and held its dripping coolness up to her cheek. Ah, the delight of having ice delivered to the house daily during the summer. She thought back to the heat and humidity of the hospital and lifted her chin to let the coolness of a breeze in the shade of the old oak tree caress her neck.

"What have you heard from your mother? They must be coming pretty soon."

Thorliff took a long swallow of his drink and shook his head, his eyebrows arching slightly. He glanced down at his hands, and when he looked up again, his eyes wore a shroud of sadness.

"They aren't coming. Anji's brother Swen was gored by a bull and died. Our families are so close, and Swen was like a brother to me. I can't begin to imagine how they all are handling the sorrow of this." The slump of his shoulders betrayed the weight of grief he carried. "Some of the other families are having real problems too, so Ma has been taking care of them all. Harvest is going now, and she can't leave. Too much work to do." He stared at the glass in his two hands, suspended between his knees.

"Oh, Thorliff, I am so sorry. Here we've been having such a good time, and I-I had no idea. . . ."

He raised one shoulder in a slight shrug. "Yeah, well, that's life. The Lord giveth and the Lord taketh away." He looked across the table to Elizabeth. "But sometimes it is mighty hard to say, 'Blessed be the name of the Lord.' "

"I know. Sometimes in the operating room when we lose a patient, like when we lost Moira and her baby, I want to scream at the heavens." She held the glass to her cheek again. "Your mother and I have a lot in common, don't we?"

"Ja, you do."

"Are you going to go home for a few days?"

"No, I don't have the time. Perhaps I'll go this year at Christmas."

"I won't be here for Christmas." Sadness struck like a lightning bolt, her heart splitting like a mighty oak. Tears burned the back of her eyes, but she wasn't sure if it was for herself or for the young man sitting near enough that she could touch his hand if she leaned forward. The hands that clasped a cool glass had carried her book satchel, had helped her into the sleigh. Hands that ran the printer and penned marvelous stories. Hands that she wanted to hold in an act of comfort, in the hope that the comfort she so desired to offer would flow from her to him.

The breeze lifted a lock of hair off his forehead. He sighed and drained the glass.

She picked up the pitcher, and when he set his glass on the table, she refilled it. "There you go." Keeping her gaze locked on his, she gently pushed the plate of cookies closer to his hand. "Cook will be disappointed if there are any left." Adding to her own glass, she leaned back in her chair, wishing for a fan, grateful he couldn't hear her heart slowing to a slumberous beat.

She held her glass in hands that shook slightly, making the bottom of it rattle on the heavy glass tabletop. She glanced up to catch him studying her, and her neck heated to burning, making her wish for a fan all the more.

"Warm, is it not?"

"Ja, it is." His voice had dropped to a whisper.

The breeze chuckled in the oak branches above them. Languor stole from her feet, curled in her middle, and wound its way upward to blossom in her smile.

"Cookie?" Thorliff's voice seemed to come from far away.

She nodded, but her hand failed to obey the prompting of her mind and stayed in her lap.

"Okay, I caught it." Thorliff set her glass on the table. "And I get the message." He finished his drink and, setting the glass on the tray, picked it up as he stood. "You quit fighting nature and move to the chaise where you can be comfortable." He pulled her to her feet and over to the chaise lounge. "This is the perfect place for an afternoon nap. I will see you again this evening at supper."

Elizabeth thought perhaps she answered and was sure she heard his departing whistle but couldn't be confident of anything but the comfort of sleep.

She awoke some time later to Jehoshaphat's train-loud purr and his front paws kneading her belly. He stared at her through slit eyes, the pink tip of his tongue protruding under his whiskers.

"Ugh, you weigh a ton." She shifted him to lie beside her and stroked his head, making sure to give his ears their fair share as he tilted his head to make it easier for her.

She blinked to clear her eyes and glanced up at the lilac hedge, again feeling that someone had been watching her at the same time as the branches moved—and not from the breeze.

"What? Who's there?" She shot up, sending the cat leaping to the flagstones at their feet. Her skin crawled, but did she really have any proof someone had been there? Most likely it was children from the house two doors down, but surely they would have answered, with a giggle if nothing else. "Some watch cat you are." She scooped up the well-fed gold-and-white cat and, with another glance over her shoulder, headed for the house. The tranquility of the backyard had vanished in the rustle of lilac branches.

"You all right?" Cook paused, the knife that had been smoothing frosting on a three-layer cake hovering above the delicacy.

"Just felt like someone was watching me." She shivered and let her cat leap to the floor. "Sometimes I wish we had a dog."

"Must have been those rascals down the street. They've been very obstreperous the closer they come to school starting."

Elizabeth kept herself from smiling at the unusual word spoken in Cook's still recognizably Norwegian accent. She inhaled the familiar scents of freshly baked cake, vinegar and spices from the pickles made just that morning, and now the ginger from the refreshing drink and the faint smell of vanilla from the morning's cookie dough.

"It smells heavenly in here."

"Thank you. Looked like you had a good lie-down out there."

"I can't get over how I fall asleep every time I sit down. How embarrassing. Thorliff slammed me into the lilacs even." She thought back to retrieving the ball from the hedge. She'd not felt any sense of being watched then. "Think I'll go play the piano for a while. I've been needing music like a duck needs water."

"You need some refreshment first?" Cook nodded toward the cookie jar she'd kept full ever since Thorliff became part of the newspaper staff.

"No thanks." Elizabeth made her way to the grand piano, the lid raised and the keyboard uncovered as if it had newly dressed itself in anticipation of her arrival. She sat down on the bench and, starting at the right, finger danced her way down the keyboard, reveling in the notes that fed her spirit. She played chords for a bit, then meandered into her favorites of Bach and Debussy, hymns and popular tunes, whatever pleased her fancy. Eyes closed, she swayed to the waltzes and let the music knit her raveled edges back together again.

When Annabelle came in the front door, she stopped in the music room before going upstairs to freshen up. "Oh, how this house has needed your playing. Even the walls are applauding."

Elizabeth let her hands drift to a stop, resting them in her lap. "Thank you, Mother. How were things at the office?"

"I can't tell you how much I enjoy my time down there. Wait until you see the accounts. And we have so many new subscribers since we started sending the paper out in the mail. We've hired the Hansen girl to come in and fold for the mail delivery as it has gotten to be too much for Thorliff and your father. There's talk of even going to twice a week. Now, wouldn't that be something?"

Elizabeth lowered her eyelashes so she could contain the humor that pleaded for release. Such enthusiasm in her mother's voice and for the newspaper no less.

"I even write some of the news now, like the obituaries and the church events."

Elizabeth kept her mouth from dropping open but almost had to use her hand to snap her chin back in place. "You are writing?"

Annabelle tapped her with the point of her parasol. "You know I've been an avid letter writer for years. This is just one more thing to add to my repertoire. It has refreshed my spelling and punctuation. I had no idea I could learn to write so fast. Your father can be a real taskmaster." But her accompanying smile was genuine, not covering a criticism like in the former days when Annabelle's biting sarcasm was frequently directed at her husband's business.

"Mother, is that ink I see on your chin?"

Annabelle's mouth dropped open. Her hand automatically went to her chin. "Oh." She turned and with a swirl of skirts headed for the stairs. "I'll be down after I wash up."

Elizabeth chuckled to herself. And all those years her mother had been appalled at ink under her husband's fingernails. Placing her hands back on the ivory keys, she started to play ragtime like she had heard from the pianos of Chicago but instead drifted into "Clair de Lune."

When she felt that all the raucous sounds and smells of the hospital had been washed away, she went on upstairs to take a bath before supper, something she had never before considered a luxury.

Her mother woke her from where she'd fallen over on the pillow while brushing out her hair after the languid bath. "Supper will be ready soon, or would you rather continue sleeping?"

"No, I'll come down. I can't believe I fell asleep again. Makes me wonder if I've contracted sleeping sickness." Elizabeth sat up and stretched her arms over her head. "You have no idea how I appreciate the quiet, the peace, and the smell of your roses." She leaned over and sniffed a pink cabbage blossom. "Have you made any potpourri yet? I'm going to want some to take back with me. A hint of home."

"Of course, I—"

"You've been too busy?" Elizabeth enjoyed the flustered look on her mother's face. "I think you like being a woman working outside your home."

Annabelle smiled with a tiny nod. "But don't tell your father. He thinks I am still doing this as fill-in until he finds someone else."

"And has he been looking?" Elizabeth dabbed a bit of scent behind her ears and at the base of her throat, taking an extra sniff of the bottle stopper.

"You can be sure I have not reminded him of it. And while my needlepoint has been sadly neglected, we have so many things to talk about now at night. You'd think we'd get them talked out at the office but . . ." She raised both hands in a classic shrug.

Elizabeth stood and put both arms around her mother. While the hug was gentle, she packed it with feeling. *Thank you, God, for caring for my mother in a way I never would have even thought to pray for. You are so wise and mighty, answering my prayers before I even think of them. Thank you, indeed.* "Do you have a special dress you would like for me to wear?"

Annabelle's eyes widened slightly before a smile twitched and grew into delight. "Why yes, this blue-sprigged dimity that we bought in Chicago. I know your father will love seeing you in it."

Elizabeth removed the scoop-necked dress with an empire waistline from her wardrobe. Matching blue piping divided white lace from the bodice at the neck and around the hems of the puffed sleeves and also peeked out at the bodice seam, tying in a bow at the front. The same trim decorated the full hemline.

When Elizabeth sat down to fix her hair, her mother took the brush from her hand. "Let me."

"You're not going to braid it so my eyes go like this?" Elizabeth put her fingertips at the outer edges of her eyes and pulled back slightly.

"No, I think I'll put it up on the sides with curls gathered on top and down in the back." Within minutes she accomplished just what she wanted and stood back. "You need something more."

"I think not. Is there anything that you don't do well?" Elizabeth touched a finger to the curls on top. "I can never get it to do anything but go into a bun, like at the hospital, or pull it back with a ribbon. Although a braid would probably be better than a bun at work. You saw those triangle scarves we wear to keep our hair back?"

"Not especially attractive." Annabelle pulled a blue ribbon out of a drawer and threaded a creamy cameo on it before tying it at the back of her daughter's neck. "There."

"Unattractive, my big toe. They are ugly. Downright ugly." Elizabeth nodded while she looked in the mirror again. "Thank you."

They descended the stairs together but stopped when Phillip and Thorliff greeted them with claps of approval.

"Thank you, kind sirs." Elizabeth bobbed an almost curtsy, laughing with her father. When she looked at Thorliff, she caught her breath. His eyes, that incredible blue, shone with more brilliance than ever.

She's beautiful. Thorliff swallowed and swallowed again to force the action past his Adam's apple. Like someone out of a painting. *Don't be silly. It's just Elizabeth.* He ignored that voice, feeling his lips stretch and tilt upward with a mind of their own. The scent of roses wafted down and circled on an air current from the open French doors. Every hair on his body tingled, as if standing to attention. Words like *adoration* and *beauty* and *grace* tripped through his mind and tickled his mouth to further expansion. As if propelled by a sense not his own, he stepped forward and extended his crooked arm.

Elizabeth stepped off the bottom stair as if onto a cloud. She returned his smile, her head slightly tipped to the side as if listening for an inner music. *It is only Thorliff.* She ignored the voice and laid her hand on his arm as though she were a princess meeting her prince.

His muscles flexed beneath her fingertips, responding without his intention. If he turned his head just a bit, her fragrance teased him further. "It appears your naps have done you well." *You sound like her father or her doctor. Can you come up with nothing more brilliant than her health, of which you are not supposed to be aware anyway?*

"Ah, did I look so terrible then?" *Elizabeth Marie Rogers, you are flirting!*

"No, I mean—of course not, I . . ." *If my neck gets any hotter, my tie shall burst into flame. Why didn't I stay at the paper?*

Elizabeth smiled, a small smile that along with the slight lift of her eyebrows said she knew she'd sent him into the hinterland to sort out his mistakes.

"Let us search for a breeze on the back verandah." Phillip took his wife's hand and tucked it within his arm. "Cook said we have about fifteen minutes until supper is ready."

In the few short seconds before they passed outside into the cool shade, Thorliff wished he could pull his collar away from his flaming neck. Whatever was the matter with him? After all, he and Elizabeth had been trotting up and down the hill, working together at the paper, and even playing croquet a few times, let alone the hours they'd spent arguing over politics, religion, women's rights, novels read, studies, and even Greek philosophers. So what was going on here?

"I've had the funniest thing happening to me." Elizabeth stood between her father and Thorliff, sipping from the glass handed her off the silver tray.

"And what is that, my dear?" Phillip handed his wife a glass also before getting one for Thorliff and then himself. "I do hope you plan to play for us this evening. That piano has been pining for you as much as I have." He looked down at his daughter. "Excuse me. You said something about funny things? I could use a good dose of humor."

"I think I must be getting paranoid. Not even trusting my shadow."

"What?"

"I get the oddest sensation that someone is watching me."

"You are lovely enough that I am sure you turn young men's heads everywhere you go."

Elizabeth smiled up at her father. "That is not what I mean at all. This is more a sinister thing. Even just this afternoon after my nap out here, I thought I saw the lilac hedge move. Just hallucinations, I am sure." She felt a shiver raise the hairs down her back. "And yet . . ."

Phillip stared into his daughter's eyes. "You are no flibbertigibbet to spook at a shadow. If you feel that again, you will let one of us know."

She could tell his response was not a request but an order.

She tried to laugh. "Surely we are making too much of this."

"When did it start?" Thorliff asked quietly.

"At the hospital." She shook her head at Thorliff. "Now you sound just like my father."

"Is this what you referred to in your letter?" He kept his voice to a low murmur for her ears only.

"Supper is served," Cook announced from the doorway.

"Come now, let us have a pleasant evening." Elizabeth gave Thorliff a nearly invisible nod. "I'm sorry I brought it up. I thought it would give us all a good laugh." She covered her sigh of relief with a chuckle. *They did not laugh at me, so perhaps I didn't want that after all. Oh, I don't know what I want, other than to not have that feeling ever again.*

CHAPTER TWENTY

Northfield, Minnesota

"Don't say nothin' and ye won't be gettin' hurt."

Elizabeth struggled against the solid arms imprisoning her. The black covering over her head smelled rank, making her gag. *Dear Lord, what is happening?* "Who are you? What do you want?"

"Ow!"

Her heel connected with his shin. She tried to free her arms, kicking and twisting, but while her feet landed more blows, they weren't enough to deter her attacker.

"Ugh!" She grunted as he wrestled her to the ground and, with one knee in her back, roped her feet together, cursing as one final kick connected with what she hoped might be his head. *Not get hurt? What did he think he was doing to her now?* She twisted her face to the side so she wasn't inhaling dirt.

He finished tying the rope around her legs, rolled her over and, wrapping it twice around her arms, hefted her trussed-up body over his shoulder and strode off, each step jolting into her rib cage.

"Let—me—go. You—are—making a—terrible mistake."

"Shut up, or I'll be shuttin' ye up permanent-like."

His voice. Where had she heard it before? *Father God, I know you hear me. Please get me out of this.* "What do you want?" With all the blood rushing to her head and the man's shoulder in her belly, she was having difficulty thinking. *Think, Elizabeth, think.*

Her captor stopped, his heavy breathing indicating that carrying her was not an easy chore. In fact, she could feel his heart thundering underneath her.

Walking in the twilight had always been one of her favorite activities. On her way to the riverbank this time, she'd heard someone begging for help. She'd stopped and turned to look into the band of trees when someone had thrown a bag over her head in spite of her frenzied efforts to thwart him.

Rage and fear joined hands to lock down her tears. "Who—?" He turned and banged her head against something solid, setting her ears to ringing and her temple to thudding with pain. She moaned, fighting nausea.

"Please, I need . . . air."

"Shut up!" He started out again, long strides bouncing her tender flesh against his bony shoulder, an arm of steel clamped across her knees.

"L-look, if y-you want money—"

"I said shut up!" He thumped her posterior with a heavy hand.

Lord God, where are you? Please, I beg you, come to my rescue.

"Elizabeth surely is staying out late."

Phillip looked up from the book he was reading to see his wife standing at the front windows looking out. "She must have stopped to talk with someone."

"Folks are really happy to see her home, that's true. You think she stopped by to see Thorliff?"

"We can call down there and check. He was going to spend the evening working on his latest story. At least that's what he told me."

"I'll call Mr. Stromme. Was Thorliff going to work at the office?"

"Most likely. You know how Henry loves to talk, so there's not much chance to work there until after bedtime."

"I believe I'll call."

"You worry so." Phillip returned to his book. "Elizabeth's going to tease you about this." But Phillip put his book down and started to rise when Annabelle came back in the room.

"She's not there. Thorliff said he hasn't seen her." Worry dug channels in her forehead.

"Annabelle, dear, our daughter is growing up. She's even been on her own in Chicago. What could possibly happen to her here in Northfield?"

She took the front of his shirt in both hands and stared into his eyes. "Something is wrong. I feel it clear to the marrow of my bones."

Phillip clasped his hands over hers. "I'll go look for her, then, if that will set your mind at ease. Did she mention what direction she might be going?"

"No, just that she'd be back before dark. Thank you, dear, and if I'm wrong you can tease me all you want."

"Please, God, that you be wrong."

The sun had set by the time Phillip left the house. Trying to think like his daughter, he turned left toward Main Street but then decided that she'd probably gone right where she'd see more friendly yards than buildings huddled close to one another.

Why couldn't she have asked him or her mother to go with her? Because she's a young woman now and perhaps after all the pressures of the hospital would want some time alone. His thoughts darted faster than bats on a bug quest. She loved the river walk, so he turned down the next street to pick it up, although the mosquitoes would be fierce by now. If he'd started earlier, he might have been able to ask people sitting on their porches if they had seen her, but now the bugs had probably driven everyone indoors. True to what he'd thought, the only occupants of the river walk were fireflies twinkling in the grass and whining bloodsuckers wanting to suck him dry.

Phillip picked up a jog and kept it up in spite of lungs that started complaining after a hundred yards or so. He kept at it until his heart thundered, his legs took on lead, and a stitch in his side forced him back to a walk.

Lord God, give me strength. He checked in at Mrs. Sitze's Ice Cream Parlor, and though he was greeted by several customers, none of them had seen Elizabeth. Nor had Thorliff when he pushed open the office door.

"You want I should come with you?" Thorliff laid down his pencil. "I'm on my way home now anyway."

"You think she might have walked up to the college?"

Thorliff shrugged. "I have no idea, but I'll go look if you want."

"Please do. That will make her mother happy, but let's stop first at the house and see if she is home yet."

"I said, shut up!" The man bopped her another one on her rear. He staggered under her weight and finally dumped her on the ground, her legs buckling on impact. She twisted around until she lay on her side, her feet and legs full of stinging bees as the circulation returned.

Other than his stentorian breathing, she heard no sounds of the town. Missing were the laughter, dogs barking, wagons and buggies on the streets. She listened hard, hoping to hear something that sounded familiar. Was that the river? She held her breath to make sure. Yes, they weren't far from the river, so that meant he'd headed west. But how far? Far enough to not hear the town. She tried to think what lay out here besides farms, none of which were close together.

A dog barked off in the distance. A cow bellowed.

She flexed her hands, which were still tied down at her sides. Fear tasted metallic, like old blood in her mouth.

A stick or rock dug into her hip, so she scooted back only to encounter another. When she heard her captor get to his feet and walk away, she listened to which direction he headed. Where was he going? Would he leave her here, trussed up like a rolled rug? Quieting her breathing, she listened with every sense. When she heard him relieving himself, she clamped her teeth together. He'd be back. She wriggled her arms, bit by bit easing the ropes upward. *If he leaves me here, I know I can get free,* she thought as she heard him returning, brushing branches and grass aside as he came.

His sigh as he sat down again made her wonder if he had any idea what he was doing. She wriggled again to find a place on the ground that didn't poke her. For once she wished for the heavier skirts and petticoats of winter. At least she'd have had more protection.

"Could you please take this thing off my head so I can breathe better?" She kept her tone conversational, as if they were acquaintances out on a picnic. A grunt that she took for no was her only answer.

Mosquitoes whined, and she heard him curse and slap. "Ye buggers."

Perhaps she'd rather keep her trappings. At least she was protected from the blood-sucking critters.

She waited a bit. "Sir, would it be permissible for me to sit up and lean against a tree trunk or something?"

He grunted and slapped at a buzzer again. About the time she'd figured he had no intention of making her more comfortable, he thrashed his way over to her, grabbed her by the shoulders, and hoisted her into a sitting position. Then he dragged her backward until she felt something solid behind her back. "Thank you."

Leaning her head back against the tree trunk, she could breathe more easily, and with her knees bent and her feet flat on the ground, the cramps in her legs let up.

Get him talking. How do I get him talking? Skilled as I am at parlor chitchat, I should be able to find something to talk about. What would my mother say I should do now?

"No. No one's seen her," Annabelle said when Roger and Thorliff arrived at the house. "I asked Ina Odegaard to send a message out to everyone over the telephone. People are calling for her, but no one has seen Elizabeth." Annabelle glanced at the clock on the mantel. While it seemed like hours had passed, the hands had moved only thirty minutes.

"Okay, Thorliff, you go on up the hill then and I'll . . . I'll . . ." Phillip used both hands to scrub his hair back. The telephone rang, and he snatched up the earpiece. "Rogers here." He held up a finger and nodded as the voice continued. "Okay, thank you very much." He hung up, a sigh slumping his shoulders. "Mrs. Stonebridge saw Elizabeth heading past her house toward the river. But I was down there, and I saw absolutely nothing."

"You still want me to go up the hill?"

"No. Let's both go toward the river. We'll go west this time."

"You could go faster on horseback. Or I could."

"Good idea. You saddle up my horse, and I'm going to talk to Sheriff Meeker." Phillip picked up the receiver again and barked into the mouthpiece. "Get me the sheriff, will you, Ina?"

Thorliff headed out the door to the small pasture behind the carriage house. *Where could Elizabeth be? Perhaps she had fallen or had some other kind of accident. For one usually so conscientious, something must be preventing her from calling home or coming home. Or someone? But who?* Elizabeth Rogers was loved or admired by most everyone in town. At least it seemed that way. He rattled a can of oats and the horse trotted up to him. "Good boy." Thorliff looped the reins around the horse's neck and led him up to the tack room. Tossing the feed can back in the bin, he slid the bridle in place and tied the horse to the post. He retrieved the flat saddle from the tack room and, after buckling that in place, led the horse outside to mount and trot down the lane. As soon as he reached the street, he nudged his mount into a canter and turned right at the first street. Once on the dirt track by the river, he leaned forward and gave the horse his head. A run would do them both good.

"Please, sir, I need to use the facilities."

A bark of what might have passed for laughter made her flinch. "Ain't no facilities out here, and if I let you loose and you take off, then where would I be."

Much safer than you are now. Surely Father will come looking for me. Wherever I am. But she felt certain that her captor had followed the river trail until he entered the brush, and he hadn't staggered very far through that.

"If you thought to ask for a ransom, my parents are not wealthy. And I have nothing to offer you."

"Money ain't me purpose."

Elizabeth heard him rustle around as if he were trying to get comfortable. Where had she heard that voice before? She closed her eyes and tried to think back, but the fetid odor from the sack made concentrating difficult. When had she spoken with a man recently? Thorliff, her father, Mr. Stromme, Dr. Gaskin . . . Think back further. The porter on the train, the manager at the hotel, the hack driver, Patrick at the hospital, a patient? She coughed, wishing for a chance to wipe her nose. Maybe he was a patient, but she hadn't treated any men other than in surgery, and they were in no condition to talk. Why did the word *patient* keep coming back? *God, help me, I need you.* Was that someone coming? She stopped breathing to listen.

"You make a noise, and I'll be slittin' your throat right now." His whisper carried all the venom of an attacking cobra, a hiss as he fumbled his way to her and clamped a hand across her mouth. He blocked her nose at the same time. She threw her head back, banging it on the tree. Fighting for air, she grunted, the words screaming in her mind but getting no further than his palm.

"Stop it!" He hissed the words in her ear, and she could feel her body going slack as darkness of a different sort descended. Had she really heard someone calling her name, or was it a figment of her brain suffering loss of oxygen?

"Elizabeth!" Thorliff stopped the horse so he could hear better if there were a response. Nothing. He called again and listened before nudging his mount back into a canter.

God above, if she is in danger, please surround her with your protection. And Lord, if she is visiting someone in town and been too careless of time, please keep me from ripping into her when I see her. Somehow he knew in his heart that the latter wasn't the case.

Something had indeed happened to Elizabeth. He knew it down to his innermost self. Thorliff stopped the horse and called again. Thinking he might have heard something rustling in the woods off to his left, he waited silently, but when nothing else happened, he shook his head. Probably scared up a bird of some kind. He walked the horse a ways before picking up the canter again. How far could he be from town now? A mile and a half? Two? Or more. Grateful for a horse that had better vision at night than he had, he finally turned around and headed back to town. With no moon and overcast skies, he could only faintly see the trail, let alone anything down at the river or off into the brush. Every so often he paused and called her name again. Nothing answered but a dog barking at some farm off in the distance.

He rode back to the Rogerses' home, hoping and praying they had heard something.

"Only thing we've heard is Henry Stromme's report that he saw a stranger in town." Clyde Meeker, the county sheriff, stood with Phillip by the fireplace. "Sorry, Mrs. Rogers, Thorliff. We'll all set out soon as dawn half lightens the sky and search every inch we can. Maybe she just got lost in the woods and is waiting until morning herself."

But Thorliff knew that was wishful thinking. There weren't woods with that density close enough that Elizabeth would have gone walking to. She didn't take the bicycle, and he'd ridden the horse.

"Oh." Elizabeth sucked in a deep lungful of air. What had happened? She blinked, but unless her eyes weren't working properly, full darkness had fallen. She wiggled her fingers and feet and relaxed her cheek against the cool ground. She was back to lying on her side, but he hadn't suffocated her, much as she had thought he did. Something teased the outside of her mind. Had she heard someone calling her name? Was someone looking for her?

"Sir, could you help me sit back up please?" When there was no answer, she waited without breathing herself. She could no longer hear him breathing either.

"Are you there?" Was he waiting for her to scream, and then she'd feel the knife like he promised? She waited awhile longer, her heart thudding, fear eating like acid in her stomach. If he wasn't there any longer, had he run away? Where was she? What dangerous wild animals lived in these woods? She'd heard tales of bears and bobcats and once in a great while a wolf or two.

"Well, I'm certainly not going to lie here and wait for something to attack me." Speaking aloud offered only slight comfort, but slight was a far cry better than nothing. And trying to get loose would at least give her something to keep her mind busy.

Pushing her heels into the ground, she scooted on her back, rubbing the ropes down her arms. She banged her head into a tree trunk and grunted at the pain.

"Time to go the other way." Turning around took more rolling in the dirt and duff. She froze as something or someone crashed through the woods. Was he coming back? She waited, calming her breathing so she could hear better. Nothing. After what seemed like hours of more rolling and pushing and wriggling, Elizabeth had one hand free. With a muffled squeal of joy, she ripped the filthy sack off her head and shook out her hair. Ah, clean air. Stopping to listen frequently for any sound of her returning attacker, she released her other hand and clasped her hands around her bent knees. "Thank you, Father. Thank you. I know more than I ever have that you live up to your promises to be with us no matter what. I don't know what made him run off, but I sure am grateful." She loosened the rope, untied it from around her ankles, and finally, using a tree for support, stood on her own two feet. Now, which way was home?

"Would that tonight was a full moon instead of no moon. And here in the woods, dark is even darker." She held her breath to listen for the river, but the singing crickets and whining mosquitoes, along with other chirping, fluttering, crying, and squeaking noises that seemed to thunder through the leaves and branches, thoroughly buried the sound of the summer river that meandered rather than roared like the spring torrents. *"If you are ever lost in the woods, stay in one place, and I will find you."* Her father might as well have been standing behind her, she heard his voice so clearly. After banging into one tree after another, falling flat after tripping over a stump on the ground, and nearly losing an eye to a broken branch, she heeded her father's long-ago advice.

Hoping she had gotten far enough away from the place her abductor had left her, she sat down to lean her back against a tree trunk. But as soon as she was still, a horde of needle-nosed scavengers attacked all her exposed skin. Elizabeth leaned over, separated her skirt from her petticoat and, wrapping her petticoats tight around her feet, threw the skirt up over her head, effectively covering every square inch of her tender skin. "So there." She leaned back to wait for morning and willed herself to keep watch should her abductor return. But soon exhaustion took over, and she fell into a fitful sleep.

"Thorliff, you join that group and go out on the river trail again to search the woods. Phillip, you go with the group up the hill, and Reverend Johnson, you take that group west. Ask at every farm. Check the barns too, in case someone is hiding her." Sheriff Meeker finished giving the instructions, then turned to Annabelle. "If you hear anything, you let Ina know, and she'll find us somehow." He tipped his hat. "We'll do our best, ma'am, to bring her back to you safe and sound."

"Let us pray first." Reverend Johnson took off his hat, and the others followed suit. "Lord God, you who can see through the darkest night, we beg you to help us find Elizabeth. Please keep her safe from harm and free from fear. Lord God, we beg you for your loving care to extend to all of us as we search for this young woman who is so dear to us all. In Jesus' name, amen."

"Okay, let's go."

Dawn had yet to paint the silver skies pink when they all rode out of the Rogerses' yard.

"That woods is too thick to ride these horses through," the man riding beside Thorliff muttered.

"Well, we can ride out that far and then tie up the horses so we can beat through the underbrush," one man suggested. "Sure wish we had Jefferson's old hound. She could find about anybody."

"Yeah, but she can't see good enough anymore to keep from running into trees herself."

Thorliff only half listened to the men's discussion as they trotted down the streets and turned left on the trail. Elizabeth could be lying out there wounded, or . . . He refused to allow his mind to explore the *or*.

They stopped and dismounted, tying the horses to tree branches before entering the woods. Their cries of "Elizabeth" echoed and reechoed as they beat through the brush.

Elizabeth woke with the twittering of the birds. Remembering her harrowing ordeal of the night before, she cautiously looked around. No sign of her abductor. *Thank you, God. You delivered me.* Just thankful he was gone, she unwrapped herself and stretched, then stood and turned in a circle. Which way was the river? Remembering an old saying she'd heard that moss grows on the north sides of the trees, she inspected the trunk of the elm she'd used for a bedroom. Sure enough, one side did sport green lichen. She followed the north sides of the trees a hundred feet or so. When she paused and listened with every sense, she could hear the water and continued toward it. As she finally stepped out on the dirt trail, she heard someone calling her name.

"I'm here!" But her throat was so dry that the shout came out as nothing more than a croak. Not quite thirsty enough to drink from the muddy river, she headed toward the rising sun. Surely she would be home soon.

"Let's go back to the trail and ride further west," Thorliff suggested as they turned back from the south side of the woods that bordered a field with grain already standing in shocks, ready for the threshing machine. Again, they shouted her name as they beat their way back toward the river.

"I'm here" came a barely audible answer.

Thorliff stopped in midstride. "Did you hear that?" The man next to him shook his head, but they both stopped to listen. "Elizabeth!"

"Here." The voice came faintly from the northwest.

"Let the others know," Thorliff said and left his partner to call to the others. He tore through the brush, leaping fallen logs and pushing aside branches that reached with tenacious fingers to stop him.

"Elizabeth!"

"I'm here by the horses," she called.

"I'm coming." He burst out of the woods and charged down the trail, arms pumping, mouth stretched open, sucking in the air that his screaming lungs so desperately needed. When he saw her standing by one of the horses, he slowed to a trot and then to a stumbling walk as she broke into a run and flung herself into his arms.

"Oh, Elizabeth, dear Elizabeth. I thank God you are all right." Thorliff stroked her grimy hair back from her even grimier face, its translucent skin showing through the tear tracks. "What happened to you?"

"Some man crammed a bag over my head and threw me over his shoulder. He carried me for forever it seemed, until he could go no further. I was all trussed up like a turkey for roasting, but for some reason, he ran off and left me—"

"All bound up?"

She nodded.

His hands cupped her face and his thumbs stroked the tears away.

"I . . . I . . ." She threw her arms around his neck and burrowed her face into his collarbone. "I was so scared. He . . . he said he was going to kill me. That he would cut my . . . my throat if I screamed." A shudder shook her so hard, he trembled.

With his arms around her slender waist, Thorliff thought he'd reached heaven for sure.

Until his Beatitude reminded him. Was he thinking impure thoughts? He hesitated. And almost shook his head. No, his thoughts were pure. Could fear make one realize how much one cared for another? This wasn't friendship, this was . . . He hesitated to use the word. *Remember, you thought you loved Anji, and you had to get over that. Now be careful so you aren't hurt again.* He listened to his voice and took a step backward. Or at least part of a step. He dug in his back pocket and pulled out a handkerchief, extending it to her with a shaky hand.

"Here, wipe your tears. You can ride the horse back."

"You really found her!" The men broke from the woods and came trotting to where the two stood, now separated by a proper distance.

Elizabeth retold the story of her abduction, but when the men persisted in trying to figure out who the culprit was, she just shook her head. "I don't know. I never saw his face. I had a bag over my head."

Once back home and reunited with her parents, Elizabeth told the sheriff her story. He nodded. "Good thing you didn't see his face, or he would have been forced to kill you. You could incriminate him."

"Oh." Elizabeth sank back in the chair, regardless of her filthy garments. *But I think I know his voice.* The reminder stayed where it was in her head. Until she knew for sure, she promised herself to say nothing.

Annabelle sat beside her daughter, never letting go of her hand.

"Do you think he'll be back?" She asked the question they'd all been thinking.

"I doubt it." Sheriff Meeker ran his tongue around the inside of his right cheek. "But if you get any inkling of who it might have been, you got to tell me, Miss Rogers. Promise?"

Elizabeth studied her filthy hands. What could she say?

"If I ever find out who it is, I swear to God, I'll tear him limb from limb." Phillip spoke with a deadly certainty that sent chills up Elizabeth's back. She looked up to see a matching frozen look in Thorliff's eyes. Elizabeth closed her eyes and tried to take a breath around the knot in her chest. Would another sin make the first sin right?

CHAPTER TWENTY-ONE

Blessing, North Dakota
Late August

"Do you think I could go with you?"

Haakan stared at the young man standing before him. Gerald Valders wore the look of a boy trying to be a man and not yet able to leave the bonds of sharp elbow and bony knees, of an Adam's apple that stuck out of a skinny neck as if he really had an apple in his craw.

"I promise to work real hard." The boy's voice cracked on the *real*. "I know I ain't worked with big machinery much, but I learn fast."

"I'm sure you do. Let me think on it."

Gerald turned away, his shoulders slumping like he'd borne too many defeats for his young age.

"Don't you have to start school in a couple weeks?"

"Ja, but I asked Pastor Solberg if I could take time off. He said since I get straight A's, he didn't see a problem with that. I promised I would make up all the lessons I missed."

"I see. How about if you help on the farms around here, and if you work out okay, you can go along. But I got to warn you, harvesting is hard work."

"I know I don't look very strong, but I don't mind hard work. Thank you, Mr. Bjorklund. You won't be sorry."

"You'll need a bedroll and an extra change of clothing. Oh, and we don't pay until the end of harvest, so if you want spending money, not that there is anyplace to buy anything, you need to bring it along."

"Okay, thank you." Gerald took off his hat and clutched it to his chest, then clapped the tattered hat back on his head with one hand, waved with the other, and took off down the land as if swarming hornets were after him. A war whoop floated back and brought a smile to Haakan's face. That war whoop echoed of pure boy joy.

"Sure hope I did the right thing." Haakan slapped the reins on the rumps of the patiently waiting team and walked them back out to the field to hitch up to the binder and continue cutting wheat. He watched over his shoulder as the wheat fell before the sickle bar, laid back on the bed, and when enough reached the binder it was tied into a bundle and kicked out the rear of the machine. Someone would come along later and stand three up together to make a shock so the grain could continue to dry for threshing.

When Astrid came running across the field, her braids bouncing as she leaped a bundle and Barney barking at her heels, Haakan called the team to a stop and stepped off to take the jar of buttermilk she offered.

"What did Gerald want?" she asked, digging in her pocket for the packet of cookies she'd brought along. After handing the cookies to her father, she dug out two carrots from the other pocket and walked around to give the horses their treat and to stroke their noses and ears.

"Pa working you too hard? Poor things, out here in the heat. Bet you'll be glad to be turned out tonight." She gave them one more pat and ambled back to her father.

"So?"

"So what?" His twinkling eyes gave away his innocent expression.

"You know. What did Gerald want? I thought he'd come up to the house, say howdy at least."

"He asked if he could work harvest for us this year."

"What did you tell him?"

"That if he wanted to help with the locals and he worked out all right, he could go along."

"Andrew won't be too happy to hear that, being as he has to stay home."

"I know." Haakan took another swig from the jar and handed the now empty container back to his daughter. "But someone has to stay home and take charge of the milking. Your ma is so busy making cheese, she don't have time to milk twenty head or more."

"Mr. McBride is a good milker now."

"I know. Sure wish Abe Mendohlson would have stayed around. I could've used him this fall." Haakan checked the fittings on the binder as he spoke, then climbed back up on the seat. "Call your dog."

He waited to *hup* the horses until Astrid had a good hold on the pup, and with a *clickety-clack* of the binder bed, the rig moved forward again.

"Mange takk," Haakan called, and Astrid took off back across the field, her "You're welcome" floating back like birdsong.

"You gave Gerald Valders a job on the threshing crew?" Andrew's fork paused halfway to his mouth as he looked toward his father.

"Not exactly. I told him to help out here with our local farmers first, and then we'd see."

"But why?"

"Because he asked, and because I think being away from his younger brother would be good for him."

"Being away from Toby would be good for anyone," Andrew muttered around a mouthful of baked chicken. "Far away would be best."

"Andrew." Ingeborg laid a hand on his shoulder as she set a refilled platter of sliced tomatoes on the table.

"I suppose you're going to let Toby go too."

"Not at all." The corner of Haakan's mouth quivered slightly upward.

"Good. Please pass the potatoes."

Supper continued with talk of harvesting both field and garden.

"I went over to see Dorothy today," Ingeborg said. "Joyce has broken off with Knute. She wanted to get married, and he said he wasn't ready. So she went to visit her aunt in Grand Forks."

"They been seeing each other for near on two years, haven't they?" Haakan leaned back in his chair and patted his stomach. "That was mighty good. Nothing better than corn on the cob and fresh tomatoes. Your garden is doing you proud this year."

"Enough rain makes a mighty big difference. We got Thorliff's newspaper today. Astrid, you want to go get it and read some to us?"

Astrid took her plate and Andrew's and slid them into the soapy water waiting in the pan on the stove. When she brought the paper back, she took her chair over to the window to make full use of the sun.

Andrew fetched his carving knife and began turning a block of wood into a hump-backed creature that he'd only seen in pictures, a camel for the Nativity set.

Haakan scraped his pipe bowl clean and tamped in fresh tobacco, the fragrance of it both acid and sweet. He lit it with a flaming spill brought to him by his wife, who also brought him a cup of coffee.

Astrid read of an ice cream social held at Carleton College, a lecture by a visiting professor, predictions for harvests, a haystack that was struck by lightning. She read an editorial by Phillip Rogers on the pros and cons of Darwinism, and when she looked up to her mother, Ingeborg raised her hands shield fashion.

"Don't ask."

"But Mor—"

"All I know is what the Bible says, and I don't care how long the days were. God created, and he goes on creating today."

Astrid returned to her reading. "Here's an article about the new books in the library. Wouldn't it be wonderful to have a real library with rooms full of books and not just three or four shelves?"

"Many people would be exceedingly grateful for a whole shelf of books to choose from."

"I know, but I've already read some of the ones on the shelves at school two and three times. Oh, here's an article about a lady who wrote a book about a dog. It's called *Beautiful Joe*."

"I sure would like to read that book," Andrew put in.

"Me too. We should tell Thorliff to write a book about Paws. If that lady can write about a dog, why not Thorliff?"

"You write and suggest that to him."

"I will."

"Thank you, Astrid, for reading. Let's save some for tomorrow night. As you go help your mor with the dishes, how about handing me my Bible?"

"You better read fast. You look about asleep already." Ingeborg poured water from the reservoir into the rinsing pan. "You want to wash or dry?" she asked Astrid.

"Dry." Astrid handed her father the big leather-bound volume that had come from Norway with Roald and Ingeborg. "I think we should get a Bible written in English."

"Why? Reading in Norwegian helps you remember your mother language." Ingeborg dunked a plate in the rinse water and handed it to Astrid to dry.

"But since I was born in America, why is Norwegian my mother language?"

"Good question. I guess it isn't. But I still think it is important that you can read and speak both languages. Just think, Thorliff can read Greek and Latin too."

"Whatever good *that* will do him."

"Hey, Andrew," Trygve called from the door, "you want to play hide-and-go-seek?"

"Sure." Andrew scooped all his shavings and dumped the bits of wood in a can in the woodbox kept there specifically for his shavings to use for tinder.

"Hurry, Mor, I want to go play too." Astrid quickly dried another plate and added it to the stack.

"You go on ahead. We're about done." Ingeborg took the dish towel from her daughter. "It's a perfect evening for hide-and-seek."

Astrid kissed her mother on the cheek. "You're the best mother ever."

When Ingeborg finished the dishes, she dumped the wash water out the door on her rosebushes and hung the pan on the hook behind the stove.

"More coffee?"

Haakan shook his head. "But I'll take a cookie if you have any."

"Sure." Ingeborg set a plate of cookies on the table and took out the canister of sugar.

"What are you making?"

"Raspberry swizzle. You know they'll be thirsty after running like they do." She paused to listen to the laughing and shrieking. She could hear Sophie teasing Andrew and Sammy calling Astrid. The dog added to the din, his joyous barks giving away the hiding place of one child after another, bringing shrieks of "No fair" and "Go away, Barney."

Ingeborg stirred the sugar and ginger in warm water until it melted, then she added the vinegar and poured in the canned raspberry juice.

She poured the drink into glasses, set out more cookies, and went to the door to call the children in.

"Thank you, Tante Ingeborg. How did you know we wanted something special to drink?" Sophie took another long sip, then wiped her mouth with the back of her hand. "Ma is sewing us new dresses for school. Ours are too short."

"I think you each grew half a foot this summer. What has your mother been feeding you?"

Grace's eyes lit up. "Fertilizer." She spoke slowly but precisely and giggled behind her hand when she saw all of them laughing.

"You made a joke, Grace. You made a joke." Astrid grabbed her hands and danced her around in a circle.

"How's the arm, Trygve?" Ingeborg held out the plate of cookies.

"Good. Never hurts anymore. But not as strong as the other." He rubbed the weaker arm that had yet to become as tanned as the left.

With gentle fingers, Ingeborg probed the once broken arm. The bone felt straight and true. "God healed you well."

"Mor said the same thing. Thanks for the dessert. We better get home."

The four ran out the door laughing with Astrid and Andrew waving good-bye.

"That was fun, but next time Barney has to stay inside. He goes and finds everyone." Astrid pouted at the pup, whose busy tail gave the floor a good dusting.

The next morning Ingeborg took her first cup of coffee outside and stood on the top step of the porch looking out across the wheat fields, no longer shimmering like waves in the morning breeze. Shocks stood in orderly rows awaiting the lifting pitchforks that would throw them onto the wagon and from there onto the conveyor belt. When they finished up with their own fields, the men would follow the tractor that would haul the steam engine and separator to the next farm and the next, heading westward as the wheat ripened. The changing of the unchanging seasons.

Lord, I really don't want Haakan to go this year. I mean, I never do, but this year more so than ever. With all the work here . . . She shook her head. What could she say? Threshing brought in cash money, as the threshing crew received a percentage of each farmer's harvest, paid at the granaries along the railroad tracks. She sucked in a breath of the cool morning air, already tasting the hint of fall. Turning, she reentered the house and started breakfast. Not long before she'd be cooking for the threshing crew. For the local farmers, the women took food to help out whoever had the crew there that day. Meals were almost a party, as everyone got together for a welcome visit.

Three days later harvest began in earnest with the firing up of the steam engine that ran the threshing machine.

Less than a week after that, Ingeborg kissed Haakan good-bye and headed for the cheese house. Another batch of curd was ready for pressing, and several wheels were ready for their wax coating, after which they could be put on the cooler shelves to age. A batch of soft cheese was ready for sale, so she would ship some to Grand Forks and take the rest to Penny to fill the orders she had waiting at the store.

"I know, Lord, I should be grateful for the work that we have and the blessings you have given us through this farm. Your Word says to sing praises to your name, to give thanks in all things. I am doing that. I praise you. I give you thanks. I worship your holy name, but Lord, this is truly a sacrifice of praise because I don't feel thankful or grateful at all right now." She slammed the weights down on the glutinous mass that would eventually be a rich wheel of cheese. Whey poured from between the slats and into a trough that fed to a spigot. The cans that brought milk from other farms would go home full of whey for pigs and other livestock. Nothing was wasted.

"I will sing praises. I praise thee, my God." She gritted her teeth and kept on with the words. A bit of a tune tiptoed into the far reaches of her mind and lifted up a word or two, then three and four, and finally she sang to herself. *I will praise thy name. I praise thee. I worship thee, Lord God, heavenly king.* The song left her mind and forced itself out of her mouth until she was singing along with all her work.

"That's a pretty tune, Mor," Astrid said when she came in the cheese house door.

"Thank you. I guess I made it up." Ingeborg sluiced a bucket of clean water over the cheese forms, then took a brush and scrubbed out the crevices, all the while humming her new song.

"How come you are so happy?"

"I'm not happy. I'm—" Ingeborg stopped. After laughing at herself, she amended her words and thoughts. "I wasn't happy; in fact I was downright mad because Haakan left."

"But Pa always leaves for harvest." Astrid turned off the spigot to the cans, capped the full one, spun it out of the way, and placed an empty one in its place.

"I know he does, but I don't have to like it."

"And so you were singing 'cause you were mad?" Astrid's face told how clearly she didn't understand her mother.

"No, dear heart, I took God at His word. He says we are to praise Him in all things, so even though I didn't want to, I did, and pretty soon my heart was happy again. And it started singing."

"So . . ." Astrid shook her head. "Doesn't make sense."

"I know, but since when does God have to make sense? He says to do something, and when we do it, He can make good out of it."

"If you say so."

"I say so. Now that this is all cleaned up again, let's go visit Bestemor and Tante Penny. You start school next week and we won't have time for many more visits together."

The two linked arms and headed for the house.

"Where's Andrew?"

"Checking his snares to see if he has any rabbits for Metiz; then he said he and Trygve were going fishing."

"Good. We'll have either fried fish or fried rabbit for supper."

"And if I know Bestemor, we'll have dinner at the boardinghouse."

"We're not canning today?"

"No, today is our holiday. No men to cook for and the summer about gone." *And the dark of winter will come far too soon, and we better get out of here before I feel too guilty to leave. It's not like there is nothing here for me to do. Lord, please take care of the men as they travel, and bring them home safely.*

CHAPTER TWENTY-TWO

Northfield, Minnesota
September

"I am afraid of going back to Chicago."

There, she'd said it, even if only to her friend the mirror on the dresser in her bedroom. "And I don't want to tell Mother, because she is still nervous from that stupid abduction." She ground her teeth for a moment. And it was worse now that she had finally remembered who that voice belonged to.

Not long after "that night," as she referred to it, she started having nightmares, dreams so terrible she would wake up shaking with her hands clutched around her throat, trying to protect her vulnerable jugular from a slashing knife. The glittering knife was always poised just above her, held in the hands of a man with a stained and filthy gunnysack over his head.

But one night her dreams had reverted back to the hospital and to the day that Moira and her baby had died and her grief-stricken drunken husband had carried Patrick like a sack of potatoes under his arm and had thundered vengeance against Dr. Morganstein and her hospital for butchering his wife.

That was when she knew.

It was the same voice that threatened to slit her throat if she screamed. And she'd believed him.

But how did Ian Flannery get to Northfield? And why did he come after her instead of the doctor? Or was he planning on meting out his brand of justice to both of them? Should she call Dr. Morganstein?

Elizabeth recognized the purple shadows under her eyes, painted there by sleep just before he stole off instead of taking up residence for the night. And soon her mother would be asking what was wrong, and then she would have to lie and say that nothing was wrong. She rubbed her forehead where a headache had formed in the wee hours when she'd been turning and tossing and pounding her pillow into submission.

"So you want to say what is bothering you?" Cook caught her before her mother did.

"Just nightmares. I am having a hard time sleeping." Elizabeth took the proferred cup of coffee, already laced with cream, the kind called café au lait in France, where she'd learned to like it. She and her mother had spent a month in France the summer before her senior year in high school, supposedly to improve her French and introduce her to real art and to the world beyond American borders. In actuality she had found a hospital to visit. Her mother had not been pleased. Today she really needed the dark brown, near to black sludge kind of coffee from the hospital. Something that would pop her eyes open and put apples on her pallid cheekbones.

"Looks like more than nightmares to me. Although with what you went through, not having them would be more surprising." Cook set a plate with warm buttered cinnamon bread down on the counter Elizabeth leaned against. "You've not been eating either."

"I think my abdomen is still bruised from bouncing on that man's shoulder." Elizabeth rubbed her middle with the hand not holding the coffee cup, still inhaling the fragrance rather than drinking. Whenever she closed her eyes, she could see dark lines in front with faint light between the mesh. No matter that she'd taken baths and wore perfume to kill the stink, her nose refused to forget. Finally the coffee fragrance took over, and she sipped while reaching for the bread.

"Made just this morning, right?" Sometimes she wondered if Cook ever slept.

"Don't get many chances to make your favorite things anymore, least not with you here to enjoy them." She nodded toward the outside. "You go on out and lie back in that chair out there, and I'll bring you scrambled eggs with bacon." When Elizabeth started to protest, Cook pointed a long finger toward the door.

Feeling as though she were eight years old again, Elizabeth did what she was told. Inside, she chuckled at the sight. How good it felt to be where someone was trying to take care of her instead of . . . She blocked the rest of the thought and swung by the rosebush to sniff the perfume of the late bloom. Her mother's roses didn't look quite as well cared for as usual; in fact she picked off a yellowing leaf with black spots and stuck it in her pocket. Her mother was spending more time at the newspaper than in her yard. And Old Tom was not as careful as she.

After sitting on the chaise, Elizabeth held her coffee with both hands, sipping like a little girl at a tea party. But she'd never been one for tea parties. She enjoyed playing hospital far more. Her dolls had worn splints on their arms and bandages on their heads.

"Here you go." The plate held enough food to feed three people. Elizabeth groaned.

But Cook just shook her head and refilled the coffee cup. "The cream is there in the pitcher."

"The tray is lovely." Elizabeth smiled up at her longtime friend. Yellow and rust-red nasturtiums, their round leaves still bright green, smiled out of a small cut-glass vase. A bit of parsley graced the eggs, and sliced peaches cozied in a shallow layer of cream, lightly sugared.

"I will remember this." She swallowed back the tears that hovered so near the surface.

"We're having peach pie for dinner."

Elizabeth nodded and laid her napkin in her lap. "Thank you." *And how am I supposed to eat dinner in two hours after all this?*

As she ate, Elizabeth thought back to an earlier conversation with Thorliff when they'd been sitting out here under the oak tree.

"What do you hear from your family?" she'd asked him.

"Mor is busy with all the normal gardening and fieldwork, and she is making more cheese than ever."

"All by herself?"

"No, she has several women working for her, but summer is her busiest time because the cows produce so much better when feeding on grass. I'm not surprised that she and Astrid can't get away to visit me."

"But you were hoping."

"Yes, earlier in the summer it looked like they might squeeze in a trip. As Alexander Pope said, 'Hope springs eternal in the human breast.' But from the reports I've heard, North Dakota looks to be having a good harvest, barring grasshoppers or hail or too much rain or—"

"I guess living in town as I have, I never realized how precarious a farmer's life is. It is easy to take flour and milk and such for granted."

"Yes, but if the prices go up because of crop failure, city people scream the loudest, accusing the farmers of selfishness and wanting too much money." Thorliff shook his head. "They don't realize how many hands make up the chain from the farm to the city table."

She took another bite of Cook's incredibly light and fluffy biscuits. Perhaps the flour for the baking had come from the Bjorklund farms. And they often had Bjorklund cheese when they could get ahold of it. Thompson's Grocers sometimes stocked several Bjorklund cheeses.

She looked over to the chair where he'd been sitting and felt warmth creeping up her neck. Often lately, thoughts of Thorliff made her feel slightly mushy inside. Until she reminded herself that mushy feelings for a man did not coincide with her life's dream.

"Do you have time to go for a walk?" Elizabeth asked Thorliff that evening. They'd just finished supper, and Phillip was heading back to the office.

"Go ahead, Thorliff. I'll keep an eye on the press." The older man waved his hand.

"You sure?"

"Now, how often do you get an invitation like that from such a lovely young woman?" Phillip shook his head, eyes twinkling. "Not often enough to turn it down. You two go on, and I'll see you later at the office."

Thorliff and Elizabeth followed Phillip down the hall to retrieve Thorliff's straw boater from the hat rack.

"So where would you like to go?" He set his hat firmly on his head when they stepped out the front door.

"You don't have to do this, you know. It is not required of an employee to walk with his employer's daughter."

Thorliff stopped on the step below and stared at her, eyes slightly slit. "I don't walk with you for any other reason than you are my friend and I enjoy your company." *And miss you when you are gone, and wish for more walks and talks and family concerts and . . .*

"I'm sorry." Elizabeth had the grace to look ashamed. "I was teasing you, but I can tell it wasn't funny." She touched his arm but snapped her hand back as if she had been burned.

He glanced at the spot on his arm, every sense aware of the reaction that ran from the skin under the sleeve of his shirt to all points south, north, west, and east on his body.

"You're forgiven." Without further thought, he took her hand and tucked it under his arm. His look suggested she not try to take it back. "Now that we have that all straightened out, where shall we go?"

"Down along the river."

"Are you sure?" Thorliff stopped walking to turn her toward him. He waited until she looked up, reading resolution in her eyes and the lift of her chin. Only the slightest quiver of her lower lip betrayed her.

"Yes. I cannot let fear rule me." She inhaled a breath deep enough to raise her shoulders. "And the longer I put this off, the more I dread going there. You know that has always been one of my favorite places. I can't let that man take it away from me." She paused with a slight shake of her head. "I can't."

The desire to take her in his arms and shield her from all harm swept through him like a fierce wind. She'd been in danger, and he hadn't been able to protect her. And this was in their very own town. How helpless he would be with her back in Chicago.

With a sigh he tucked her arm through his again, and they picked up their leisurely pace. Tilting at dragons took a steady heart and firm footing. *Lord, please protect her; keep her safe from harm, and give her the strength to overcome whatever lies ahead.*

Thoughts whirled through him, mind and heart, as they reached the river. Their pace slowed.

"Right or left? We don't have to slay all the dragons at once."

"Left, and then we'll come back and go for a soda at Mrs. Sitze's."

Elizabeth's step faltered only slightly as they walked westward, the river flowing gently on their right.

"Tell me where you are on your story."

"Better than that, I'll let you read it if you like."

She flashed him a smile. "I'd like that a lot."

When Thorliff started classes again, Elizabeth felt a pang at being left out. For all these years she'd gone to school every September, and now she wasn't even looking forward to October and her lifelong dream of attending medical school. Instead, she felt that part of her heart was missing. The mailman left her an envelope from Dr. Morganstein, and she stared at it a long time before slitting it with a pewter letter opener. Unfolding the paper, she read,

> Dearest Elizabeth,
>
> This place just doesn't seem the same with you gone. It is like you have become part of our family, and there is a hole with you not here. The children ask after you, and so do some of the outpatients. Dr. Fossden grumbled at one of the surgical nurses that his third hand was missing and she wasn't an adequate substitute.
>
> This is not to lay pressure on you to return earlier than the starting of school but to let you know how valuable you are, and not only to us. I know your Dr. Gaskin hates to see you leave again.
>
> I am still set on having you teach physiology and anatomy, and if you get stuck, one of us will help you out. I have already ordered the textbooks and all the charts, and we have an articulated skeleton to hang in the corner of the classroom. You can name it when you come or have the other students assist. As a designated second year

student, you will officially be given the title of Doctor because of your copious experience.

I am honored that you want to join us in our mission to provide doctors who are more skilled and experienced than might be available otherwise.

Please greet your mother and father for me and know that we await your arrival with joy.

In God's love,
Althea Morganstein, M.D.

A tear dripped on the paper. *Lord, I cannot let fear rule my life, but Ian Flannery is most likely back in Chicago. What if he tries again? But if I told Sheriff Meeker what I believe, there is no way I could prove that it was Mr. Flannery who abducted me. I never saw his face. I only know it was his voice.* She clenched her fists into her diaphragm, where even the thought of the man brought spasms.

Lord, what do I do? I know that you protected me from death or violation. I know that you will continue to do so because that is one of your promises. You said you will guide me, to the right or to the left, you will set my path before me and, Father, I want to walk on it, for I feel you have set my path and my feet on it. She opened her Bible and laid her clasped hands on the fine pages. *Lord, I confess my fear, and I ask, I plead with you, to deliver me. I will trust you and your Word. I will. I will. I do.* Tears rained down her cheeks, cleansing tears that washed the fear away and left her feeling as though she could float right up to the ceiling. She leaned back in her father's chair, the library around her a safe place, a haven for her to remember that here, at 10:40 A.M. on September 14, 1895, she gave God her fear.

"Good morning, ladies and gentlemen." Reverend Mohn waited for the whispers and rustlings of the St. Olaf students to cease. He laid his Bible on the podium, flipping through the pages until the room was silent enough to hear the whisper of fine sheets of paper brushing against each other and the clearing of his throat.

Thorliff turned at the clatter of boots on the stair and the tiptoe thuds as Benjamin tried to sneak in late.

"Good of you to join us, Mr. Dennison."

"Sorry I'm late, sir, I . . ." Benjamin collapsed in the wooden chair next to Thorliff.

"We will discuss this later." Reverend Mohn shifted his attention to the entire student body. "Let us begin in the name of the Father and the Son and the Holy Ghost."

Thorliff nudged his friend. "Oversleep again?" He kept his whisper low, his attention on the man in front.

"For those of you who were here at our final meeting last spring, I want to refresh your memory of the challenge I left with you and explain our exercise to the new members of our body. We will start with the reading of the Beatitudes in Matthew five."

Thorliff's ears kept listening to the list, but his mind flew back to the incidents over the summer. Mrs. Karlotta Kingsley and her . . . her attentions. Even the thought of her brought a rush of heat to his ears and to his entire body. He was sure everyone noticed, and he resisted squirming in his seat only with steely determination. When Reverend Mohn glanced from student to student, Thorliff was sure the man could see right into his heart, his sadly impure heart.

"What I asked each of you to do was to choose one of these Beatitudes, to memorize it, and to live your verse to see how your dreams and actions correspond with Jesus' plan for living. We will now go around the room, and those of you returning students will stand, recite your Beatitude, and briefly share with us what you learned from this assignment. We'll start here at my right. Miss Syverude?"

As one by one the students stood, each shared an incident and then admitted that they couldn't always be merciful, or meek, or peacemakers, or whatever their Beatitude called for.

Thorliff could feel his throat growing more dry by the second. Was he the only one to choose pure in heart? When his turn came, he stood and tried to force words past the sawdust of his throat.

"I—" he cleared his throat—"I chose . . ." He swallowed hard and willed some spit to return to his mouth. "I chose 'Blessed are the pure in heart. . . . ' " He paused. How could he explain that he'd never noticed bosoms and ankles before like he had after choosing the verse? How could he explain his perverse and disobedient thoughts and the number of times he'd had to plead for God's forgiveness? He cleared his throat again and began. "All I can say after trying to do this assignment is that I must use the apostle Paul's words when he said, 'O wretched man that I am! who shall deliver me from the body of this death?' 'For the good that I would I do not: but the evil which I would not, that I do.' " He raised his hands and let them fall to his sides. "I don't know what else to say, sir."

Reverend Mohn nodded. "Martin Luther had something to say about this. He said he couldn't stop the birds from flying over his head, but he could keep them from nesting in his hair." He paused and looked around before turning his attention to Benjamin, who would be the last.

Thorliff thought about the quote as he half paid attention to Benjamin shuffling to his feet. Was he so dimwitted, like the disciples so often had been, that he had to ask for an explanation of a parable? Flying overhead? Nesting in the hair?

"Isn't it interesting that not one of you has had any degree of success in living up to such simple actions in order to receive blessings? And I know each of you well enough to know that you desire God's blessings. I know that you did not take this lightly. All I have to do is see the sorrow on your faces. And so I must ask myself . . ." He paused and his gaze seemed to nail Thorliff to his chair. "Did I give you too difficult an assignment, or . . ." His pause stretched again. "Is it that God's Word on the way we should live is never easy, but the eternal rewards are out of this world?"

At their smiles, he nodded and smiled back.

"Now for those of you who were confused with my story of Martin Luther, let me explain. Thoughts flit into our mind and out, and we have no control over that. What we have control over is in letting them stay—like mulling over a thought, letting it take up residence so that we begin to stew or worry or take pleasure in the thought. Then the thought grows like some awful weed and sets down roots, and we become consumed by it. But Paul says we should take every thought captive. That means to take charge of our thoughts. Choose to think on Jesus, on those things that are true and good and pure." His eyes crinkled, and he half smiled, just enough to let his students know that he was not castigating them but teaching them.

"I have good news for you regarding your chosen Beatitude. There is no way you can ever live up to any of them perfectly. They are examples of the way that God would have us act, to guide us onward, and that, my dear young friends, is what grace is all about. God knows we cannot measure up, and that is why He sent His son, His only son, to live here with us and to die on the cross to pay for our sins. Grace, eternal abiding grace. Grace that says I love you, no matter what. It is the character of God to love, and God is unchanging. So we confess our sins and our failings, and He covers us with His grace and forgiveness.

"But . . ." He held up an index finger. "In love and gratitude we must never stop striving to live the way he wants us to. Through this exercise you became more aware of your own inadequacies, and I hope and pray that you drew closer to your heavenly Father as you prayed to live a Beatitude."

Thorliff studied his hands clasped in his lap. *I did draw closer.*

"Let us pray. Father in heaven, we thank thee for thy word, for thy Son, for these young people gathered here in thy name. I pray that they will continue to study thy Word and to apply thy principles to their lives. In Jesus' precious name, amen."

Thorliff stood along with the others, and with his books tucked under his arm, he trailed out of the room. Grace. It's all about grace.

Three weeks later Thorliff stood in front of Elizabeth at the train station. "I hate to see you go," he said, their hands nearly touching the way they seemed to do so easily after he had brought her home from her ordeal in the woods. Not only their hands, but arms and shoulders and eyes saying more than their lips. She'd looked forward to the evenings when he stayed after supper and sometimes she played the piano. Other times they went for a walk or played croquet or joined in one of the rousing political discussions that so often occurred when Phillip invited people over for an evening. Talk turned to the savage fighting going on in the Orient as Japan tried to take over both Korea and China. They discussed the growing number of electric power plants and what that would mean to people in general.

"I-I know," she responded. *But at least I'm not afraid any longer. Since when did you become so important to me that my heart wants to see you at least every day?* She felt herself swimming in those blue eyes of his, eyes that revealed so much more of Thorliff Bjorklund than ever did his well-shaped mouth. She kept her fingers from reaching up to stroke his square jaw.

"Will you write?"

"Of course, and you?" *No matter how busy I am, Thorliff, I will find time to write to you.* "What is it?"

"What?"

"Your eyes. They went dark for a moment, like a cloud passing over the sun."

"Ah, nothing."

But she knew it was something. "No, what?"

"I-I'm not a real faithful letter writer." *Look how much I let Anji down. Will I do the same again?*

"You who writes all the time? I look forward to your letters. Tell me stories in them."

"Really?" His brows knit together in a most fetching way.

Again her fingers tingled to touch him.

Her father cleared his throat. "There are others of us waiting here to tell you good-bye."

"Oh, sorry, sir." Thorliff stepped back. He could feel his neck growing hot.

"Now, dear, you embarrassed them." Annabelle tapped her husband's arm with her fan, but her eyes twinkled as she put her arms around her daughter. "I'll make sure he writes to you," she whispered in Elizabeth's ear. "God bless and keep you." Her voice broke on the *keep*. She swallowed and kissed her daughter's cheek. "I will miss you dreadfully."

"The train runs to Chicago every day." Elizabeth kissed her mother back.

"And you would take time off to visit?"

"Dr. Morganstein assured me that I can, even though we don't get long holidays off. Not like college where we had summers off and semester breaks." Her gaze traveled over her mother's shoulder to lock into Thorliff's again.

Phillip put an arm around each of his women. "Who knows? Perhaps even Thorliff and I will come looking for news." He hugged his daughter. "I'm proud of you, dear. Never forget how much we love you and are waiting to see you again. Letters are wonderful but . . . ." He cleared his throat and looked up as the conductor called, "All aboard."

"You better get on up there before you have to run to catch it." When he reached down to pick up her satchel, Thorliff had beat him to it.

Thorliff climbed the stairs and reached back a hand to assist Elizabeth. She turned and waved before allowing him to help her up the last step.

Within moments Thorliff appeared in the doorway and stepped to the ground. He looked up at the window where she sat, her deep purple hat with a fine feather perched forward, the point of it nestled onto her forehead, making her look like a fashionable young woman.

He waved and kept on waving until only the end of the caboose could be seen down the tracks with the smoke from the engine trailing above. The long cry of the whistle echoed the loneliness already filling his heart. How long would it be before he saw her again?

Monday morning in class on the hill, Benjamin took his place next to Thorliff. "You look like you lost your last friend, but that can't be, because here I am." He set his book bag under the chair and grinned at his classmates. This year there were seventeen students in the junior class. While several had dropped out, others had come back, and now they were the upperclassmen and in charge of many of the college activities.

Surely I don't look that bad. Thorliff nodded his greeting. "Did you have a good Sunday?"

"Life sure is easier living here in the dormitory. You missed a good time at the social. Ah, the singing and the games. You work too hard. All work and no play makes one boring, old man." He clapped Thorliff on the shoulder.

Mr. Ingermanson entered the classroom and looked around to make sure they were all present. The conversation stopped as soon as he reached the front of the room.

"Good morning. I do hope you all have your essays finished. You can lay them right on the corner of my desk on your way out. Today we will be discussing your assigned reading of John Milton. Who would like to begin with any questions your reading raised?"

Thorliff raised his hand. "I thought it interesting that it was only after Milton was forced to retire from political life and went blind that he wrote his greatest work. Why was that, do you suppose?" The discussion was off and running.

When they gathered in the dining room for dinner, Benjamin picked up his tray and joined Thorliff and some of the others at their usual table near the back wall. "I do hope Cook sent extra cookies today. Nothing beats her cookies, no matter what kind she blesses us with."

"Benjamin, you ever thought of letting Thorliff eat his own cookies? It's not like they are starving you here."

"I have it on good report that you had seconds at dessert again last night. And after that we popped corn, and there were enough apples to take some upstairs with us."

The conversation flowed around Thorliff as he reread the article he had just completed for the *Manitou Messenger*, St. Olaf's student newspaper. While he really didn't have time to work on the paper, Mr. Ingermanson had convinced him that it would be to his benefit to take part. Between articles for the *Northfield News* and the *Manitou Messenger*, his classwork, and the novel he was already writing in snippets to send to Elizabeth, his hand felt permanently cramped. Let alone trying to live up to the promise he'd made to himself to write home once a week.

Blessing seemed as if it existed on another plane or another continent, not only distant in miles but in reality. No matter how many letters he read from folks there, he realized he no longer thought of that as home. Home as in where he'd been reared, yes, but not where he belonged now.

Benjamin bumped his arm. "Here she comes."

Thorliff looked up in time to see a young lady enter the dining room. A transfer student, Miss Anne Boranson had caught Benjamin's eye from the first day, and now he declared himself madly in love with her even though they'd spoken to each other no more than two or three times.

"So go ask if you can sit with her." Thorliff nudged Benjamin with his elbow.

"I'm better at adoring from afar."

"You're chicken, that's what. Surely you could sit by her at one of the sing-alongs." Thorliff finished his beef sandwich as he reread the last sentences he'd just written.

"I know. Why don't you go and invite her to join us over here?" one of the others asked.

"She's sitting down with her friends."

"Like she does every day." Benjamin sighed, and the others laughed.

"Good grief." Thorliff reached for an apple from the bowl on the table. "See you later. I've got more studying to do."

"Hey, Bjorklund, are you going to take part in the debate? The new topic is Should Our Government Support Public Work Projects?"

Thorliff stopped to answer the question.

"I'd like to. What about you?"

"We could do the pro side this round. We made a good team last time."

"Let me give it some thought. My schedule is pretty full right now."

"When is it not?" The editor of the *Manitou Messenger* tipped his head back to see Thorliff better. "You finished with that article?"

Thorliff handed the papers to him. "I'd thought to get another quote from Professor Ytterboe, but he's out of town again, so that's impossible."

233

"Good, good. I want this first edition for this year to be exemplary. You have any other suggestions, you let me know."

"I will. Excuse me, please." Thorliff backed off as he spoke. How easy it would be to sit down and while away the remainder of the dinner hour like the others were doing, but he had type to set in the evening and other chores around the newspaper. Besides, he wanted to stop by and see Henry Stromme. He was no longer living there, because a new student had taken his place, but he missed the old man and his cackling laughter.

Reverend Mohn had said that morning in chapel that life was meant to be lived to the fullest in the service of God. Sometimes Thorliff wondered if all he did was in service to God. Like trying to live up to the Beatitudes. One could never do enough, let alone too much.

Leaves had donned their fall dancing gowns and crackled merrily beneath his boots on the way down the hill. At times like this he really missed Elizabeth and their walks to and from school together.

Perhaps today there would be a letter. He broke into a trot, inhaling the rich, fecund flavor of fall.

"Thorliff," Phillip said as soon as Thorliff entered the office, "you need to go over to Mrs. Kingsley's house. She has a story she has written for us and was unable to bring it by. I promised her you'd be there as soon as you got down from the hill."

Thorliff groaned inside but struggled to keep his thoughts from his face. Mrs. Karlotta Kingsley could ruin all his vows of purity of mind faster than he could make them. And how could he confess this to his employer when Phillip had pretty much figured out that Thorliff and Elizabeth were thinking of each other as more than friends. At least he knew he was, and he was fairly certain she was too. At least he hoped so.

CHAPTER TWENTY-THREE

September 15, 1895
Dear big brother Thorliff,

I decided to write that to remind you who you are and that we miss you every day. As you know, school started again, and I think Toby Valders is only getting meaner and sneakier than ever. Do you think some people are born mean and maybe they can't help it? I wonder because if I had to chop all that wood, I would certainly change my ways.

Mor and I wanted to come visit you so bad, but with all the terrible things happening here, harvest was on us before we could take time to even breathe. But Pa says we had good harvests for a change, and while they had grasshoppers out towards Devil's Lake, they never made it here.

Anji and Mr. Moen were married after all. Mrs. Valders said they were unseemly in not waiting for the year of mourning after Anji's brother died, but Mor said, "Uff da, some people have no spirit of compassion." Anyway, they are traveling in Norway, Anji and Mr. Moen, I mean, not Mrs. Valders, and I hope they are happy. Anji is now a mother, as he has two daughters who will come back to America with them.

Baptiste wrote a letter to Metiz. Can you believe it? Anyway, Mor read the letter to us, and the news is that Manda is in the family way. When they brought the horses from Montana two weeks ago, I could see she has gotten fat around the middle. I sure hope they bring the baby next year when they come. I'm big enough to care for it. I have grown two inches since last spring and Pa says I am growing like pigweed.

Thank you for sending us copies of your articles and stories. I read some of them at school. Pastor says I am a good reader, but I already knew that. I think sometimes that I would like to be a teacher when I grow up. I help with the little kids, and it is so exciting to see them learn to read and know that I had a part in that. I make them learn all the sounds of the letters and then show them how to turn the sounds into words. Some words are such wonderful fun like anthropomorphic and analgesic, though I don't use those for the little kids. I try to do as you say and learn a new word every day. I try to work something like misanthropic into a sentence in everyday conversation. It's a predicament all right. Isn't that a good word? I like to say it over and over.

Mor is calling me to set the table, so I will write again sometime. Please think of coming home for Christmas. I want to make sure you are not a figment of my imagination. I read that in a book.

Love from your sister,
Astrid

October 12, 1895
Dear Thorliff,

I didn't realize what a fine poet you are, but I shouldn't be surprised, as you do everything well. At least in the writing department. Thank you for sending what you call your *little drivels* to me.

I hadn't been back two minutes when there was an emergency, and without even unpacking I changed into my scrub apron and assisted Dr. Fossden in the surgery. He has aged in the few weeks

I have been gone. Perhaps it was going on all the time, but sometimes one needs distance to see what is right in front of one's face. He is only supposed to be operating here on a part-time basis, but we seem to be busier than ever. Accidents, like time, wait for no man. I start teaching tomorrow. Today, or this evening rather, Dr. Morganstein had a reception in her quarters for all of the students. As each of us introduced ourselves and told about our medical schooling and experience up to now, I realize how indeed blessed I am. I must send Dr. Gaskin an unending stream of gratitude for all he has taught me and thank my parents again for sending me to college to learn all that I have.

Thorliff, my dear friend, I am so blessed. Sometimes it takes a tragedy, or in my case an almost tragedy, to make us realize all or even part of the innumerable blessings our Lord showers upon us.

One of the children who'd been here this summer came to see me and brought me a fistful of daisies he had picked in a vacant lot. I cannot begin to describe how I felt at seeing him walking with barely a limp. I helped operate on his leg, and it healed so straight and true. If you had seen the break, you would have thought him to be lame for life or that he would lose the leg altogether. I thank our God for privileges like that.

And I thank you for making my time at home such a joy to look back on, in spite of my abduction. But that too is giving blessings beyond measure. I will tell you more about that in another letter. I must get some sleep in preparation for the morrow.

Yours faithfully,
Elizabeth

October 22, 1895
Dear Elizabeth,

You have piqued my curiosity, that is for sure. What other good than what we have already discussed could come of your frightening experience? I know and believe that God's promise of working everything for good for those who love him and are called according to his purpose is true now and forever, but other than increased faith and trust, what could be added? I know you are doing a superb job teaching the beginners. I shall never forget what you said of Dr. Morganstein's principle for the school: "See one, do one, teach one." That is an adage that applies to all of life. I am using it in training the young man your father has hired to help us here. Curtis Jessop has taken over my job of cleaning up after printing. He learns quickly and is willing. What more can you ask?

Life on the hill is lonely without my favorite walking partner to argue with on my trek up and down. Fall is my most favorite time of the year, but I know you will tease me and remind me that I say that in the spring too. Like you, winter is my least favorite, but there is much to be said for the brilliance of sun on new snow and the exuberance of a snowball fight.

There is not much other news from Northfield. I dislike bragging, but Edward and I trounced the opposition in the debate on state's rights last week. We received a hearty round of applause and have now challenged the debating team from Carleton to a match. I will let you know how that goes.

In the meantime, remember that you are held up in all our prayers, mine especially.

Your friend,
Thorliff

November 1, 1895
Dear Thorliff,

When the wind blows off Lake Michigan, it goes right through you, freezing cold and damp to the core. And winter has yet to roar in, which according to my sources will be fierce. One of the boys brought in a woolly caterpillar, and his stripes are wide and really woolly, so that is supposed to indicate a hard winter. This is a city of extremes. Hot and so humid in the summer, cold with a wind that wants to rip one apart in the winter. We had heavy rains this fall and already we are seeing the effects of lack of warmth in our patients. Some of the tenement owners do not heat their buildings anywhere near enough, and the minimum upkeep of replacing windows and walls is ignored. I do not know how they can in good conscience get a decent night's sleep. I would hope guilt plagues them and gives them nightmares. Dr. Morganstein says I have not begun to see the suffering, but I am already wishing there were more that I could do. You want to write editorials? I can give you real-life stories that would make your hair stand on end.

Remember when you asked me if something was wrong and I said no? Well, there was something wrong, but I felt I shouldn't tell anyone for fear of worse things happening. I know that might not make sense to you, but now the story has come full circle and I feel I can share. Perhaps this will work into one of your stories someday. Goodness knows, it will read like a novel. I did finally realize who the man was who abducted me. He is the husband of the woman I told you about who died when we did a Cesarian section to try to save the baby. Her husband had pushed her down the stairs, which precipitated the whole thing. Anyway, he'd been shadowing me in Chicago, thus the feeling of someone watching me. When I came home he followed me to Northfield and shadowed me until he got the opportunity to grab me. He wanted to kill me but was already realizing that he couldn't do that, and then when he heard you calling my name that first evening, he took off into the woods, figuring I would be found or would escape or something. How do I know all this now? He came into the hospital. When I saw him here, I nearly collapsed, thinking he was after me again, but he asked to speak to Dr. Morganstein and me. He confessed the whole thing, begged my forgiveness, and said he has sworn never to drink again. He had gone to confession with his local priest, and the priest said he must give his terrible mixed-up life over to the Lord, and his penance is to never drink again and to confess to us and ask for a way to make restitution. He also had to go to the police and confess, and they kept him in jail for a time, but since I was not hurt and refused to press charges, he is hard at work. I know my father would want him imprisoned forever, so I have yet to tell my parents the whole story

And yes, I forgave him. I already had in my heart, for as Reverend Johnson said, I cannot let a root of bitterness grow, and I add fear to that, for fear is nearly as choking as bitterness. So Dr. Morganstein has made him into an orderly, and he is such a help with heavy things.

Can you believe what a gracious and amazing God we have who could work all of this out for good?

I am sorry to go on for pages and pages like this, but I had to tell you what had happened. If you would, please show this to my mother and father; first ask my father to not threaten dire destruction when he reads it. I want them to know what happened, but I have no time to write this twice. Please prepare them, as I know you can, and I thank you in advance.

Blessings, my dearest friend.
Elizabeth

November 10, 1895
Dear Elizabeth,

Dare I write Dearest Elizabeth? For that is what I am feeling. I know that there was a deep change in my feelings during and after the horror of that night. And you were right. I had to take a long, hard, fast walk to keep from getting on that train and coming to Chicago to first of all, beat that man senseless, and second, to haul him off to the police. But with the walk and your wise words and reading and rereading God's Word where He says that He will repay, that vengeance is His, I finally calmed down. I took those verses printed out with me when I gave the letter to your father and mother. I think forgiveness comes easier for women, but both your parents are calmed down again and talking rationally. Evening was probably the best time for them to read the letter because there was no train leaving before the next day.

I stand in awe and amazement at your forgiving attitude. Even remembering how you looked when I found you makes my blood boil, and I have to listen to Paul's instruction on taking every thought captive. Reverend Mohn spoke on that very thing at chapel, telling how our minds can tear off in all kinds of directions and we can believe things that aren't true and be frightened with fears that never come about. I think forgiveness fits into this, for if I allow myself to dwell on what that man did, I shall soon be in jail for murder, but if I rely on God's promise to be my avenger and believe what He says about living a life of forgiveness, I am then the man He desires me to be. I cry out with the man who said, "Lord, I believe; help thou mine unbelief."

Please do not laugh now, but I had to go out to Mrs. Kingsley's to pick up her story for the paper. I believe your father delights in teasing me about this bodacious woman, but I think she has a new conquest, for I met a young man from Carleton exiting her home as I arrived. He wore the same shocked, red-eared look that I'm sure I wore when she first accosted me. I still believe that at times there is safety in running. And this has given me another chance to learn about taking every thought captive in order to maintain purity of heart.

Old Tom is predicting early snow this year, and it was cold enough this morning that it could soon be on the way. At least you don't have to trudge the hill any longer, but I miss your sweet presence by my side.

Yours,
Thorliff

November 30, 1895

Forgive me, Thorliff, for not writing sooner. We had a tenement go up in flames due to a faulty furnace, and since we are the closest hospital, we received most of the victims. Caring for the badly burned patients has taken every moment of the day and night. Please pray for us, as we are weary beyond measure. I ask special prayers because my hand slipped in surgery, and it could so easily have caused terrible repercussions. I have tried to determine the cause of this sudden weakness but so far to no avail. It is hard to remember to praise God in the midst of all this.

Yours,
Elizabeth

December 1, 1895
Dear Mor and Far, Astrid and Andrew,

Thank you for your letters and the package of cheese. I have taken orders and will need three wheels shipped before Christmas.

I could go into the cheese distribution business without much effort. You must tell me what price I am to charge, as I have lost contact with the prices of goods since all my meals are provided by someone else. I am sorry to say that I will not be able to come home for Christmas because Mr. and Mrs. Rogers are planning a trip to Chicago to have Christmas with Elizabeth. She cannot get away from the hospital long enough to come home. I have mailed a box to you, and I hope it arrives in good condition.

School is going well, as is the latest novel I am working on. I get so little time to write on it that it might take me ten years to finish. I cannot believe I managed to churn out a chapter a week for all those months. However, perhaps that is the kind of deadline that I need. I am more involved at school, serving on the monthly paper, which is almost like a magazine, and I really enjoy the debate team. We have a match with Carleton coming up, and my partner and I will be arguing on the pro side of whether or not our government should sponsor public works projects. I guess arguing comes naturally to college students. Debates are going on all the time.

My coursework is heavy this year, so I spend a lot of time studying. The Beatitudes and the Sermon on the Mount continue to cause discussions as to what Jesus actually meant and how His words apply to us. I am always grateful Pastor Solberg taught us that the easiest way to understand the Bible is to just read what it says and not try to second-guess the meaning. Although there certainly are passages that manage to be in conflict with each other. Thus all the arguments, or rather discussions.

Elizabeth is back in Chicago at the hospital where she worked for the last two summers, only now she is in medical school there.

How are Knute and the others doing? It was so hard to believe such an accident could happen and just when Swen was so happy. And Mor, what about you? You have been very silent on the subject, but I know this must be so hard for you to bear.

Andrew, is that new dog anywhere near as smart as Paws? If so, I'm sure you have him trained to bring up the cows by now.

My love to all of you. I remain your dutiful son and brother,

Thorliff

December 27, 1895
Dear Thorliff,

Christmas without being at home seemed stilted, even though Father and Mother tried their best to make the holidays here in Chicago a celebration. I missed playing the piano for all of our friends, and though Cook sent nearly a trunk of good things, it certainly wasn't the same. Is this part of growing up? Learning to make the best of holidays away from home? Now I know how you must have felt last year, and this year you didn't even have our house to celebrate at. What did you do?

We have snow and that horrendous wind that tries to blow you over when you go out or at least freeze your blood in your veins. The adjoining passageway between the school and the hospital was finished just before this big storm hit.

I should have sent you a note with Mother and Father, but the hospital is full, and we are running our legs off. We need more nurses, let alone doctors and other staff. Dr. Morganstein says this is a chronic problem, so she is now thinking of starting a school for nurses like we have for doctors. She's going to need another building soon at the rate she is dreaming up new ideas.

I like teaching. Are you surprised? Two of the students really keep me on my toes; they memorize so quickly while the others struggle along. You can hear them muttering *tarsal, metatarsal* as they pass in the hallway. One of the more clever ones has come up with a way to memorize all the bones of the hand.

We sent the last of our burn victims home just before Christmas. The woman is so terribly disfigured that I am afraid children will run screaming when they see her. I wonder if someday there will be more we can do to help people like her.

I so enjoy your letters, and you are a dear to send your stories. I read them sometimes to patients in the wee hours of the morning when they cannot sleep. Your stories make me very popular.

I must get to bed, but I do love to spend this time with you. I picture you sitting at your desk or huddled under a quilt in your room, books spread around you while you cram in the final bit of knowledge that will give you an A on an exam. Thank you for being so much more than just an employee to my mother and father. They think the world of you.

From the cold and dreary land of Chicago, I remain,
Yours,
Elizabeth

January 5, 1896
Dear Thorliff,

I am sorry I have not written more often, but between school and chores I sometimes fall asleep at the table. I think of you writing after we all went to bed, and I do not know how you did it.

Everyone was here for Christmas as usual, and Tante Kaaren read your Christmas story aloud to all of us. Mor had tears in her eyes, and Pa had to blow his nose. He said he must be catching a cold, but he wasn't. Metiz came too, but she would have stayed home if we didn't go get her with the sleigh. Mor tried to talk her into moving into the soddy for the winter, but you know Metiz. She would have none of that.

One reason chores take up so much of my time is that Hamre left soon after harvest. He said he wanted to see the ocean again, so he headed west where there is a fishing fleet out of Seattle. As you know, he never has much liked the prairie. I would like to see the ocean too, but I think there is nothing more beautiful than our flat land. Not that I have a lot to compare it with, but as you know, we can see forever here. I climbed up on the barn roof to check some shingles, and I thought sure I'd be able to see the mountains. When I asked Pastor Solberg why not, he explained the curvature of the earth. You must be able to see a far distance from the mountains in Montana. Manda and Baptiste said there is nothing like it.

We go back to school in two days. I want to thank you for the book on farming. I've read a lot of it already.

I sure wish Toby Valders would behave himself so that I wouldn't have to chop so much wood.

Your brother,
Andrew

PS: Mor has been sad for a long time. I think more letters from you would help cheer her up.

January 15, 1896
Dear Elizabeth,

We had a skating party last night at the pond on the hill. As you know, I don't usually attend those things, but Benjamin coerced me into it. I think he needed a bit of moral support in his pursuit of Miss Anne Boranson. But he didn't need my help at all. He asked her to skate with him, and they never skated with anyone else all night. I thought of asking her to skate with me just to rile him up, but I stayed the good friend and didn't tease him.

Have you been reading the newspaper articles about the grave robbers? They sell the cadavers to medical schools and laboratories. Perhaps you should ask Dr. Morganstein where she purchased the cadavers you are studying. While your description of the nerves and muscles was interesting, I'm sure most people would rather not know quite so much about the human body. Since I grew up on a farm, I am not so squeamish.

Have you heard from Thornton? Reverend Johnson mentioned him in his sermon on Sunday, saying that he needed prayer for a health problem. You know me, I immediately wanted to know all the details.

Enclosed you will find my newest contribution to *Harper's Magazine*. I do hope they take it.

I need to get back to my books. How I dream of a piano concert by a certain pianist that I long to see.

Yours,
Thorliff

CHAPTER TWENTY-FOUR

Blessing, North Dakota
February 1896

"What is it, my Inge?" Haakan rolled on his side toward her.

Ingeborg stared toward the ceiling now hidden in the darkness. The wind and snow howling around the house almost drowned out the song of the wolves.

"I just feel so sad, and the pit yawns ever before me. Life is so heavy that I just want to lie down and let it roll on by. Instead, I am being squashed more each day." She clenched the flannel sheet in her hands, the quilts along with the featherbed keeping them warm in spite of the dropping temperatures.

"I read my Bible, and all that I read sounds like God is scolding me, and He certainly has justification."

"I don't think He is scolding you. Like the part I read tonight at the supper table. He said, 'Come unto me, all ye that labour and are heavy laden, and I will give you rest.'"

"Ja, that is good." Her sigh spoke more than words were able.

"I just feel that perhaps God no longer wants me to take care of the sick and the birthings and such. So much death, Haakan. So many have died."

"Ja, I know, but death is a part of life, and only God knows the hour or day. Those people wouldn't have died did he not ordain so." He took her hands in his and raised one to kiss the palm. "God has given you these hands, and he has used them to heal people, to comfort, and to bring forth new life. Whyever would He take away the gift He has given you?"

"Perhaps I misused it."

"Ingeborg." His tone chided her gently.

"Or maybe I have grown proud."

Haakan moved closer and pulled her spoon fashion against his chest. "Lord God, free your Ingeborg from this weight of sadness and bring her back into your joy. Let her know how much the things she does please you."

She could hear his voice fading just before the amen.

"Thank you."

His first snore, a little like a hiccup, made her want to turn and kiss him, but she didn't want to wake him again. *Thank you, Lord, for giving me this man. I will try harder tomorrow to spend time praising you instead of fearing the pit. Thank you for my children, and please keep Thorliff safe, and his Elizabeth.* She shivered at the sound of the wolf's howl. Barney barked in the kitchen by the back door where he slept. *He must think the wolves are right outside. Thank you, God, for this sturdy house that protects us from the storms. And now, please calm the storm that rages inside me.* Like Haakan, she drifted off before the amen.

They woke in the morning to a stillness that screamed for attention after the rage of the storm. Haakan left her in bed and went to put wood in both stoves before returning to the warmth of the quilts and his sleepy wife's arms.

"Warm me up." He shivered as he snuggled her close.

"Did you hear the wolves last night?"

"Who didn't?"

"One sounded like it was right outside the back door."

"Hmm, they must be hungry to be so brave."

"I think I better go check on Metiz this morning. Since the storm is past, I'll just ski on over. I think being out in the sun, if it doesn't cloud over again, will be good for me."

"I wish she had come to the soddy."

"I know. Me too. But we Norwegians aren't the only ones who are stubborn."

"Well, ja, and if I don't get my stubborn body out of bed, the cows will think something has happened to the feed man." He grabbed his wool pants and shirt, along with hand-knitted stockings, and charged out to dress by the now blazing fire. Ingeborg followed him, her quilted petticoats and long wool stockings over her arm. When dressed, she brushed and braided her hair and wrapped the braid around her head like a crown. She tied a clean apron around her waist and set to making the coffee. Pouring the beans into the coffee grinder, she inhaled the pungent fragrance of the dark beans. Nothing smelled as good on a cold winter morning, or any morning for that matter, as a steaming cup of rich, near-black coffee.

After adding flour and eggs and lard to the potato water yeast bubbling on the shelf behind the stove where it always stayed warm, she kneaded the bread, knowing that the more she beat her frustrations into the dough, the lighter and finer the bread would be. Bread needed lots of air worked into it to make it rise. Setting the crockery bowl back on the shelf, she poured herself a cup of the now ready coffee and inhaled the fragrance again.

Astrid wandered into the room, rubbing sleep from her eyes. "How long have Pa and Andrew been out at the barn?"

Ingeborg glanced at the clock. "Better than an hour."

"How come you let me sleep?" Astrid leaned her head against her mother's shoulder and yawned again, causing Ingeborg to do the same.

"Oh, I don't know, but you better hurry now and get washed and dressed so you won't be late for school."

"You say that every morning."

"Not in the summer."

Astrid left the room, a giggle drifting back over her shoulder.

"Thank you, God, that I can at least make someone else laugh." The cat went to the door and asked to go out. "And I can take care of those close to me. You are going to freeze your toes if you don't come right back in." The big orange-and-white cat slit his eyes at her and slipped through the door like a shadow.

She had the ham sliced and frying before Astrid returned. Like her mother, she was wearing long woolen stockings, quilted petticoats, and a woolen vest under her dress. She handed Ingeborg the hairbrush.

"Can I have one braid today instead of two?"

"I guess, but it won't stay as well. Why?"

" 'Cause Toby tied the two together yesterday when he sat behind me. It hurt."

Ingeborg shook her head as she separated the thick fall into three strands. "That boy. Uff da." She stopped what she was doing. "How about if I braid from both sides as usual and then join them and finish as one?"

"That sounds nice. Thank you." Astrid sat on the stool, humming a song as her mother looped the strands over one another. "Soon I will be old enough to wear my hair up."

"Don't be in too big a hurry. Time is flying by as it is."

"It is? Not when I do my arithmetic. How come I have to do arithmetic?"

"How else would you be able to help with the bookkeeping in the cheese house if you didn't know your numbers?"

"You do all that."

"Ja, but you are getting old enough that you can learn."

"Tante Penny lets me help in the store. She says I make change really good, er, really well."

"I'm sure you do." Ingeborg dropped a kiss on the straight part in her daughter's hair. "There you go. Let the cat back in before he has a fit."

"I need to go feed my chickens."

"The door needs to be dug out first. Far will do it later."

Astrid took out the silverware and set the table while they talked. "Are we having porridge?"

"No. Ham and eggs and fried bread."

"Yum. With syrup?"

"If you like." Ingeborg dug a hunk of rising dough out of the bowl and smoothed the rest back into a smooth mound. Laying the dough on a floured board, she cut it into roll-sized pieces and flattened each one to then be dropped in the sizzling lard in an iron skillet on the back of the stove. They puffed up as they fried, and when browned, she turned them over, standing them on their sides in a warming pan on the shelf of the stove.

She'd just finished when they heard the men knocking snow off their boots at the door.

"You pour the coffee, and I'll fry the eggs. Oh, and open a jar of applesauce too. Andrew likes dipping his bread in that."

By the time the men were washed up and seated, Ingeborg set the serving platters in front of them. They all bowed their head for grace and at the amen reached for the platters to pass around the table.

"Mor, you make the best breakfasts."

"Why, thank you, son. We haven't had fried bread for a long time."

"Nor fried cornmeal mush either. I like that." Astrid dipped her bread in the puddle of syrup on her plate.

"You have a drop of syrup on your dress." Ingeborg pointed to a place on her own front to show where and nodded when Astrid used her napkin to dab it away. Many was the time her daughter just pulled her dress up enough to suck off the syrup or jam.

"You might want to use soap and water on that too. Sticky syrup will attract more dirt."

When the children were out the door to jump in the wagon bed set on skids that Lars drove up, and Haakan returned to clean out the barn, Ingeborg wrapped some cheese, bread, and a jar of jam for Metiz. She stuck them in a backpack, and after getting into her heavy coat, scarf, and mittens, she slung the pack over her shoulders and took down the skis from the pegs on the wall in the porch.

Ingeborg blinked against the brilliance of the sun on the new snow. She raised her face to feel any warmth, shutting her eyes against the glare. With the loops of the poles over her wrists, she set off, reveling in the pull of the muscles in her legs. Her breath clouded in front of her face, and flying down a long, high drift made her laugh. The silence of a land shrouded in new snow struck her ears, her breathing and the hiss of the skis the only sounds.

She took in a deep breath and exhaled, the plume of steam dampening her cheeks as she surged ahead. *Free, I'm free!* The thought brought a laugh that came out part choke. *Thank you, God, the weight is gone! Thank you for bringing me back to life! Thank you, thank you.* If she could have twirled in place on skis she would have.

As she drew nearer to Metiz' little house, she slowed. No smoke rose from the chimney. The front porch had not been swept off. She glided up to the buried step and unbuckled her skis.

"Metiz!" Her voice rattled in the cottonwoods around the house. "Oh, God, please, not Metiz." She pushed open the front door and stepped inside where the temperature seemed the same as outside.

"Oh, Metiz!" She stood in the light from the doorway and stared at the small body barely evident under the covers. No movement, only an intense sense of no one being there.

Ingeborg crossed to the bed and tried to see through the tears already raining down her cheeks. "When, oh Lord? How long has she been gone?"

She touched the leathered cheek, the lips curved in a slight smile. Her dark eyes that spoke so much of life were closed. "You went the way you wanted, in your sleep. But oh, my dear friend, how I am going to miss you. Lord, please . . ." But she wasn't even sure what she was asking for. Pulling over a chair, she sat by the bedside, her breath rising in steam clouds like outside. Had the fire gone out in the night and she froze? "Oh, Lord, I hope not." The peaceful look on her friend's face brought more tears.

The wolf howled last night. The thought brought her halfway to her feet, but she sat down again. "It couldn't have been." She stood and walked to the front door, almost afraid to look out. She stepped outside and studied the area where snow had not drifted. Big dog tracks? She looked closer. No. Wolf's track, his deformed foot a signature like none other. She found more tracks at the back door and circling the house.

"She saved your life all those years ago, and now you returned to announce and mourn her passing. How fitting." Ingeborg blinked back the renewed onslaught of tears. "She died last night, didn't she? We saw smoke yesterday morning. And he came." But her only answer was a deeper sense of peace.

"I'll be back, my friend." She strapped her skis on again and headed home. She had to see if Wolf's tracks were at their door too.

She skied up to the barn and, leaning the skis against the barn wall, stepped inside the warm and cow-scented interior.

"Haakan?" When there was no answer, she raised her voice. "Haakan?"

"Back here," he called from the horses' stalls.

Ingeborg found him brushing the horses. "She's gone."

"Metiz?"

"Ja. I think in the night. I didn't check for coals in the stove, but the house was real cold. Remember the wolf howling so close last night?"

He stopped grooming and came to lean against the stall post. "Ja."

"Help me check, but I think it was Wolf. His tracks are all around her cabin."

Haakan cleaned the brushes by scraping them, bristle on bristle. He set the brushes on a shelf and came to take Ingeborg in his arms. "I'm not surprised. Metiz has been getting weaker and weaker. Why, we were just talking about her last night." He rested his cheek on her head where her knitted scarf had pulled back. "I am so sorry for us, you, but not for her."

"Do you think Pastor Solberg will bury her in the church cemetery?"

Haakan sighed. "There might be a ruckus over it."

"I was thinking, what if we burned her house down?"

"Is that what the Indians do?"

"I've heard of it." She sighed, her cheek shifting against the rough wool of his coat. "How would we find out?"

"Pastor Solberg has been in contact with the Indian agent for the reservation. He will tell us."

"I will miss her so. She taught me everything. If it weren't for her, we might not have made it that terrible year." She looked up at her husband. "Do you think she knew?"

"Knew what?"

"That her time was coming. She had that extra sense so often, of knowing things."

"Could be." He tilted her chin up and kissed her. "Another sorrow for you."

Ingeborg shook her head. "She lived a long life, and this is right. I am sad, for I will miss her dreadfully, but sorrow? No. She's gone home to be with our Great Spirit. How she loved to say that when I said God or our Father. I think that's why it was easy for her to believe in Jesus. He is the Son of God, so He is our brother."

"Some here will disagree with you."

"They did not know her as I did and do." She hooked her arm through his. "Come, let's go look for Wolf's tracks."

They found them to the side of the house where the snow didn't drift in as deep.

"He was letting us know?"

Haakan shook his head. "I . . . I just don't know about that."

"What other explanation is there?"

He sighed. "I don't know that either. But then, there are a lot of things I don't understand. I'm just glad God does."

"You want a cup of coffee?"

"Ja. I will stop in to tell Pastor when I go for the children. You want to tell Kaaren and Ilse?"

"I'll ski over there later."

Ingeborg rattled the grate and laid more wood in on top of the coals. As soon as she had the lids back in place, she brought the coffeepot forward to the hottest part of the stove and crossed to the crock that held cookies baked the day before.

Haakan sat down at the table. "I got the chickens shoveled out and cleared the path to the cheese house. There's enough milk out there to start a batch." Due to the reduced milk production in the winter when many farmers let their cows go dry, the Bjorklunds made far less cheese. So that was when they cleaned out the cheese house and prepared for spring and the new crop of calves.

Ingeborg took a knife out of the drawer to cut the cheese and stared at the blade sunk in a deer horn handle—Metiz' specialty. Tears stung again and she brushed them away with the back of her hand. So many things to remember her friend by, but wasn't that the way it was supposed to be between friends? "I'll write to Manda and Baptiste tonight. And Thorliff—he'll want to know."

"I think I'll take a hammer and boards out there and board her house up until we decide what to do."

"Good." She set the coffee in front of him. Only into the new year two months. What would the rest of 1896 bring?

CHAPTER TWENTY-FIVE

Blessing, North Dakota
April 1896

Ingeborg stood at the kitchen window, hands cupping her elbows. Snow still covered the land with not a hint of a thaw, and heavy clouds hung over the earth. "Will this winter never be over?"

The cat stretched in his place in the rocker by the stove and jumped to the floor to wind around her skirts. She leaned over and picked him up, cuddling him under her chin like Astrid did. The heavy purr vibrated her arms, and his ear tickled her chin.

"Good thing I have quilting tomorrow or I swear I will go stark raving mad. It's not like I have nothing to do, but I am sick and tired of that wind. Here it is almost Easter and spring hasn't even shown its nose."

With a sigh she left the window and checked the cake she had baking to take to the church with her the next day. She'd already made a pot of beef barley soup, since it was her turn to serve, and the simmering the next morning would only improve the flavor.

She set the cat back in the chair, opened the oven door to gently press the cake top to check for doneness, and closed the oven door again to let the cake bake a few more minutes. After the cake was resting on the counter to cool before frosting, she returned to sorting through her leftover pieces of fabric to see what to take for the quilting.

Feeling more restless by the moment, she picked up the family Bible and took it over to the rocking chair by the stove to read but first gently nudged the cat to the floor.

"Goodness sakes, it's too dark to even see to read." Laying the Bible aside, she rose and lit the kerosene lamp, setting it up on the warming shelf of the stove to shed a pool of light over the rocker.

The cat had taken over the chair again.

She paused in picking him up. Was that a wolf howl? In the daytime? If they were that hungry, perhaps she'd better go out to the sheep shed and check on her flock.

The sound came again. Either the wind or a wolf howling. She plunked herself back down in the chair. The howling reminded her.

"Ah, how I miss Metiz." The cat jumped back up in her lap, kneading her thighs and pleading for some long overdue petting.

Two tears dropped on his fur.

Ingeborg opened her Bible to the Psalms, and in every one she read, David seemed to be lamenting. Reading aloud, as if to drive off the bleakness, she said, " 'My God, my God, why hast thou forsaken me? why art thou so far from helping me . . . ?' " On and on she read, gaining strength from the words. " 'Unto thee will I cry . . . be not silent to me. . . . Hear, O Lord, and have mercy upon me: Lord, be thou my helper.' "

Hearing the sleigh arrive with the schoolchildren, she hastily wiped her eyes, closed the Bible, and rose to build up the fire. Andrew would want something hot to drink before going out to help with the chores.

Andrew and Astrid laughed their way through the door, stamping the snow off their boots and shedding their coats to hang them on the pegs on the wall.

"Guess what, Mor?" Astrid flipped her braid back over her shoulder.

"What?"

"Pastor Solberg sent Toby Valders home from school today. He cannot come back until he apologizes to Ellie."

Ingeborg glanced up at her son, whose mouth had been laughing, but his eyes still wore the glint of anger.

"Don't worry, Mor, I didn't touch him."

"He didn't have to. Pastor Solberg got really white around the mouth and then said, 'Tobias Valders, you go home until you can comport yourself as a young man of God in this school.' What do you think Mr. and Mrs. Valders will do to Toby?"

"I don't know." But Ingeborg flinched inside. Mr. Valders was known to have a temper, and Mrs. Valders would be terribly embarrassed.

"I'm glad I'm not Toby." Astrid picked up the cat, which had been mewing at her feet.

"I'm going to change clothes. Is Pa out in the barn?"

"I think so. Ellie is all right, isn't she?"

Andrew nodded. "He wouldn't dare touch her." His quiet voice wore barbs of steel.

The next day Ingeborg pulled her things together, fetching the tall pot of soup from its place on the back porch, where it had partially frozen during the night. When she had everything settled in the sleigh, she gathered the reins and drove next door to pick up Kaaren and Ilse. With all the deaf students at school, they could both attend the monthly quilting bee at the church.

"Sounded like Pastor Solberg had a pretty bad day yesterday." Kaaren arranged the buffalo robe over her legs and Ilse's.

"More than Toby Valders?"

"Ja. Two other boys got in a fight, one of them from the deaf school. They got to chop wood as a reminder that fighting is not the way to settle a disagreement."

"However did Andrew stay out of it?"

"I don't know. Maybe chopping enough wood is an effective way to learn to control your temper."

"But Andrew only fights when someone younger or weaker is being bullied. He doesn't just get mad and punch someone." Ilse spoke up from her nest under the robe.

"I'm certainly happy to hear that." Ingeborg clucked the horse to a trot, setting the harness bells to jingling merrily.

"Do you know if Penny is bringing her machine today?" Kaaren asked. "I could have put mine in."

Ingeborg shook her head. "No idea."

"Are you all right?"

The concern in Kaaren's voice made Ingeborg swallow hard. "I will be if spring ever comes again."

"It has been a long winter. And a sad one. That makes it seem even longer. Would that I could help you."

"You do, as much as possible. I guess grief is just something you need to wade through, like the mud in the spring. It pulls at your feet, but you don't sink down beyond getting out. And when it dries, the soil is richer than ever."

"That's a beautiful description. All of us waiting for spring for seeds to sprout, and if God planted them, we have no idea what wonderful plants are going to flower, such glorious colors, such sweet fragrances. Just think, some of the most sweet smelling bloom only at night, like the nicotiana. I planted some of that last summer right under our bedroom window. I saved the seeds, so I shall bring you some."

Ingeborg whoa'd the horse and stepped from the sleigh to throw a blanket over the horse and slip the bridle off, then tied the rope to the halter and the hitching rail. While she took care of the horse, the other two unloaded the sleigh, and by the time they had everything inside, others were arriving.

Women filed in, carrying baskets of food, sewing supplies, and their Bibles, ready for a day they all looked forward to for the entire month.

"All right, ladies, let's get started." Penny Bjorklund clapped her hands and turned to answer a question. "No, let's set the sewing machines up by that window and the quilting frames over there. That sun should feel most welcome for a change. I know I was beginning to think spring had passed us by too."

"Don't plan on it being over yet. Mr. Valders says another storm is

258

still on its way." Hildegunn Valders set a platter of fresh cinnamon rolls in the center of the table. "I brought these to go with coffee."

"They smell heavenly, but I sure hope your husband is wrong. The only storm I want to see is a gentle rain that smells like spring and melts all this white stuff very gently so that it all soaks into the ground and gives us the best crops possible. Now, if that isn't asking for a lot, I don't know what is, but God says, 'Ask, and ye shall receive.' "

"Ja, well, I am asking that Kaaren read and we get started. Einer Junior is home with a sore throat, and I cannot be gone all day." Mrs. Helmsrude shrugged as she finished her sentence. "Why do they get sick on quilting day? This is the first school he has missed, and now he will not get a perfect attendance."

Penny clapped her hands again. "Let us begin. Ingeborg, will you carry around the coffee tray? Bridget, would you take over stretching that quilt on the frame so we can get it basted? Mrs. Valders, will you be in charge of the cutting, please? We need to get another wedding ring started. Who knows who'll get married next. Goodie, how are the blocks coming for the quilt to be auctioned?"

"We're about half done." Goodie Wold looked up from counting blocks in a stack and glanced around the room. "Everyone has to remember to sign their blocks. Some are coming back without signatures."

"Oh, I forgot." Mrs. Veiglun shrugged and made a funny face. "I was just so glad to get them finished."

A chuckle rippled through the room. They all knew that sewing was not one of her favorite things to do, and she did not have a sewing machine like some of the others.

"That's all right." Mary Martha Solberg patted her hand. "I'll do that for you if you'll bake some more of that wonderful apple pie. I don't know what you do, but yours is so much better than mine."

And you are a master at making others feel better, Ingeborg thought. *So often I wish I could remember to pause and say the best thing and not necessarily the first thing that comes to mind.* She caught herself from shaking her head or Kaaren would know she was misthinking again. Kaaren and Mary Martha both had the gift of pouring oil on troubled waters, while she would most likely strike the match. That thought made her almost smile, not exactly an appropriate response either, since Kaaren had the Bible open on her lap.

"Anyone have any favorite passages they would like read?" Kaaren held up her Bible. After several suggestions she began reading in the Psalms as requested.

Ingeborg set her tray back down and took her place at the quilting frame.

"Your soup smells so wonderful," mouselike Mrs. Magron said in a whisper.

"Thank you," Ingeborg whispered back. Even so, Mrs. Valders across the frame raised an eyebrow. Ilse nudged her with her foot, which made Ingeborg almost smile again.

When Kaaren finished reading and leading in prayer, talk picked up as needles flashed in and out, scissors cut through fabric, and sewing machines whirred, the treadles thumping in unison.

Ingeborg got up to stir her soup when she heard Mrs. Valders say, "Did you hear that they are planning on burying Metiz in our cemetery?"

Ingeborg tried to ignore the flash of anger that nearly melted her camisole. She glanced over at Kaaren, who gave a slight shake of her head. But Ingeborg ignored her.

"And why wouldn't she be buried in the *church*"—she emphasized *church*—"cemetery?"

"The church cemetery is for baptized Christians, not for heathens."

Ingeborg tried to clamp back the words galloping off her tongue but failed. "You have no idea what Metiz believed because you never talked with her." Ingeborg tried again to swallow her anger but almost choked instead. "Metiz lived out her faith. She didn't just talk about it. She's a better Christian than you will ever be with all your judgmental ways." She gripped the back of her chair until her knuckles whitened.

"Why, I never . . ."

"That's right, you never gave her credit for helping when Mr. Valders nearly lost his life instead of just his arm. You never spoke to her as a friend. You never offered any kind of Christian love." With each word

Ingeborg leaned farther over the chairback until it was cutting into her midsection.

"Ingeborg, would you come help me at the cutting table?" Kaaren took her arm and literally dragged her away from the quilting frame.

Ingeborg followed her, but instead of joining the cutting, she made for the door, snatching her coat and scarf off the chairs where they had laid them and slammed out the door. Her flaming face didn't even feel the biting wind that had kicked up, nor did her bare hands as she wrapped her long knit scarf about her head and neck. She crammed her hands into her pockets and strode out across the prairie. Snow crunched beneath her laced and well-greased shoes, and even the sun reflecting off the snow could not prevent the tears from freezing on her cheeks.

"I could rip that woman limb from limb right now with my bare hands." She took her hands out of her pockets and stared at them. They'd even formed the shape of her anger, clenched and rigid.

She rammed them back in her pockets and kept on walking, her strides so long that she wound up at her own porch before she realized where she was.

When Haakan came in for dinner, he found her setting the table.

"What are you doing home? Where is the horse?"

"At the church. I walked out of there before I attacked and perhaps injured Hildegunn Valders."

"I see. That bad, eh?"

"She doesn't believe Metiz should be buried in the church cemetery." Ingeborg slammed a plate on the table hard enough that it cracked right in two.

"Ah."

She stared at the broken plate, her hands flying to cover her cheeks. As if mesmerized by what she'd done, she picked both pieces up and held them together again.

"It's broken, Ingeborg, but it's only a plate." Haakan took the pieces from her shaking hands and threw them in the box of garbage.

"No. I have to fix them."

Haakan grabbed her hands before she could dig the pieces of plate out again. "Ingeborg, listen to me. Glue won't hold dishes together. They just break again." He put his arms around her and held her writhing against his chest, trying to get free. "Ingeborg!"

She burst into tears, collapsing against his chest. "Sh-she is so hateful, a-and she thinks she knows it all. No wonder Toby is such a terror, having to live with someone so self-righteous as she." Sobs broke her words just as the plate had crashed on the table. "I-I will never speak to her again, and if Pastor Solberg refuses to bury Metiz in the cemetery, I swear, I will never enter the door of that church again either."

Wisely, Haakan just held her, rocking gently from one foot to the other, murmuring soothing nothings and rubbing her back.

When she sagged against him, he guided her into the bedroom and sat her down on the edge of the bed. He unlaced her boots and pulled them off, then covered her when she fell on her side.

"You will feel better when you wake up."

"No, I . . ."

He pushed her back down. "Sleep, my Inge. Sleep."

Some time later she thought she heard Kaaren's voice asking about her, but sleep claimed her again before she could rouse enough to respond.

Lord, what have I done? The thought jerked her upright. The setting sun reddened the sky and set the room to glowing. Where had the afternoon gone? Had she slept it away? She flopped back on the pillows. *How will I ever face people again?*

With the back of her hand over her forehead, she stared at the sunset-pinked ceiling.

"You think Mor is going to have to chop wood?" Andrew's voice broke through her stupor.

"Shush. Don't you go making things worse." Astrid sounded remarkably like her mother.

Andrew's chuckle echoed as he headed out the door to help with the milking.

If only she could pull the covers over her head and will this day back to the morning.

Lord God, please forgive me for yelling at Hildegunn yesterday. But I cannot say I'm sorry. For I'm not. I am still so mad at her that my hands shake. Yet I know that your Word says to forgive as we have been forgiven. But why doesn't she have to apologize? She is so . . . so like the Pharisees, and even you called them names. Ingeborg sighed and shook her head. *Why did I have to go and yell at her like that?*

The cat arched against her skirt as she sat in the rocker by the fire. Outside, icicles dripped merrily and the warm chinook wind called her to come out and play. Or at least to stand on the porch and feel the warmth after such a long, cold, and dark winter.

She'd heard the change in the wind sometime during the night when she was arguing with a silent God instead of sleeping.

By the next morning, after even less sleep, guilt weighed around her neck like one of the millstones the Bible referred to.

"Lord, I don't want to do this. I don't want to talk with Pastor. I don't want to go anywhere." Speaking aloud in the quietness, she clenched the sides of her skirt. "But I don't want to carry this burden around any longer either. Is there no other way?"

She took down the bowl with the rising bread dough and, dumping it out on the floured board, pushed her hand down into its yeasty softness. Within three strokes, she changed from kneading to pummeling, pounding the air into it, flipping and turning the dough as if it were alive and had desecrated the memory of her dear dead friend.

Tears dripped as she locked her elbows and leaned on the table. "Lord God, I cannot stand this. I give up."

She formed the bread dough into a round ball again and set it back to rise once more.

"Such irony, beat up the dough to get the lightest bread—when I would rather be beating up that woman. No wonder Andrew uses his fists at times. It must feel immensely satisfying, like the bread dough. How can I ask him to not do so when I almost did?"

Was that a chuckle she heard or the dropping of ashes in the firebox?

After serving leftover beef barley soup for dinner along with fresh bread still warm from the oven, she took a loaf and a wedge of cheese, loaded a basket, and headed for the barn to harness the horse. The snow was too wet for skiing.

Half an hour later she stopped the horse and sleigh in front of the Valderses' home and tied the horse to the hitching post. Surely she saw the curtain twitch shut in a front window, but no one came to the door. She knocked and waited, then knocked again. Hildegunn Valders opened the door and stood there, arms locked across her chest.

"I have come to beg . . ." Ingeborg swallowed and began again. "I brought you a peace offering and came to beg your forgiveness for the things I said the other day at quilting. I am truly sorry." Her words finally finished in a rush. *Will she not even invite me in?* Ingeborg held out her basket. "I just baked today. I thought—"

"I forgive you only because our Lord says I must, but I shan't forget what you said." Hildegunn closed the door without another word. The click of the catch cracked like a rifleshot in the stillness.

Ingeborg took a step back, the urge to bang on the door swelling within her like the rage of the days before. Instead, she closed her eyes. *Lord, I have done what you commanded. Now what?* Turning, she walked down the unshoveled steps and out to the waiting horse. After settling herself in the sleigh, she backed the horse and, turning, headed home. She thought of going on out to the Solberg place, since she was already out, or stopping by the store to see Penny, but instead she headed on home.

"Back so soon?" Haakan met her at the barn door.

"She said she'd forgive me but would never forget and slammed the door in my face."

Haakan's jaw tightened. "That's not forgiveness."

"Not the way I understand, but I learned something. I did what I had to do, and now I leave the rest in God's hands. Come on up to the house for coffee. I'll heat up that gingerbread and whip some cream."

"Done." He took the bridle off the horse and led him into the barn.

"And, Haakan, don't you go getting your dander up over this. One of us has to sleep nights."

She heard his chuckle as she turned toward the house, her basket on her arm. Amazing how much brighter the sun shone now than on her way into town.

The funeral service for Metiz and two others occurred as soon as the ground thawed enough to dig the graves, as usual. Ingeborg looked around at the other mourners, and the only one missing besides Bridget was Hildegunn Valders. Even her two closest friends, Mrs. Magron and Mrs. Odell, were present. Pastor Solberg caught her gaze with a slight nod. He'd already visited one day and commended her for her efforts.

"I should never have acted like that," she'd said to him.

"No, you shouldn't have, but you did right in going to her. Now it is up to you and the rest of us to pray for her that she can truly learn what forgiveness means, the way God forgives, He who remembers our sins no more."

Ingeborg brought her attention back to the three graves dug in the prairie sod.

"Dust to dust, ashes to ashes, we commend the souls of these brothers and sister to the care of our almighty God. In the name of the Father and the Son and the Holy Ghost. Amen."

Ingeborg mopped her tears and glanced over to the graves of Agnes and Joseph Baard, of Swen, and two other very small graves. Her chest tightened and yet felt empty as more tears followed the earlier ones.

Penny placed an arm around her shoulders. "Sometimes it seems the Lord does more taking than giving, but we know that is not really true. Bridget asked if you would come by the boardinghouse. She had planned on coming, but a group of people got off the train and needed dinner."

"Of course. Is she all right?"

"No different than usual. She doesn't say much, but she has really missed Metiz too. Says she and Henry are now the oldest living in Blessing, which is true, but it would be hard to guess by looking at her."

Ingeborg glanced over to the Valderses' house. Actually Hildegunn, with her sober mien, looked older than Bridget with her welcoming smile. Even though Bridget probably had twenty years on her.

Ingeborg linked arms with Penny. "Let's get the coffee poured and everyone served at the church. Then I'll go see Bridget, and after that you show me the new bolts of cloth you have. I feel the need to make a new dress of my own. And Astrid is growing so fast I've let down her hems as far as they can go. I better get some sewing done before the garden is ready to plant."

"I already started some tomatoes. Do you think it is too early?"

"No, I guess it is about time already."

The two climbed the three steps to the church, and others followed.

"When do you think Anji and her husband will be back?" Ingeborg asked Knute as she served his coffee.

"Soon, I hope, although from her letter, I think she is having a good time in Norway. She said she is missing home and the plains here, where you can see forever. Says the mountains are beautiful but give her a bowl of sky any day."

"Good. And her new daughters?"

"She said they call her Mor and are ready to come to America."

Ingeborg caught his glance toward Dorothy, who stood with her baby on her shoulder, patting his back while she visited with Martha Mary. Young Swen had made his arrival between snowstorms and with little fanfare.

Hmm, thought Ingeborg, *so that is the way the wind blows. Perhaps Penny was right and we might be needing another wedding ring quilt by summer.*

CHAPTER TWENTY-SIX

May 1896

"Will Thorliff be coming home this summer?" Penny asked.

Ingeborg shrugged. "I doubt it. He hasn't said anything about it." She nodded toward the coffeepot on the back of the stove.

"No, thanks." Penny put her hand over her cup. "I'm coffeed out. But you have no idea how I appreciate your taking me under your wing like this. A whole afternoon of not waiting on anyone in the store, not answering to little voices calling Ma-a-a, and not even having to make supper." She tipped her head back against the chair. "Between you and Astrid . . ." Penny's voice faded.

"I'm glad we could do this for you. After all, it was Astrid's idea."

"What a special daughter you have raised. Would that mine would grow up to be just like her."

"The years go so fast." Ingeborg picked up her knitting from the basket at her feet. "Astrid is asking if we can go to Northfield to see Thorliff."

"Why don't you go?"

"The expense and the time needed. Who would cook for the men? And the weeds would take over my garden. Besides, it wouldn't seem fair to go off and leave Haakan and Andrew like that."

"Haakan went to the Grange meeting in Grand Forks."

"Only over one night though. We'd need to be gone a week or so." Ingeborg kept her fears to herself. They'd have to change trains in Grand Forks and again in St. Paul. Hjelmer said the Twin Cities had doubled or tripled in size since the time she came through there on her way west to Dakota Territory. And then she'd had Roald to keep her safe.

After Penny left, Ingeborg took out Thorliff's last letter.

May 15, 1896
Dear Mor,

How swiftly this year has flown. It is hard to believe I am truly finishing my third year of college. They have asked me to be editor of the college paper next year, but I believe I shall decline the honor. I get enough newspaper work every day, and I want to use every spare minute I have on rewriting this book I am working on. I thought to have it finished by now, but playing baseball took up a lot of my time. I play the game, then replay it when I write it up for the paper. I do truly enjoy the sport. Who ever would have thought that those games of stickball in the pasture would have taught me how to hit like I do. There is a certain satisfaction in hearing the solid connection of bat and ball and seeing that ball lift in an arc and fly away. Hearing the spectators cheer does one's heart good also.

Elizabeth is not looking forward to another summer in Chicago. But once this one is done, she will officially be a licensed medical doctor and can practice anywhere she wants. Her mother is still hoping she will return to Northfield and join Dr. Gaskin in his practice. I am hoping for that too.

Thank you for your letters. I beg your forgiveness for not responding more faithfully.

This promises to be a busy summer with Mr. and Mrs. Rogers going to Chicago to see Elizabeth and then going on to New York to a newspaper convention. They will be gone for three weeks the latter part of June and into July, and the thought of being in charge for that long a time is both exciting and terrifying. Although I will have help from my friend Benjamin, and Mr. Ingermanson has said he will help if I need him. Mr. Rogers says he has complete confidence in me, but I'm glad I have my confidence in our heavenly Father instead. I covet your prayers that I will have all the wisdom I need.

Greet everyone in Blessing for me. I need to answer a letter from Pastor Solberg too. Give Astrid an extra tug on her braids to remind her that her elder brother has not forgotten her. There is a package coming for her one of these days. I'm glad you all enjoy our newspaper, even though the news is old by the time you get it.

I remain your loving son,
Thorliff

Ingeborg took out her paper and pencil.

May 30, 1896
Dear Thorliff,

I know you will do well with the paper, and that answers my question as to whether you will be coming home this summer. It also answers Astrid's plea that we come visit you. Late June is the only time I could think of being away, and from the sounds of things, you would have no time for company then. Perhaps you could come home for Christmas this year.

She laid her pencil aside and went to the window to see what the dog was barking at. Astrid ran up the lane, braids bouncing.

Ingeborg thought of how Astrid would love to see her big brother and how surprised he would be at how grown up she'd become. She put away her writing things, not wanting to have to tell Astrid she had for sure decided not to go. If only they could travel in the wintertime, when the farm chores were so much less demanding. But then school kept them home. Not that she wanted to be like Hjelmer, who seemed to be gone most of the time.

She thought back to what Penny had said about that. *"Why can't he be content with our store and selling machinery and even blacksmithing again?"* She didn't like her husband being involved in politics.

269

Ingeborg sighed. So many questions for which she had no answers.

"Mor, guess what?" Astrid burst through the door with a slam.

"What?"

"Onkel Olaf is thinking of moving."

"No!"

"That's what Mrs. Valders said to Mrs. Magron."

"Were you eavesdropping?"

"No, well, yes. Well, sort of. But it isn't eavesdropping is it when you would have to clap your hands over your ears to not hear. And besides, they were in the store, and I was in Tante Penny's kitchen, so—"

"All right, you weren't eavesdropping, and"—Ingeborg shook the grate in the stove—"I expect you won't tell anyone else what you heard."

"No, but Mor, did you know about it?"

Ingeborg shook her head. "But I wouldn't take that as gospel truth. You know how rumors can spread."

"All right. But if Ellie has to move away, Andrew won't be fit to live with."

"Then you better make sure you are not the one to worry him."

"I won't. Did you pick the eggs?"

"No."

"I will. Do you have any scraps for the chickens?"

"In the bucket on the porch." Surely Penny would have said something if this were indeed true. *Oh Lord, poor Andrew. He and Ellie Wold have been like two peas in a pod for . . . well, forever, it seems. What will he do if she leaves?*

The summer passed without further notice of anyone moving, other than to find the nearest shade. Crops were good, and for a change, the weather cooperated with just enough sun and rain. Other than Mrs. Valders still refusing to speak to Ingeborg, all was well.

After church one Sunday, Kaaren shook her head. "Doesn't she realize she is just making a fool of herself?"

Hildegunn Valders had just then turned away when Ingeborg

greeted her. For a long time Ingeborg had just ignored the silences, but now she made it a point to greet Hildegunn, and not just with a smile and a nod.

Ingeborg looked across the gathering to where people were visiting and children were running and playing. "Isn't there an old saw about killing someone with kindness?" Ingeborg's right eyebrow lifted slightly.

"I take it that will be your campaign?"

"That and a commitment to pray for her every day."

"Where did this all come about?" The two made their way back to their wagons.

"I guess it was God's idea, and He shared it with me."

August 10, 1896

Dear Thorliff,

Harvest is about to begin. The wheat is heavy and looks to be a wonderful harvest, as long as nothing happens before we get it in.

Mrs. Valders has yet to speak to me since my terrible outburst of last winter. Everyone pretty much ignores the way she acts, and I continue to pray for her. One has only to look at her face to know that she is a very unhappy woman.

Astrid had hoped something miraculous would allow us to come to Northfield, but then, I know she has written you herself. At the rate she is growing, I shall soon be the shortest one in our family. I am glad your weeks of running the paper went so well. You proved to yourself how very capable you are, something I was already convinced was true.

George McBride has agreed to take charge of the milking so that Andrew may at last go along with the threshing crew. He is so excited, as you can well guess.

We had a letter from Manda. She is in the family way again and will not be coming with the horses this year, nor will Baptiste. I shall miss seeing them.

That is all the news for now. Know always that I love you.

Your mor

271

"Mor, I never thought I'd miss Andrew so much." Lamplight cast a circle around Astrid's head as she sat at the kitchen table writing a letter to Thorliff as her mother did the same.

"I know."

"I mean, I miss Pa every harvest season, but Andrew has always been here." She tapped the end of the pencil on her teeth. "Do you think they miss us like we miss them?"

"Most likely not. They are seeing new places and different people. They work so hard, there isn't much time for being homesick."

"How come they don't write us a letter?"

"Too busy."

"Andrew had time to write Ellie a letter."

"Ah, but that is different."

"A friend is more important than your own and only sister?"

"Not more important, just different." Ingeborg turned her head to hide her smile. "Finish your letter and we'll make fudge."

"Really?" Astrid bent her head back to her paper and signed with a flourish. "I didn't have any more to say anyway."

Would that life were that easy, Ingeborg thought. *Haakan, I do wish you would write. No matter how well I handle things here, I need to hear from you.*

CHAPTER TWENTY-SEVEN

Chicago, Illinois
October 1896

Looking back, Elizabeth could not believe how fast the year had flown.

"So are you ready?" Dr. Morganstein asked.

"As I'll ever be." Elizabeth straightened her gown and patted the upsweep of her hair.

"Then let us begin." Dr. Morganstein gave the signal and all the medical students began filing into the room reserved for them at the Plaza Hotel in Chicago. When the last of the eighteen doctors in training cleared the doorway, Elizabeth smiled at her trainer and friend. "After you."

Dr. Morganstein walked past the rows of seats where her students sat and continued up to the platform to join Dr. Fossden. Elizabeth followed ten paces behind her. While the next graduating class would have nine members, she walked alone. Before taking her place on the aisle, she smiled at her parents and at Thorliff sitting beside them, at Dr. Gaskin and his new wife, the former Nurse Browne, and Thornton

Wickersham, who had returned from the mission field to recover his health, and at another of her benefactresses, Issy Josephson.

The ceremony passed in a blur, as did the legal conferring upon her of the title of Doctor of Medicine. When she accepted her diploma, the audience applauded.

"Dr. Elizabeth Rogers is our first graduate." Dr. Morganstein looked down at the students. "Next year, God willing, we will see nine more walk across the platform. We live by our creed of 'See one, do one, teach one.' You second-year students will teach the first-year students, and so it goes. And as our school grows, so will the medical care provided to our great country. May God bless us all." Smiling as she looked out over the attentive audience, she said, "You are dismissed."

Everyone clustered around Elizabeth, congratulating her and wishing her great success.

"But I'll still be at the hospital," she said with a bubble of laughter. "At least until the holidays, which I will spend with my family this year and then return. You can't get rid of me that easily." She smiled over at Dr. Morganstein, who stood with her parents and friends. *Not that you've tried very hard.* The thought brought another smile. Dr. Morganstein was getting her wish of having Elizabeth become a part of the hospital staff—at least for a time.

At dinner an hour or so later, Elizabeth joined her family and friends, taking the empty chair between Thornton and Thorliff at a long table.

"You're not here to try to talk me into going to Africa, are you?"

"No. I came because I wanted to congratulate you for accomplishing your dream."

"All the way from Africa?" Thorliff looked over Elizabeth's head to ask.

"No. I was sent home to regain my health. The bugs there seem to like me, and my body really detests them."

"What did you have?" Elizabeth switched into doctor mode.

"Things that are not appropriate for dinner conversation."

"Oh. Will you go back?"

"I don't know. I found I learn languages very quickly. I might be of more help in translating the Scriptures into Swahili or another major language so at least those who can read, can read the Bible to those who can't. Right now I am not sure how the Lord plans to use me."

"But your health is better?"

He shrugged. "I am feeling much improved."

"That is good." Elizabeth resisted the urge to take his wrist and check his pulse. He looked so gray that if he was now much improved, what had he looked like before? And what had he contracted in the dark continent, where strange and horrifying diseases seemed to proliferate like mosquitoes in a swamp?

She glanced up to catch Dr. Gaskin's eye. "So, dear Doctor, when did you finally gain your wits enough to marry Nurse Browne?"

"*Tsk, tsk.* And here I thought medical school might teach you to curb your tongue." He smiled at the beaming woman beside him. "But to answer your question, I don't know why I wasted all that time." He patted Matilda's hand lying on the table. "I feel like I have a whole new lease on life." He looked straight at Elizabeth. "So much so that I rescind my offer for you to take over my practice. I would be honored if you would join me, but I'm not ready to give up the harness yet."

"Bravo. I'm glad to hear that, because I plan to stay in Chicago for at least a few more months."

"She'll be with me forever if I have anything to say about it." Dr. Morganstein spoke from the head of the table on the opposite side of Thorliff.

Dr. Gaskin leaned forward. "Would the idea of a hospital in Northfield make a difference in how you feel?"

Elizabeth laid down her fork. "Really?"

"We are working toward that end. My small surgery with three beds is just not enough. We even thought of putting more beds in the parlor, but I'm kind of partial to that parlor now that I have someone to sit in it with me."

"We've been talking with Dr. Johanson and the city fathers. There is a great deal of interest." Mrs. Gaskin turned to smile at her husband.

Elizabeth recognized the love in her eyes. How wonderful for them both. Her thoughts took off. All this past year of exchanging letters with

Thorliff, she had been given the chance to look into his soul and realize even more what a fine man he was. No wonder her father thought so highly of him. Not only did he have a good mind, but he was a godly man of character. True, he wasn't as polished in the social graces as Thornton, but he learned quickly and, unless his head was lost in a story, usually had a good sense of humor.

Are you comparing the two? The thought caught her by surprise. *Not in the least, just finishing out an idea.* Besides, they were both just good friends. After all, that was what men would be in her life, just good friends.

You sure you don't care for Thorliff as more than just a friend? When she tried stuffing that voice down in a corner and clapping a lid on it, she raised her attention from her meal at the clearing throat next to her. "Ah, did you ask me something?"

"Not exactly, but I did expect a response to my comment." Thornton wiggled his eyebrows when she looked at him.

Elizabeth covered a snort of decidedly unladylike manner with her napkin. "I'm sorry. I was thinking. Could you repeat yourself?"

"I said that I'll be remaining in Chicago for a few weeks."

"Oh, really?" *Oh, please don't expect to take up where we left off. I have no more feelings for you now than I had then.*

"Perhaps we could attend a symphony or something."

"That would be lovely." She caught the stolid look on Thorliff's face and looked across the table to catch Dr. Gaskin chuckling at what he realized was her predicament.

Why had whoever arranged the table put her between the two young men after all?

Because they were both her friends. That was an easy answer but not an easy situation.

As the waiters removed the plates, she glanced down the table at her mother and father. They were talking with Mrs. Josephson and seemed to be really enjoying themselves. She would always have a special place in her heart for Mrs. Josephson, as she was the person who introduced a young girl dreaming of medical school to the woman in Chicago who could help make her dreams come true.

Which they had.

Ah, Lord, how blessed I am. Now please get me out of this situation that is growing more uncomfortable by the moment. She glanced at Thornton, who smiled at her, then at Thorliff, who smiled too, a forced smile with clouds dimming the incredible blue of his eyes. Tonight they looked dark, like water at twilight. Her arm brushed his, and she felt her breath catch. The desire to lean closer made her sit upright, like a prisoner laced to a pole.

Dr. Gaskin winked at her.

He knows. Knows what? Knows that I really don't look on Thorliff as a brother like I do Thornton. As if I really know the difference when I've never had a brother, but that thrill I feel with him surely doesn't come with brothers and sisters.

She rubbed her forehead to stop the voices shouting at each other, or at least it seemed they did.

A waiter dimmed the lights as the chef brought in a tray with flames burning blue on the cherries jubilee.

"In your honor, Dr. Rogers." He set the beautiful dessert on a table slightly off to the side and began serving. When the waiter set the first plate in front of her, she turned to offer her thanks.

Again she brushed Thorliff's arm. This time her back grew warm, as if that flame had moved on over to take up residence within her.

When the coffee was served at the end of the meal, Elizabeth rose and looked around the table, waiting to catch glances so she could speak. When the conversations quieted, she said, "I want to thank each one of you for coming to my graduation but even more for the parts you have played in bringing me to this place. You have encouraged me, provided me with experiences that I needed, and helped me financially, and I know that all of you have prayed for me too. I would not be where I am today were it not for all of you. Thank you, Father and Mother. I know this wasn't your dream for me, but you helped me anyway. Mrs. Josephson and Dr. Morganstein, you saw something in me that cried out for your attention. Thank you for being aware and then pursuing a way for me to walk. Dr. Gaskin, under your tutelage I delivered my first baby, I stitched the first laceration, and I cried when we lost my first patient. Thank you for all those years of answering unending questions and challenging me to think things through. Thornton and Thorliff, you have made me laugh, beaten me at croquet, and argued both theology and politics, neither being a subject for polite company. What would I do without friends like you? Again, thank you all for coming, and may God continue to guide us in the paths where we should go." She smiled at each one as she closed her impromptu speech and applauded along with them before sitting down again.

"Whew," she muttered under her breath and heard a chuckle on either side.

"You spoke beautifully," said Thornton.

"I'm proud of you," whispered Thorliff.

"Are you really?"

"More than I can say." Thorliff's whisper soothed her like a gentle rain that settles the dust and makes the world smell all fresh and alive again.

She thanked each guest at the door and finally took the elevator to the family's suite, where she collapsed on the bed and let her mother help her undress.

"Good night, dear. You sleep as late as you want in the morning. If we aren't here, we will leave a message."

"Good." Elizabeth didn't even hear her mother close the door.

October 23, 1896
Dearest Elizabeth,

Our brief visit in Chicago was far too short, and though the holidays are not too far away, right now it seems forever.

I have something I need to ask you, and I had hoped we'd have more time together when I was there, but since we didn't, here goes. Elizabeth, I have come to care for you deeply, far beyond that of friendship, although that is surely the basis for my caring. I need to know if you care even a bit for me as more than a friend. When I am with you, I forget the lonely hours when you are away, and when we are apart, I remember how much I love to hear you laugh, to discuss something important with you, and to hear the music in your voice. I feel tall and strong as an oak tree when you are by my side, and my day lights up as with the sunrise when I receive a letter from you. There, now that I've poured my heart out to you, I ask that God keep you safe and bring you home again swiftly.

Yours,
Thorliff

November 10, 1896
Dearest Thorliff,

Such beautiful words you write. How can a young woman's heart but quicken to know that someone she holds in the highest esteem speaks with such fervor!

You know my calling is to be a doctor, and that is what I am doing, and I do not know where that will lead. I commend us both to God's keeping and leading as I pray for you every day.

Life goes on here at the hospital as busy as ever. I no longer only assist at surgeries but am in charge of some of the more mundane operations. Several of the second-year students assist me, besides the nurses, of course. I am thinking of attending a special clinic at Johns Hopkins in January. Dr. Morganstein feels I will benefit from learning some of their procedures. The thought both terrifies and thrills me. How will I measure up being the foremost question in my mind. I will write more later when I know for sure.

Your still-in-training doctor,
Elizabeth

PS: Remember when I told you about dropping things with my right hand? You noticed it at dinner one day too. I finally took my courage in hand and asked Dr. Morganstein about it. She examined me but had no idea what it might be since it is so intermittent. She suggested I make a record of all the events and what was going on at the time. She feels that the pattern may be due to extreme fatigue, because it never happens when I've had plenty of rest. So the prescription is to get enough rest. How one does that when working at this hospital is a question without an answer. But it has not happened lately, and for that I am very thankful. I need not describe to you my relief.

Yours,

E.

Elizabeth tied on a clean apron and adjusted the triangular scarf that covered her hair. She glanced at the clock. Fifteen minutes until she was due in the operating room. Without thinking she massaged her right hand and arm as she took the stairs to the lower floor. She'd not had a problem with dropping things since before graduation, but then, she wasn't as exhausted all the time either. Thank God. It seemed Dr. Morganstein was right. Elizabeth thought ahead to the surgery and murmured her constant prayer before beginning. "Lord, give me wisdom and sure hands to help heal this woman. And give her the strength to come through the surgery and get well. Thank you that I can be part of your plan for healing. Amen."

CHAPTER TWENTY-EIGHT

Northfield, Minnesota

December 15, 1896

Dear Mor,

How I hate to have to write this, but due to circumstances here, I will not be able to come home for Christmas after all. I guess I did my job too well last time Mr. Rogers was gone, so now he feels free to travel more.

Thorliff stopped writing. Was that really the reason he wasn't going back to North Dakota, or was it he wanted to spend every minute he could with Elizabeth? Yes, Phillip would be gone for three days. Yes, he needed to be in Northfield through the twenty- second, but . . . He ripped his letter in half and dropped it in the wastebasket. His mother would be appalled at the waste. Paper was too precious to just throw away, that is, unless you worked in a newspaper office.

He started again.

December 15, 1896
Dear Mor and my family,

Please forgive me for not coming home, as we had talked about. I could possibly come on the twenty-second after Mr. Rogers comes back from his trip, but since I would need to be back on the twenty-eighth, that leaves so little time with all of you. As you said in your last letter, Mor, more frequent letters would be helpful, and I promise to write more often. I'm praying that one of these days you will have telephones like we do here. Such a convenience, and hearing a voice that you love over lines from far away is nothing short of miraculous. I am thinking that Tante Penny will be able to install one at the store in the next year or so, as the telephone lines follow the train tracks like the telegraph did. Perhaps they will use the same poles even.

School is going well. I am on the debate team again, and we royally trounced Carleton. Would that we could do the same in baseball.

Elizabeth is home through the holidays and enjoying the time off. I might win a debate tournament but have yet to out-debate her, especially on anything to do with medical issues. I think she figures out where I stand and deliberately chooses the opposite. They say that iron sharpens iron, and you know that I have always held strong opinions myself. I wish you could hear her play the piano. Someday she will come to Blessing, I do hope and pray. Or when you come for my graduation, you will have the privilege of hearing her.

He stopped again. Was he saying too much about Elizabeth? How much would his mother read between the lines?

He stared at the paper, seeing Elizabeth's face without even making an effort. Hearing her laugh, standing behind her, intoxicated by the scent of her hair. Rejoicing at seeing her after months of being content with letters.

Lord, if only she feels the same way. Lord God, all I ask for is a miracle.

He returned to his letter and, after sending special greetings to each in his family, signed his name and addressed the envelope. Before folding the paper, he added a P.S.

The cheese arrived yesterday, and you should have seen the delight on the faces of those who ordered from the school. "Better than candy" is what Mr. Ytterboe said.

Again, my love to you all.

T.

After dropping the letter in the outgoing mail pouch, he sighed. Was it relief at having finally done something he knew he should have done a week ago, or was it sadness and truly missing the family he had left behind?

He mentally squared his shoulders and headed for the pressroom. Time to start the run. And this edition carried this year's winners of the annual Christmas writing contest, which meant running double or perhaps even triple the normal run.

The holidays passed like an out-of-control freight train, leaving Thorliff feeling as though he'd been caught and carried on the cow catcher far beyond his station. Looking back he wished he'd pushed for some kind of an answer from Elizabeth, but then he comforted himself with the times they'd stared deep into each other's souls and enjoyed holding hands while skating on the pond. Watching her play the piano made the music even more glorious, and bringing her Christmas punch and spiced cider gave him a glimmer of the joy of service to someone he loved.

The pounding of the press that now ran a full eight to ten hours a day, sometimes five and six days a week, thundered a drumbeat for the words pouring from his pencil. He'd used the holidays to catch up on his novel, and now he could hardly leave it alone. He resented going to school, using any spare minute to finish his assignments so he could devote as much time in the evenings to writing as possible. He'd even taken to bringing supper to the office to avoid wasting a minute.

"Good night, then, Thorliff. You'll remember to bank the furnace?" Phillip leaned against the doorjamb in the office they'd created for Thorliff by partitioning off part of the new addition. Early in the fall,

Phillip had bought out the business next door and had expanded the newspaper office, so they now had a folding room, a shipping room, more storage, and Thorliff's office. Phillip was also talking about purchasing more machinery.

Thorliff looked up from his papers. "I won't forget. I just want to finish this chapter."

"I know, and get started on the next. Good thing you are young and strong to get by on the little sleep that you do."

"When I do go to bed, I sleep hard and fast."

"Amazing that the paper is all printed and it is not even nine o'clock yet."

Thorliff struggled with being polite, as he was anxious to get back to his story.

"Good night, then."

"Good night." He bent his head and was immediately engrossed in his story.

December 26, 1896
Dearest Thorliff,

How we would have loved to have you surprise us for Christmas. Astrid kept hoping you would do that, but then, she didn't realize you had sent your Christmas box on ahead, just in case. First of all, let me thank you for the lovely coat you sent me. I have not had a new wool coat in years, and the rich burgundy color makes me feel like royalty when I wear it. I tried to say it is much too fine for an old farm woman like me, but your far took me to task for such hogwash, as he called it. Astrid and Andrew will be sending their own letters, but I wish you could have seen the look of total awe on Astrid's face when she opened your box. She fingered the doll's garments and caressed her curly hair gently, as if touched too indelicately, the doll might disintegrate. "Do you think I might ever look like that?" she asked me, and what could I say? She is far more lovely already, and I am certain I am not a bit prejudiced.

Your far and I look downright stylish when we dress up for church, him with his new coat and me with mine.

There was such an empty corner where Metiz used to always sit. Her little stool is still there, but no one else took it over. I miss her every day but comfort myself with pictures in my mind of her and Agnes telling tall tales and entertaining others around them with stories of all of us in Blessing. So we have one more angel watching over us, which we surely need.

Before Christmas we had a big party, the first in a long time. Knute outbid everyone for Dorothy's decorated box. I thought we might be preparing for a wedding, but Anji tells me Dorothy is still mourning the loss of Swen. Little Swen is a happy baby. I got to hold him in church last Sunday, and when I rubbed his little back, he fell asleep right in my arms. Such a precious little one.

We had no baby for the manger this year. Swen is the youngest in Blessing, and he's too busy to lie still in a manger.

Anji thought her baby might be here for that, but she is still "waddling around," as she calls it. Her two little girls are doing well in school; they had started learning English before they came. Astrid and Ellie took them under their wings and made sure no one harassed them. As if you don't know who the only one to act like that would be!

Not much other news around here but for the change in Hildegunn Valders. She finally gave in and spoke to me after all this time. God does answer prayer, and I am only more convinced again that He has a wonderful sense of humor. I think by the end of her silence some of the more irreverent men were laying bets on who was stronger, me with my smiles and cheerful greetings or her with her sullen face and terrible unhappiness. Now we wait to see what God will do next. Perhaps He'll turn the Valderses' home into one of love and not judgment. Lest you laugh, remember, our God is always about the business of miracles.

I do hope your Christmas was both enjoyable and blessed. It is hard for me to believe that you will be graduating in June. The years have flown by so fast. Will we even recognize you? I am rejoicing that God has given you such amazing gifts in writing and blessing you with friends at school and in Northfield.

Thank you for sending us your newspaper all the time like you do. I feel I have a peek into your life from the articles you write and, as always, your stories. Each gets better and better. Pastor Solberg sends his greetings. He so often says he always knew you had a fertile brain, but these days you surprise even him.

I must finish and get to bed. The wolves have been howling of late, but we never see any signs of Wolf's tracks now that Metiz is gone. Tell Elizabeth thank-you for the receipt for cough syrup. It is most effective. I will write her myself but thought you might also thank her for me.

All my love,
Your mother

April 1, 1897
Dear Elizabeth,

I think spring might be on its way. Although we have had plenty of snow, you can smell a change on the breeze. I am glad to hear of your new techniques for surgery and that the weeks you spent in Baltimore were worthy of your time and effort. I wish you'd take long train rides more often so I can get epistles like that last one to read. If you weren't a doctor, you would make a good writer too. Your descriptions are superb.

My family has said they will come for graduation whether all the spring fieldwork gets done or not. I know Onkel Lars and some of the other neighbors will help out if need be. On one hand I wish I could go back with them to help out again, but on the other, I know that I am needed here.

I had the strangest dream last night. I dreamed that I had moved back to Blessing and started a newspaper. I talked of that years ago but had given up the idea.

I know that Dr. Morganstein dreams of sending her trained doctors out to areas that have no medical care. Have you ever thought of the plains of North Dakota as a possibility?

Your dreamer,
Thorliff

CHAPTER TWENTY-NINE

Blessing, North Dakota
April 1897

"I think it might rain forever." Ingeborg sighed.

"Only seems that way." Haakan looked up from reading the *Northfield News* that Thorliff sent them every week. "If the river doesn't open up, we are going to have heavier flooding this year."

"Ja, that is one advantage of a dry year—the river doesn't flood."

Winter had locked the land longer than usual, and now with all this warm rain, the snow was melting too quickly, compounding the problem since the Red River flowed north to ice-blocked Lake Winnipeg.

"I'm glad we moved the dry cows and young stock over to Solbergs' today. Hopefully he's high enough. He said he had enough hay for a few days, but we should take some of ours over tomorrow."

"You took the horses too, right?" At his nod, she did the same. "Good thing the cheese house is so close to empty, though I hate cleaning out all that mud again."

"We could move to Montana."

"Haakan Bjorklund, get that thought right out of your head. I'm not starting over again at this time of my life."

"I sure know how to rile you, don't I?" His eyes twinkled through the wisps of pipe smoke that circled his head. He beckoned to her. "Come on over and read with me." He patted his knee. "You can sit right here."

Ingeborg did as he suggested and leaned her head on his shoulder. "I wish we had driven the milk cows up in the haymow tonight."

"We'll have time for that in the morning if the river keeps rising."

The dog barking woke them while blackness still covered the land. When Barney didn't stop, Haakan threw back the covers. "Wonder what it could be this time?" He stepped into icy water. "Ingeborg! We are being flooded! Get as much food and household things upstairs as you can."

"Where are you going?" They could hear the cows bawling.

"Out to the barn to let the cows loose, no time for the haymow. Oh, why didn't I do that last night?"

"If the flood is high enough to have water in the house, you cannot make it to the barn." While she spoke she grabbed clothing off the hooks and bedding and headed for the stairs.

"Andrew, Astrid, come help!"

The two came thudding down the stairs.

"Get all the food you can and take the lamps. Put the dog and cat up there too."

"I'll go help Pa." Andrew sat down to pull on his boots.

"No, I don't think he can get to the barn, and he is taller than you." The water already had moved up toward her ankles.

"But my chickens!" Astrid started for the door.

"No! They are already gone." Ingeborg handed her the armloads she carried. "You stay there and run things up and down the stairs."

Andrew snatched the cat off the back of the horsehair sofa and yelped when the terrified animal dug its claws in his arm. He handed the cat to Astrid. "Be careful," he warned and rubbed the claw marks to take out the sting.

"Here, let's get the trunk upstairs. That's the only thing we can't replace." Ingeborg and Andrew each took a handle.

Haakan, dripping muddy water, pushed open the back door. "God forgive me, I couldn't get the doors open." He scrubbed his hands over his face, shaking his head all the while. For a moment he leaned against the wall, then took down all the coats and, without another word, handed them to Ingeborg and took up the handle of the trunk in her place.

"I'll cook what I can," she said, handing off the coats to Astrid, who'd come back down for more. Then throwing dry wood from the top of the box into the stove, she retrieved the ham and eggs from the pantry and, with water creeping up her legs, went about cooking what they had, her prayers for their safety and those around them a litany running through her mind. While she did that, the others carried the bed upstairs, the spinning wheel, and the Singer sewing machine. *Please, God,* she prayed as she went on cooking, boiling the remaining eggs and the potatoes, *save the livestock we moved yesterday. Protect all the people of Blessing and up and down the river. Thank you that Haakan built us a sturdy house. Though we've ridden out other floods, this is the worst so far.* Andrew and Haakan picked up the rocking chairs and kitchen chairs, pots and pans and dishes. When the water reached the firebox and doused the fire, Ingeborg carried what she could up the stairs along with the others. While there wasn't much room to move around, at least they had saved what they could.

"Let's eat while the food is hot. This might be our last warm meal for some time."

"Another of those things I planned on doing—putting a small stove up here. So many things . . ."

Ingeborg covered Haakan's hand with hers. "But all that really matters is right here. Please say grace." She waited so long that she began to doubt he could pray right now, but just as she opened her mouth, he began.

"Father God, please forgive me for not taking better care of all that thou hast given us. Had I listened to your prompting, more of our livestock might have been spared. Now I beg of you, protect us all from the ravages of this flood—our friends, our families, and all those who are fighting the torrents. I thank thee for this food and the loving hands that prepared it. And most of all, I thank thee for thy great mercies. In Jesus' name we pray, amen."

Day lightened the sky, but the rain continued, no longer in sheets but heavier than a drizzle. Ingeborg moved her sewing machine to under the window in Astrid's room and took out the dress she'd been sewing for her daughter. Lowering the presser foot, she rocked the treadle into motion with her foot and sewed the seam.

Astrid, with the cat draped over her shoulders, leaned against her mother.

"Did God need my chickens and our cows in heaven, Mor?" She sniffed and wiped under her tear-swollen eyes.

"I . . . ah . . ." *Lord, why does she have to ask such hard questions?*

"Astrid, could you please find that last paper that came from Thorliff?" Haakan looked underneath a stack of bedding. "We brought up all the stuff from the kitchen, so it must be here somewhere."

Andrew sat cross-legged on the floor, carefully using one of the gouges on his latest carving. "I saw it in with the dishes."

Astrid found the paper and handed it to her father. "You could read aloud to all of us. Please?"

"Good idea." So Haakan read, starting with the articles that carried Thorliff's byline.

"Far, do you think it is flooding in Northfield too?" Astrid sat at her father's feet, the cat curled asleep in her lap.

"It could be. But the Red River is different from the others. Northfield might not be getting all the rain we are either."

"I know. But when you look out the window, it seems all the whole world must be under water."

"Like in Noah's flood?" Andrew looked up from polishing his camel with a piece of deer antler.

"God promised not to flood the whole earth again, so I think we can be safely assured that is not what is happening." Haakan snapped the paper and folded it to make easier reading. He chose an article about the upcoming Easter concert to be put on by the orchestra and choir of St. Olaf and continued reading.

"Pa, do you think our house will stay where it belongs?" Astrid stared up at her father, fear pinching her mouth.

"It has before, and I believe it will again. That is why we must all continue to pray that God will keep it and us secure." He laid a hand on Astrid's head and drew her closer to his knee. "God has always been faithful, and He always will be."

Ingeborg hoped the children didn't hear the slight tremor in her husband's voice. Or was she only hearing her own?

The river continued to rise at a much slower pace through that day and the next. Through the windows they watched trees and dead cattle drift by, pieces of buildings, furniture, and wooden boxes. The water came halfway up the stairwell and no farther. Haakan and Ingeborg exchanged glances of relief when the same step remained visible.

"I was figuring the best way to get us all out on the roof," Haakan whispered when the children were both standing at the window looking out.

"Me too." Ingeborg shuddered. *Please, Lord, keep our house on the foundation.* That morning when they'd awakened, they realized that sometime during the night, Metiz' little house had floated away. They'd just been able to see the roof line before.

"Easter is tomorrow."

"I know." Ingeborg finished hemming the dress. "And this is what you would have been wearing to church." She held it up and gave it a shake to remove the loose threads.

"I sure could use a cup of hot coffee." Haakan stared out the window, a place he'd taken over.

"At least we have food. Others might not even have that." Ingeborg went to the north window and waved a dish towel out it to let those at the deaf school know they were all right. Kaaren waved back.

During the night the wind picked up, and by morning, the waves were breaking over the house. With each wave the house shuddered as if it might be rent asunder from its foundation. Water leaked through the shingles in myriad places, and they used all the bowls and pots and pans to catch the dripping water.

"Come, let us pray together." Haakan gathered them on top of the mattress from his and Ingeborg's bed. Another wave crashed against the roof, and Astrid let out a shriek, muffling it in the bedding.

Ingeborg gathered her into her arms and sat rocking. "Heavenly Father, you are our refuge in the storm," she began.

"Protect us, keep our house solid on the foundation you helped us lay. Calm us, comfort us. We know we are your children," Haakan continued. He flinched as another wave broke on the roof. "Guess this just shows how tightly we shingled this, although I never thought it would be keeping out waves, eh, Andrew?"

Andrew nodded and bit his lip, his eyes wide as he glanced at one of the windows.

The dog whined and snaked his way into Andrew's lap, giving the boy a quick kiss on the chin.

The house shuddered with another onslaught from the waves that splashed up on the windows, black and gray.

"Don't worry about the windows, son. The waves are hitting the roof instead of the glass. Good thing we set the house at the angle we did." Haakan patted Andrew on the shoulder. The glance he sent his wife let her know how deep his gratitude ran.

She nodded in return and continued with her hemming. "And so we continue to pray. We have our very lives to be thankful for and so much else." She hoped she sounded more certain than she felt.

God, help us. Keep our windows safe from debris and from the terrible waves. Ingeborg hid her fears by laying her cheek on Astrid's head. "Come, let us sing."

So they sang hymns, then "Yankee Doodle," "Red River Valley," and a song about the Shenandoah River, although Ingeborg wondered if that one was appropriate considering their river was causing all the problems. When they ran out of songs, they played hide the thimble and button, button, who's got the button, along with guessing games and Bible quizzes. They worked on spelling words and arithmetic, and everyone took turns reading when one person's voice gave out.

"Tell us a story, Mor," Astrid asked. So Ingeborg told them of the early days when they came to Dakota Territory; of the time Andrew got lost in the high grass and Wolf saved him; of hunting and fishing when the game was so abundant; of starting the school with Tante Kaaren teaching all the children.

And when Ingeborg played out, Haakan took over with tales of felling timber in the north woods of Minnesota and his travels as a young man in a new land.

Haakan and Andrew even carded wool after Astrid gave them a refresher lesson. Ingeborg spun it, and both she and Astrid kept their knitting needles clicking and the sewing machine singing.

When the wind finally died down and the house was still standing firm, they cheered and sang praises.

Men came by in boats to check on the farmers, but the Bjorklunds stayed safe in their upstairs like most of the others, visiting with the boaters through the windows and sending the men on their way to those who really needed help.

"I have to go home." Thorliff stood in front of President Mohn's desk at St. Olaf College. "You've read of the floods in North Dakota?"

"I have, but what can you do?"

"Help clean up the mess. I'm sorry, sir, but my family needs me."

"How long will you be gone?"

"I don't know. I just know I have to go."

"How will you get there? The trains aren't crossing the Red River."

"I'll have to find a boat. Perhaps it will have begun to recede before I get there. We've never seen such flooding since we settled there in the valley."

"That's what I've heard. I cannot promise that you will graduate if you take this time off. I will have to discuss this with the board."

"I understand." Thorliff fought to keep his feet from carrying him out without permission.

"Do what you must, and God keep you. Don't do anything foolish. You can't help your family if you drown or something."

"I know. Thank you, sir." Thorliff gathered his books, let Mr. Inger-manson know he was leaving, and trotted down the hill. Perhaps for the last time. By the time he reached the newspaper office, he had a hard time catching his breath as he pushed open the front door, setting the bell to jingling.

"You are here early." Phillip glanced at the clock on the wall. "Are you all right?"

Thorliff nodded and sucked in a deep breath. "I got permission from Reverend Mohn to go home. He tried to talk me out of it, but I have to be there." He raked long fingers through his hair, standing it on end.

"But, Thorliff, what will you be able to do?" Phillip leaned forward in his chair.

"I just feel I have to be there. What good can I do them here?"

"If you stay here, they won't have to worry about you."

"They won't know I'm coming. There is no communication without boats. I'm sure our rowboat went sailing down the river at the first surge."

"Then how will—"

"I will find a boat in Grand Forks."

"Thorliff, I think you are cockeyed crazy. Wait until the river goes down and then go. That's when you will be able to help." Phillip threw his hands in the air. "All right. I see nothing I say will change your mind." He rose. "Do you have enough money?"

"Yes. Thank you."

"You'll take the morning train tomorrow?"

"Yes. I missed today's."

"Mohn is right. You should stay until—"

"I can't." Thorliff reached across the desk to shake his friend and employer's hand. "I'll be back as soon as I can." *I hope.*

CHAPTER THIRTY

The train stopped at Glyndon, Minnesota.

"Sorry, son, we can't go any farther. There's water over the track, and a train is already waiting ahead of us." The conductor shrugged as he pointed out the window. "Can't see it from here, but once you step outside . . ." He shook his head. "Never seen it so bad before."

"How long will we be stopped here?"

"I don't know. You can stay on board or go into town. As soon as the water recedes, we'll go on. 'Course they have to check the tracks first to make sure they aren't washed out or anything." The conductor continued on, making his announcement as he went along.

Thorliff stared out the window. From what he could see, the small hills showed green grass already shooting up, even though piles of snow still skirted the buildings where it had slid off roofs. But when he stepped off the train, he could see that muddy water covered the land ahead. The conductor hadn't exaggerated. Thorliff swung back up on the train and took out a textbook to study for the final exams he might never be taking. When he'd read the page three times and still had no idea what he'd been reading, he stared out the window. Had he acted in haste and run ahead of what God planned for him to do? He thought back to his decision to leave school. Had he prayed?

Of course I did, he firmly answered the questions in his head. But doubt loomed like the water ahead of them. *I prayed, all right, but was it for my family or for my decision to come now? Would God have me sitting on this train for a reason, or is this my own fault?* He could hear Reverend Mohn's question regarding the same. He'd been so sure he was doing the right thing. Yes, they needed him at home. Or would need him when he could get there. Calling himself all kinds of names, none of which were complimentary, he forced himself back to his textbook. Were there any trains running east from North Dakota? Of course not. They were stopped on the other side of the flood.

When darkness fell, he ate the last of the food Cook had packed for him and settled down for a long night. The conductor came by with blankets for those who'd chosen to remain on the train, and cushioning his head on his rolled-up coat, Thorliff fell into a restless slumber that wasn't much better than being awake.

Somewhere in the night he woke, thinking he heard Elizabeth calling his name. He snapped upright and then slumped back. He was not in Northfield. He was trapped on a train going nowhere. Pounding his fist on the wall seemed an appropriate response, but instead he slammed the seat and settled back down. If only he had asked Elizabeth to come with him. He hadn't written to her to inquire, because he wasn't sure how she would feel about making the long trip from Chicago. *If people start getting sick, I'll send her a letter immediately.* With that thought solid in his mind, he closed his eyes and willed himself back to sleep. He'd be no good for helping anyone if he didn't sleep.

In the morning he bought coffee and food in the dining car, hating to spend the money but knowing that he'd brought this on himself. He walked the streets of the small town in a slight drizzle, casting longing looks toward Blessing. As deep as the water was, where was his family? Were they safe? Would the house and barn stand against a flood of this magnitude?

Lord, forgive me for running ahead of you. When will I learn? But please, you are keeping them safe, aren't you? The conversation, although seeming one-sided, brought him comfort. He swung back up into the car where he'd left his satchel and settled back into his studies. Whenever the worries about home and family grew too loud to ignore, he took out his Bible and read again how God cared for the Israelites as they wandered in the wilderness. At the moment he had a fair idea how they must have felt.

A cheer broke out when the conductor came through the second day and announced they were checking the tracks to make sure the route to Grand Forks was clear. Trains would not be able to cross the bridge into Fargo yet, but the tracks heading north were water free.

Thank you, heavenly Father. Now get me to Blessing, please.

Getting to Grand Forks was easier than getting out of Grand Forks and on to Blessing. No one had a boat. All those that hadn't been carried off in the flood were being used in rescues on the swollen river. Much of Grand Forks was still under water, leaving Thorliff no place to stay. When he contacted one of the Lutheran pastors in town, the man invited him to share a room at the home of a member of his congregation who lived beyond the flood line.

"I should have stayed in Northfield until the trains were running again." Thorliff shook his head.

"Hindsight is always perfect," Pastor Ness said with a smile. "I know your father through Pastor Solberg. He speaks highly of all of you, and now I get to meet his prize pupil."

"Not much of a prize but eternally grateful for all he has done for me. Have you heard anything about the folks at Blessing?"

"Sorry, not a word, but the waters are receding rapidly, so perhaps tomorrow the train will run again. The tracks are high enough above the ground that they dry out more quickly than the rest of the land."

While it took two more days before the train ran across the river and north, Thorliff had never been so happy to see anything as the bedraggled town of Blessing. Mud covered the walls and roofs of all but the two-story houses and barns. Soddies lay in heaps of rubble.

"Thorliff!" Penny shouted his name as she ran to throw her arms around him. "Oh, they will be so happy to see you!"

"Everyone is all right?" Thorliff hugged her back and, glancing around, shook his head. "Where did you stay?"

"At the boardinghouse. Bridget took in any who needed help. We had a regular party up there." She rolled her eyes, telling him the time hadn't been all fun. "But we are safe and cleaning up to start over. That is all that counts. Livestock lost but not one man, woman, or child. Although I hear some are falling sick now that the flood is gone."

"I need to get on home. Any chance the telephone lines have come to Blessing yet?"

"No, but the telegraph is working again. Grand Forks has telephones though, so who knows, perhaps one of these days we'll have all kinds of newfangled gadgets here too."

"I hope so. They are real handy. Will you be able to save anything from your store?"

"Some, I'm sure. Canned goods and things in glass or tins. Some things we'll be able to clean up, like boots and perhaps materials if I can wash the mud out. One thing about our rich river mud, it stains like permanent dye. I got the kitchen stove cleaned out and working though so we can cook the food we can find. Thanks be to God that we canned so much last summer."

Thorliff nodded and kept from shifting from one foot to the other with an act of will and his mother's insistence on good manners.

"I know you want to get going out there. If you walk fast enough, you might not sink in past your ankles." She patted his arm. "Sure good to see you."

"Ja, God bless." Thorliff headed out, his coat folded over his shoulder since the sun seemed to be trying to make up for lost time in drying the land. Several times he slipped and slid, barely keeping upright. Every so often he leaned against a friendly fence post to scrape the pounds of mud from his boots, gray black mud and grasses hanging from fence wires and piled around the bottom of posts mute testimony to the recent submersion. Trees wore dresses of gray black, pitch cleansing the wounds of missing branches as spring leaves forced their way through the coating.

The stench of putrid death rose like the steam from puddles. Instead of the verdant fragrance of spring, rotting carcasses stank in the fields to feed crows and other scavengers.

Silence, other than the slop of his feet as he strode the once leveled lane, lay across the land. Ahead he could see the black mud line above the windows on their house and up on the roof of the barn. But at least the buildings were standing and people were working. The joy of that brought tears to the back of his throat. "Thank you, Father, thank you. I have a family still, and I was right in that they need me." If he could have run, he would have, but instead he scraped the mud off again and plowed forward.

A dog barking brought everyone's attention to see him coming.

"Thorliff!" Astrid dropped the broom she was using to clean the mud off the house and tore across the yard, the dog running and barking along with her. "You came!" But when she tried to stop her feet slipped in the mud, and without Thorliff's grabbing her, she would have slid right into him. She wrapped both arms around his middle and clung like lichen on the sides of the trees. "I'm making you all messy," she muttered into his chest.

"Who cares." Thorliff hugged her and grinned at the others running to meet him. "Careful, I can't catch everyone at once." Barney danced around Thorliff, barking and half growling, not sure if he should know this person or not.

Ingeborg hugged both Thorliff and Astrid, who still had not let go, with Andrew clinging right behind her. "What are you doing here? You're not out of school yet."

Thorliff leaned back to look in his mother's face. "I had to know if you were still alive."

At his words, Astrid burst into tears and tightened her grip on his waist. Thorliff fought the burning in his own eyes, and the tears streaming down his mother's face almost undid him.

"Thanks be to God, no one drowned in Blessing." Haakan clapped his arm around Thorliff's shoulders and the other around Andrew so that they formed a circle with Astrid safe in the middle.

"Hush, Barney." Andrew's voice broke as he commanded the dog. "This is Thorliff, and he is family."

Yes, thank God, we are still family. All of us together. Thorliff recognized the new crevasses on his father's face. Worry did that to a man. "It was bad?"

"Terrible. Still is. But we are alive, and eventually we will plant crops as usual. We still have the teams. I sent them west along with the dry and young stock, so we have something to begin with again."

Thorliff listened to the words and realized the loss behind them. There'd been no mention of the milking herd.

"The water came up so fast in the middle of the night, there was no time to escape. Barney woke us up with his barking. If it hadn't been for him, we'd have lost more of the household things. As it is, there is a lot to clean." Ingeborg hugged him again. "I have never been so happy to see anyone in my entire life."

Thorliff looked over her head to his father. Haakan stood, his normally straight shoulders now rounded forward as if the burden were so heavy he could no longer stand straight. Was there something besides the flood? "Far, are you all right?"

Haakan gave an almost imperceptible shake of his head with a slight glance toward the barn. Cow carcasses littered the area in front of the open barn door. Thorliff fought the gagging in his throat.

"What are you going to do?"

"Burn them. Can't dig a hole deep enough. It fills with water fast as we can dig, and I got to get the barn cleaned out. Kerosene will work, soon as I get enough. Drying wood too, so we can use that."

"My chickens died too." Astrid looked toward where the hen house used to be.

"Looks like I should have brought chickens and pigs and—"

"Grain to feed them. Heard tell some farmers west of here are shipping hay and grain from what they have left to help us out. All our stock is still over to Solbergs'. Pastor ran some up in his haymow, and the rest made it through on a haystack. Good thing we had plenty of hay last year. It's saving us now."

Ingeborg took his hand. "Come, you must be hungry. Soup is ready, and I baked the first bread just this morning."

The smell of mud and wet wood didn't stop them from eating and talking around mouths full of food. "I need to go check on Sam's family this afternoon," Ingeborg said after refilling the coffee cups. "And the Valderses. They are both down with terrible vomiting and the runs. I have so little to offer. I just don't know what to do for them."

"Perhaps Elizabeth will come. And bring medical supplies."

Ingeborg stopped by the newly scrubbed stove. "That would be a godsend but a lot to ask. Even if she could just tell me what to do."

"I'll get a letter ready later, and you can mail it when you are at the store." Thorliff said. "I believe she will want to come."

After dinner Thorliff wrapped a bandanna dipped in vinegar around his nose and mouth like Haakan did, and the two headed out to the barn. The stench overwhelmed even the vinegar smell, but he kept his meal in place in spite of a bout of gagging. They wrapped chains around the cows' legs, then hitched the horses to the chains to drag out the bodies.

"If we had a ramp, we could drag them up into the pile," Thorliff suggested later in the afternoon.

"Good idea." Haakan unwrapped the chains and drove the horses back to the side corral to remove their harnesses. "I've got some planks that didn't float off because they were in the barn. Some wet, but that don't matter. Get the hammers out of the toolbox on the steam engine."

Thorliff went to do as told, realizing yet again how disturbed his father was. Any other time, Haakan would have thought of the ramp. And already had it built.

"Lord, please take care of my pa. He isn't himself, and this scares me worse than the flood."

CHAPTER THIRTY-ONE

That evening Thorliff retrieved his satchel, dug out paper and pencil, and sat at the table to compose a letter to Elizabeth. He hoped she would be agreeable to coming.

April 26, 1897
Dear Elizabeth,
The trains are running again, and the people here are trying to clean up the horrendous mess and get on with their lives, but we need a doctor. Dr. Morganstein said she was training doctors to go where there are none, and we are in desperate need right now. People are near death. Please come. You can send a telegraph as to when you will arrive. Send to Thorliff Bjorklund in Blessing, North Dakota. We have no medical supplies here, and my mor is doing her best.

Yours,
Thorliff

Between flood cleanup and increasing numbers of very ill people, Thorliff sometimes wished he had stayed in Northfield. But he knew he was where he had to be. As the land dried, getting from one house to another became easier. The men worked on the machinery, scraping, cleaning, and oiling. The women and children scrubbed houses inside and out. Hjelmer brought in a cattle car of livestock donated by Minnesota farmers, along with hay and grain to feed them. And Penny restocked the store as soon as it was clean enough to hold the merchandise.

Every day Thorliff hoped to hear from Elizabeth. How long could a letter take? But when he checked the calendar, only five days had passed since he'd sent his letter, days that felt like weeks or even months. While waiting to hear from Elizabeth, he received a letter from Reverend Mohn telling him of the board's decision to allow him to return to take his examinations as soon as he was able.

When he brought the letter home to read to his family, he found his mother lying in bed.

"I'll be all right if I can just sleep awhile." But her greenish white face told him otherwise. He saddled one of the horses and headed for Penny's store to send a telegram.

"I was just coming to you with this." Uncle Olaf waved a paper when he saw Thorliff dismount in front of the store.

"Mange takk." Thorliff read the brief telegraph to himself, then aloud. "Arriving on the morning train Stop Will need wagon Stop Love Elizabeth Stop." He thumped the man on the shoulder. "You brought good tidings. We are getting a doctor here to help, and she brings medicines."

"Good thing, if she gets here in time. My Goodie took sick this morning. Don't look too good for the baby. He was born just before the flood, you know." Olaf shook his head. "Don't think I can take too much more of this. If the flood wasn't bad enough, now everybody taking so sick." He turned and headed back toward his house, his back more bent than Haakan's.

～≈≈≈

"When did your mother get sick?" Elizabeth stood at Ingeborg's bedside studying her patient.

"She kept on going until yesterday. She has used up all her energy taking care of the others." Thorliff knelt by his mother's bed. "Mor, Elizabeth is here. She will take care of the others." *And you. Father God, please don't take my mother.* "You don't need to worry about them now. Just rest."

Ingeborg nodded but barely, as if that took too much effort. Her lips twitched in what might have been a smile.

Elizabeth sat on the edge of the bed and took her hand. "I am glad to meet you, though these surely aren't the circumstances either one of us would have chosen."

"A . . . Astrid?"

Elizabeth glanced up at Thorliff, who now stood slightly behind her with his hand on her shoulder.

"She's a bit better, Mor."

"Good." Her fingers clenched Elizabeth's and relaxed.

"Mor?" Thorliff fell to his knees.

"She is only sleeping. Rest and plenty of fluids are what she needs." She led the way back to the kitchen. "You have been boiling all the water you use in the house?"

"All that we drink, ja."

"No, you must boil all the water. For dishes, for washing your hands, for cooking." She glanced around the kitchen. "This room was under water?"

"Ja, all but the upstairs."

"How awful. What about your well?"

"It is sealed since we got the windmill, so no animals or trash can get down in it."

"Good. How deep is it?"

"Ten, fifteen feet, if that much."

"Still, you better boil all the water. Use carbolic acid to clean out the reservoir on the stove, and you need to boil all the dishes and silverware."

Thorliff gave her a questioning look.

"I know your mother keeps a clean house, but germs live on. And germs make us sick. Something so small we can only see it with a microscope can and does kill us."

"I will begin to boil, then."

"You have glass jars?"

"Ja."

"Boil them first and pour the clean water into them."

"Like canning?"

"Yes. What other families are the sickest?"

"I'm not sure. I've been taking care of them here for the last couple of days. Far and Andrew are helping some of the others."

Elizabeth thought for a bit. "This is what we will do. You must get your mother and Astrid to drink every fifteen minutes, even if you are spooning water into them. The more frequently the better. Do you have any beef to boil?"

He shook his head.

"Chicken?"

"No. The flood took everything. My uncle Hjelmer went to Minneapolis to buy a boxcar of supplies for all of us. He should be back yet today."

"I could have brought ham or . . ." Elizabeth shook her head. "No sense looking back. I will take care of things here, and you go tell the others to boil everything. Just like I told you."

"I will go to Tante Kaaren's first and send Trygve to the others. I told Far I would take care of Mor and Astrid."

"All right. Will they believe Trygve?"

"Yes. He will say you said to do so. Most of them know of you because of my letters home."

"Good. Please fill that kettle with water so I can begin the boiling. Jars, where would I find them?"

"In the basement, where we still have standing water. I'll get them."

After getting the jars for her, Thorliff flew over the small pasture where grass was already poking green spears through the layer of mud.

Trygve listened carefully, then took off for the Baards', running as if wolves were after him.

"I can send Ilse over to help you since we sent all of the students home early." Kaaren, who so recently had been lying sick in bed herself, lifted the lids and put more wood in the fire. "Sophie is well enough to help here."

"How's Gracie?"

"On the mend. George is still bad."

"Ilse will leave him?"

"I can make him drink while she is gone." She shook her head. "While I'm thanking God no one died here, so many others have. And from what I hear, Blessing isn't as hard hit as some of the other communities."

"I have to get back. Make sure you boil everything."

"I will, and thank your Elizabeth for coming. I so look forward to meeting her."

Not that she's my Elizabeth, but . . . He waved from the door. *My Elizabeth, how I wish she would be my Elizabeth.*

Haakan brought home two chickens from the relief train and within an hour had them boiling, overriding the rank flood stench that permeated the house.

"Thank you for coming," he said to Elizabeth after Thorliff introduced them. "The train brought coal too so that people can cook again. We were so fortunate that all of our wood didn't float away. So many things we take for granted, like wood to burn, dry wood that is, and chicken for supper."

"So true. I have a suggestion, Mr. Bjorklund."

He nodded.

"What if we bring Astrid downstairs to share the bed with Mrs. Bjorklund? That will make caring for them both easier."

"Of course, Doctor. Anything else?"

"We must get the word out to all of Blessing that boiling all utensils and dishes is as important as boiling drinking and cooking water. That everyone drink only boiled water, that those who are ill need to drink boiled water and broth, as much as can be poured into them. Tea made of peppermint will help calm the digestive tract. I brought a big bag of leaves. And sunshine and fresh air will help restore them also."

"I will take care of that. Would you be willing to write up instructions? Penny could post them at the store, and I know Pastor Solberg would read them on Sunday."

"I could make copies," Andrew offered.

"I will write out the instructions."

"Now, what can I do for Ingeborg?"

"Make her drink more."

The next two days passed with Elizabeth spending part of her time going from farm to farm and making recommendations in the care of the sick.

"I'm hungry," Astrid said the following morning, struggling to sit up. Elizabeth rushed to help her, holding her while Thorliff plumped a pillow behind her.

"That's the best news I've heard in a long time." Thorliff stroked his little sister's hair.

"I'll get you some broth."

"Can I have a piece of bread?"

"Broth first and then bread." Elizabeth stood and went to the kitchen.

"Who is that?" Astrid whispered.

"Dr. Elizabeth Rogers."

"Your Elizabeth?"

Thorliff nodded and shrugged at the same time. "My friend, Miss—er—Dr. Rogers, yes."

Elizabeth returned with two cups of broth and two spoons. "Here, you help Astrid with that, and I'll give some more to your mother."

Sitting on the edge of the bed, Elizabeth touched Ingeborg's arm. "Mrs. Bjorklund, listen to me. If you want to get better, you have to swallow this." Elizabeth held the spoon to Ingeborg's mouth. She waited and finally Ingeborg's mouth opened, and she swallowed.

Father, please, she is so weak. Thorliff didn't dare look at either his mother or Astrid for the certainty they would see the fear in his eyes.

Astrid looked over at her mother in the bed beside her. "Is Mor . . ."

"She is getting better just like you."

"Good." Astrid curled over on her side and laid her cheek on her hands. "God, please make my mor better." Her eyes drifted closed almost before all the words were out of her mouth.

"Please, God, let it be so." Thorliff's words fell soft on the spring breeze that drifted through the open window.

That night when Elizabeth and Thorliff changed shifts at the bedside, he asked, "Is Mor any better?"

"I don't think so, but she is no worse either. That is a good thing."

Thorliff sighed. "She is a strong woman, my mor, and a fighter." Staring down at the pale face on the pillows, he fought the tears that threatened. *Please, God, you said that by the stripes of your Son, we are healed. Let it be so, here and now. Let your Word be so.*

"Call me if you need me." Elizabeth rose and offered him her chair.

"I will." Thorliff took the hand she held out and clasped it to his cheek. "Thank you."

She'd not been gone long when Haakan drifted in. "Any change?"

"She's holding her own."

"I could take this shift. I'm awake anyway."

"You sit here, and I'll go get more broth."

Haakan sat and took his wife's hand in his. The stoop of his shoulders and the weariness in his eyes smote Thorliff right in the heart. His pa looked like he'd aged ten years in the last week. He watched as Haakan's lips began to move in what Thorliff realized was nearly continuous prayer.

Surely God was listening. Surely.

He returned with cup and spoon and offered them to his father, then took his place on the other side. They had moved Astrid back to her own bed that evening.

"Far, you look done in. Go on to bed."

"Can't sleep anyhow. Close my eyes, and I see those cows drowning in the barn when I could have saved them. I thought to move them west too and didn't do it. God forgive me. He tried to help me, and I ignored him."

Thorliff closed his eyes, prayers fluttering upward as though borne on eagles' wings. "He says He forgives, no matter what. That's what you've always told me, you and Mor and Pastor Solberg. The Scriptures never lie."

"I know that. My head knows that. I've been reading and rereading all the passages I know. But somehow I just can't let this go. I thank Him for saving us, but my prayers don't even make it to the ceiling."

"You got to have faith, Far, you've got to."

"And now Ingeborg, if . . ." He spooned more broth into her mouth. Thorliff closed his eyes. *What do I say? What do I do?*

Her only movement was the faint motion of her throat as the broth trickled down.

Some time later Thorliff caught himself nodding off and jerked upright. Haakan lay back in the chair on the other side of the bed, gentle snores puffing his lips. Other than that, the silence in the room made Thorliff close his eyes again. *Please, God.* He forced himself to look at his mother, fear gnawing at his mind like a snarl of rats. Was she gone? He studied the bedclothes, relief pouring through him. While the rise of her chest was so faint as to scarcely move the covers, they did move. She was breathing.

He picked up the spoon and the now-turned-cold cup of broth and, ordering his hand to hold steady, held the full spoon to his mother's lips. "Please, Mor, drink this. You have to drink!" He put all the force of his love into the words, at the same time his mind screaming to his Lord for help. While she swallowed, albeit faintly, part of the liquid dribbled down her chin. Thorliff held another spoonful, tipping it slowly, but the same thing happened again. He mopped her chin with the bed sheet. *Is this doing any good, Father? Where are you?*

Haakan jerked awake with a snort. "Is . . . is she . . . ?"

"About the same."

"Here, let me try. You go on to bed."

Thorliff handed over the cup and spoon, then took the cup back. "I'll go heat this up again. Talk to her, Far. We've got to keep her here."

Haakan gave his son a questioning glance, then looked back to his wife. "Ingeborg Bjorklund, you cannot die. You hear me? You got to live." He swallowed and knelt by the bed, clasping her flaccid hand. "Please, God, don't take her. We—I need her here, for a long time yet." He kissed her hand and smoothed her hair back. "Hear me, Inge? You got to want to live."

Thorliff ignored the tears blurring his vision and turned away to fetch warm broth. He returned in a couple of minutes to see Haakan sitting back in his chair, still clutching his wife's hand.

"Here, Far. Try some more." He handed Haakan the cup again. "Unless you want me to do it." Thorliff felt his own tears burning again when he saw the tear tracks on his father's face.

"Haakan?" The name came faintly.

"Yes. Inge, my dear Inge." The spoon and cup clattered to the floor at the same time as Haakan's knees hit the braided rug.

"Ja, I . . . I . . ." The pause caught at Thorliff, but she continued. "I am still here."

"Ja, you are. Please stay. Don't leave me."

"I . . . I . . ." A slight smile tugged at her chapped lips. "I will."

"Drink more." Tears rained down Haakan's cheeks as he spooned more broth, the shaking of his hand causing some to dribble down her face. "Sorry."

"It's . . . all . . . right."

His mother spoke. For the first time in three days, his mother spoke. Was that a bit of color in her cheeks?

Thorliff took a handkerchief from his back pocket and, after wiping his eyes, blew his nose. "Praise God."

"Ja, praise God."

The next Sunday as many of the people of Blessing as were able gathered for the regular service at the church.

"Welcome. We are gathered in the name of the Father and the

Son and the Holy Ghost, amen." Pastor Solberg glanced around the congregation, his smile reaching every soul there gathered. "We will sing 'O God, Our Help in Ages Past,' for we have indeed been delivered from a stormy blast."

Not all of us, Ingeborg thought as she glanced around. Many families were missing a member, thanks to the cholera scourge. *And I . . . I was almost one of them.* She raised her head to catch Haakan watching her. "I'm fine." She whispered the words when she'd rather have shouted them to the heavens. Now she truly understood what weak meant. Weak before had meant just birthing a baby, but there was a rope of joy in giving birth that there hadn't been when she was too weak to even swallow. Never would she have thought she might have to force herself to swallow broth.

She joined her voice with the others, noticing after a few bars that singing took strength too. Like several others, she sat back down at the end of verse one, waving away Haakan's concern.

After a sermon, short by normal standards since Pastor Solberg had been one of those struck down, and communion had been served, he leaned on the pulpit and took a deep breath.

"I never thought leading worship would wear me out, but thanks be to God, I am still here to do so. Our thanks to each one of you who helped us through this vile illness, and special thanks belong to Dr. Rogers. Please stand and accept our hearty thank-you." He nodded to Elizabeth, who rose and returned his smile. When he began clapping, the others joined in—hesitantly at first, after all, they were in church— then with full accord.

When Elizabeth sat back down after nodding her acknowledgment, she whispered to Thorliff, "Why didn't you warn me?"

"I didn't know."

Pastor Solberg raised his hands, the tremors visible only to those closest to the front. "Now the Lord bless and keep thee, the Lord make his face to shine upon thee and give thee His peace, in the name of the Father and the Son and the Holy Spirit, now and forever, amen."

Ingeborg felt herself swaying and caught hold of Haakan's arm.

"I told you that you shouldn't be out yet." He wrapped his other arm around her waist.

"Maybe not, but I wouldn't miss church this morning for anything. To think there was no service at all last Sunday." She shook her head. "Pastor must have been terribly sick."

"Not as sick as you were."

"That's because she took care of everyone else until she keeled over." Elizabeth moved closer to Ingeborg and lowered her voice as they made their way out of the sanctuary. "You might want to consider taking it easy."

Ingeborg both smiled and nodded in a small motion and leaned more heavily on Haakan's arm. She caught a look between Elizabeth and Haakan. "And don't you two go ganging up on me." When Thorliff cleared his throat, she added, "You three. It feels wonderful to be out and about."

"Mor." Astrid skidded to a stop. "Can—" She stopped at the look her mother gave her and started again. "May Ellie come home with us? We are working on a play for school, and I thought maybe Thorliff would help us."

"I s'pose. Ask Goodie if—"

Haakan squeezed her arm. "Not today. You are not cooking for a group today."

"Oh." Ingeborg glanced up at her husband to see concern wrinkling the space between his eyebrows. Usually they had a houseful of company on Sundays, but not since the flood. She caught a sigh before it flew to other ears. *Lord, please give me the patience to get well at your speed, not mine, and thank you for a man who cares like my Haakan does.*

They stopped to talk to several other families on the way to the wagon. Kaaren was still home nursing young Samuel, who'd been the sickest in their family, and Penny stopped to visit for only a minute.

"I told Bridget I would come help serve dinner. Mrs. Sam still isn't as well as she could be, and Henry is still doing poorly too. I do hope we never go through anything like this again."

On the ride home Ingeborg turned to Elizabeth. "Isn't it strange how the cholera attacks one person and not another?"

312

"Like with other diseases, usually the very young and the very old go first. The human body can throw off a lot of disease if it gets enough rest, good food, and clean drinking water. I think we are just beginning to learn where illnesses come from. The more I read about the germ theory, the more I wonder how much we don't yet know."

Haakan cleared his throat. "I, for one, want to say again our thanks. Not just for us but for the whole community. This cholera epidemic just shows even more clearly how much we need a good doctor close by. You saved lives here, and we will never forget it."

Ingeborg slid her hand under his arm and leaned slightly against his shoulder. She knew he was thinking of her when he spoke. Thinking back, she realized how close she had come to death. The light had beckoned her, but Haakan's voice had called her back. She'd heard the pleading, the agony as he called her name. How could she leave him if she had a choice? If she spoke of this to Elizabeth, would she understand, or was it all a figment of her imagination? Sometimes illness brought on delirium. *One day I'll know the answer,* she promised herself. *When God figures the time is right.*

On Tuesday the men took a break from cleaning up the mud-encrusted machinery.

"Good to see stock back in the pasture." Lars leaned on the fence rails.

"Ja." Haakan lifted his hat to stroke his hair back and resettled it where it belonged.

Lars glanced over his shoulder. "We got a lot to be thankful for."

Haakan nodded, but the furrows remained between his eyebrows.

"Can't keep stewing over what might have been."

"You been talking with Ingeborg?"

Lars shook his head. "No need. How many years we been working together now?"

"Ja, I know." Haakan sucked on his teeth. "Just that—"

"Pa!" Andrew called from the barn. "Old Maple, she's starting to have her calf."

The two men turned and ambled over to the open barn door and into the box stalls where the old caramel-colored cow, one of the earliest they'd bought, paced the stall, tail twitching. She lay down, then pushed to her feet again.

"You think she's all right?" Andrew stroked the cow's muzzle and rubbed her throat. She stood a bit for his attentions, then resumed her pacing, checking out each corner and the stall door. "She'd rather be out in the pasture, I think." Andrew dipped pieces of hay out of the water bucket in the corner rack.

"She'd pick the muddiest low land and get herself all mired in. Perhaps even lose the calf. No, she stays here," Haakan said.

"Well, I better be getting on home. Kaaren will have supper ready. You take good care of that cow, Andrew. She'll calm down the way you keep petting her." Lars headed out the barn door.

Just then Ingeborg called them for supper.

"I'll stay here," Andrew said.

"No. She'll be a while yet. She knows what she's doing, not like a dumb young heifer."

The two of them walked up to the house.

"Will be good to have a cow to milk again, huh, Far?"

"Ja, that it will."

After washing up, Haakan sat down at the table where Thorliff was already seated and waiting, something apparently on his mind. "Far, you know how you and Pastor Solberg always say there is a Bible verse for everything?" Thorliff laid the Bible on the table next to his father's place.

"Ja, and I'm about to hear one, right?"

"Right." Thorliff pointed to the page. "It says here that God will restore all that the locusts devoured. I figure if you substitute flood for locust, the meaning stays the same."

"Ja, well . . ." Haakan stirred in his chair and glanced at the others. "Elizabeth still out?"

"Ja, she might be there all night. That baby must be thinking it's too dangerous to try his way in the outer world yet."

Astrid looked up. "You think babies have a choice on when to be born?"

"Seems that way at times."

"I read where a wild mare can be having her colt and if something spooks her, she can stop the birthing to run, then have her baby when it is safe." Andrew wiped his hands and sat down.

When everyone was seated, Haakan bowed his head. "Heavenly Father, we thank thee for this food we have and for the health to eat and talk and work. Amen."

"So you think that verse might be a good one to chew on?" Thorliff glanced at his father with one eyebrow raised.

"Please pass the potatoes. Good thing your mor canned so much last summer."

Ingeborg shook her head with just the smallest hint of a smile. "He heard you, son."

After a rather silent meal, Andrew headed back out to the barn. When Haakan finished smoking his pipe, he followed. Thorliff finished a letter to Benjamin before joining them.

Maple lay on her side, two small hooves protruding from under her tail. Andrew sat in the corner, his back against the wall. He smiled up at Thorliff when he joined his father leaning on the stall's half wall.

"She's doing just fine."

"I see." Thorliff returned his brother's smile.

With each contraction, the hooves emerged farther, retreating less with each relaxation. With a final push from the cow, the calf slid out onto the straw. Andrew picked up a handful of straw and wiped the mucus from the calf's nose to make sure it was able to breathe. The calf shook his head.

"Strong one, eh?"

"Ja, and a heifer." Andrew used the straw to clean the sac away from the calf. He glanced over his shoulder to catch his father's eye. "The first in the new herd that God will bring us. Like Thorliff said, to repair what the locust has eaten."

Haakan looked from one son to the other. "You know, eating one's own words is never easy, but when it is your own son pointing out the error of your ways . . ." He shook his head. "Like your mor says, 'I give up.'" He raised his hands and let them fall to his sides again. "Sometimes accepting forgiveness is harder than giving it."

Maple surged to her feet and began licking her calf, emitting soft moans encouraging her baby to get to her feet so she could nurse. On the third try, the little heifer tottered to her mother's side and, after bopping the full udder, latched on to a teat, her metronome tail flashing in the dim light.

Two weeks later Thorliff and Elizabeth stood at the Blessing train station.

"You could stay longer." Thorliff looked down at her, his eyes sending a message not yet uttered.

"I know, but I am not needed here any longer."

Yes you are. I need you. He reached for her hands. "You are going back to Chicago, then?"

"For now. When will you return to Northfield?"

"Soon."

"Will they let you graduate?"

He nodded. "I have to take the examinations, but they will let me graduate with the others." *Tell her. Tell her.* He sucked in a deep breath. "I love you, Elizabeth. With all my heart."

Her eyes widened, and she stared into his. "But . . ."

"I know you have always said you cannot be both a doctor and a wife, but I believe we could make it work. I believe God has brought us together, and with His guidance and help, Dr. and Mr. Bjorklund could become a family."

"I . . . I . . . Thorliff, I . . ."

"Please think about it, about us." The arriving train filled the air with screeching and steam hissing.

Lord, please change her mind. Let her love me as I love her.

"All aboard!" The conductor stood at the open door of the first car right behind the coal carrier.

"I . . . I have to go."

"God be with you." He fought to keep a smile on his lips. "I'll write to you." *And plead and plead until you give in. Whatever it takes to win this woman, Lord, I will do it.*

Instead of letting her hand go, he drew her into his arms and held her close. "Go with God."

Eyes glittering from the tears that spilled over and glistened like diamonds down her cheeks, Elizabeth stepped back and accepted the conductor's assistance.

Several other passengers mounted the steps as Thorliff waited to see where she would sit. Would she wave good-bye? But all the window seats were filled with other passengers, and he resigned himself that this was good-bye—for now.

"All abo—ard?" The conductor's call sounded as sad as the train whistle when it wept over the prairie.

Thorliff blinked several times and straightened his shoulders. *Well, Lord, the battle isn't over yet, is it?*

The train chugged forward, the screeching of the gears and the pistons that turned each wheel laughing in derision. She was leaving.

He stood until the last of the four passenger cars showed no Elizabeth at the windows. Thorliff raised a hand and turned to go. At least at home he was still needed.

"Thorliff!" The call rang out.

Was he hearing things? He spun back around. "Elizabeth!" He leaped the tracks and swept her up in his arms. "What did you do? Get off the other side?"

"Yes. It was too crowded on your side. And yes."

He set her back on the plank platform. "What?"

"I said yes." She put her hands on both sides of his face. "Yes, I will marry you."

"You will?" He dropped his arms and took her hands. "But—you said—what changed your mind?"

"I guess I never before knew what love felt like. And I had to tell you something."

"What?"

She stared into his eyes. "I love you, Thorliff Bjorklund."

317

"And you will marry me?"

"I said yes."

He cupped her face in his hands and kissed her. *Ah, Lord, she is indeed more than a dream. Thank you. Thank you.* "Thank you!" That last one he shouted so even the angels would hear.

ACKNOWLEDGMENTS

Writing a book is a community project, although the actual writing is mine. When I get stuck or frustrated, I call or e-mail my Round Robin supporters or those on ChiLibris, and help comes. How blessed I am. Thanks also to Kathleen for reading my roughs and giving me excellent suggestions.

In addition to these people, Jeff Sauve, the assistant archivist at St. Olaf College, provided books, papers, and copies from their archives describing early life at St. Olaf. Otherwise I would have had little idea of what went on there besides classes. Thanks, Jeff.

No writer is her best without good editors, and Sharon Asmus and the others are the greatest. Thanks to everyone at Bethany House Publishers for your excellent work. I thank you again for the thrill of holding a new book in my hand.

My friends and family not only support me but listen to me grumble when the words are hard to come by. They remind me that this too shall pass and we've been here before. I love you all. And as Tiny Tim said, "God bless us everyone."